BIRDS IN THE HAND

BIRDS IN THE HAND

Fiction and Poetry About Birds

Edited by DYLAN NELSON AND KENT NELSON

North Point Press

A division of Farrar, Straus and Giroux

New York

North Point Press
A division of Farrar, Straus and Giroux
19 Union Square West, New York 10003

Distributed in Canada by Douglas & McIntyre Ltd.
Printed in the United States of America
First edition, 2004

Bird illustrations copyright © 2004 by Bailey Escapule

Owing to limitations of space, all acknowledgments for permission to reprint
previously published material can be found on pages 371–374.

Library of Congress Cataloging-in-Publication Data
    Birds in the hand : fiction and poetry about birds / edited by Dylan Nelson
        and Kent Nelson.— 1st ed.
        p.   cm.
    ISBN 0-86547-673-x
    1. Birds—Literary collections.   2. American literature.   3. English
literature.   I. Nelson, Dylan.   II. Nelson, Kent, date.

    PS509.B5B57 2004
    810.8′03628—dc22

                                                              2003066232

EAN 978-0-86547-673-8

Designed by Jonathan D. Lippincott

www.fsgbooks.com

10   9   8   7   6   5   4   3   2   1

This book is for Nanoo

Contents

Preface

The Great Gray Owl is the largest owl in North America, but it is difficult to see. Scarce and secretive, it has been called "Phantom of the North" and "Great Gray Ghost." The summer I was nine years old, my father, younger brother, and I went to look for the owl in the dense forests of Yosemite National Park. It was a crisp late August afternoon, sun shafting through the trees and all around the smell of pine needles. Our destination was an out-of-the-way meadow where a Great Gray had been spotted. If we were lucky, we might see it, near dusk, swoop across the clearing, hunting mice.

We walked for an hour. No owl. Nuthatches and creepers crawled the tree trunks; woodpeckers drilled; warblers skittered through the high branches. We reached the clearing and sat in the fragrant grass. My brother ran in circles. A doe grazed quietly at the edge of the meadow. Still no owl. When darkness fell, we started along the trail back to the car. As we reached the edge of the meadow, a gray shape slipped through the trees with a brush of tremendous wings, and was gone.

What did the bird mean? It was the fulfillment of a quest, a shared experience with my brother and my father, an evocation of wildness and solitude. As a threatened species, the owl was a quiet rebuke and a reminder that we are all endangered. And it was, simply, magnificent to see. These are only partial answers. What does any bird mean, within a moment's experience or the sweep of a life?

I grew up birding with my father and co-editor, Kent Nelson. For every numinous encounter like our glimpse of the Great Gray, there were dozens of fruitless searches through swamps or scrub desert, hours of boredom in the car, smelly walks around sewer ponds, and assaults by ravenous mosquitoes. But I loved the unpredictability of what we might see. I loved the adventure. Birding took my father and me places few people go: talus slopes outside Valdez, Alaska; anonymous washes east of L.A.; burned-out forests in coastal Maine. For me, birds were a reason to move through the landscape. They taught me to pay attention and linked me to a world outside my own. When I became a writer, it seemed natural for birds to show up in my stories. Birds often appeared in my father's work as well. He and I grew curious: How many others found writing about birds irresistible? What did other writers have to say about the relationship between humans and birds?

In David Wagoner's story "The Bird Watcher," a Winter Wren provides a moment of stillness, of secrecy—a pact between the protagonist and the universe. For Louise Erdrich, the screams of Barred Owls summon dread and frustrated desire. For Jan Epton Seale, the appearance of a mystery bird releases the power of legend. Hummingbirds help the narrator of Sheri Joseph's "The Elixir" come to terms with her daughter's agonizing death; through a parrot's eyes, Robert Olen Butler takes a hilarious look at envy and infidelity. Billy Collins envisions his poetic voice as a hood ornament shaped like a bird. A blackbird embodies the sin of John L'Heureux's troubled priest. For Mark Helprin, a dove evokes age-old associations of purity, innocence, and peace. My father and I sought out fiction and poetry that used birds to illuminate the human experience—that explored the complex, often startling connections between birds and human beings. *Birds in the Hand* is the result of our search.

Birds can evoke nobility and cravenness, cruelty and mercy, life and death. When birds fly, they show us we cannot. When birds seem innocent, they show us we are not. Yet birds also reveal to us our better selves: our generosity, our kindness, our capacity for wonder. Through birds, we see the brightest and darkest aspects of our natures. The stories and poems in *Birds in the Hand* are as varied as the birds themselves. Many of our selections use birds to examine human mortality; others use birds to express life's joy. Several, like Flannery O'Connor's "The Turkey" or Eudora Welty's "A Still Moment," investigate religious faith. A number invoke the idea of rescue. A child finds a hawk with a broken wing and, against terrific odds, gets him to a veterinarian; a canary momentarily distracts a schoolyard bully; inmates at a federal prison escape in the form of birds. Many pieces in this collection describe the ecstatic and mysterious ways birds link us to nature, and others chronicle man's relentless degradation of the natural world. In "Bringing Down the Birds," Maxine Kumin writes, "[H]ow long / would it take us logging and drilling and storing up / treasures to do them all in again?" That birds don't judge man's recklessness makes our often-tenuous coexistence even more moving. As William Wenthe writes in "Birds of Hoboken," "They don't exclaim: again, as if willing / to forgive, they arrive."

Birds were central to storytelling long before the first person wrote with a quill. From Leda's swan to Noah's dove, from Coleridge's albatross to Keats's nightingale, birds are a familiar and powerful presence in the literary canon. Rather than collect the recognized classics, which on their own could fill several books, we chose instead to showcase more recent, yet equally compelling, bird literature from both celebrated and emerging authors. We tried to select work that reflects a variety of settings, styles, and sensibilities. While our primary criterion was artistic merit, we also tried to vary the bird species as much as possible. Crows, starlings, geese, grackles, pigeons, and sparrows are, it turns out, as onmipresent in literature as they are in life, and we selected several pieces in which these ubiquitous species evoke singular insight; but we also included work about herons, cranes, and sandpipers; hawks and eagles; kingfishers, thrushes, and waxwings. Sometimes the birds in these stories and poems are rare or extinct. Sometimes they are imaginary.

When dealing with the natural world, our inclination is to classify, to explain. Indeed, one of the deep satisfactions of birding is to point out that yes, that is *this* bird and no other. However, the stories and poems in *Birds in the Hand* don't fall into neat categories. An environmental poem is also a love poem; a funny story turns suddenly heartbreaking. Instead of organizing the work by habitat, or species, or theme, after much discussion my father and I simply arranged it by feel. We mixed content and setting, species and tone, four or five poems for every two stories. Birds, after all, surprise us. Seeking one, we find another, and the most ordinary species create uncommon delight. We read fiction and poetry for the same reason we search for birds: because we hope to be startled, because we love to see the everyday world turned over and made new. We hope you will go into the book and look around, the same way you'd look for birds in a forest or park. We hope you will explore, and be surprised.

Dylan Nelson, June 2003

It was a dramatic summer. Shortly after finding the Great Gray Owl in Yosemite National Park, Dylan, her brother Taylor, and I drove to Southern California in search of another rare bird species: the California Condor. I gave them a choice between going to Disneyland and looking for the condor, a bird I'd seen several years before and of which there were only six left in the wild. Taylor was five, and Disneyland perhaps appealed to him more, but Dylan knew she wanted to see the condor. Taylor went along, of course, and we were all eager. On the way to our campsite we detoured up steep, windy Mill Potrero Road and joined fifteen or so birders already at the viewing site. Within minutes we had three distant condors in the scope. A short time later one flew overhead, so close we saw clearly the bare orange head and white wing linings. We got to Disneyland the next day, but it's the condors we remember.

I grew up on the outskirts of Colorado Springs, and I was ten when birds first captivated me. Lewis's Woodpeckers, Gray Catbirds, and Broad-tailed Hummingbirds nested in my yard, and I explored the creeks and woodlands around my house. Scaled Quail abounded in the foothills. I remember vividly one afternoon in spring finding a male Rose-breasted Grosbeak, unusual for central Colorado, singing from the top of a wild lilac near the creek. These species are gone from my boyhood haunts. Houses now proliferate along the creek, and shopping malls have sprung up where the quail lived. Magpies, starlings, House Finches, and crows are the birds in my mother's yard. Still, the experiences of my early years translated into a lifelong fascination with birding.

Many birders keep life lists, a catalog of the birds they've seen in particular states, countries, or continents. Some take part in team Big Day competitions to see how many species they can find in twenty-four hours. Others compete in Big Years—there is even a Hollywood movie in development about the phenomenon. There have been 910 species recorded in the American Bird Association area (North America, excluding Mexico); a team from Texas saw an astounding 258 of them in one day. The biggest year was Sandy Komito's 745. The biggest current life list in the ABA area is 864 species, seen by Macklin Smith, whose poem "Birding the Battle of Attu" is in this volume. But many birders don't chase birds; they view birds in their backyards or limit their travel to local parks, marshes, and woodlands. These birders are just as devoted to their pursuits as the competitive listers. Selecting the stories and poems in this book, Dylan and I hoped to appeal to everyone who appreciates birds—the backyard birder as well as the birder in search of rare or hard-to-find species. But you don't have to be a birder to know a good story. In fact, few of the writers in this volume are birders. Writers observe what's around them, including the mundane birds, and they use the landscapes they know, whether these are urban, as in Gladys Swan's "Dreaming Crow"; on a southern river, as in David Bottom's "Under the Vulture-Tree"; or in the arid landscape around the Salton Sea, as in Maya Sonenberg's "Beyond Mecca." Our task was to choose stories and poems that were challenging and accessible, intellectual and emotional, serious and entertaining. We hope we have made choices broad enough that readers will experience birds within a variety of created worlds.

Dylan and I decided not to include our own work in this anthology, preferring to highlight stories and poems by other writers we admire. However, we both use birds frequently in our fiction. In Dylan's story "Calving," a woman struggling with guilt over the death of her child kayaks across Prince William Sound. Her boyfriend quizzes her on the bird life, which she pretends not to know. Yet at the close of the story, terns show her a way back into her own difficult life: "Arctic Tern. She knew the name; she couldn't forget it. They ranged farther north, overlapping with Aleutian Tern. Solid black caps. Pointed wings. Impossible grace. And they flew, every year, from the Arctic to the Antarctic and back. Thirty thousand miles to go away and then come home." In my novel *Language in the Blood,* the protagonist, Scott Talmadge, a bird guide and troubled soul, takes his friend Tilghman to see a Yellow Rail at a marsh in Minnesota. On the way there Tilghman asks how Scott came to care about birds, why he wants to see the Yellow Rail. Scott thinks about his answer: he could say that birds are beautiful in their myriad forms, that he is fascinated by flight, that the songs of birds enthrall him. "But the Yellow Rail was not a bird of beauty or grace or power. It was not even yellow, but rather a tawny brown and drab ocher, with blackish crosshatching on its back and wings; it had a dull yellowish bill, and a white wing patch visible only when it flew. And it was a poor flyer." He finds no answer to give Tilghman. At the end of the book, though, Scott decides he knows. "I wanted to see the rail because birds are in me. They are in my blood like a language. They were what I first knew how to love."

Kent Nelson, June 2003

BIRDS IN THE HAND

LI-YOUNG LEE

Praise Them

The birds don't alter space.
They reveal it. The sky
never fills with any
leftover flying. They leave
nothing to trace. It is our own
astonishment collects
in chill air. Be glad.
They equal their due
moment never begging,
and enter ours
without parting day. See
how three birds in a winter tree
make the tree barer.
Two fly away, and new rooms
open in December.
Give up what you guessed
about a whirring heart, the little
beaks and claws, their constant hunger.
We're the nervous ones.
If even one of our violent number
could be gentle
long enough that one of them
found it safe inside
our finally untroubled and untroubling gaze,
who wouldn't hear
what singing completes us?

LESLIE NORRIS

The Kingfisher

On the morning of his fourteenth birthday, James met his father in the kitchen. His father came to him and held him by the shoulders, at arm's length, and looked at him with such wry and compassionate warmth that the boy was at once convinced of the imminence of some great cataclysm. Almost the same height, they stared at each other for nearly half a minute.

"So you're fourteen," James's father said. "It seems no time since I first held you in my arms. With great trepidation and very gingerly, but I held you. And here you are, fourteen."

"That's it," James said.

"Fourteen," his father said. "Always a sad anniversary for men of our family. A sad day."

He picked up his cup of coffee, walked to the window, and stared seriously over the garden. When he turned away from the window, he smiled almost shyly at James, as if they shared an enormous, obligatory knowledge—some ominous secret. "Come into the dining room with me, James," he said.

The dining room was cold and quiet. Its mahogany furniture sat solidly in place, heavy, smelling of polish. James remembered it arriving at the house when he was a small boy, sent south from his grandmother's home in Yorkshire. The room was rarely used.

"Sit down," James's father said. "It would be best if you sat down."

James sat on a hard chair. Its seat had been broken long ago and repaired with some old craftsman's adhesive. James felt with his finger the small ridge of the mend. He could see a black streak of dry glue running the length of the wood.

"How do you feel?" his father said. "We can postpone this if you don't feel up to it."

"Get on with it," James said. "Whatever it is."

"Admirably stoic," his father said. "I wish I had been as stoic when my father told me."

"Told you what?" James said.

His father didn't answer. He moved quietly into a corner of the room, and then he spoke. "James, when the men of our family reach the age of fourteen, they are thought old enough to bear a terrible knowledge. Generation after generation, from father to son, we have been told this secret, pledged to pass it on in our turn. Although what we learn has in many ways blighted our lives, made saddened men of us, we have all borne our sorrow bravely. I know you will do the same."

Oh, God, thought James, rigid on his chair, we suffer from incurable hereditary madness. All over the country my cousins, tainted and cretinous, are shut away in stone towers. We are descended shamefully and illegitimately—incestuously, probably—from some nameless criminal family. He pushed away other terrors, too hideous to think of. "Tell me," he said, his voice a croak.

His father, upright and slim and still, stood in the shadows of the room. He was remote and impersonal. His face was dark. "Remember, it is my duty to tell you this," he said. "I would willingly have spared you and kept this knowledge alone."

"Hell's flames!" yelled James, his control at an end. "Tell me!"

For a long moment, until the imagined echoes of his cry had left James's ears, his father waited. Then he spoke. "There is no Father Christmas," he said.

That had been almost two weeks ago, and James still laughed at the memory, although he had been wild with rage at first. He lay in bed listening to his father's voice through the open window, and little uncontrollable giggles made him shake. It was not yet seven o'clock, but his father was already in the garden. James knew what he was doing. He was standing among his rosebushes, encouraging and cajoling. Every morning he spoke to them, full of praise if they were flowering well, like a general before battle if he felt they could do better. James got up and looked out at his father.

The lawn carried a heavy summer dew, and the marks of his father's footsteps were clear. He had wandered all over the garden, but he stood now near the rose bed, talking quietly and fondly. James could not hear what he was saying. His father's thin shanks stuck out below his silk robe. It was a glittering paisley robe in green and blue, tied at the waist with a sash of darker colour. Watching his father bend above the subservient shrubs, James thought he looked like an exotic bird, a peacock of some kind.

His father loved birds to come to his garden. He had widened the trickle of a stream that bordered this plot into two small pools, so that he could keep in comfort a pair of ancient mallards, Mr. and Mrs. Waddle. This morning, hearing the man's voice, they hopped out of the water and hurried loudly to him. Mrs. Waddle, always the braver, marched to his feet and pecked at his brown slippers. She paused to look up, her head on one side, out of a round black eye. A yard away, Mr. Waddle looked on benevolently. He was in his summer glory, his green head glossy, his speculum a trim bar of reflecting blue. James's father went off to the garage, where he kept a sack of poultry food.

It was then that a kingfisher flew in, paused above the stream, and dived. He was blue lightning, an arrow of light; his flight was electric and barbarous. He took instantly from the shallow water a small fish, stickleback or minnow, and perched on the wooden post that had held a clematis, killed by harsh frost two years back. James saw the brilliant turquoise of the bird's back, the warm chestnut breast, his sturdy beak. The kingfisher held the small fish struggling across his beak and whacked it savagely and expertly against the wood before he slid it down his throat. Then he flew, seeming to leave behind a visible echo of his flight, a streak of colour. James's father came out of the garage, holding a bowl of pellets. His ducks begged and skidded before him. He had missed the whole appearance of the kingfisher.

That afternoon, because his mother had gone to Birmingham to see her sister, James went with his father to the nursing home. His father would not go alone.

"Charles Emerson, to see his mother," he said to the receptionist. "And James Emerson, to see his grandmother."

The nurse smiled at them and told them to go ahead.

The old lady lay inert in her white bed, her thin hair damp and yellowish against the pillow. James's father held her hand and spoke softly to her, but she didn't answer. Her eyes were closed. She didn't know anybody. Sometimes she had spoken, but her words were disjointed and incoherent. Now she neither spoke nor moved. James watched his father grow quiet and sad as the slow minutes passed. The small room was too hot. It smelled of sickness. The voices of boys playing tennis in the park came faintly to them. James was glad when it was time to leave.

His father drove furiously out of the car park, showering the neat red gravel behind the wheels of the car. He spun the big car roughly through Redmond Corner, his tyres protesting. It was always like this. He always left the nursing home in a rage of frustration, in an agony over his mother's decay.

James tapped his father's knee. "Too fast, Dad," he said. "You'll get a ticket."

His father braked, but said nothing. For several miles he drove carefully down the road, heavy now with afternoon traffic—the cars of businessmen, files of trucks taking their loads around Oxford to Southampton.

"You see what we come to," he said at last, as if he were very tired. "You see what time brings us to. We lie insensible in strange rooms, not knowing we are alive. The tyranny of the breath keeps us going. Your grandmother has committed the crime of growing too old."

James had known these moods before. He sat at his father's side and waited for him to recover. He did not understand his father's anger and impotence. It was natural to grow old, natural for the body to wither and break; it was common mortality, the human condition. He wished very much for some comfort to bring back his usual ebullient, unpredictable father.

They stopped at the traffic lights near the Queen's Theatre. "Tell me, Holmes," James said to his father, "what do you make of that old lady on the other side of the road, dressed in black?" It was an old game of theirs, although they had not played it for a long time.

His father's head jerked about, his long neck stiff—like an old heron stalking a frog. He was smiling. "Ah," he said, "you mean the retired Irish parlour maid, Watson? With a ne'er-do-well son in the Army and a pipe-smoking husband?"

"Holmes," James said, "you astound me! How on earth did you gather that information? Do you know the woman?"

"Never saw her before in my life," his father said. "But you know my methods, Watson. I knew she was a parlour maid because her right arm is six inches longer than her left—the result, Watson, of many years of carrying heavy buckets of coal to the upstairs parlours in which her employers sat."

James laughed, turning in his seat to look at his father. "Good gracious, Holmes," he said. "You do astound me. Go on."

"A mere nothing," his father said. "I know she is retired because, apart from evident maturity, she would not be about so early in the evening were she still employed. And as she is still wearing, although St. Patrick's Day is long past, a bunch of faded shamrock at her collar, she is undoubtedly Irish."

"When you put it like that, Holmes, it's quite simple," James said. "But what about her son in the Army and her pipe-smoking husband? I have you there, I think."

"Not at all," said his father. He was well into the game now, his gloom forgotten. "The shamrock is fastened to her coat by an old brooch, on which the word *Mother* is clearly to be discerned. The parcel she carries is addressed to a private in the infantry named McCarthy. It is safe to assume he is her son. That he is a ne'er-do-well is evident from the woman's dress. No decent son would allow his mother to go out so shabbily garbed."

"Great," James said. "Pretty good. What about the husband?"

"That," said his father with relish, "is the easiest deduction of all. Did you not observe that the woman's clothes are spotted all over with tiny burns, small marks of scorching? They prove beyond all doubt that she has spent many years in the close vicinity of a man who is a careless pipe-smoker, undoubtedly her husband."

"A full score," said James. "You haven't lost your skill."

His father took the car past a row of parked vehicles outside the library. "Your turn," he said. "Tell me, Holmes, what do you make of the sinister-looking man who stands outside the filling station?"

"You mean," James said, "the ex-sailor who subsequently became a policeman, was dismissed for taking bribes, and now earns a casual living as a gardener?"

"Holmes," said his father, "you astonish me."

They ate supper together, silently, contentedly, and afterward James walked in the garden. The evening was still warm, and Mr. and Mrs. Waddle muttered from their stream. High up, the seagulls were trailing their irregular columns back to the beach. A little tatter of silk, Oriental in its brilliance, had blown from somewhere onto the lawn. James bent over it. It was the kingfisher. He picked it up, and it lay dead on his hand, light as dust. Its head rolled loosely of its own tiny weight, as if its neck were broken. James examined the short, blunt wings, touched the dry beak.

From the house his father began to sing. "Questa o quella," he sang, his voice breaking comically on the higher notes, "per me pari sono."

James held the dead bird on his open palm. He carried it to the long grass beneath the maple tree in the corner of the garden. He placed the bird in the dark grass behind the tree and stood above it, rubbing his hands together briskly. He would not tell his father about the kingfisher, not about its vivid morning flight across the garden, not about its small, irrevocable death. He would spare his father that knowledge.

Angel of Mercy, Angel of Wrath

On Eleanor Black's seventy-first birthday a flock of birds flew into her kitchen through a window that she had opened every morning for forty years. They flew in all at once, without warning or reason, from the ginkgo tree at the corner, where birds had sat every day since President Roosevelt's time. They were huge and dirty and black, the size of cats practically, much larger than she had ever imagined birds. Birds were so small in the sky. In the air, even in the clipped ginkgo ten yards from the window, they were nothing more than faint dots of color. Now they were in her kitchen, batting against the ceiling and the yellow walls she had just washed a couple of months ago, and their stink and their cries and their frantic knocking wings made it hard for her to breathe.

She sat down and took a water pill. They were screaming like wounded animals, flapping in tight circles around the light fixture so that she got dizzy looking at them. She reached for the phone and pushed the button that automatically dialed her son, who was a doctor.

"Bernard," she said, "there's a flock of crows in the flat."

"It's five in the morning, Mom."

"It is? Excuse me, because it's seven out here. I forgot. But the crows are flying in my kitchen."

"Mother?"

"Yes?"

"Have you been taking all your medicines?"

"Yes, I have."

"Has Dr. Gluck put you on any new ones?"

"No."

"What did you say was the matter?"

"There's a whole flock of crows in the flat."

Bernard didn't say anything.

"I know what you're thinking," she said.

"I'm just making the point that sometimes new medicines can change people's perceptions."

"Do you want to hear them?"

"Yes," he said, "that would be fine. Let me hear them."

She held the receiver up toward the ceiling. The cries were so loud she knew he would pick them up, even long distance.

"Okay?" she said.

"I'll be damned."

"What am I supposed to do?"

"How many are there?"

"I don't know."

"What do you mean, you don't know?"

"They're flying like crazy around the room. How can I count them?"

"Are they attacking you?"

"No, but I want them out anyway."

"How can I get them out from Denver?"

She thought for a second. "I'm not the one who went to Denver."

He breathed out on the phone, loud, like a child. He was chief of the department at Denver General. "I'm just making the point," he said, "that I can't grab a broom in Colorado and get the birds out of your place in New York."

"Whose fault is that?"

"Mom," he said.

"Yes?"

"Call the SPCA. Tell them what happened. They have a department that's for things like this. They'll come out and get rid of them."

"They're big."

"I know," he said. "Don't call 911. That's for emergencies. Call the regular SPCA. Okay?"

"Okay," she said.

He paused. "You can call back later to let us know what happened."

"Okay."

"Okay?"

"Okay." She waited a moment. "Do you want to say anything else?"

"No," he said.

She hung up, and a few seconds later all the birds flew back out the window except for two of them, which flew the other way, through the swinging door that she had left open and into the living room. She followed them in there. One of them was hopping on the bookshelf, but while Eleanor watched, the other one flew straight at the window from the center of the room and collided with the glass. The pane shook, and the bird fell several feet before it righted itself and did the same thing again. For a few moments Eleanor stood watching, and then she went to the kitchen, took the bottle of cream soda out of the refrigerator, and poured herself a glass. Yesterday it had been a hundred degrees out. When she finished, she put the bottle back, sat down again, and dialed 911.

"Emergency," said a woman.

Eleanor didn't say anything.

"911 Emergency."

"There's a flock of crows in my apartment."

"Birds?"

"Yes."

"You have to call the SPCA."

"They're going to break the window."

"Listen," she said, "we're not supposed to give this kind of advice, but all you have to do is move up quietly behind a bird and pick it up. They won't hurt you. I grew up on a farm."

"I grew up here."

"You can do that," she said, "or you can call the SPCA."

She hung up and went back to the living room. One still perched itself on the edge of her bookshelf and sat there, opening and closing its wings, while the other one, the berserk one, flew straight at the front window, smashed into it, fell to the sill, and then took to the air again. Again and again it flew straight at the window, hitting it with a sound like a walnut in a nutcracker, falling to the sill, then flapping crookedly back toward the center of the room to make another run. Already the window had small blotches of bluish feather oil on it. The bird hit it again, fell flapping to the sill, and this time stayed there, perched. Through the window Eleanor noticed that the house across the street from her had been painted green.

"Stay here," she said. "I'm going to open the window."

She took two steps toward the bird, keeping the rest of her body as still as she could, like a hunting dog, moving one leg, pausing, then moving the other. Next to her on the bookshelf the calm bird cocked its head in little jerks—down, up, sideways, down. She advanced toward the window until the berserk one suddenly flew up, smashed against the glass, fell to the sill, flew up again, smashed, and perched once more. She stopped. It stood there. To her horror, Eleanor could see its grotesque pulse through its skin, beating frantically along the wings and the torso as if the whole bird were nothing but a speeding heart. She stood perfectly still for several minutes, watching.

"Hello," she said.

It lifted its wings as though it were going to fly against the window again, but then lowered them.

"My husband was a friend of Franklin Roosevelt's," she said.

The bird didn't move.

"Why can't you be like your friend?" She pointed her chin at the one on the bookshelf, which opened its beak. Inside it the throat was black. She took another step toward the window. Now she was so close to the berserk one that she could see the ruffled, purplish chest-feathers and the yellow ring around its black irises. Its heart still pulsated, but it didn't raise its wings, just cocked its head the way the other one had. She reached her two hands halfway toward it and stopped. "It's my birthday today," she whispered. She waited like that, her hands extended. The bird cocked and retracted its head, then stood still. When it had been still for a while, she reached the rest of the way and touched her hands to both sides of its quivering body.

For a moment, for an extended, odd moment in which the laws of nature didn't seem to hold, for a moment in which she herself felt just the least bit confused, the bird stood still. It was oily and cool, and its askew feathers poked her palms. What she thought about at that second, of all things, was the day her husband, Charles, had come into the living room to announce to her that President Kennedy was going to launch missiles against the Cubans. She had felt the same way when he told her that, as if something had gone slightly wrong with nature but that she couldn't quite comprehend it, the way right now she couldn't quite comprehend the bird's stillness until suddenly it shrieked and twisted in her hands and flew up into the air.

She stepped back. It circled through the room and smashed into the glass again, this time on the other window next to the bookshelf. The calm bird lighted from its perch, went straight down the hall, and flew into her bedroom. The berserk one righted itself and flew into the glass again, then flapped up and down against it, tapping the wide pane with its wings like a moth. Eleanor went to the front window, but she couldn't open it because the Mexican boy who had painted the apartments last year had broken the latch. She crossed into the kitchen and looked up the number of the SPCA.

A child answered the phone. Eleanor had to think for a second. "I'd like to report two crows in my house," she said.

The child put down the phone, and a moment later a woman came on the line. "I'd like to report two crows in my house," said Eleanor. The woman hung up. Eleanor looked up the number again. This time a man answered. "Society," he said.

"There are two crows in my house," said Eleanor.

"Did they come in a window?"

"I always have that window opened," she answered. "I've had it opened for years with nothing happening."

"Then it's open now?"

"Yes."

"Have you tried getting them out?"

"Yes. I grabbed one the way the police said, but it bit me."

"It bit you?"

"Yes. The police gave me that advice over the phone."

"Did it puncture the skin?"

"It's bleeding a little."

"Where are they now?"

"They're in the living room," she said. "One's in another room."

"All right," he said. "Tell me your address."

When they finished, Eleanor hung up and went into the living room. The berserk one was perched on the sill, looking into the street. She went into the bedroom and had to look around awhile before she found the calm one sitting on top of her lamp.

She had lived a long enough life to know there was nothing to be lost from waiting out situations, so she turned out the light in the bedroom, went back into the living room, took the plastic seat cover off the chair President Roosevelt had sat on, and, crossing her arms, sat down on it herself. By now the berserk bird was calm. It stood on the windowsill, and every once in a while it strutted three or four jerky steps up the length of the wood, turned toward her, and bobbed its head. She nodded at it.

The last time the plastic had been off that chair was the day Richard Nixon resigned. Charles had said that Franklin Roosevelt would have liked it that way, so they took the plastic off and sat on it that day and for a few days after, until Charles let some peanuts fall between the cushion and the arm and she got worried and covered it again. After all those years the chair was still firm.

The bird eyed her. Its feet had four claws and were scaly, like the feet on a butcher's chicken. "Get out of here," she said. "Go! Go through the window you came from." She flung her hand out at it, flapped it in front of the chair, but the bird didn't move. She sat back.

When the doorbell rang, she got up and answered on the building intercom. It was the SPCA. When she opened the door to the apartment, she found a young black woman standing there. She was fat, with short, braided hair. After the woman had introduced herself and stepped inside, Eleanor was surprised to see that the hair on one side of her head was long. She wore overalls and a pink turtleneck.

"Now," she said, "where are those crows you indicated?"

"In the living room," said Eleanor. "He was going to break the glass soon if you didn't get here."

"I got here as soon as I received the call."

"I didn't mean that."

The woman stepped into the living room, swaying slightly on her right leg, which looked partly crippled. The bird hopped from the sill to the sash, then back to the sill. The woman stood motionless with her hands together in front of her, watching it. "That's no crow," she said finally. "That's a grackle. That's a rare species here."

"I grew up in New York," said Eleanor.

"So did I." The woman stepped back, turned away from the bird, and began looking at Eleanor's living room. "A crow's a rare species here, too, you know. Some of that particular species gets confused and comes in here from Long Island."

"Poor things."

"Say," said the woman. "Do you have a little soda or something? It's hot out."

"I'll look," said Eleanor. "I heard it was a hundred degrees out yesterday."

Eleanor went into the kitchen. She opened the refrigerator door, stood there, then closed it. "I'm out of everything," she called.

"That's all right."

She filled a glass with water and brought it out to the woman. "There you go," she said.

The woman drank it. "Well," she said, "I think I'll make the capture now."

"It's my birthday today."

"Is that right?"

"Yes, it is."

"How old are you?"

"Eighty-one."

The woman reached behind her, picked up the water glass, and made the gesture of a toast. "Well, happy eighty-first," she said. She put down the glass and walked over and opened the front window. Then she crouched and approached the bird, which was on the other sill. She stepped slowly, her head tilted to the side and her large arms held in front of her, and when she was a few feet before the window, she bent forward and took the bird into her hands. It flapped a couple of times and then sat still in her grasp while she turned and walked it to the open window, where she let it go and it flew away into the air.

After the woman left, Eleanor put the plastic back on the chair and called her son again. The hospital had to page him, and when he came on the phone he sounded annoyed.

"It was difficult," she said. "The fellow from SPCA had to come out."

"Did he do a decent job?"

"Yes, decent."

"Good," he said. "I'm very pleased."

"It was a rare species," said Eleanor. "He had to use a metal-handled capturing device. It was a long set of tongs with hinges."

"Good. I'm very pleased."

"Are you at work?"

"Yes, I am."

"Okay, then."

"Okay."

"Is there anything else?"

"No," he said. "That's it."

A while after they hung up, the doorbell rang. It was the SPCA woman again, and when Eleanor let her upstairs, she found her standing in the hall with a bunch of carnations wrapped in newspaper. "Here," she said. "Happy birthday from the SPCA."

"Oh my," said Eleanor. For a moment she thought she was going to cry. "They're very elegant."

The woman stepped into the apartment. "I just thought you were a nice lady."

"Why, thank you very much." She took them and laid them down on the hall vanity. "Would you like a cup of tea?"

"No, thanks. I just wanted to bring them up. I've got more calls to take care of."

"Would you like some more water?"

"That's all right," said the woman. She smiled and touched Eleanor on the shoulder, then turned and went back downstairs.

Eleanor closed the door and unwrapped the flowers. She looked closely at their stems for signs that they were a few days old, but could find none. The ends were unswollen and cleanly clipped at an angle. She brought them into the kitchen, washed out a vase, and set them in it. Then she poured herself half a glass of cream soda. When she was finished, she went into the bedroom, took a sheet of paper from the drawer in the bedside table, and began a letter.

Dear President Bush:

I am a friend of President Roosevelt's writing you on my eightieth birthday on the subject of a rare species that came into my life without warning today and that needs help from a man such as yourself

She sat up straight and examined the letter. The handwriting got smaller at the end of each line, so she put a paper aside and took out a new sheet. At that moment the calm bird flew down and perched on the end of the table. Eleanor jerked back and stood away from the chair. "Oh," she said, and touched her heart. "Of course."

Then she patted her hair with both hands and sat down again. The bird tilted its head to look at her. Eleanor looked back. Its coat was black, but she could see an iridescent rainbow in the chest-feathers. It strutted a couple of steps toward her, flicking its head left, right, forward. Its eyes were dark.

She put out her hand, leaned a little bit, and, moving her hand steadily and slowly, touched the feathers once and withdrew. The bird hopped and opened its wings. She sat back and watched it. Sitting there, she knew that it probably didn't mean anything. She was just a woman in an apartment, and it was just a bird that had wandered in. It was too bad they couldn't talk to each other. She would have liked to know how old the bird was, and what it was like to have lived in the sky.

PATTIANN ROGERS

The Hummingbird: A Seduction

If I were a female hummingbird perched still
And quiet on an upper myrtle branch
In the spring afternoon and if you were a male
Alone in the whole heavens before me, having parted
Yourself, for me, from cedar top and honeysuckle stem
And earth down, your body hovering in midair
Far away from jewelweed, thistle and bee balm;

And if I watched how you fell, plummeting before me,
And how you rose again and fell, with such mastery
That I believed for a moment *you* were the sky
And the red-marked bird diving inside your circumference
Was just the physical revelation of the light's
Most perfect desire;

And if I saw your sweeping and sucking
Performance of swirling egg and semen in the air,
The weaving, twisting vision of red petal
And nectar and soaring rump, the rush of your wing
In its grand confusion of arcing and splitting
Created completely out of nothing just for me,

Then when you came down to me, I would call you
My own spinning bloom of ruby sage, my funneling
Storm of sunlit sperm and pollen, my only breathless
Piece of scarlet sky, and I would bless the base
Of each of your feathers and touch the tine
Of string muscles binding your wings and taste

The odor of your glistening oils and hunt
The honey in your crimson flare
And I would take you and take you and take you
Deep into any kind of nest you ever wanted.

Duck Blind

He was a judge in Louisiana—this is a story told by his daughter over dinner—and duck hunting was the one passion in his life. Every year during the season when the birds migrate, green-headed mallards and pintails and canvasbacks, blue-winged teal and cinnamon teal, gadwall and widgeon and scaup carried by some inward reckoning down wide migration routes in orderly flocks from Canada to Yucatán, he rose at three in the morning and hunted them. Now, at seventy-five, he still goes every day to the blind; he belongs to a club with other white men who, every morning, fathers and sons, draw lots before sunup and row quietly in skiffs to their positions. When he misses a shot, he shakes his head and says, "To shoot a duck"—it is what hunters often say—"you have to be a duck." And many mornings now he falls asleep. When five sprig circle, making a perfect pass above his blind, and all the men hold their breath and hear the silky sound of wind in the oiled feathers of the birds, and nothing happens, only silence, one of his companions will whisper to his son, "God-dammit, I think the judge is asleep again." And if it happens twice, he says, "Lennie, you better row over there and see if the judge is asleep or dead." And the son, a middle-aged man, balding, with thick, inarticulate hands, rows toward the judge's blind in the ground mist, and watches the birds veer off into the first light of the south sky.

ROBERT HILL LONG

The White Ibis

Absolution, there is none anywhere
but I saw its ghost in the wingspread
of the ibis, a black-tipped cross soaring
in the humid blue-white over the barrier

islands—I heard its ocean-breath
a mile away. Then it croaked and was just
a bird again, alarmed off its nest by
our trespassing. John and I had crossed

the Cape Fear River by canoe to this rookery
developers were blueprinting into someone's
idea of perpetual vacation. A ferry
dock already bit into the sawgrass.

Parked in raw muck at the end of it,
the first earthmover. Soon, brushcutters
and minimum wage laborers piling stumps
for bonfires. Through the twisted

yaupon groves, red-flagged stakes
outlined the idea: condos, pebble paths
curving between pampas grass borders
to the yacht slips, the tennis club.

It was egg-time for egrets, snowy
and American, for the yellow-crowned
and the little green and the great
blue and the Louisiana herons,

and for the white ibis, whose
Egyptian god-headed dignity
testified how inhuman this sliver
of the island-world might have stayed.

I clapped my hands: hundreds of white
wings rose over us with the noise
of a huge tent being lifted and shredded.
A few feet ahead, one ibis hung

head down, red legs hobbled to a branch
in the rings of a six-pack grip.
Its wingtips feebly flicked the dirt.
The legs broken, the eyes already

filming over; we were its last wrong
image. I pinioned the wingspan. John
shook his head. "Who," he asked, "are we
doing this for?" He stroked the neck's

long shiver, then twisted, hard.
The moment our canoe slid ashore
we'd stayed too long. Into the island's
arid sandspur scrub we moved

with nowhere to go that didn't cross
another line of stakes defining the one
perspective to come. I jerked a stake loose,
flung it, imagined harvesting stakes

like carrots, dumping a bunch under the nests.
But I stopped after one. John kept walking.
A quarter mile behind us, with no past
like ours, without much future,

a thousand wings resettled in waves.

R. T. SMITH

Hardware Sparrows

Out for a deadbolt, light bulbs
and two-by-fours, I find a flock
of sparrows safe from hawks

and weather under the roof
of Lowe's amazing discount
store. They skitter from the racks

of stockpiled posts and hoses
to a spill of winter birdseed
on the concrete floor. How

they know to forage here,
I can't guess, but the automatic
door is close enough,

and we've had a week
of storms. They are, after all,
ubiquitous, though poor,

their only song an irritating
noise, and yet they soar
to offer, amid hardware, rope

and handyman brochures,
some relief, as if a flurry
of notes from Mozart swirled

from seed to ceiling, entreating
us to set aside our evening
chores and take grace where

we find it, saying it is possible,
even in this month of flood,
blackout and frustration,

to float once more on sheer
survival and the shadowy
bliss we exist to explore.

DAVID WAGONER

The Bird Watcher

Stone had been sitting still by the switchbacked, disused logging road for half an hour, trying to be less human, trying to outwait the supposedly short attention span of the birds.

Every living creature in the twenty-acre grove of fir trees and the small swamp near the middle of it had gone dead quiet when he'd arrived on foot, having left his car a quarter of a mile behind, and now his own attention span had begun to dissolve into daydreaming fragments left over from the city he'd escaped for a day, the intrusive reminders of errands that needed running and letters that demanded answers. He hadn't lost his city-self yet, the half-stunned shape that had to sit at a desk and put its forefinger into the holes of telephones.

The temperature was about fifty, and his parka wasn't insulating him well enough from the moist forest duff, the layer of dead evergreen needles and other rich debris cast off from high overhead. But here, under what remained of the hundred-and-fifty-foot Douglas firs, he strained to stay alert, listening, watching the nearby undergrowth, the beautifully intermingled ferns, vine maple, devil's club, Indian plum, hazel, salmonberry, and ancient moss-covered upended first-growth stumps.

Suddenly he heard a winter wren singing too far away to be in sight, the amazing 16-note-per-second, 112-note song blurred a little by distance, and he tensed, waiting for a possible nearby answer. None came. Instead, a flash of movement, partly yellow even in the green-filtered light, caught the corners of his eyes, and he turned them instead of his whole head in time to see a pair of Wilson's warblers flitting high and low among the leaves of a clump of young cottonwoods, darting so quickly and perching so seldom he didn't consider trying to get his binoculars on them. They were feeding on small flying insects, making no sound now—that would come soon, he remembered, as spring deepened into nesting time—and they were so graceful and filled with life, he found himself smiling at the mere fact of their existence. He watched them pass deeper into a thicket and disappear, alert, expert, completely admirable.

He relaxed his spine slightly, having permission to breathe again, and behind his back, from below him and below the humpbacked bend in the road, came the unmuffled, crack-throated roar of a car going too fast on the steep, potholed road full of blind turns, and in a moment it came jouncing into view, a cut-down, drag-tired, high-shocked twelve-year-old Chevy, swerving to keep from barrel-rolling into a salmonberry patch, then accelerating at the end of the skid to pick up momentum for the dip at the small swamp before the even steeper leg of the next switchback.

The exchange of looks as the car lurched by, buffeting Stone with its following wind, was blank on both sides: the flushed, arrogant-seeming teenage kid at the wheel, streaky blond hair flowing backwards, and his happy-scared girlfriend rigid beside him, her white face a mask of stoic concentration while they swiveled in ruts and headed out of the grove and up into the shambles of the clear-cut mountainside.

Stone tried to imagine how the young man had made that date. Had he simply said, "Wanta see how fast this beast'll go up a god-damn mountain?" or had he needed to say anything at all? Maybe he just took it for granted that if there was some showing off of reckless skill to do and some noise to make while he was at it, he did it automatically, and his audience came along automatically too.

Whatever birds might have been nearby, about to come out of hiding after the first disturbance of his silent arrival, would now have all their protective behavior renewed and reinforced. So instead of waiting for them to forget again, Stone stood up, did his best to ignore the chainsawing sound of the car as it swiveled up slope out of sight, and pulled his wading boots all the way up his thighs and snapped the tops securely. He picked up his broom-handle staff and looked around for a place to cache his identification books and clipboard full of blank, mud-stained paper. And then he heard the second car.

It was a deeper sound, less frenzied, and for a moment he was afraid the logging trucks had come back after a year to finish off his grove, the only full stand of trees left on this side of the mountain. But there was no diesel blast in the sound. In half a minute the large pickup rounded the curve toward him, slowed on the downhill stretch, and stopped beside him.

A skinny man with a weathered face and a blue stocking cap leaned out of the cab and looked him over carefully, and while he was having his look, Stone did the same by glancing over the two hang gliders folded in the bed of the pickup, their metal joints and ribs gleaming, the plastic wings bright yellow and red.

"Hi, man," the skinny man said. "Hunting?"

His passenger, a heavyset younger man in a red quilted parka, muttered something, and the skinny man gunned the engine without moving.

"Something like that," Stone said. There seemed to be no particular hostility in the man's look, just curiosity, as if Stone might know something he didn't. Or was it more like an old resident giving a new neighbor a carefully casual once-over? In this case, however, Stone was the old resident: he'd been coming here since before the trees had been cut down, and it was only clear-cutting that had made hang gliding possible—or at least less suicidal.

The passenger spoke again, impatiently, and the skinny man said, "Surveying?"

"Something like that too," Stone said.

"You with the lumber company?"

"Rather be against them."

A kind of understanding lit up the narrow face, and the skinny man nodded. "Oh, one of *them*." He grinned for one second only. "You collecting bugs or something?"

"Not if I can help it." Stone smiled to take any sting out of the answer.

"Save me a couple of bullfrogs for lunch, will you?"

"Help yourself," Stone said.

"Come *on*," the passenger said.

The skinny man winked at Stone and said, "I'll yell on my way over, and if you see any hunters, tell them I'm no chicken hawk, okay?"

"Sure," Stone said.

Looking at the binoculars again, the skinny man said, "Bird watching! You a bird watcher?" Eyes wide open, mouth half open, he seemed ready to have the joke confirmed so he could laugh.

His partner beat him to it with a snicker and a high-pitched, "Well, ain't that cute?"

"Up yours," Stone said mildly.

The skinny man smiled and nodded as if he agreed wholeheartedly with both of them and zoomed off uphill, jouncing deep on the springs.

Stone didn't watch them go. He'd thought it was too early in the year for hang gliders. They mostly preferred the more predictable weather toward the dead of summer. But here they were already, working their buddy system of at least three men and probably two pickups, and they'd be gunning past his swamp all afternoon if the wind and rain held off. He felt like quitting now, calling it a bad day, and going home.

Instead, on impulse, he hid his clipboard and books behind a dense clump of swordfern and tried to figure out how to go wading in the choked pond whose depth he wasn't sure of. Yet at the same time, he was worrying. He hadn't told many people, after the first few at the office, that he'd become a bird watcher. Besides, it wasn't the right name for what he did. He watched birds, all right, but the most intense pleasure came just from *being* somewhere natural. He didn't need anything as grand as a whole landscape: a small clearing in the woods could do it, or a bend in a creek or a place like this small, rain-fed, permanently shaded swamp, where he could look and learn and renew a powerful and healing sense of belonging momentarily to a dependable order. He didn't meditate. His mind went nowhere else in time, didn't even go into itself. It was an intimate joining with the Here and Now, as reassuring as love, as valuable and memorable, though not as long-lasting. And he was afraid of giving these sometimes prolonged moments any kind of important name for fear they'd stop happening.

He simply told himself and his wife, on some of his days off, that he was going into the woods, into the foothills of the Cascade Mountains, maybe to some river or creek, and he would drive out of a man-made and man-damaged world and find a place where other, older processes were still at work, and there he'd yield to those places if he could, sometimes (like now) having to struggle in order to yield, a depressing paradox that told him only too clearly that much of his life was *un*natural.

His concentration—or whatever it might be called—was temporarily broken now, his willingness to give himself up. His attention had been called back to a world that required figuring out instead of one to be joined, and he tried to forget the intruders by focusing on the swamp.

It was full of cross-fallen, moss-backed cedar and fir logs, some far older than others, more like mud than wood, some entirely underwater. And there was almost no clear surface water: milfoil, duckweed, watercress, water starwort, and white water crowfoot had claimed the little available light with densely interwoven claims on this territory, but none of them would support his boots wherever he put a foot down. He would have to test every step, like a climber crossing a glacier whose snow and ice had small, almost unknowable relationships with each other and the unaccustomed burden of a two-legged man.

As slowly and safely as he could, he went in up to his knees, pausing after each movement to be sure nothing was going to slip out from under him or send him staggering sideways or sliding off balance down an invisible slope. The water chilled his legs and numbed them in spite of the boots, made him feel half-bodied, a part of the rich spoils barely holding him up now: if he moved too quickly, without testing the next foothold with his staff, he would nearly trip himself in a strange kind of slow motion, yet if he stood still too long, he would begin to sink, as if the soft bottom would take all of him if he waited. Twice, his staff—as long as he was tall—went all the way under without seeming to touch anything but water weeds along the way. He avoided those places.

After five slow minutes, every imaginable shade of green surrounded him, from the black-olive dimness of fringed liverwort to the nearly chartreuse half-dead club moss of last season, and he felt dazed with it. He was in a place where everything was dying and changing and being reborn whether it wanted to be or not, and he was a part of it, a slow part of it, making no more noise than the hemlock nurse-log beside him, out of whose rotten, lichen-covered side a healthy, fully needled three-foot hemlock had sprouted and from whose mass of old roots now a winter wren darted.

Stone held still, not caring whether he sank or not, while the wren perched on a gnarled root and inspected him. It was one of the smallest of birds, smaller than his thumb, chestnut-colored, incredibly quick-moving, black-eyed, its stub of a tail aimed forward over its back. He had never been so close to one before. It was within arm's reach, but he knew if he moved that arm an inch, the wren would be gone instantly. He must have looked dead enough to get by because the wren tilted its head back, opened its beak, and sang.

But it wasn't the loud cascade of notes he'd heard earlier. It was so quiet, he knew if he'd been back near the road only fifteen feet behind him, he wouldn't have heard it at all. The bird sang three times at three short intervals in the same pattern as the loud song but down at the very edge of silence, and he realized he was hearing (as only a few others had) the winter wren's "whisper song." It was the only bird that did such a thing, and no one had explained why it sang so softly at times. Then it was gone, back among the roots.

He felt numb and happy and knew he'd never be able to tell anyone about it successfully. He didn't even try to tell himself about it, merely stood there, slowly sinking into the marshy bottom. But when he glanced up at the sky, both to stretch his tense neck and to trace a movement he'd half-sensed there, he saw the hang glider coming.

Between the tall trunks of the firs he could see the skinny man under a yellow and red wing-shape more colorful than any bird (except a western tanager, maybe), his body braced in the underrigging, his legs trailing at an angle like a hornet's, sailing downward with a directness and serenity that showed the air currents were cooperating so far, not moving fast but oddly slow for the size of the contraption, the ratio of weight to lifting-power probably all in his favor, and when he passed nearly overhead, missing the tops of the firs by ten or fifteen feet, he kept his promise and yelled something.

Stone didn't yell back. Yelling in the woods was for other people. Instead, he watched the hang glider clear the barrier of the grove and approach the landing site hundreds of feet below and hundreds of yards away: a field of corn-stubble some amiable farmer must have okayed as a target. The skinny man landed, not with the limp, collapsing violence of a parachutist but without even kneeling.

He started wading again, but halfheartedly now. Why was he doing what he was doing? He had a sudden sense of his own ludicrousness, and it was almost like catching a glance of himself in a mirror en route to a costume party. He was a grown man wading in a swamp without *having* to, up to his thighs in muck and with nothing much in his head. Not one particle of the greenness around him had the slightest doubt about what *it* was doing; crowding to catch what little light there was with a desperate, calm, age-old ingenuity. And the wren, though its ambitions might be more secret, undoubtedly knew exactly what its next move was.

After a few minutes he heard an engine straining uphill, and the skinny man braked a different-colored pickup as close as possible and leaned out the window. "Howja like that?"

Stone kept it simple. "It looked hard to do."

"Easy as falling off a cliff, only it takes longer," the skinny man said. He had a different partner this time, taking a long pull at a beer can, and the skinny man took it away from him, finished it off, and jerked his head at the folded hang gliders in the truck's bed behind him. "Hey, man, want a lesson?"

"No thanks," Stone said.

"If you like birds so much, why don't you want to fly like one?"

"I doubt if I'd be any good at it," Stone said.

The skinny man laughed, taunting a little, then gunned the engine and took off, waving once.

When the woods and the swamp were silent again, he tried to remember how happy the wren had made him feel, but the pleasure had escaped him. He could tell how deflated he was by the way his eyes refused to focus on anything for long, by the way his boots were making sloshing and twig-snapping noises. And he felt cold. It was time to fold up.

But once on the dry road bank again, he lingered and dawdled, made a few incoherent notes on his clipboard, read the "winter wren" entry in one field guide, wished he had something to drink, and finally realized he was waiting to see the skinny man fly again. The fact depressed him further.

At last he saw the hang glider coming once more down over the clear-cut, over the eroded ridges and draws and the huge splinters of gray slash jackstrawed thickly and deeply enough to keep everything but bracken, fireweed, and a few brambles from reseeding themselves among the weathered stumps. Stone tried to imagine himself doing it. The skinny man had mentioned hawks, and it must have had something of that in it, the use of thermals for soaring, the sense of being all-seeing, superior to groundlings, the rush of the lifting air under his breast, the knowledge of how to move in more than one element, the simple enjoyment of a dangerous situation in which he himself could feel dangerous, and maybe the sheer pleasure of performing.

But as the red and yellow, slightly umbrellalike wing with its strange trapeze supporting a man approached the barrier of the grove, it bucked suddenly and faltered, lost airspeed almost as if it had run into something, tilted and sideslipped briefly, nearly recovered but too late to avoid tangling with the relatively flexible new growth at the top of a fir tree, snagged in it, and fell halfway through it, with the skinny man still hanging on.

Stone's view was partly blocked by other branches of other trees, but he went down into the swamp again and began wallowing in that direction, not taking time to sound the bottom with his staff and three times going in over his boot-tops so that by the time he had slogged his way onto relatively dry, firm duff, he felt as heavy-legged as a dreamer unable to run away from a nightmare.

But he managed to half-run toward this one, waterlogged and

trying not to panic. The tree the hang glider had caught was only forty or fifty yards away, but they were wild yards of hard and soft hummocks, rotten logs, and clumps of thorny bushes, and twice he had to stoop under half-decayed, moss-heavy potential deadfalls of old maple and alder, during which he couldn't even hold his breath, since he was already panting with the strain.

Between watching the uneven ground for fear of breaking an ankle and trying to keep track of the hang glider, he missed what must have been for the skinny man some bad moments: the wing, with its struts now half-crumpled, had fallen farther down through the branches as Stone glimpsed it for the third time, then even farther at the fourth look, and when he came, finally, dizzy and raw-throated, to the base of the right tree, the hang glider and the skinny man had slid into and were momentarily caught by the last few branches before the trunk turned completely bare, twenty or twenty-five feet overhead.

The skinny man's legs were swinging back and forth limply, and for a few seconds Stone thought he'd been knocked out and wouldn't be able to help himself by squirreling his way along a branch five feet to the trunk and sliding down it like a bear cub. But then he saw the pale face peer downward at him and seem to focus with a kind of recognition. His stocking cap was gone, and his long dark hair was getting in the way, but he steadied his attention like a drunk and said, "Hi, man."

Stone said, "Don't move."

"I wouldn't if I could."

Which sounded like the right frame of mind or like a mind with the frame still around it. "Hang on," Stone said. "Were your buddies watching? Will they come?"

"Yeah." The wing jerked and crumpled a little more but didn't lose its hold on the last branches.

"Are you hurt bad?"

"I don't know," the skinny man said. "Got a cigarette?"

Stone didn't bother to laugh. "Even if I could climb a bare trunk that high, all I could do is help you fall down. So keep still, hang on, and when the others get here, we'll work something out. Do they have any rope?"

"Who knows?" the skinny man said, sounding groggy.

Again the glider lurched and now seemed to be snagged by too narrow a branch to depend on for long. Stone stationed himself directly under the skinny man's dangling legs, feeling like a circus roustabout standing under a solo balancing act without a safety net, ready to break the fall with his arms, to lower an accident from fatal to serious if he could. But what if the glider, with what he could see were broken struts, fell too? How was he supposed to catch that?

He could see the skinny man fumbling at some cords, and for a moment he let himself hope there could be a climb-down after all, but suddenly the skinny man was free of every entanglement and falling all by himself, leaving the glider stuck in the tree, and Stone thought as fast as he could and braced himself with bent knees and bent elbows and his forearms as tense as he could make them, and in spite of every bit of thinking he could do in that single second, he wasn't ready for the slamming impact.

The skinny man seemed to pass through his arms as if they hadn't been there, and the simultaneous jarring of Stone's knees, hips, ankles, and elbows made him think he'd done the falling himself. Yet there he was on all fours with the skinny man lying flat on his back on the soft, moss-patched duff in front of him.

The eyes half-opened. "Thanks, man."

"No thanks," Stone said. "Don't move." He took a moment to forget the pain in his joints, the strained ligaments, the bruises on their way. "Take your time now and hold still. Figure out how you feel. *Slow.*"

"Lousy, man."

"Move your fingers," Stone said.

The skinny man moved almost all of them like a child learning a trick.

"Hold still now," Stone said, recollecting garbled first-aid lessons from some other life. "Now move your feet a little." He waited, but the skinny man's feet were motionless, his boots flopped outwards. "Go on, move them."

"If they're not moving, man, they're not going to." He was staring up at the branches he'd just come from, scratched across cheeks and forehead but not bleeding badly.

Stone was shaking but tried not to let the skinny man see it. Just to keep the conversation going, he said, "I think maybe you hit a tree."

"Yeah, they should've cut the bastard down with the rest of them."

Swallowing something that tasted more like despair than anger, Stone said, "Well, it cut *you* down, man. And right now you'd better stay put and practice keeping still for a change. You're going to do a lot of it for months, because if you try to sit up or even roll over, you're going to kill yourself. I think your back's broken."

"I think it is too," the skinny man said. Cold sweat was beading his face now, his pale lips were fluttering, and he was breathing shallowly and not often enough.

Stone took off his parka and covered as much of the middle torso as he could. "I mean *really* broken."

After a short serious silence, the skinny man said, "Well, at least I didn't bust my balls."

"You wouldn't know it if you had," Stone said. "Right now your lower half is out of business. Lie still. Your buddies will be here in a minute." Already he could hear at least one engine roaring. "You may be going into shock, so don't let it throw you."

The skinny man tried to come up to his elbows, and Stone forced him back as gently as possible, keeping hold of the thin, bony shoulders quivering under his own quivering hands. Blinking and seeming to give up the idea, the skinny man said, "Okay, doc." His teeth were beginning to chatter now. "It sure was beautiful up there. Maybe I should've stayed up there."

"Maybe so, but it wasn't bad down here either." They could probably make a stretcher out of the broom-handle and a cottonwood sapling and parkas, and he scraped the bottom of his brain trying to remember where the nearest hospital was. The roaring was closer.

"See any special birds besides me?" the skinny man said, squeezing his eyes shut against what seemed to be pain.

"All birds are special," Stone said.

A pickup was jouncing around the humped downhill curve, and the skinny man said, "I mean really good ones."

"All birds are really good," Stone said. "Now hold still, you knothead."

"Wiseass," the skinny man said.

Stone heard a car door slam behind him, and he broke his own rule about yelling in the woods, hollering, "Here!" A voice answered, and he braced the skinny man's narrow, light-boned shoulders against the forest floor, keeping him still, waiting for them both to understand each other better while there was still time.

ROBERT OLEN BUTLER

Jealous Husband Returns in Form of Parrot

I never can quite say as much as I know. I look at other parrots and I wonder if it's the same for them, if somebody is trapped in each of them paying some kind of price for living their life in a certain way. For instance, "Hello," I say, and I'm sitting on a perch in a pet store in Houston and what I'm really thinking is, Holy shit. It's you. And what's happened is I'm looking at my wife.

"Hello," she says, and she comes over to me and I can't believe how beautiful she is. Those great brown eyes, almost as dark as the center of mine. And her nose—I don't remember her for her nose but its beauty is clear to me now. Her nose is a little too long, but it's redeemed by the faint hook to it.

She scratches the back of my neck.

Her touch makes my tail flare. I feel the stretch and rustle of me back there. I bend my head to her and she whispers, "Pretty bird."

For a moment I think she knows it's me. But she doesn't, of course. I say "hello" again and I will eventually pick up "pretty bird." I can tell that as soon as she says it, but for now I can only give her another hello. Her fingertips move through my feathers and she seems to know about birds. She knows that to pet a bird you don't smooth his feathers down, you ruffle them.

But of course she did that in my human life as well. It's all the same for her. Not that I was complaining, even to myself, at that moment in the pet shop when she found me like I presume she was supposed to. She said it again, "Pretty bird," and this brain that works like it does now could feel that tiny little voice of mine ready to shape itself around these sounds. But before I could get them out of my beak there was this guy at my wife's shoulder and all my feathers went slick flat like to make me small enough not to be seen and I backed away. The pupils of my eyes pinned and dilated and pinned again.

He circled around her. A guy that looked like a meat packer, big in the chest and thick with hair, the kind of guy that I always sensed her eyes moving to when I was alive. I had a bare chest and I'd look for little black hairs on the sheets when I'd come home on a day with the whiff of somebody else in the air. She was still in the same goddamn rut.

A "hello" wouldn't do and I'd recently learned "good night" but it was the wrong suggestion altogether, so I said nothing and the guy circled her and he was looking at me with a smug little smile and I fluffed up all my feathers, made myself about twice as big, so big he'd see he couldn't mess with me. I waited for him to draw close enough for me to take off the tip of his finger.

But she intervened. Those nut-brown eyes were before me and she said, "I want him."

And that's how I ended up in my own house once again. She bought me a large black wrought-iron cage, very large, convinced by some young guy who clerked in the bird department and who took her aside and made his voice go much too soft when he was doing the selling job. The meat packer didn't like it. I didn't either. I'd missed a lot of chances to take a bite out of this clerk in my stay at the shop and I regretted that suddenly.

But I got my giant cage and I guess I'm happy enough about that. I can pace as much as I want. I can hang upside down. It's full of bird toys. That dangling thing over there with knots and strips of rawhide and a bell at the bottom needs a good thrashing a couple of times a day and I'm the bird to do it. I look at the very dangle of it and the thing is rough, the rawhide and the knotted rope, and I get this restlessness back in my tail, a burning thrashing feeling, and it's like all the times when I was sure there was a man naked with my wife. Then I go to this thing that feels so familiar and I bite and bite and it's very good.

I could have used the thing the last day I went out of this house as a man. I'd found the address of the new guy at my wife's office. He'd been there a month in the shipping department and three times she'd mentioned him. She didn't even have to work with him and three times I heard about him, just dropped into the conversation. "Oh," she'd say when a car commercial came on the television, "that car there is like the one the new man in shipping owns. Just like it." Hey, I'm not stupid. She said another thing about him and then another and right after the third one I locked myself in the bathroom because I couldn't rage about this anymore. I felt like a damn fool whenever I actually said anything about this kind of feeling and she looked at me like she could start hating me real easy and so I was working on saying nothing, even if it meant locking myself up. My goal was to hold my tongue about half the time. That would be a good start.

But this guy from shipping. I found out his name and his address and it was one of her typical Saturday afternoons of vague shopping. So I went to his house, and his car that was just like the commercial was outside. Nobody was around in the neighborhood and there was this big tree in the back of the house going up to a second-floor window that was making funny little sounds. I went up. The shade was drawn but not quite all the way. I was holding on to a limb with arms and legs wrapped around it like it was her in those times when I could forget the others for a little while. But the crack in the shade was just out of view and I crawled on along till there was no limb left and I fell on my head. Thinking about that now, my wings flap and I feel myself lift up and it all seems so avoidable. Though I know I'm different now. I'm a bird.

Except I'm not. That's what's confusing. It's like those times when she would tell me she loved me and I actually believed her and maybe it was true and we clung to each other in bed and at times like that I was different. I was the man in her life. I was whole with her. Except even at that moment, holding her sweetly, there was this other creature inside me who knew a lot more about it and couldn't quite put all the evidence together to speak.

My cage sits in the den. My pool table is gone and the cage is sitting in that space and if I come all the way down to one end of my perch I can see through the door and down the back hallway to the master bedroom. When she keeps the bedroom door open I can see the space at the foot of the bed but not the bed itself. That I can sense to the left, just out of sight. I watch the men go in and I hear the sounds but I can't quite see. And they drive me crazy.

I flap my wings and I squawk and I fluff up and I slick down and I throw seed and I attack that dangly toy as if it was the guy's balls, but it does no good. It never did any good in the other life either, the thrashing around I did by myself. In that other life I'd have given anything to be standing in this den with her doing this thing with some other guy just down the hall and all I had to do was walk down there and turn the corner and she couldn't deny it anymore.

But now all I can do is try to let it go. I sidestep down to the opposite end of the cage and I look out the big sliding glass doors to the backyard. It's a pretty yard. There are great placid maple trees with good places to roost. There's a blue sky that plucks at the feathers on my chest. There are clouds. Other birds. Fly away. I could just fly away.

I tried once and I learned a lesson. She forgot and left the door to my cage open and I climbed beak and foot, beak and foot, along the bars and curled around to stretch sideways out the door and the vast scene of peace was there at the other end of the room. I flew.

And a pain flared through my head and I fell straight down and the room whirled around and the only good thing was she held me. She put her hands under my wings and lifted me and clutched me to her breast and I wish there hadn't been bees in my head at the time so I could have enjoyed that, but she put me back in the cage and wept awhile. That touched me, her tears. And I looked back to the wall of sky and trees. There was something invisible there between me and that dream of peace. I remembered, eventually, about glass, and I knew I'd been lucky, I knew that for the little fragile-boned skull I was doing all this thinking in, it meant death.

She wept that day but by the night she had another man. A guy with a thick Georgia truck-stop accent and pale white skin and an Adam's apple big as my seed ball. This guy has been around for a few weeks and he makes a whooping sound down the hallway, just out of my sight. At times like that I want to fly against the bars of the cage, but I don't. I have to remember how the world has changed.

She's single now, of course. Her husband, the man that I was, is dead to her. She does not understand all that is behind my "hello." I know many words, for a parrot. I am a yellow-nape Amazon, a handsome bird, I think, green with a splash of yellow at the back of my neck. I talk pretty well, but none of my words are adequate. I can't make her understand.

And what would I say if I could? I was jealous in life. I admit it. I would admit it to her. But it was because of my connection to her. I would explain that. When we held each other, I had no past at all, no present but her body, no future but to lie there and not let her go. I was an egg hatched beneath her crouching body, I entered as a chick into her wet sky of a body, and all that I wished was to sit on her shoulder and fluff my feathers and lay my head against her cheek, my neck exposed to her hand. And so the glances that I could see in her troubled me deeply, the movement of her eyes in public to other men, the laughs sent across a room, the tracking of her mind behind her blank eyes, pursuing images of others, her distraction even in our bed, the ghosts that were there of men who'd touched her, perhaps even that very day. I was not part of all those other men who were part of her. I didn't want to connect to all that. It was only her that I would fluff for but these others were there also and I couldn't put them aside. I sensed them inside her and so they were inside me. If I had the words, these are the things I would say.

But half an hour ago there was a moment that thrilled me. A word, a word we all knew in the pet shop, was just the right word after all. This guy with his cowboy belt buckle and rattlesnake boots and his pasty face and his twanging words of love trailed after my wife through the den, past my cage, and I said, "Cracker." He even flipped his head back a little at this in surprise. He'd been called that before to his face, I realized. I said it again, "Cracker." But to him I was a bird and he let it pass. "Cracker," I said. "Hello, cracker." That was even better. They were out of sight through the hall doorway and I hustled along the perch and I caught a glimpse of them before they made the turn to the bed and I said, "Hello, cracker," and he shot me one last glance.

It made me hopeful. I eased away from that end of the cage, moved toward the scene of peace beyond the far wall. The sky is chalky blue today, blue like the brow of the blue-front Amazon who was on the perch next to me for about a week at the store. She was very sweet, but I watched her carefully for a day or two when she first came in. And it wasn't long before she nuzzled up to a cockatoo named Gordo and I knew she'd break my heart. But her color now in the sky is sweet, really. I left all those feelings behind me when my wife showed up. I am a faithful man, for all my suspicions. Too faithful, maybe. I am ready to give too much and maybe that's the problem.

The whooping began down the hall, and I focused on a tree out there. A crow flapped down, his mouth open, his throat throbbing, though I could not hear his sound. I was feeling very odd. At least I'd made my point to the guy in the other room. "Pretty bird," I said, referring to myself. She called me "pretty bird" and I believed her and I told myself again, "Pretty bird."

But then something new happened, something very difficult for me. She appeared in the den naked. I have not seen her naked since I fell from the tree and had no wings to fly. She always had a certain tidiness in things. She was naked in the bedroom, clothed in the den. But now she appears from the hallway and I look at her and she is still slim and she is beautiful, I think—at least I clearly remember that as her husband I found her beautiful in this state. Now, though, she seems too naked. Plucked. I find that a sad thing. I am sorry for her and she goes by me and she disappears into the kitchen. I want to pluck some of my own feathers, the feathers from my chest, and give them to her. I love her more in that moment, seeing her terrible nakedness, than I ever have before.

And since I've had success in the last few minutes with words, when she comes back I am moved to speak. "Hello," I say, meaning, You are still connected to me, I still want only you. "Hello," I say again. Please listen to this tiny heart that beats fast at all times for you.

And she does indeed stop and she comes to me and bends to me. "Pretty bird," I say and I am saying, You are beautiful, my wife, and your beauty cries out for protection. "Pretty." I want to cover you with my own nakedness. "Bad bird," I say. If there are others in your life, even in your mind, then there is nothing I can do. "Bad." Your nakedness is touched from inside by the others. "Open," I say. How can we be whole together if you are not empty in that place that I am to fill?

She smiles at this and she opens the door to my cage. "Up," I say, meaning, Is there no place for me in this world where I can be free of this terrible sense of others?

She reaches in now and offers her hand and I climb onto it and I tremble and she says, "Poor baby."

"Poor baby," I say. You have yearned for wholeness too and somehow I failed you. I was not enough. "Bad bird," I say. I'm sorry.

And then the cracker comes around the corner. He wears only his rattlesnake boots. I take one look at his miserable, featureless body and shake my head. We keep our sexual parts hidden, we parrots, and this man is a pitiful sight. "Peanut," I say. I presume that my wife simply has not noticed. But that's foolish, of course. This is, in fact, what she wants. Not me. And she scrapes me off her hand onto the open cage door and she turns her naked back to me and embraces this man and they laugh and stagger in their embrace around the corner.

For a moment I still think I've been eloquent. What I've said only needs repeating for it to have its transforming effect. "Hello," I say. "Hello. Pretty bird. Pretty. Bad bird. Bad. Open. Up. Poor baby. Bad bird." And I am beginning to hear myself as I really sound to her. "Peanut." I can never say what is in my heart to her. Never.

I stand on my cage door now and my wings stir. I look at the corner to the hallway and down at the end the whooping has begun again. I can fly there and think of things to do about all this.

But I do not. I turn instead and I look at the trees moving just beyond the other end of the room. I look at the sky the color of the brow of a blue-front Amazon. A shadow of birds spanks across the lawn. And I spread my wings. I will fly now. Even though I know there is something between me and that place where I can be free of all these feelings, I will fly. I will throw myself there again and again. Pretty bird. Bad bird. Good night.

JOEL BROUWER

Abracadabra Kit

Because the Evil Knights, who chewed Skoal
in sixth grade and wore matching black jackets,
beat me to jelly almost every day,
the joy buzzers, pepper gum, and fake puke
on offer in Batman's sooty back pages
seemed meager, trifling, idle junk. Even
the X-ray specs which turned skirts clear left me
cold: so you see their panties. Then what?
All these were mere pranks. I needed power.

And so with the last of my birthday cash
I ordered the Abracadabra Kit.
The ad promised rivals would flee me in terror
and pictured grownups swooning (eyes X's)
as a boy in tails drove swords through his sister.
I checked the mailbox every day and dreamed
the damage I'd do the Knights, the magic words
I'd speak to blanket them with zits, shrivel
their cocks, cripple their families and pets.

The kit came and of course was crap.
Three thimbles and a marble for the shell game,
a wand which bloomed paper roses just once
before its spring broke, a hank of clothesline
for knot tricks. Most useless of all, a book:
43 Illusions for Beginners.
The book said *people need magic more than water.*
The book said *practice* and *takes years to master.*
Sent to bed at ten, I read, rapt, by flashlight.

The next day at recess the chief Knight, Pete,
brought me a dog turd, said *Here's your lunch, fag.*
I reached, pulled an egg from his ear, cracked it
in my hand, and mom's canary shot up
gold between us, pulsed above the playground,
vanished whistling over the gym. That instant—
Pete's gulp of wonder before his first savage punch
hooked my gut, the bird flying wild and oblivious—
my haven then, my labor ever since.

DAVID BOTTOMS

Under the Vulture-Tree

We have all seen them circling pastures,
have looked up from the mouth of a barn, a pine clearing,
the fences of our own backyards, and have stood
amazed by the one slow wing beat, the endless dihedral drift.
But I had never seen so many so close, hundreds,
every limb of the dead oak feathered black,

and I cut the engine, let the river grab the johnboat
and pull it toward the tree.
The black leaves shined, the pink fruit blossomed
red, ugly as a human heart.
Then, as I passed under their dream, I saw for the first time
its soft countenance, the raw fleshy jowls
wrinkled and generous, like the faces of the very old
who have grown to empathize with everything.

And I drifted away from them, slow, on the pull of the river,
reluctant, looking back at their roost,
calling them what I'd never called them, what they are,
those dwarfed transfiguring angels,
who flock to the side of the poisoned fox, the mud turtle
crushed on the shoulder of the road,
who pray over the leaf-graves of the anonymous lost,
with mercy enough to consume us all and give us wings.

Albert Goldbarth

27,000 Miles

These two asleep . . . so indrawn and compact,
like lavish origami animals returned

to slips of paper once again; and then
the paper once again become a string

of pith, a secret that the plant hums to itself. . . .
You see?—so often we envy the grandiose, the way

those small toy things of Leonardo's want to be
the great, air-conquering and miles-eating

living wings
they're modeled on. And bird flight *is*

amazing: simultaneously strength,
escape, caprice: the Arctic tern completes

its trip of nearly 27,000 miles every year;
a swan will frighten bears away

by angry aerial display of flapping wingspan.
But it isn't all flight; they also

fold; and at night on the water or in the eaves
they package their bodies

into their bodies, smaller, and deeply
smaller yet: migrating a similar distance

in the opposite direction.

WILLIAM MEREDITH

The Jain Bird Hospital in Delhi

Outside the hotel window, unenlightened pigeons
weave and dive like Stukas on their prey,
apparently some tiny insect brother.
(In India, the attainment of nonviolence
is considered a proper goal for human beings.)
If one of the pigeons should fly into the illusion

of my window and survive (the body is no illusion
when it's hurt) he could be taken across town to the bird
hospital where Jains, skilled medical men,
repair the feathery sick and broken victims.
There, in reproof of violence
and of nothing else, live Mahavira's brothers and sisters.

To this small, gentle order of monks and nuns
it is bright Vishnu and dark Shiva who are illusion.
They trust in faith, cognition, and nonviolence
to release them from rebirth. They think that birds
and animals—like us, some predators, some prey—
should be ministered to no less than men and women.

The Jains who deal with creatures (and with laymen)
wear white, while their more enterprising hermit brothers
walk naked and are called *the sky-clad.* Jains pray
to no deity, human kindness being their sole illusion.
Mahavira and those twenty-three other airy creatures
who turned to saints with him, preached the doctrine of *ahimsa,*

which in our belligerent tongue becomes *nonviolence.*
It's not a doctrine congenial to snarers and poultrymen,
who every day bring to market maimed pheasants.
Numbers of these are brought in by the Jain brothers
and brought, to grow back wing-tips and illusions,
to one of the hospitals succoring such small quarry.

When strong and feathered again, the lucky victims
get reborn on Sunday mornings to the world's violence,
released from the roofs of these temples to illusion.
It is hard for a westerner to speak about men and women
like these, who call the birds of the air *brothers.*
We recall the embarrassed fanfare for Francis and his flock.

We're poor forked sky-clad things ourselves
and God knows prey to illusion—*e.g.*, I claim these brothers
and sisters in India, stemming a little violence, among birds.

SHERI JOSEPH

The Elixir

Monday morning, another one. I'm finished with the feeding and am fetching a wheelbarrow to start mucking stalls, when I feel my boot roll something as soft and little as a mouse. It tumbles a few feet along the brick-lined hall, spinning dust and cobwebs and horsehair and specks of wood shavings about itself as it goes. When I pick it up, it's grown into a grayish cocoon wrapped around a pulse of life. I know it's alive—the way you know a cocoon has life in it, despite the fact that I just kicked it half across the floor—but it's so entangled it can't move. I hold it as gently as I can and worry some of the grime away with my fingernails. A black reed of a beak appears, like a grain of wild rice, then a glimmer of green feathers, a pumping iridescent breast the size of my thumb. Another damned hummingbird.

They come in here after the fluorescent lights. Maybe a thing with a brain the size of a needle's eye can't tell the difference between a gladiolus and a tube of electricity—I don't know—but they'll fly in here sometimes and bounce off the lights like moths. I saw one doing that for a good ten minutes, until I scooched it out the door with a broom; then it flew away. If I don't catch them in time, they'll exhaust themselves and wind up on the floor, like this one. Their metabolism's so fast they short out after a while.

Once I've uncovered her white throat, I know it's a female. Maybe she's the same one I chased out yesterday. "Stubborn," I tell her. "See where it got you." But you can't reason with a bird as if she were your teenage daughter. Then again, teenagers don't necessarily listen any better than birds—they're bound to go zinging off their own bright lights, deaf to common sense.

With Marcy, it was cities. First Atlanta, then Jacksonville, then Memphis—three times home in the back of a police car. Between those, and after, I never knew her destinations or what drew her one place or another. Something about a city. She'd show you with her glass-hard eyes and the set of her chin which way she was oriented, as if she were picking up a distant signal other people couldn't hear. As if the whole time you were trying to talk to her, she was listening to something else.

The truth was, I didn't understand that girl. I wanted reasons. Sometimes I blamed her dad for not paying any attention to her. "She's not easy to love," Jimmy would inform me like it was news, and I'd holler back, "She's your *daughter*. She's thirteen." We would fall to silence, and later Marcy would pass through to get a Pop-Tart and go back to her room, without ever looking at us—as if she walked in another reality and Jimmy and I were just a background flutter, characters on her TV.

After Atlanta, she returned armored in the proof she could take care of herself. "It's not about you," she said. "It's not about him, either." But I wanted a cause, and when she took off for Memphis I settled on Jimmy. He came home one day hauling the trailer, another horse he'd got for a bargain, and I said, "No, sir. You are not putting another horse in my barn, not at a time like this." He said, fine, he'd pasture it over at Ernie's place, and I said, "Fine, and you can go with it." I meant it, too. Since then I've lived alone, except for those brief times when Marcy was home.

The last time I saw her the way I think of her now, she was fourteen—round, pretty face, long brown hair I used to wash and comb. I didn't see her again until she was nineteen and sick, too weak to stand. "I'm dying, Mama" is what she told me over the phone, as if there would be no use arguing. "I need a place to stay for a while."

She came off the plane in a wheelchair. A flight attendant rolled her through a dazzle of sun that flooded the glass walls of the terminal, so that she all but vanished in light. Then she was before me, my daughter—wide blue eyes and crooked smile—wanting to know would I have recognized her.

She was true to her word, about the dying, though at times her body argued otherwise. Miracle drugs, first one, then another, briefly lifted her strength, and for a time she would feel well. But eventually

I had to quit my job to look after her, to feed her and clean the vomit and try, during the bad spells, to keep her in bed. She wandered. Even after she lost her sight, I'd find her bumping around the house, disoriented, looking for a door.

Once in winter at midnight, I found her outside in nothing but a nightgown, barefoot in the garden, out of her wits. "Come inside, love," I begged, tugging her chilled arm, but she persisted toward the west, chin thrust before her as if it knew the way. "Why are you so stubborn? Look where it's gotten you." Instructive, forgetting her blindness, I pointed to the coiled hose where her feet were tangled, the naked, frost-crusted vines climbing the trellis. But she didn't know me. She had somewhere to go, it seemed, and it took me a time to turn her face, to coax her back indoors. From then on, I put her down each night in my own bed, between my body and the wall.

Nine times in fourteen months I carried her to the emergency room—vomiting, diarrhea, pneumonia, blindness, dementia—words I didn't know how to attach to my daughter. An IV went directly into her chest. A tube served her last meals. I cleaned her as I had when she was a baby—never, never in all my prayers, did I imagine a child returned this way. Forty-four different medications, and each one wore itself out, or wore her out, and no sooner one horror banished than another rooted in a new spot, resisting the drugs or caused by the drugs, the internal functions in chaos and shutdown and revolt.

It seemed wrong, after all that, that the one to end it would be a strain of tuberculosis only birds get. The doctor thought she'd carried it for some time, that she'd probably picked it up from pigeon droppings. In a city, he said, she could hardly have avoided exposure. It was in the air everyone breathed.

This spring, five years after her death, the hummingbirds started showing up. I find them buzzing along the walls a few inches from the ground or panting in the horses' bedding, their little feet rimed with cobwebs. One I found actually caught in a new web, suspended from a crossbeam like some spider's lunch with its miniature wings outspread. I looked up, and it blinked—I swear I saw it blink at me with its black pin eyes.

After Marcy died the way she did, I never wanted to touch a bird, any bird. Dirty things, they seemed. And these minute visitors so often arrive coated in a filth denser than their own bodies. But I can't leave them to die. Hummingbirds never touch the earth if they can help it, so once they're down they must have no capacity to cast off the lint of the world. Perhaps their bodies even attract it somehow. But underneath the matted debris, they're like jewels still; lift it off and they shimmer again.

I admit it's a trial to clean a thing so delicate, always feeling that one unfortunate twitch of your finger could crush it beyond repair. But I always try. I know some magic too. This little female I carry up to the house this morning—she's weaker than most, still partly cocooned, won't even lift her head to give me a defiant look like some of them do. On the back porch, I drop two sugar cubes in a coffee mug, add some water, pop the mug into the microwave. While it warms, I use a pair of tweezers, still out here from last time, to remove the remaining cobwebs and one long, dark horsetail hair that has the bird bound like a package. When she's free, she lies on her side in my palm, breathing five breaths for every second.

"You're going to use up your life awful fast at that rate," I tell her. They never listen. "Sorry about kicking you," I add. "That probably didn't help."

I take the mug out of the microwave and stir the water, then scoop out a teaspoonful. Specks of sugar are still visible in the spoon's silver bowl, but I hold it up to the bird anyway, submerge the tip of her reed-like beak. At first she doesn't move. Then her black lash of a tongue flicks out once, experimentally. Pretty soon the tongue is going like the needle of a sewing machine, ravenous. I'm freshly amazed. Even caged in my loose-curled fingers—surely she's terrified of this giant—the bird knows sugar when she tastes it, knows her body needs it, and she drinks.

For a full minute she drinks, then seems to tire. She looks at me.

Her stiff, matchstick wings are spread against my palm like little flippers, propping her upright—what intricate mechanisms of the body must be required to beat those wings into a blur, to zip quick as a bee to a flower cup and then hover, poised there in startling visibility. What strength. I've never kicked one across a floor before, can't imagine the damage. But I go outside onto the step and open my hand.

There is no moment of waiting, hoping. Like magic, she rises. Her wings hum with effort, and her leaving is slow, gradual, as if her body is heavier than she remembers. But still she rises, over the barn and past it. To the limits of vision, she is a dark seed lofted into the morning, and I clap my hands to my face, forgetting the dirtiness of birds.

All I wanted, in the end, was one last drug. Marcy lay in a hospital bed, her long, clean hair spread on the pillow around her upturned face. She weighed eighty-two pounds. She didn't know me, didn't know where her body lay, spoke urgently in words—as clear as daylight—that made no human sense. There has to be another drug, I insisted. Someone's lab must hold a cure, newly cooked, experimental, untested. I'll take anything.

What a slap from God to see these exhausted birds revived, again and again, with a single spoonful of kitchen sugar. But I never get tired of it.

BARBARA KINGSOLVER

from Prodigal Summer

She sat cross-legged on the floor of the porch, brushing out her hair and listening to the opening chorus of this day. A black-and-white warbler had started it long before dawn, breaking into her sleep with his high-pitched "Sweet *sweet!*" Deanna could picture him out there, circling the trunk of a poplar, tilting his tiny little zebra-striped head toward the first hints of light, tearing yesterday off the calendar and opening the summer of love with his outsized voice. She'd rushed out to the porch in her nightgown and bare feet, the hairbrush mostly an afterthought lying on her lap. She needed to listen to this: prodigal summer, the season of extravagant procreation. It could wear out everything in its path with its passionate excesses, but nothing alive with wings or a heart or a seed curled into itself in the ground could resist welcoming it back when it came.

The other warblers woke up soon after the black-and-white: first she heard the syncopated phrase of the hooded warbler with its up-beat ending like a good joke, then the Kentucky with his more solemn, rolling trill. By now a faint gray light was seeping up the edge of the sky, or what she could see of the sky through the black-armed trees. This hollow was a mean divide, with mountains rising steeply on both sides and the trees towering higher still. The cabin was no place to be if you craved long days and sunlight, but there was no better dawn chorus anywhere on earth. In the high season of courtship and mating, this music was like the earth itself opening its mouth to sing. Its crescendo crept forward slowly as the daylight roused one bird and then another: the black-capped and Carolina chickadees came next, first cousins who whistled their notes on separate pitches, close together, distinguishable to any chickadee but to very few humans, especially among this choir of other voices. Deanna smiled to hear the first veery, whose song sounded like a thumb run down the tines of a comb. It had been the first birdcall to capture her fascination in childhood—not the calls of the meadowlarks and sparrows that sang outside her windows on the farm every morning, but the song of the veery, a high-elevation migrant that she encountered only up here, on fishing expeditions with her dad. Maybe she'd just never really listened before those trips, which yielded few trout and less conversation but so much silent waiting in the woods. "Now, 'at's a comb bird," her dad had improvised, smiling, when she asked, and she'd dutifully pictured the bird as a comb-shaped creature, bright pink. She was disappointed, years later, when she discovered its brown, ordinary birdness in the Peterson field guide.

The dawn chorus was a whistling roar by now, the sound of a thousand males calling out love to a thousand silent females ready to choose and make the world new. It was nothing but heady cacophony unless you paid attention to the individual entries: a rose-breasted grosbeak with his sweet, complicated little sonnet; a vireo with his repetitious bursts of eighth notes and triplets. And then came the wood thrush, with his tone poem of a birdsong. The wood thrush defined these woods for Deanna, providing background music for her thoughts and naming her place in the forest. The dawn chorus would subside in another hour, but the wood thrush would persist for a long time into the morning, then pick up again in early evening or even at midday if it was cloudy. Nannie had asked her once in a letter how she could live up here alone with all the quiet, and that was Deanna's answer: when human conversation stopped, the world was anything but *quiet.* She lived with wood thrushes for company.

Deanna smiled a little to think of Nannie down there in the valley. Nannie lived for neighborly chat, staking out her independent old-lady life but still snatching conversation wherever possible, the way a dieter will keep after the cookies tucked in a cupboard. No wonder she worried for Deanna.

The sky had a solid white cast by now, mottled like an old porcelain plate, and the voices began to back off or drop out one by one. Soon she'd be left with only the thrush song and the rest of her day. A few titmice and chickadees were congregating at the spot underneath a chokecherry, a dozen yards from her cabin, where she always scattered birdseed on top of a flat boulder. She'd chosen a spot she could watch from her window and had put out seed there all winter—ordered birdseed by the fifty-pound bag, in fact, along with her monthly grocery requisition. The Forest Service never questioned it. It wasn't exactly policy to feed chickadees and cardinals, but apparently the government was willing to do whatever it took to keep a wildlife monitor sane through the winter, and in Deanna's case it was birdseed. Sitting at the table beside the window with her coffee on snowy February mornings, she could lose hours watching the colorful crowd that gathered outside, envying the birds their freedom in the intense cold. Envying, even, their self-important fuss and bustle. A bird never doubts its place at the center of the universe.

CHARLES BAXTER

Cataract

At the dinner table Walter Lundholm, Sr., toys with the silver pepper shaker, wondering how to announce his plans for an early retirement to his wife. They have both been eating overcooked beef burgundy, and now Jane is relating an anecdote about what happened at the A&P this afternoon. It seems that a rather shabby-looking man with a broad, piggish face fell down in a dead faint in front of the meat counter and had to be revived by two grocery boys. While Jane is telling this story, the sound of rhythmic clapping leaks out from the kitchen, where the Lundholms' cook, Vernice, is listening to Pentecostal radio while she does the dishes.

Walter is following Jane's story, but he is looking at the fleur-de-lis pattern wallpaper. Every thirty seconds, he nods. What he wants to say to his wife is that they don't need more money and he wants to stop earning it. In worldly terms, this is not a large problem, but it happens to be associated in his mind with the unpleasant aching glow he has lately felt radiating out of his chest. What he does not want to say to Jane is that if he works much longer at developing real estate properties along high-intensity freeways, he too will eventually fall to the floor in supermarkets. He listens as she concludes her story, with the piggish man coming to, and walking home by himself.

"And with no groceries," Jane says. "Imagine. What do you suppose he was doing there?" She waits. "Walter, why are you playing with that pepper shaker? You've finished your meal."

"I've been thinking."

"What? What have you been thinking about?"

"Giving up the office." He watches her reaction. "I'm going to let Gordon and Kenny buy me out. They've made offers. I'm tired of the business. I've been meaning to tell you."

"Well," she says, reaching for the string of pearls around her neck.

"My goodness. This is quite a surprise. You're not being silly, are you? This isn't one of your moods? You *do* get obsessive about things."

"No." He is gazing at the pearls. "It's not a mood. I've thought about it for months."

"Months. Well, this is the first *I've* heard. What will you do?" She has a sip of wine. "Start a new business?"

"No. Not that. No more money. I want to try something different." He smiles and looks directly at her. "I want to paint again."

"Paint?" She clasps her hands together. "*Paint?* Walter, dear, you haven't painted since your college days. Why on earth did you think of that? *What* do you want to paint?"

He folds his napkin. "Well, landscapes, to start with. I have this idea about a barn." He draws a barn in the air. "An image. I think about it quite often. I've even dreamt about it." From the living-room FM stereo comes the sound of dinner music, the Brahms Clarinet Quintet. He arranges his fork and knife on the plate. "I want to drive out to the countryside and paint whatever I see."

"Well." She tilts her head back. "I am trying to take all of this evenly and calmly. Believe me, it's not easy." She touches her hair. "I don't know *what* our friends will say. I suppose we shall make some accommodations. I can't say I was prepared for this piece of news, but I will do my best. Do you think you'll be able to fill all the hours of the day with this new hobby of yours?"

"I don't know."

"I don't know either. We'll see." She gives him a social smile. "I imagine it'll be good for your blood pressure. One hundred sixty-five over ninety is no joke." She looks as if she is adding numbers. Apparently the results of these calculations do not cause her excessive distress, because she picks up her wineglass and looks out the bay window toward the driveway. "Painting," she says. "Now whatever put that into your mind? Whom were you thinking of? Rembrandt? Degas?"

He looks down at his plate. "No. Not them."

"Well, then. Who inspired you?"

"Winston Churchill," he says. "I want to paint like that."

Now, a month later, Walter's canvas, easel, floppy hat, chair, and oils are loaded up in the back of his Buick Electra, and he is driving out from suburban Minneapolis along Highway 7 into rural Minnesota, looking for a scene to paint. He wants a barn. A barn stands in the right-hand background of his imagination, with the rest of the canvas filled with fields and sky. Many barns have been torn down to make way for Walter's development properties, and now, in his own small way, he wants to save one. He thinks of the barn as reddish-brown but has not decided what color the fields should be.

In central Minnesota Walter finds himself off the freeway and the state highway he meant to follow. He is speeding down a dirt road at forty-five miles an hour. His car throws up a turbulent wake of light brown dust. Where is the right barn? Most of them are marred geometrically by deep-blue Harvestore silos that put them in shadow. What Walter wants is an individual barn, by itself, a proud symbol of something or other.

Ahead and to his right he sees a barn and decides that, yes, this one will have to do. Red, with the proper slanted rooflines, and a wide door at its loft with hinges at the top, it shows some age in its mottled texture, as if it needed carpentry work and two coats of paint. Slit windows look out from the loft on the north side. A weather vane perches at the center, a blue glass bulb in its stalk.

What is the etiquette of painting a stranger's field and barn? Permission is required. Farming is not a business for tourists. He drives off the dirt road and up the driveway, stopping fifty feet from the house. This house is white, and, more important, it *looks* like a farmhouse; it even has four lightning rods at its cardinal points. The yard itself has a rose arbor ten feet away from a clothesline, on which hang two yellow bath towels and two white bedsheets. A black cat is asleep underneath one of the sheets. Everything looks exactly the way it's supposed to. To his left stand a rickety shed and a doghouse with broken shingles, but no dog in view. A broken toy windmill flaps far back in the yard. And then there are the fields, passive and flat, stretching far away, holding their seedling crops he cannot identify.

Careful to leave his sunhat in the car, he knocks at the door; he does not ring the doorbell. At a farmhouse, a knock is more appropriate, more in the spirit of things. After waiting a moment, he is greeted by a slender boy, ten or eleven years old, wearing orthopedic shoes and thin wire glasses.

"Yeah?" he says, looking down at Walter, who stands on the bottom step. "Do I know you?"

"No," Walter says. "We haven't met."

The boy swallows. "You want something?"

"I'm a painter. I want to paint a picture of your barn. From the road, so I can get the fields in it, too."

"Is that all?" the boy asks. "You're a painter? You're asking if you can paint our place?" He shrugs. "Suit yourself, mister."

"If you want me to do something," Walter says, "I will."

"Huh?" The boy turns on the porch and looks at him. "Do what? You aren't a doctor or something, are you?"

"What? No, I'm not." He waits. "I'll pay you if you want."

"Mister," the boy says, "we're busy here, okay? I've got things I got to do. Go ahead and paint your picture."

"Thanks," Walter says, backing through the yard to his car. He smells compost, as he opens the door and turns on the radio to static. He parks off the country road, making sure that the car is almost in the ditch, out of everyone's way.

An hour later, with his easel set up, Walter feels the sun at his back, front-lighting the barn so that it appears to have a brilliant uncompromised visual integrity. Protected by his hat, his canvas in front of him, his oils ready, he is ready to paint what he sees. The only trouble is that he feels awful. His chest is glowing and aching, and he feels displaced, the one thing that is visually wrong in this landscape where everything else is right.

As he paints, a portly man in a gray Oldsmobile arrives at the farmhouse and carries a leather bag inside. Yes, this *would* be the doctor. Thirty minutes later the same man leaves, waving at the boy, who stands inside the screen door sucking an orange Popsicle. The boy glances at Walter and goes back inside. The doctor slows down to look at Walter's painting, opens the window, and shouts, "Not bad!" and then spins his tires on the dirt road. By now Walter has drawn the outlines of a barn, and he has the mix of colors right, ready for the painting-in. His throat is itching.

Now another car turns into the farm's driveway, a blue two-door Ford. Will this parade of cars ever stop? A woman wearing jeans and a pale-pink blouse gets out, followed by a black Labrador dog. She crosses the lawn and steps up to the porch. Walter, working on the horizon line across the top third of the canvas, glances at the farmhouse, not in the painting but the one in his line of sight, and there at the window on the second floor is a man's face, probably the boy's father, looking straight out at him, pale and accusatory.

Walter adjusts his easel, hiding behind it for a moment. His back aches, and his throat feels dusty. He paints quickly, hoping that if he skips lunch he can finish enough of the picture to complete it at home. His image of Churchill, smoking Havana cigars and sitting on the cliffs at Cornwall while he paints the immense apolitical ocean, doesn't correspond to what he is experiencing now, in this claustrophobic field. Twice he catches himself painting with his eyes on the farmhouse where the man stares down on him, and for a moment Walter thinks of the way animals look out from behind bars in the zoo.

Insects are making their crazed noises behind Walter, and gnats cluster over his head, tiny dots of leaping aggressive life flying into his ears and hair. In the painting, the barn stands placid and self-contained, settled to the ground, mixed and concentrated by proportioned midwestern sky. Walter pours himself Lipton tea from a thermos into a red plastic cup. There is that man. *What does he want?* Late in the afternoon, Walter packs up and leaves, giving one last glance at the emptied upstairs bedroom window.

When he walks into the house at six-thirty, Jane examines him with genteel shock. "You look awful," she says, inspecting his face. "You poor dear, you've been in a war. Is *that* how they treat gentlemen in the countryside?" She takes off his hat and brushes his hair with her hand. "We've had a crisis here, too," she says. "Benchley messed the carpet, and the vet says it has to do with his age. We can't go on cleaning up the carpet because our dog is senile. I'd like a suggestion." She pauses. "Well, dear, did you find your lovely little barn?"

"I found it," he says. "I'll discuss everything after a shower and a martini." He begins to walk toward the stairs, then notices that he is tracking in mud and dirt on the front-hall carpet. He returns to the front entryway to wipe his shoes.

An hour later he is sitting in the den, sipping his second martini. He feels conspiratorial with the books and the furniture. "My God, it was hot," he says. "I don't know how those people stand it."

"You sound like Marco Polo," she says.

"I might as well be. They were looking at me. As if *I* were a sideshow. I didn't care much for it."

"You don't have to care for it. It's a hobby. You're supposed to *enjoy* a hobby, you know. Well, are you going to leave me in suspense forever? Where's the famous picture?" At this moment Benchley pads into the room and settles with a groan in his favorite corner. Jane glares at the dog, then sighs. "Let me see what you did," she says.

"I'll bring it in if you promise you've had enough gin to feel uncritical."

"I promise."

Walter goes to his car, lifts out the painting from the backseat, and brings it back into the den, setting it on the couch so that the light from the window illuminates it. He hears Vernice, the cook, tapping dishes in the kitchen.

Jane gazes at his painting for a long time. At last she says, "Well, it's not Velasquez, but it's very nice. School-of-Hopper, or somebody like that. You still have your touch. I had almost forgotten. But what's all this?" She points to the middle of the painted field.

"What?"

"This."

"What do you mean, 'this'?"

"This figure."

"There's no figure there. What figure?"

"Where I'm pointing to. It's almost like a ghost, green in the middle of green, standing there with its arms clasped. You've painted someone here. In the distance, small, but *I* can see him. I don't mean *much* of someone, just the outlines. Just a few lines."

Walter looks down where she is pointing but sees nothing but what he has drawn to indicate the field. "You're seeing things."

"No, I'm certainly *not* seeing things. *This* is a figure." She waits. "And quite an unpleasant figure, too, I would say. Look at how it's standing. It's not a woman or a man, it's an in-between, this thing. Why on earth did you paint this? Was there someone out there?"

"Of course not."

She turns toward him, and her face is set. "You think I'm making this up? I'm not. How can you be so blind to it? Should we call up the Erlandsons? They'll be home." She looks through the curtains at the side window toward the neighbors' yard. "Yes. They're home. Let me give them a buzz."

"No," he says, but she is already dialing.

"Irene? Jane. Listen, darling, would you and Ted do us a neighborly favor? No, no, we're just fine. It's just that Walter's brought back his first painting from the wilderness and . . ." She waits. "Yes, dear, a painting. He *paints*, for heaven's sake. No, I'm *not* joking. Anyway, we disagree about what's in it." She laughs politely. "Yes, in the *picture*, darling." Another pause. "No, it's not abstract, silly. It's a picture of a *barn*." She is interrupted but then continues. "Yes, on a farm. One of those. It looks like a barn, all right, but there's a field, and we've been having a tiny spat about the field. We need two brilliant and impartial art critics like you and Ted. No, I'm not joking. Please come over. There's a drink in it for you if you help us out."

Standing in front of Walter's painting, giving off a faint odor of Chivas Regal, Ted Erlandson offers a first tentative opinion. "I didn't know you were an artist, Walt. I must say, this is very impressive. Not beginner's work. And very, um, picturesque."

"I was an artist in college."

"Who wasn't? I was an actor. We all had talent, years ago. But you've been sitting on yours all this time. Imagine making all the money you've made when you could have been alone, starving in a garret, eating catsup and cottage cheese and living the life of bohemia." He turns to Irene. "Did you know we had such a talented neighbor?"

Irene shakes her head. "No. I certainly did not. Walter has always kept it a secret from me. And I thought he had no secrets." Irene Erlandson throws back her head and laughs; she is a tall woman, almost six feet, and her laugh sounds electrically amplified. "I thought he was just like us," she says, and sips her drink. "Mmmm, this is delicious, Walter. You could take up bartending if your new vocation fails you. Now, what're we supposed to be looking for?"

Walter says, "Jane sees something in the picture."

Jane transfers her drink to her left hand and points. "You see Walter's field, here? Well, do you see this figure? This sort of person with its horrible hands clasped in front of it, in the distance? This creature? You do see it, don't you?"

Irene scowls at the painting and shrugs. Ted closes one eye and looks puzzled. Then he nods. "Sure. Okay. If you say so."

"No," Jane says. "Look. You *must* see it."

"Well . . ." Irene nods. "It's there and it isn't. Like those vases that are faces and then are vases." She giggles. "You know, when I was a little girl, I used to wake up and see camel shapes in the folds of my bedroom curtains."

"Ted?" Jane gazes at him.

Ted Erlandson also shrugs and nods. "Okay, maybe I see it. I think you have a case, Jane. A definite case." He smiles. "I wouldn't've seen it if you hadn't told me it was there, but now that you mention it, I suppose it *is* there."

Looking at his own painting, Walter can almost see what she is talking about. And then he can't.

One week later he is sitting next to Minnehaha Creek, his easel in front of him. Once again the insects annoy him. Impatiently, Walter outlines the stones, the sand, the logs, the leaves, and the water.

Two days later, when he is mostly finished with it, he shows it to Jane, again during the cocktail hour. She examines it a long time.

"Oh my," she says finally with admiration. "I like this one much better than the other one. Technically, I mean. So many more difficulties here."

Walter nods.

"With all those different textures," she says, moving her pale hand with its diamond ring across the canvas as if in slow motion, "you had a much more difficult job." She stops and breathes in deeply. "Walter."

"What?"

"*Look* at this," she says emphatically, then points. "Look at what you've put into the water. Walter, dear, *why* are you doing this? Is it a joke? A joke on me?"

He looks where she is pointing. "What do you see this time?"

"It's not a matter of what *I* see, my darling. It's a matter of what is *there*. Of course you see it. Of course."

"No," he says, "I don't. Sorry." Benchley walks into the room, and Walter pats the dog on the head.

"This face," Jane says, looking at him. "This terrible face."

"Where?"

"Look! For pity's sake, look at what you've done!" Her voice is rising. "This face! Down under the water, between those stones! It looks like it's *screaming*. How can you say it isn't there when it's there for all to see? It's like Munch, underwater. And," she continues, "it's worse, because you've put this horrible thing in a babbling brook, in the center of this nice forest, with all this lovely dappled sun around. I don't believe you didn't know what you were doing this time."

Gazing at his painting, at the silent shouting watery face Jane claims is there, he says, "You have to believe me when I tell you that I can't see it."

"Well." She pulls a handkerchief out of her sleeve. "I don't know if I believe you."

"Why shouldn't you?"

"It seems like a joke." She examines her fingernails. "You gave up a good career to paint these . . . these Rorschach blots in oils. Walter, dear, I wish you'd stop."

"But I've been enjoying it," he lies.

"I don't know," she says. "Maybe you have cataracts."

"Cataracts," he says. "I don't think so."

"Then where are these *things* coming from?" she asks. "You say *you* don't know. *I* don't know. But I can tell you how I feel. I feel as though these things are making fun of me."

"They're not."

"Then don't paint anymore!" She holds the handkerchief up and blows her nose. "Don't paint until you can paint a picture that doesn't have this dreadfulness in it. I'm sorry, dear, but that's how I feel. Can we talk about something else now? I want to go into the dining room and have our dinner as we usually do. We'll have a pleasant time. We won't say any more about this. Is that all right?" She looks at him. "Please?"

He looks at her face. Her expression is on the edge of desperation.

"I'll think about it," he says. When he glances away from her face, he sees that she glitters: her fingers and wrists, where the jewels are positioned to catch the light, have their lines of age, their own creases. The usual liver spots dot her hand. "Yes," he says at last. "Let's do that."

Now, a week later, he is driving his Buick Electra across the flatlands of central Minnesota, his white canvas, easel, and paints stored in the trunk, his two paintings in the backseat. A map is unfolded next to him, and he sees that the road he is on appears on the map as no more than a thin gray line, almost invisible. He cannot remember where that farm was or how he found his way there, to that wretched barn. He taps his right index finger on the map, following the rhythms of Bach on the radio. This music is growing fainter, and soon it will be gone. He turns the dial to a blank spot on the band, where he can listen to the random static, which calms him.

Listening to static, driving down a dirt road with no particular goal, lost, Walter sees the barn in the distance, his subject. By now it is midafternoon, cloudy, with no wind. He stops the car at the side of the road and opens the window. The smell of dirt and heavy moist air enters the car and mixes with the scent of leather and carpeting. For five minutes Walter gazes at the barn he once painted and at the farmhouse nearby. Where is Jane's ghost that found its way into his painting? He is feeling irritable and moody. Finally he opens the door, steps out into the road, and takes in both hands the two paintings he had placed on the backseat.

When he reaches the house, he presses the doorbell. There are patterns in the dust of the driveway. He looks at them. He sees a dog, and then a plant. Then a fabric of broken twigs.

"Yes?" It is the boy again, looking down at Walter through his glasses from behind the screen door.

"Hello," Walter says. "I don't think you'll remember me. I'm the man who—"

The boy interrupts him. "Sure. I remember. You painted our barn."

"That's right." Walter looks at the boy through the screen. The boy's face through the mesh has taken on a colorless rural-Seurat appearance of textured points. In the background Walter can hear a radio playing Bach, the same station that faded out in his car. Who listens to Bach in a farmhouse? He says, "I have the point . . ." He stops. "The *painting* with me. Right here."

"Are you tryin' to sell it? I don't think we can buy it." The boy puts his hands in his pockets. "I'm sure about that. We don't have much money right now."

From another part of the house, a woman shouts, "Who is it, Davey?"

"It's that guy who painted our barn."

"What does he want now?"

"I think he wants to sell his painting or something."

Walter joins in. "No, no, I don't! I don't want to sell it! I'm just here to show it to you!"

Now the woman appears behind the boy, her face, like his, patterned by the screen. "How do you do?" she says, wiping her hands on a towel. "I'm real sorry, but we're busy." He stares at her: her face, bland, blank, and pale, is totally illegible.

"May I come in?"

"What do you want?"

"I want to . . . I really must show you the painting."

"Please," she says. He isn't sure how to interpret this word. Therefore he opens the door, which squeaks like a parakeet, and steps inside.

"I appreciate this," he says. "You don't know my name. I am Walter Lundholm, and I'm retired, and I've taken up painting as my hobby. I live in the city. I used to be a real estate developer. I'm *not* asking for your money. What I wanted to do was, I wanted to show you the painting I did of your barn."

"Well," she says, "come into the living room."

He crosses the porch with its four rocking chairs and small pile of *National Geographic*s and steps into the hallway to the kitchen. On the wall is a picture of Jesus speaking to a group of American schoolchildren, and to the side is a finished wood table and four stainless-steel chairs with pink plastic cushions. The linoleum is midway between blue and gray. The living room is dominated by a console television set and a calendar from an auto-parts store, which has an illustration of a mountain lake whose water is a thick granular blue. Walter remains standing.

"Your husband?"

"Upstairs. He's sick."

"I know it," Walter says. "I think I want to give these pictures to him."

She places her right hand under her throat, the thumb on one side of the neck, the fingers on the other. "He's sick," she repeats. Walter looks at her again: when she stands, she seems to lean backward, to stand against things.

"I wonder if I might go upstairs with these paintings," he says.

At that moment they hear a voice, from the second floor, which sounds as if it is coming over the radio. "Joyce," he shouts, but only with enough strength to make the shout achieve the level of slightly intensified speech, "who's there? Who're you talking to?"

"It's this man. Says he wants to give you two paintings he did."

There is a long pause, as if the voice is trying to gather some energy. Then he says, "Send him up."

Walter smiles for a split second. How much this procedure resembles the elaborate mannerisms of a business conference! Closed door, secretary, waiting period in the outer office: they have it all. The woman, Joyce, seems displeased by her husband's willingness to invite Walter upstairs. Sullenly, she guides him toward the stairway by holding her left arm out stiffly and walking toward the brown banister. In her rigid position is the suggestion that she might fall, but instead of falling she simply grasps the rail with her freckled fingers. Then she waits with her eyes down while Walter climbs the creaking stairs, one painting in either hand.

As he climbs, he feels time slowing down unpleasantly. He has never felt so silly in his life. At least, he thinks, I didn't buy a beret. Nevertheless, he wants to drop the paintings on the stairs and rush straightaway out of this house, past Joyce, past the boy in his orthopedic shoes. As he glances down to see if he would have a clear escape, he expects to see the woman scowling at him and blocking his path, but her place has been taken by the boy, who now has a birdhouse in his hands, held there as an offer of interest: look at what I have. Walter nods, as if to say that he'll look at it when he's finished.

At the top of the stairs, Walter feels a pang in his knees. He takes a deep breath. The second floor is rich in the fetid odor of medicine and bedclothes, and something meant to disguise it, the sugary wintergreen stink of air freshener.

"In here," the voice says from the one darkened room facing the front of the house. Walter looks into the first room, the boy's, and sees photographs of birds scissored out of popular magazines and Scotch-taped to the walls: sparrows, juncos, wrens, crested flycatchers, owls, pheasants, egrets, and on one wall scores of bluebirds, a collage of photos from floor to ceiling, apparently cut out of bird books. On this wall in the middle of the bluebirds is a left-profile picture of Jesus. "I said I'm in here," the voice rasps irritably. Walter advances into the room.

The man of the house lies propped in bed, lips drawn back over his teeth, his skin the color of school paste. He does not turn his head, though he holds out his thin-knuckled hand for Walter to shake. Shaking this thin hand makes the hair on the back of Walter's neck stand up. The man in bed is wasting away. He is a male Medusa: sunken eyes and hair like watercress. Medicines are scattered on a bedside table, and a television set on the other side of the room is tuned to a rerun of *The Honeymooners*, the sound so low that only Ralph is audible, as he points his finger straight in the air and shouts at Alice.

"Hello," Walter says. "I'm sorry to intrude on you."

The man nods. "I know you."

"Yes. Yes, you do. I want to give you the picture I painted," Walter says.

"You do."

"Yes."

"Well, it's not much good to me," the man says. "My health ain't too hot right now." He waits, tugging at the sheets. "Still and all, if you want to give me your picture, I guess it's none of my business." The smell in the room makes Walter want to gag. The man in bed points down. "That it?"

Walter holds up the painting so that it is displayed on the foot of the bed. The farmer stares at it a long time.

"You did that."

"Yes."

Walter waits for a pardon. Just then the man says, "It's nice." Before he can respond to this compliment, the man continues in a half-whisper. "It's nice for someone to do up your place like that. You know, I worked here since I was twenty." Walter tries to nod. He feels the presence of the man's wife watching from the doorway. The farmer continues talking. "I like it. You painted this place like it was important. A fellow from the city. Well, fine. I want you to know I appreciate it." The effort to say all this makes him sink down into bed.

"Thank you," Walter says. "I have another one here of a stream." He holds it up.

The farmer stares at it. "That's nice, too."

"If you want it," Walter says, "it's yours. My wife doesn't like it. She doesn't like the other one either. She doesn't want them in the house. My wife," Walter says, "doesn't like nature."

"Too bad."

"Well, you can have them both. Free."

The man does not smile, but he nods again. "Thank you. Joyce'll put the picture of the barn up on the wall. I never had a painting before. We were too busy."

Walter nods.

"But anyway," the farmer says, beginning to wave Walter away, "I appreciate your coming out here and I only wish I could get up and offer you a beverage." He is staring at the painting of his barn. "But I can't. I'm real sick, y'know." Walter nods again, idiotically. "That's a nice thing, that barn," he says, "and thank you." He holds out his hand again, and Walter stares at it, dreading to grasp it, but at last he does, and on cue the hairs on the back of his neck stand up. "Goodbye."

"Goodbye." He steps past Joyce, who doesn't move out of his way, and is heading down the stairs, his eyes half closed, when he sees the boy, who still holds the birdhouse in his hands.

"You talk to my dad?" the boy asks, but before Walter can answer, the boy says, "This is something I made downstairs in the basement during my free time. It's too small for squirrels, and chipmunks don't want it. I'm going to put it up on the catalpa outside the kitchen window even though the wrens aren't going to come and use it until springtime." He hands the birdhouse to Walter, who examines it and hands it back. But this gesture is not enough. The boy holds it up to Walter's eye level. "See?" he asks. The wren house is painted blue, the same shade as the kitchen linoleum.

"Yes," Walter says.

"Davey," Joyce calls at the top of the stairs, "don't bother the man. Take him out to his car, would you?"

"Okay, Mom." The boy tucks the birdhouse under his left arm and marches through the living room out onto the porch, and out through the porch into the front yard. "We don't get too many birds around here," the boy says as he walks. "Last week I saw a scarlet tanager. It was on its way somewhere. Only the sparrows and chickadees stay around here. And the bluejays and the crows. They're related, did you know that?" He stops and turns around. "Did you give my dad a picture of the barn?"

"Yes," Walter says.

"I bet he really likes it."

Now Walter is standing by his car while the boy continues his monologue about birds. The house sparrow, he says, was introduced into North America by travelers from Europe. In some places, the boy continues, the sparrow was once considered a messenger of news from the gods. If you put a sparrow into a cage, it will not chirp. A princess was once turned into a sparrow by her father, in a story. The state bird of Minnesota is the loon. When it flies, its big feet are stretched out past the tail. They're hard to spot on lakes. When they dive, they can stay under for a minute. Finches are easier to see, what with their yellow and purple color, and their nesting rituals. And their song is easy to remember. Suddenly the boy puckers his mouth and sings: *swit-wit-wit.*

"I don't know anything about birds," Walter says. "At the end of the day, I don't look for a bird. I look for a martini. Did you know," he says, staring at the boy, "that many people now put ice cubes into their martinis? That's a great mistake. Martinis are meant to be poured straight up, preferably with an olive in the glass, and sipped. Poured," he says, wiping his forehead with his sleeve, staring toward the dusty dirt road, on which a red pickup truck is now passing, "from a silver cocktail shaker, with condensation from the air beaded on the sides. *That's* what I want right now, young man. A drink."

"We don't drink here."

"I believe it." He walks toward his car. "Actually, I do know something about birds. They are the most beautiful of God's creations." The boy begins to nod, then stops himself. Walter makes his way to his car, and suddenly the boy begins talking about woodpeckers. Walter opens the car door and slides in behind the wheel while the boy is still in midsentence. He manages to wave and starts the car. As he drives off, he looks in the rearview mirror to see the boy observing his departure. The boy doesn't look like a bird; he doesn't even suggest the image of a bird.

Driving back to Minneapolis, Walter considers his retirement plans. He has no more mental images of paintings he wants to paint. He has no idea of what he will do with his time. Start a business, he thinks, turning on the radio. A new business. Building wren houses, using low-cost lumber.

He is almost inside the city limits when he sees traffic slowing down in his lane. For fifteen minutes he crawls and creeps forward, until he reaches the source of the trouble, an accident. The ambulance has arrived; one car is accordioned in front; another is turned over. Broken glass everywhere on the pavement, a cop gesturing him past. Men bent over. Over what? Walter keeps his eyes fixed ahead and inches forward until the congestion clears. He accelerates, rushing home.

S HERMAN A LEXIE

How to Obtain Eagle Feathers
for Religious Use

F OR G. S.

> The Federal law protecting bald and golden eagles makes provisions for the use
> of eagle feathers by Native Americans for religious purposes.
> —U.S. Government Bulletin

Page 1

Picture an eagle or parts of an eagle. That has nothing to do with it.
Remember: I am the Indian who wrote the obituary for the obituary
editor and have come to know these things. Often, I have stood in
places where nothing has happened. For instance, the summer I
worked forestry for the BIA and found a strand of barbed wire fence
still nailed to a pine tree. Stapled to the barbed wire was a hand-
painted sign: NO TRESPASSING. INDIAN LAND. 1876. I have no memory of the artist.

Page 9

An Indian plays piano somewhere on the reservation when we close
our eyes to sleep. The song is familiar, something close to Elvis before
he grew fat, useless. Believe us: an Indian waits by the Dumpster outside the trading post. He swears he is Elvis in braids. He wears feathers and Levis. We give him a quarter or two every time we go to the
store. Soon, it will be enough.

Index

Arrowheads and Alcohol, BIA and Basketball, Commodities and
Clear Cut, Department of Interior and Dogs, Errors and Eagles, Forgiveness and Fancydancing, Gasoline and God, Hell and Heroes, In-

dians and Ignorance, Jerky and Jumpshots, Keno and Kerosene, Love and Lust, Mothers and Madmen, Necklaces and Notebooks, Orgasms and Oranges, Porcupines and Playing Cards, Quilts and Quotas, Roaches and Receiving Docks, Sin and Sunburn, Terror and Towels, Underarms and Underachievers, Victories and Variables, Weed and Wonder, X-Rays and X-Rated, Yesterday and Youth, Zeroes and Zip Codes.

Page 7

Applications for a permit to acquire eagle feathers for religious use may be made by completing the macaroni & cheese dinner, by opening the bag of commodity noodles, by shredding the commodity cheese, by pulling the cast-iron pot down from the shelf, by boiling water and adding a pinch of salt, by paying the light bill, by renting the HUD house, by working for the BIA, by running the four-minute mile.

Rough Draft

All of this is excellent, Stan, but where's the human interest angle? How many parts of an eagle equals one eagle? Also, what is the average number of feathers per eagle? Does the bald eagle have fewer feathers than the golden? Goddammit, Stan, it's like asking someone to hand you a piano. Which came first, Christopher Columbus or the eagle?

Page 5

Photograph: an Indian with a stoic face. No, he's brown-skinned and smiles, holds a flashlight above his head. No, it's an eagle or parts of an eagle. But none of this has anything to do with it. There is a photograph of another Indian, not a totally different man, but different enough to make the two photos separate. This other Indian in the photograph is holding a flashlight. He is not smiling. He walks slowly through the powwow grounds and searches for something. What is it? What is it?

Do you remember the eagles who came to Little Falls Dam every summer? Yes, they came the summer we went to Disneyland. Every Spokane Indian climbed into cars, trucks, wagons, and traveled north to the Magic Kingdom, leaving the eagles alone at Little Falls Dam. I was locked in the trunk of a '65 Malibu and no one let me out until all the complimentary tickets were gone. Lester FallsApart is still there, going crazy in a teacup. Revolution after revolution, he continues, past history and the television's uninterrupted news. Picture an eagle or parts of an eagle. *It will not be enough for the twenty-first century.*

Eagle Poem

To pray you open your whole self
To sky, to earth, to sun, to moon
To one whole voice that is you
And know there is more
That you can't see, can't hear
Can't know except in moments
Steadily growing, and in languages
That aren't always sound but other
Circles of motion.
Like eagle that Sunday morning
Over Salt River. Circled in blue sky
In wind, swept our hearts clean
With sacred wings.
We see you, see ourselves and know
That we must take the utmost care
And kindness in all things.
Breathe in, knowing we are made of
All this, and breathe, knowing
We are truly blessed because we
Were born, and die soon within a
True circle of motion,
Like eagle rounding out the morning
Inside us.
We pray that it will be done
In beauty.
In beauty.

Martha Silano

At the Shorebird Festival:
Grays Harbor County, Washington

We're learning their names: dunlin, black-bellied plover.
Sandpipers: western and least. Styles of probing:
run, stop, run; incessant sewing machine. What's
diagnostic: upturned bill of the slender, elegant
avocet. Ruddy turnstone's crimson feet.

Wired for wind and cold, bills conveniently tuck
beneath scapulars; feet retract to feathered bellies.
At the slightest hint of shadow, sudden movement
(ring-billed gull, drifting leaf . . .), they take to the air
like giant swirling amoebas, locust dark till they turn

in a flash of white—beautiful, undulant whirl
lowering the odds of a raptor's successful strike;
mournful *tu tu tu* of dowitcher, raucous *cur-ret* of the knot
translating unmistakably: *watch out.* Every movement,
ounce, sound, rigged for survival. But we're not thinking

life or death, the why of insulation, skittishness. We're focused
as always, on something else: *American coot, osprey near bridge
to Aberdeen* (mill stench, strip mall, equaling loss, unworthy
of note), a nearby curmudgeon's grumble ("the brochure said
thousands . . ."), what's for lunch—mortality's access,

like the nesting grounds of snowy plovers,
all but permanently blocked. Even when we turn
from mudflat to ocean, to a surfer stuck in a criss-cross
of breakers refusing to spit him out—bobbing, waving his arms—
to four Jeep Cherokees emblazoned "Ocean Shores Police"

barreling down the beach, to a man—wild-eyed, mustachioed—
heading out in a boat to save him, routine, we're thinking.
And as he guns the motor, greets each surge—head high,
bulging chest—as he enters the whirling churn,
we're unconcerned enough to admire

the sunlight pouring down in silvery rays,
magnificent concert of every-which-way waves.
Even when two massive swells converge to flip the boat
and *he's* the one who's waving *I'm okay.* Rising. Falling.
Disappearing. Surf a vortex . . . rushes . . . rips . . .

And just as we're getting nervous (police, walkie-talkies, a growing,
gawking crowd), *was he wearing a wet suit isn't ten minutes all it takes . . .*
out of nowhere a Coast Guard lifeboat nabs the surfer,
while a faint, growing louder, whir-and-heart-pounding-
clomp-clomp-clomp of a chopper lowers in

On the place where . . . *but now I don't see him is he*
he's under blinding swirl of water and blades
a man on a rope plunging into *he can't be did you see*
his eyes did you see the squall, comes up with a body,
a body, limp as a . . . limp as a . . .

he's okay, the wind knocked out that's all hoists him up
like a half-mast on a windless day *he sure looks*
dead like a dead man have you ever seen someone living hang
like that like the suit's empty . . . to shore where medics
he'll be okay those who knew him cradling their own

incredulous faces, a round of *shits* pacing static *no*
response no one asking *is he?* Huddled. Stunned.
Light draining the sky. The last *good God.*
Good night. Even after the tide erases every footprint,
and where he lay a flock of whimbrels alights.

ELIZABETH BISHOP

North Haven

IN MEMORIAM: ROBERT LOWELL

I can make out the rigging of a schooner
a mile off; I can count
the new cones on the spruce. It is so still
the pale bay wears a milky skin, the sky
no clouds, except for one long, carded horse's-tail.

The islands haven't shifted since last summer,
even if I like to pretend they have
—drifting, in a dreamy sort of way,
a little north, a little south or sidewise,
and that they're free within the blue frontiers of bay.

This month, our favorite one is full of flowers:
Buttercups, Red Clover, Purple Vetch,
Hawkweed still burning, Daisies pied, Eyebright,
the Fragrant Bedstraw's incandescent stars,
and more, returned, to paint the meadows with delight.

The Goldfinches are back, or others like them,
and the White-throated Sparrow's five-note song,
pleading and pleading, brings tears to the eyes.
Nature repeats herself, or almost does:
repeat, repeat, repeat; revise, revise, revise.

Years ago, you told me it was here
(in 1932?) you first "discovered *girls*"
and learned to sail, and learned to kiss.

You had "such fun," you said, that classic summer.
("Fun"—it always seemed to leave you at a loss . . .)

You left North Haven, anchored in its rock,
afloat in mystic blue . . . And now—you've left
for good. You can't derange, or re-arrange,
your poems again. (But the Sparrows can their song.)
The words won't change again. Sad friend, you cannot change.

HAYDEN CARRUTH

The Birds of Vietnam

O bright, O swift and bright,
you flashing among pandanus boughs
    (is that right? pandanus?)
under the great banyan, in and out
the dusky delicate bamboo groves
    (yes? banyan, bamboo?)
low, wide-winged, gliding
over the wetlands and drylands
    (but I have not seen you,
    I do not know your names,
    I do not know
    what I am talking about).

I have seen the road runner and the golden eagle,
the great white heron and the Kirtland's warbler,
    our own endangered species,
and I have worried about them. I have worried
about all our own, seen and unseen,
whooping cranes, condors, white-tailed kites,
and the ivory-bills (certainly gone, all gone!)
the ones we have harried, murdered, driven away
as if we were the Appointed Avengers,
    the Destroyers, the Wrathful Ones
out of our ancestors' offended hearts
at the cruel beginning of the world.
But for what? for whom? why?
    Nobody knows.

And why, in my image of that cindered country,
should I waste my mourning? I will never have

enough. Think of the children there,
insane little crusted kids at the beckoning fire,
think of the older ones, burned, crazy with fear,
sensible beings who can know hell, think
of their minds exploding, their hearts flaming.

I do think. But today,
O mindless, O heartless, in and out
the dusky delicate groves,
your hell becomes mine, simply
and without thought, you maimed, you
poisoned in your nests, starved
in the withered forests.
   O mindless, heartless,
    you never invented hell.
We say flesh turns to dust, though more often
a man-corpse or woman-corpse is a bloody pulp,
and a bird-corpse too, yet your feathers
   retain life's color
long afterward, even in the robes
   of barbarous kings,
still golden the trogon feather,
still bright the egret plume, and the crest
of the bower bird will endure forever
almost. You will always remind us of what
   the earth has been.

O bright, swift, gleaming
in dusky groves,
I mourn you.
O mindless, heartless, I can't
help it, I have so loved
   this world.

HOWARD NORMAN

from **The Bird Artist**

My name is Fabian Vas. I live in Witless Bay, Newfoundland. You would not have heard of me. Obscurity is not necessarily failure, though; I am a bird artist, and have more or less made a living at it. Yet I murdered the lighthouse keeper, Botho August, and that is an equal part of how I think of myself.

I discovered my gift for drawing and painting birds early on. I should better say that my mother saw that someone had filled in the margins of my third-form primer with the sketches of wings, talons, and heads of local birds. "I thought this primer was brand-new," she said. "But it's full of these bird drawings. Well, somebody has talent." After a night's sleep she realized that the pencil work was mine and was what I had been concentrating on during my school lessons. Actually she seemed quite pleased, and at breakfast the following morning said, "Awfully nice to learn something so unmistakable about one's offspring." She tore out a page full of heads of gulls and ospreys, wrote, "October 28, 1900," on it, and nailed it to the kitchen door.

Witless Bay's librarian was Mrs. Paulette Bath, a spirited woman in her late fifties or early sixties when I was a boy. She claimed to have read every one of the hundreds of books in her library, which was her own living room, dining room, and sitting room. She had not claimed that in a bragging way but as if it had been a natural obligation. Her house overlooked the wharf. She gave out hand-printed library cards. "Like in the city," she said. Each card had the silhouette of a woman reading in a bathtub, which I assume was a humorous turn on her own last name. You either remembered your card or had to fetch it. No exceptions were allowed. No book left her library without the date printed in her cramped script on a piece of lined cardboard tucked into a pocket glued to the inside back cover. She kept scrupulous records. She had taught my childhood friend Margaret Handle the fundamentals of bookkeeping. She would reprimand borrowers in public about overdue books. She featherdusted, humming, and was all but constantly alarmed about book lice. Some afternoons I would come in and immediately be aware that she had been spraying book spines with rubbing alcohol, her own remedy. On her mantel was her framed certificate of Library Science, earned in London, where she had been raised. She had left there when she was thirty-four.

In her library I discovered a few books on natural history, including *First Book of Zoology,* by Edward Morse, which was published in the United States. But it contained only technical illustrations. Whereas the volume that changed my life—I should better say gave me purchase on it—was to be found in Mrs. Bath's private collection, sequestered in a glass case that had five shelves. The book was called *Natural History of Carolina, Florida, and the Bahama Islands, 1731–1748.* It had been a gift from her Aunt Mina, a patron of libraries in London; Aunt Mina's photograph was next to Mrs. Bath's certificate on the mantel. This book was a true revelation for me. It held 220 hand-colored engravings of North American flowers, weeds, and wild animals. But what I memorized and actually dreamed about were the 109 birds. The naturalist's name was Mark Catesby. He was the first real bird artist I knew about.

I sat every afternoon, I think for two years, in Mrs. Bath's living room, the main reading area, turning the pages of Catesby's work. I can still smell her sofa. At the thick-legged oval table, with its lion's-paw feet, I would set out my scrap paper and copy. Copy, copy, copy. One morning Mrs. Bath stood next to me, looking over my shoulder. "Mr. Catesby, dead so long now," she said. "Yet his birds are so alive in these pages. To you, Fabian, I imagine this art is as important as Leonardo da Vinci's."

"Who's Leonardo da Vinci?"

"A great genius."

"Did he ever paint birds?"

"Truth be told, I don't know. He never painted them in New-foundland."

She laughed, sharpened a pencil for me, and left me alone until she closed the library, at exactly six o'clock, by the chimes of her clock.

When I finally stopped my formal schooling after fourth grade, having learned to read and write, my mother kept after me to read books. She would make lists of words, set them out on the table after supper, and go over them with me. "I'm not as good as the real dictionary," she said, "but pretty close."

I did keep up with my reading. I struggled to write clearly, too. I took pride in my secret diaries. These were not diaries full of a boy's confessions, though a few of those might have crept in. More, I made up travels to places I had read about, and described birds, landscapes, certain dangerous encounters with the local natives, and there always seemed to be earthquakes, volcanoes, and monsoons as well. Anyway, by age eight I was practically living out in the coves, the wetlands, or at Lambert Charibon's trout camp. Lambert was a friend of my father's. He let me stay around sketching kingfishers, ospreys, and his crippled pet owl. At age eleven, I put a lot of time into a field guide to coastal species, made up of my own drawings, of course. I sewed the pages together and donated it to the library. Now and then I would check to see if anyone had taken it out. "People here know the birds already," Mrs. Bath said. "They don't need a guide. Every book is a curiosity of sorts, I suppose. Yours is a local example of that. But maybe a tourist will pass through and need it. You can never tell."

All through those years her advice, given once, but very firmly, rang in my ears. "Just *draw*. It's a God-given gift." Before she died, when I was seventeen, she often provided me with money out of her own till for pens, pencils, inks, special paper. Drawing birds was what I most loved. It had been from the beginning.

Besides Mrs. Bath, I showed my drawings only to Margaret Handle, beginning when I was fifteen. Margaret was four years older than I. She lived with her father, Enoch, who piloted the mail boat the *Aunt Ivy Barnacle*, the first steam-engine vessel I ever saw. Her mother had died when she was seven. She had, I was told, her mother's red hair; colorwise, this contradicted her father's ancestry, which was part Beothuk Indian. There were no longer any Beothuks left in New-foundland by the time I was born, in 1891. As my own mother once put it, Margaret was on her own earlier than most, because Enoch was away for such long periods of time, collecting and delivering mail north and south along the coast. I might have been merely two or three years old, but I remember a night my father carried me on his shoulders past the lighthouse and all the way into the village to show me Margaret's house lit up by candles. As far as I am concerned, this was my first memory. Lambert Charibon accompanied us that night. We stood about a hundred feet away. There was a candelabrum on the dining-room table, consisting of five candles. There was a candle in each window as well. "She can't sleep, Enoch told me she told him, unless the house is lit up like Christmas," my father said.

"If that's going to be a lifelong habit," Lambert said, "she might want to learn to dip candles herself, to save money."

Lambert carried me back home.

One day when I was thirteen Margaret found me sketching scoter ducks at the wharf. She sat down next to me. She had just cut her hair. It was the shortest I had ever seen it. She looked at my drawing. "You know," she said, "my father taught me to shoot ducks, him being away so much. I've seen scoters close up. I've cleaned them. In my opinion, you've caught its likeness, except for the face. Close up, a scoter's got a more delicate face. You've got yours looking like a decoy. A wooden face. But you're an artist, Fabian, and I've never sat with an artist before." It was a hot summer day. No breeze at all off the sea. She tightened her hand around mine, the one with the pencil in it, and drew my hand to her chest and fluttered her own on top. She moved my hand to her breast for a moment. Then she got up and walked home. Well, for days after, I drew only scoters. I went too far at first, making their faces almost human, and then, after many hours of work, came around to something Margaret approved of. I thought she would put my hand on her breast again, but she did not.

For several years in decent weather we took long walks together. I brought a feeling of nervous mystery to these walks, based mostly on one thing, really: when would Margaret provoke me out of my silence? I desired not to talk. She would get annoyed. "Don't you have an *opinion*? If you don't have opinions, you're the village idiot." The actual provocation reminded me of a saying that aptly pertained to the unpredictable and sudden shifts in Newfoundland weather: *Every breeze may messenger a storm.* One time, for instance, Margaret was just talking along about this or that; then, as if interrupting herself, said, "I saw your mother touch Botho August's collar. Well, no doubt she was flicking away a moth—"

"I've seen her do that to one of our window curtains at home," I said.

"Alaric's particularly fussy about that sort of thing, I guess."

"I guess."

"Still, it was an intimate gesture, don't you think?"

"How far away from them were you, to see it?"

"Here's what. I was in Romeo Gillette's store, along a wall aisle."

"Left or right of the counter?"

"Right, facing the counter."

"And—"

"And I was looking at a pair of fancy stockings."

"I know the store pretty well. I didn't know that Romeo had ladies' stockings in there."

"Have you ever seen a pair, let alone *on* anyone?"

"No."

"Anyway, you know the customer bell Romeo has. Well, Botho and Alaric were standing at the counter. And neither of them was tapping the bell. Romeo must've been in the stockroom, maybe."

"My mother's so rarely in the store. Botho's rarely in the store, too, I'm told. What a coincidence!"

"Your mother bought sewing thread."

"This was yesterday?"

"Yes."

"That's right, then, because she brought home black thread."

"Botho told Alaric he was there to pick up gramophone records, which my father had brought from Halifax."

"So, all right. My mother was there for thread. Botho for the gramophone discs."

"Nobody was ringing the bell. They were talking with each other."

"And."

"And. With somebody midsentence, I think it was Alaric, she reached out and touched his collar. I for one didn't see a moth, though a moth might've been there. I right away stepped out and said, 'Hello, Mrs. Vas!' and she nearly jumped out of her shoes. 'I have stockings,' I said. Botho walks right up to me, takes the stockings out of my hand, holds the pair the length of my legs, impolite as an ill-bred child. Says, 'I don't yet have anyone to buy French stockings for.' At which moment Romeo steps out from the back room. 'They're not French,' Romeo says, 'they're from Montreal, Canada, though a French seamstress might well have made them.' Botho squints and tilts his head and narrows his eyes, like he does."

"I've seen him do that."

"And *Alaric*—your mother got so flustered, she rang the customer bell! Romeo is standing right there! She says, 'I'll come back for this thread,' sets it on the counter, walks to the back of the store, turns around, and pays Romeo for the thread and leaves the store."

"And Botho?"

"Says, 'Did my gramophone discs come in yet?' Yes, says Romeo. 'Well, then, I'll pick them up tomorrow,' says Botho. He leaves the store."

"Where are we walking to, anyway?"

"Guess what else? I went to the store this morning and found that Botho August had *paid* for my stockings. I have them in a dresser drawer at home."

"Wherever will you wear them?"

"Maybe only by myself, Fabian. At home. In the privacy of my house."

"We're almost to the cliff. Where are we going?"

"We can turn either left or right, or go back down the path. There's choices."

"Margaret, this conversation—Botho, my mother in the store. It feels like an insult to my father. That's my opinion."

"Probably it was just a moth."

She took my hand.

"Where are we walking to, anyway?" I said.

"We're just walking along and talking. It's enough not to be chaperoned on such a balmy night."

"I agree."

The eeriest thing about fate, it seems to me, is how you try to deny it even when it's teaching you to kiss. A few weeks after my sixteenth birthday in April, Margaret said, "I'm going to give you a lesson." Just like that. We were standing on a dock. The *Aunt Ivy Barnacle* was tied up at the end. "Fabian, you kiss like I imagine an old man does. Like you used to know how but can't quite recall. It makes me almost start laughing. And I don't want to laugh when I kiss somebody, Fabian. I want almost the opposite, whatever that is. Maybe to be on the verge of tears every second of it."

She led me from the dock onto the *Aunt Ivy Barnacle*, the wooden, two-tiered wedding cake of a boat. We climbed down into the bunkroom. Margaret said, "Lie down there. It's all right." I looked around as if there was some place other than the bed she might have meant. "The bed," she said. I got under the one blanket, fully clothed. Watching, Margaret simply shook her head back and forth. Then she took her clothes off entirely and got in next to me.

Now Margaret was at the center of my life. I did not fully recognize this fact at first, did not consider it possible while lying with her that night. Maybe I had come to believe that tenderness was the least practical part of my nature, so what could be the use of it? "It's all right," she said in the middle of the night. She may have been asleep when she said it.

I think it was about five o'clock in the morning when we heard Enoch up on deck. When he started down the stairs, Margaret wrapped her legs tightly around me and said, "Shut your eyes." We heard Enoch go back up the stairs.

"I've never been all night anywhere but my own house," I said.

"Now you have."

"I'm going to have to explain it."

"Not to me."

"My mother, I meant. My father."

"If we walk right up to your house hand in hand, stand right in the kitchen, and ask for breakfast together, I bet they'll get the hint."

"Margaret, my mother doesn't like you. You know that."

"She can't bear me. But I can keep you separate from Alaric. I don't know if she can."

"Your father's right up on deck."

"Put on your clothes, Fabian, and walk up there. Say good morning to him, because it's morning. You don't have to add anything. I'm getting more sleep."

I climbed up and said, "Good morning," to Enoch. He was mopping out the steering cabin.

He did not look up. "You know, I've let Margaret steer this boat since she was ten. Why, she could take over my job any minute, if need be! She can take apart and put together this newfangled steam engine. She just learned it with native intelligence, eh? She's always had a talent for mechanical things. That's something she might not have told you, so I thought that I would."

Roughly from 1908 to 1911, I was faithfully apprenticed to a bird artist named Isaac Sprague. I had followed up on his advertisement in the journal *Bird Lore*, which Mrs. Bath had ordered specially on my behalf. In her will, in fact, she left me all the back issues.

Sprague lived in Halifax. Above my desk I had tacked a reproduction of his painting of a red-throated loon, which I had torn from an issue of *Bird Lore*. It was so graceful and transcendent that each time I sat down in front of it to work, it made me want to give up. But then after I had stared at it, the loon became an inspiration. It was uncanny how that change overtook me. The pencil seemed to move of its own volition. The brush made a beak, feather, eye. It was as if to hesitate or think too much, to resist in any way, would impede the progress of my calling. I was convinced that birds were kinds of souls. Not the souls of people but of previous birds whose mystery and beauty were so necessary on earth that God would not allow them to be anything in their second life but birds again. This was an idea I had come up with when I was nine or ten, just after Reverend Sillet's sermon on the transformation of souls in heaven. I sometimes went to church with my mother. Witless Bay had the Anglican Church of England. I would sit antsy in the pew, or daydream. Having made my own connections between God and birds, I felt moral enough not to have to listen too closely to Sillet's sermons. Besides, I had already passed my own judgment on Sillet; I had made a few drawings of him taking potshots at a woodpecker on the church belfry.

It went like this. I would send five carefully packed drawings or watercolors to Halifax, and Sprague would comment by return mail; this might take one summer month, if the *Aunt Ivy Barnacle* was in good repair and if Enoch did not dawdle on his mail stops, and if fair weather prevailed. But when I sent drawings out just before winter, I would not get Sprague's reply until spring, because the *Aunt Ivy Barnacle* would be in dry dock. Anyway, once I did get a letter from Sprague, I would send him two dollars, a lot of money for me. For anyone in Witless Bay, for that matter. To pay my parents' room and board, which I had done since I was thirteen, I worked at the dry dock, repairing and painting schooners, trawlers, dories. I sometimes worked side by side with my father. Still and all, I was barely able to afford the inks, special paper, and brushes which I ordered through Gillette's store, especially after Mrs. Bath died.

Isaac Sprague's letters were detailed and impersonal. They kept to subjects such as the shaping of a beak, shadows, color accents. He wrote to me about consciously denying certain background landscapes the opportunity—as he put it—to dominate rather than feature a bird. In one letter he said that bird artists should *invoke* a bird, feather by feather, not merely copy what we observe in the wild. He had, for me, a difficult vocabulary and I wrote him a separate letter to say that. He sent me a dictionary for Christmas 1909, along with a note saying, "Read each of my letters from now on with this book in hand. I'm not going backwards in my education on your behalf." The dictionary had arrived in October, Christmas greetings inscribed in advance.

Sprague offered strong opinions in each letter, not just about my work but about bird art in general. Much later, after our correspondence had ended, I realized that all of his musings, asides, complaints, all of his fervor added up to a rare education, not just in craft but in his own passionate character as well. "Birds," he wrote, "and the making of a bird on the page is the logic of my heart. And yours?" He examined life closely and described things in close-up language. "That belted kingfisher you sent me," he wrote, "is pretty good—fine. A solid effort, Mr. Vas. Yet the foot does not seem to encircle the branch but to be laid on a differently pitched surface." I looked up *pitch* in the dictionary. I drew kingfisher feet on branches for hours, days in a row.

Whatever praise he divvied out I was intoxicated with for weeks, months! When I would hear that the *Aunt Ivy Barnacle* had tied up, I would drop everything and run to the wharf. I would follow the burlap mail sacks up to Gillette's store, even haul them myself, and watch as Romeo distributed envelopes into slots. My family did not have a slot. "Anything for me from Halifax?" I would ask Romeo, a question meant only to narrow down my possible disappointments to one, since Halifax was the only place from which, and Sprague the only person from whom, I had ever received a letter.

Each of Isaac Sprague's letters began: "Dear Mr. Vas, Student #12." I learned that at any given time throughout the years I worked with him, he kept three dozen or so students through the mail, and also taught a night course, "Nature Drawing," in a small museum on Agricola Street, the stationery of which he used. The date of each letter was printed below his signature, and each letter ended in an identical way:

In hopes for improvement,
Isaac Sprague

I have kept all his letters, my own inheritance from those years. "You've got a knack," he wrote on September 7, 1909, "but you are no genius."

Out of financial necessity I maintained my other employments, yet privately I considered bird art to be my profession. In secret, a journal such as *Bird Lore* truly defined my world, or a world I wanted more and more to belong to. I wanted someday to report birds back from Catesby's Florida, or from Africa, South America, Siberia, any place really; just looking at a globe would keep me awake half the night painting. I was squirreling money away to flee. And though I was stuck in Witless Bay, or thought of it that way, I was in fact able to improve, slowly, to the point where two reputable journals, *Maritime Monthly* and the more specialized *Bird Lore*, solicited my sketches and watercolors, both as fillers and to accompany feature articles. Each request, each acceptance, made me feel more hopeful, more alive to the possibility that bird art could be my life. *Maritime Monthly*, for instance, had paid $1.50 Canadian for the first work I had ever sold, ten pencil sketches of barn swallows which it did not publish yet kept on file. Sprague, of course, had recommended me. He wrote to tell me that he had. I thought of this as a generosity and it was, yet it was also an investment in his own future. The success of his students, within the small world of bird art, reflected well on him, and he asked that I mention him in any correspondence I might have with a journal's editor. I am certain that he asked the same of all his students.

In fact, when I had sold the barn swallows, Sprague requested that I send him a 25-cent commission, that one time only. I sent it; I would happily have sent the entire amount I was paid. And I enclosed a lengthy, no doubt overwrought description of a magnolia warbler, along with a torn-out page from my daily sketchbook, as intimate a document to me as any diary. However, the audacity of a student offering "a preliminary sketch," as he called it, heartily offended him. He wrote back: "I herewith return your warbler without comment." That was comment enough. Perhaps it was his custom to give his students a cold shake early on, to slowly step back once they had entered his professional domain. I cannot say for certain. When our work together ceased with sudden abruptness, it was a mystery to me, and upsetting. Late in October 1910, I had sent him the required five drawings: a murre, a crow, a gull, a cormorant, a black duck, knowing the likelihood of not hearing from him until spring. Yet in April and May 1911, the *Aunt Ivy Barnacle* made a number of round trips, and there was no letter from Sprague.

Anyway, I had been earning money from bird art and was proud of it.

In 1911 I still had a steady hand and could set aside personal torment for the duration of a drawing or painting. I still could concentrate for hours in a row, day and night, and had not yet fallen completely into the habit of drinking twenty to thirty cups of coffee a day. That happened in earnest after I had murdered Botho August and holds true of me to this day. I had never enjoyed alcohol, though I would drink whiskey with Margaret Handle, because she hated to drink alone. And she drank alone much of the time. But coffee is a different thing. It is a peculiar addiction and few people understand it. In my case, however, it can be traced back to Alaric's, Orkney's, and my household; I had drunk coffee since I was five years old. There were the long winters, you see, and coffee was what you came in to out of the cold.

So much to tell. Though I am a bird artist, you would not have heard of me. None of my paintings resides in a museum. My sketchbooks gather dust in Enoch Handle's attic. My first wife, Cora Holly, whom I married in an unfortunate arranged marriage, may still own an ink portrait of a garganey in eclipse plumage, I do not know. It was a wedding present, actually.

The garganey is a surface-feeding duck, and even Enoch Handle, who knew every bird along the coves, inlets, the entire coastline (he delivered mail from Lamaline at the southern tip of Newfoundland, to Cook's Harbour at the top; another boat, the *Doubting Thomas*, serviced the western seaboard), found it a rare visitor. Enoch was in his sixties and told me he had identified only two garganeys with total certainty. He admitted that at a glance a garganey might easily be mistaken for a cinnamon teal or a blue-winged teal. And it was true that you could live your entire life in Witless Bay, in Newfoundland for that matter, and never see a garganey, even if you were desperately searching for one.

Yet I had drawn Cora Holly's wedding present from life. It had been as though an otherwise meandering summer day, the day I had spotted the garganey, had lured me to Shoe Cove. Just before dawn I had packed my sketchbook, pens, binoculars, and had set out from our one-story blue cottage. I had already drunk five cups of coffee. I walked the half mile to the lighthouse. It was a clear morning; the lighthouse was silent except for gulls bickering along the wooden rail that encircled the light housing . . .

. . . In Shoe Cove, between Witless Bay and Portugal Cove, I saw the garganey. It was a male, asleep in the early sun, head tucked to his breast. There were no other birds or people in sight. It was a small, high-cliffed cove, and I made my way down to some flat rocks near the water, where I sat watching the garganey for a few moments. Then, moving to a more comfortable rock hollowed out almost like a chair, I sat sketching the garganey for a good two hours. I drew him as he slept. I drew him as he lifted his head, preened, skitted across the surface. He mostly held to one place, though at a certain point he flew off, circled, then lit down on what I thought was the exact same spot, hard of course to determine on a sun-glinted sea. It was as though he had enacted his own dream of flying, then had returned to his body. He fed awhile, scooping, shoveling, shaking his head, dipping, drifting, slowly turning with the random eddies. The sea brightened, the wind picked up, and there were whitecaps. I drew. Those were the elements: water, rocks, sun; the garganey, a migrant here for a short stay, whose life I had only happened upon because of that morning's particular luck. Luck like no other I had ever had, or have had since.

Three days later I purchased a simple wooden frame from Gillette's store, with money I had earned from *Bird Lore*. On the back I etched: *This is for Cora Holly, my fiancée. Begun June 26, 1911, completed June 29, 1911.*

ANDREA BARRETT

Birds with No Feet

There was no breeze that night. The sea, lit by the full moon, shone smooth and silver; the Southern Cross turned above the ship and below it squid slipped invisibly through the depths. Between sky and sea lay Alec Carrière, sprawled like a starfish in his hammock and imagining how the treasures packed in the holds were about to change his life.

Beetles and butterflies and spiders and moths, bird skins and snakeskins and bones: these were what he'd collected along the Amazon and then guarded against the omnivorous ants. Mr. Barton, his agent back home in Philadelphia, had sold Alec's first specimens for a good price, and Alex expected this shipment would finally set him free to pursue his studies in peace. He was a few months shy of twenty-one, and dreaming a young man's dreams.

Until he'd sailed for the Amazon, he'd worked in a shop making leather valises, not far from the tavern his parents ran in Germantown. But like the young English collector he'd met in Barra, near the flooded islands of the Rio Negro, he'd been saved from a squalid and unremarkable life by a few kind men and a book. With his uncle's ornithology text in his pocket he'd wandered the banks of the Wissahickon, teaching himself the names of birds and imagining wild places. His brother Frank had taught him to shoot, and behind the outhouse he'd prepared his first clumsy skins and mounts. Even then he'd known that other naturalists had taught themselves their trade. Others had risen from just such humble beginnings, and he'd seen nothing extraordinary in his ambitions.

Once every few months he went into downtown Philadelphia to visit the Academy of Natural Sciences, where a few of the members corrected his malformed preparations and taught him what they could. His interests spread from birds to other species. Titian Peale showed him an excellent way to pin and display his moths. Two of the Wells brothers, Copernicus and Erasmus, taught him how to prepare skeletons. All this gave Alec great pleasure but annoyed his father; by the time he was sixteen his father was pressing him to abandon this childish hobby and take his work more seriously. He almost gave up. But in 1850 Peale made him a gift of William Edwards's small and wonderful book, *A Voyage Up the River Amazon*.

When Alec read it a door seemed to open. What was there to keep him in Philadelphia? Edwards had been only a few years older than him when he'd set off; Alec was strong and healthy and his three brothers could look after their parents. And he had a most earnest desire to behold the luxuriant life of the tropics. Mr. Barton, a natural history auctioneer whom he'd met at the Academy, assured him that all of northern Brazil was little known, that Edwards had brought back only small collections, and that Alec might easily pay the expenses of his trip by gathering birds, small mammals, land-shells, and all the orders of insects. Among the wealthy, Mr. Barton said, glass cases filled with tropical creatures arranged by genus or poised in tableaux were wildly fashionable. And so few specimens had reached North America from the Amazon that high prices were guaranteed.

With the brashness of youth Alec wrote to Mr. Edwards himself, who provided him with letters of introduction to several traders. Then he packed his things and used his small savings to book passage on a merchant ship. His father was angry with him; his mother wept. But he saw miracles.

The mouth of the Amazon was like a sea, and could be distinguished from the ocean only by its extraordinary deep-yellow color. The Rio Negro was as black as the river Styx. Jet-black jaguars and massive turtle's nests, agoutis and giant serpents; below Baião, a crowd of Indians gathered, laughing and curious, to watch Alec skinning parrots. Driven to gather as much as he could, Alec shrugged off the heat and the poor food and the fevers that plagued him intermittently. His persistence was rewarded in Barra, where Alfred Wallace greeted him like a brother.

Wallace wasn't famous then. Except for the light that burned in him and lit a similar flame in Alec, he was just another collector, exceedingly tall, with a thatch of yellow hair and clothes as shabby as Alec's own. On the day they met the sun dropped like a shot bird, and in the sudden tropical night they compared skins and guns.

Alec was lonely, and glad for the company after months among Indians whose language he couldn't speak. He talked too much the night he met Wallace, he knew he did. But although Wallace was a decade older, wracked with fever and ready to leave for home after three hard years in the jungle, he never laughed at Alec's chatter or made him feel less than an equal. He showed Alec the blow-pipes his Indian hunters used, and the bitter vegetable oil with which he coated the ropes of his specimen-drying racks. Alec showed him the glorious umbrella-birds he'd captured in the flooded forest of the *igapo.* Standing by the side of this long, lean, wasted man, Alec took pleasure in his own youth and compact sturdiness; how his hands, next to Wallace's fine bones, were all broad palm and spatulate thumb. Around them the toucans yelped and the parrots chattered and the palms went *swish, swish* in the evening breeze. They ate fish and farinha and turtle. Later they traded stories about the books that had saved them. When Alec learned that Wallace was no gentleman scientist but was, like Alec himself, solely dependent on selling specimens to pay his way, he felt an immediate bond.

After they parted, Alec collected with even more fervor. Now the results lay snugly packed below him, and as the ship rocked sluggishly he was imagining how he'd drive up to his parents' tavern, dressed in a new suit and laden with more money than they'd ever seen.

They would be thrilled, Alec thought. As would everyone who'd helped him. How surprised the Wells brothers and Titian Peale would be, when Alec made them gifts of the especially amazing butterflies he'd set aside for them! And then the hush inside the Academy, as he lectured to the men who'd taught him. Holding up a perfect skin from one of those rare umbrella-birds, he would point out the glossy blue tufts on the crest-feathers. "When the bird is resting," he would say, "the raised crest forms a deep blue dome, which completely hides the head and beak." Then men would give him a desk, Alec thought, where he might catalogue his treasures. And he might marry, were he to meet someone appealing.

He was happy; he was half-asleep. Then the cabin-boy ran up to Alec's hammock and shook him and said, "Mr. Carrière! The captain says to come immediately. There seems to be a fire!" And Alec, still dreaming of his wonderful future, stumbled from his cabin with only the most recent volume of his journal and the clothes on his back.

The scene on deck was pure chaos: smoke rising through the masts, a sheet of flame shooting up from the galley, crew members hurling water along the deck and onto the sails. Captain Longwood was shouting orders and several of the men were unlashing the boats and preparing to lower them, while others hurriedly gathered casks of water and biscuit.

"What's happened?" Alec shouted. "What can I do?"

"Save what you can!" Captain Longwood shouted back. "I fear we may lose the ship."

Even as Alec headed for the forecastle, he could not believe this was happening. Some months after his meeting with Wallace, he'd heard that the brig carrying Wallace home had burned to the waterline, destroying all his collections and casting him adrift on the sea for several weeks. This news had filled Alec with genuine horror. Yet at the same time he'd also felt a small, mean sense of superstitious relief: such a disaster, having happened once, could surely never happen again. Although Alec's own collections were not insured, since he could not afford the fees, Wallace's bad luck had seemed to guarantee Alec's safe passage home.

All this passed through his mind as he fought his way forward. Then every thought but panic was driven away when he saw the plight of his animals.

In the holds below him was a fortune of things dead and preserved—but in the forecastle was the living menagerie he was also bringing home. His sweet sloth, no bigger than a rabbit, with his charming habit of hanging upside down on the back of a chair and his melancholy expression; the parrots and parakeets and the forest-dog; the toucans; the monkeys: already they were calling through the smoke. And before Alec could reach them a spout of flame rose like a wall through a hatchway in front of him.

Wallace's ship, he knew, had caught fire through the spontaneous combustion of kegs of balsam-capivi, but their own fire had no such exotic cause. The cook had knocked over a lamp, which had ignited a keg of grease, which had dripped, burning, through the floorboards and set fire to the cargo of rubber and lumber just below. From there the fire licked forward, downward, upward; and when the hatches were opened the draft made the fire jump and sing.

Alec was driven back to the quarterdeck and stood there, helpless, while the men prepared the boats and hurriedly gathered spars and oars and sails. The captain flew by, still shouting, his hands bristling with charts and compasses; they were five days out of Para and no longer within sight of land. The skylight exploded with a great roar, and the burning berths crackled below them. Terrible noises rose from the bow where the animals were confined. His lovely purple-breasted cotingas, roasting; the handsome pair of big-bellied monkeys, which the Brazilians called *barraidugo*—his entire life, until that moment, had contained nothing so distressing.

For a moment he thought the birds at least might be saved. One of the men dropped from his perch on the cross-trees and smashed in the forecastle door with an axe. Then the toucans, kept unconfined, flew out, and also a flock of parakeets. The cloud of birds seemed to head for the cloud of smoke but then swooped low and settled on the bowsprit, as far from the fire as they could get. They were joined by the sloth, who had magically crept up the ironwork. But meanwhile the mate was shouting, "Go! *Now*!" and hands were pushing against Alec's back, men were tumbling over the stern and he tumbled with them, falling into one of the leaky boats. Someone thrust a dipper into his hands and he began to bail, while men he had never noticed before barked and struggled to fit the oars in the oarlocks. The man pressed against his knee dripped blood from a scratch on his cheek and gagged, as did Alec, on the smoke from the rubber seething in the wreck.

The shrouds and sails burned briskly; then the masts began to catch. Soon enough the main-mast toppled and the moon-lit water filled with charred remains.

"Please," Alec begged Captain Longwood. "Can we row toward the bow? Can we try to save some of them?" His animals were lined along the last scrap of solid wood.

Captain Longwood hesitated, but then agreed. "Two minutes," he said sternly.

But when they approached the bow Alec found that the creatures would not abandon their perches. As the flames advanced, the birds seemed to dive into them, disappearing in sudden brilliant puffs that hung like stars. Only the sloth escaped; and he only because the section of bowsprit from which he hung upside down burned at the base and plopped into the water. When Alec picked him up, his feet still clung to the wood.

They were three days drifting in their leaky boats before they saw a sail in the distance: the *Alexandra*, headed for New Orleans. A fortunate rescue. Alec was grateful. But a year and a half of hard work, on which his whole future depended, was destroyed; as was the sloth, who died on the voyage. Alec reached home in one piece, but with hardly more to his name than when he'd left. As a souvenir he was given nightmares, in which the smell of singeing feathers filled his nostrils and his sloth curled smaller and smaller, and closed his eyes, and died again and again.

In November, recuperating at his uncle's house as his father would not have him at his, Alec learned that his acquaintance from Barra had written two books, one about his travels and the other about the exotic palms. Alec read both and liked them very much. They had shared a rare and terrible thing, Alec thought: all they'd gathered of the astonishing fauna of the Amazon, both quick and dead, turned into ash on the sea. Alec wrote to him, in England:

Dear Mr. Wallace: I expect you will not remember me, but we passed a pleasant evening together in Barra in September 1851. I was the young American man heading up the Rio Negro in search of specimens. I write both to express my admiration for your recent books, and to record an astonishing coincidence. You will hardly believe what happened to me on my journey home. . . .

Wallace wrote back.

Dear Alec: My sympathies on the distressing loss of your collections. No one who has not been through this himself can understand. Beyond the horrors of the fire itself, the terrible loss of animal life, and the substantial financial blow is this fact, so difficult to explain: That each specimen lost represents a double death. Our hunting always had a point; each bird we shot and butterfly we netted was in the service of science. But burnt, they now serve no one. It is very hard. I thank you for your kind words about my books. I plan to head, this coming spring, for the Malay Archipelago: an area hardly explored at all, which should prove extremely rich for our purposes. Perhaps you might like to consider this yourself?

Alec's mother, who had faithfully written to him during his absence, without understanding that he would get her letters only in one great batch when he returned to Para, was during this hard time very kind to him. She visited Alec weekly at his uncle's. And when he told her what he planned to do next, she encouraged him and secretly bought him two suits of clothes.

{Ague—1855}

It was not as if Wallace and Alec traveled together throughout the Malay Archipelago, nor as if Wallace took Alec under his wing in any practical way. Alec was in Macassar when Wallace was in Bali; Wallace was in Lombok when Alec was in Timor; they both visited the Aru Islands, but in different years. And their situations were no longer as similar as they'd been in the Amazon. Wallace was still strapped for money, but his books had made him a reputation, and the Royal Geographical Society had paid his first-class passage to Singapore aboard a fast steamer. Alec made a slow and uncomfortable voyage on three merchant ships and a filthy whaler. Wallace had with him an assistant, sixteen-year-old Charles, who helped capture, preserve, and catalogue specimens, whereas Alec was all alone, and often overcome by details.

During the wet season of 1855, Alec was in Sarawak, in northwestern Borneo. He'd heard tales of a lively Christmas house-party at the bungalow of Sir John Brooke, the English Rajah of the territory—all the Europeans in the out-stations being invited to enjoy the Rajah's fabled hospitality, and so forth. But he had not been asked to join the party, and he never suspected that Wallace was there. Over that Christmas, and into January, Alec was miles east of the Rajah's bungalow, collecting beetles and hunting orangutans in the swamps along the Sadong River.

For some weeks he'd been blessed with astonishing luck. Moving through the dense foliage he would hear a rustling overhead, then glimpse one of the reddish-brown apes swinging. Branch to branch, tree to tree, never touching the ground. His desire for possession seemed to carve a line in the air between his gun and his target; he aimed and a moment later the orangutan was his. Retrieving the body was more difficult, but here the native Dyaks helped him. As the orangutans fed on the fruit of the durian tree, of which the Dyaks were very fond, the Dyaks were happy to guide Alec to them and then, after the shooting, to fell the trees in which the bodies were trapped, or climb the trunks and lower the bodies down. With their help Alec obtained four full-grown males, three females, and several juveniles. Just before the ague hit again, he also shot another female high in a giant tree. While lashing the body to the carrying poles, one of his Dyak hunters found the orangutan's little infant face-down in the swamp, crying piteously.

This orphan Alec brought back to camp with him. He could not feel guilty about shooting the infant's mother; this was part of his work, what he was meant to do. But neither could he abandon the small creature who'd become his responsibility. While he lay on his cot, alternately burning and chilled, the infant orangutan clung to his clothes and beard and sucked on his fingers as he might at his mother's breast. For a long time no one had touched Alec. He gave the infant sugar-water and rice-water and coconut milk through a quill, and later offered bits of fruit and sweet potato. The orangutan insisted on clinging to some part of his body at all times. And Alec found this peculiarly touching, despite the weakness and lassitude brought on by his fever. When a pair of strangers walked into his hut, he was flat on his back, in a violent sweat, with the infant curled like a cap around his head.

Wallace, Alec learned from the strangers, had been at the Rajah's bungalow this whole time, staying on alone but for Charles and a Malay cook after the holidays had passed and the Rajah and his entourage had left. Having heard of Alec's plight through some visiting Dyaks, Wallace had sent these two back to fetch him. The pair carried Alec through the swamp and the forest, on a litter made of bamboo poles. Some of his helpers followed with his belongings, including all his crates of insect specimens and the skins and skeletons of the orangutans. The infant rode on his chest.

Wallace had the ague as well. When Alec arrived at the Rajah's bungalow, and first caught sight of the veranda and the huge teak beams, the wicker chairs and the spacious library, Wallace was desperately ill, and in bed. A few days later, when Wallace could get up, Alec was delirious. For ten days the men alternated bouts of fever as if they were playing lawn-tennis, but then finally, after large doses of quinine, both were well at the same time. In their weakened state they sat on the veranda, sipping arrack from narrow bamboos and talking. Wallace claimed that the bouts of ague stimulated his brain.

"Aren't these beetles astonishing?" Alec said, pawing through the box at his feet. His clothes and person were clean, he had had a good dinner, he'd slept on a real bed. He felt wonderful. This Brooke, he thought, truly lived like a king. And even though the Rajah had welcomed Wallace and not Alec, Alec was consoled by the beautiful things he had to show for his isolation.

"In two weeks I collected more than six hundred different kinds, sometimes a dozen new species a day—it's bewildering," Alec said. He held out a beetle with horns twice the length of its body. "Have you come across this one? And what do you make of the remarkable multitude of species here?"

Wallace smiled and turned the beetle delicately on its back. He said, "I have several of these; they're charming. I do not see how a reasonable man can believe any longer in the permanence of species. All species, as you have seen yourself, constantly produce varieties. If this process goes on indefinitely, the varieties must move farther and farther from the original species, and some of these *must*, in time, develop into new species—but how and when does this happen? What is the method by which species undergo a natural process of gradual extinction and creation?"

"The method?" Alec said. Wallace passed the beetle back to Alec and Alec held it cupped in his palm. Since his first day in the archipelago he'd been haunted, vaguely, by the question Wallace now posed clearly: where had all these creatures come from? But Alec had had no time to theorize, caught up as he was in the urgency of trying to capture and name everything he saw.

"There must be a *mechanism*," Wallace said.

The rain was falling steadily. From the trees three Dyaks emerged and joined the men on the veranda; Wallace produced a piece of string and tried to show them how to play the child's game of cat's cradle. Much to Alec's astonishment the Dyaks knew it better than he did. The three of them stood in a close circle, weaving figures he'd never seen before on each other's hands and passing the cradle back and forth. When Alec joined them they netted his fingers together.

Later Wallace showed Alec the lone specimen he'd found of a huge new butterfly, which had brilliant green spots arrayed against the black velvet of its wings. "I have named it *Ornithoptera brookeana*," Wallace said. "After our host." In return Alec showed Wallace how happily his little orangutan, whom he'd named Ali, lay in his arms as he brushed its long brown hair. He tried not to feel jealous when Ali leapt into Wallace's lap and licked his cheek. Wallace was Alec's friend, but also his rival, and sometimes Alec longed for Wallace to have some failing. A certain coldness, say. Or an absent-mindedness, brought on by deep thinking. But it seemed there was no part of their lives in which Wallace could not surpass him.

The ague struck them both again on the following day—and to their great sorrow, it also struck Ali. Wallace, too weak himself to rise from bed, had Charles give the infant castor-oil to cure its diarrhea, but although this worked, the other symptoms of fever continued; Ali's head and feet swelled; and then he died. Everyone at the bungalow much regretted the loss of the little pet. When Alec's own strength returned, he wept over Ali's body and then decided to bring the skin and skeleton home with him. Ali was sixteen inches tall, four pounds in weight, with an arm-spread of twenty-four inches. Alec made these measurements, but he shrank from the task of preparing the specimen and thought to have Wallace's Charles help him out. Wallace discouraged that.

"Charles is a nice boy," he said. "But quite incapable—look what he has done with this bird."

He showed Alec a bee-eater Charles had been putting up, which resembled Alec's own first specimens. The head was crooked, a lump of cotton bulged from the breast, and the bird's feet had somehow been twisted soles uppermost. Alec looked at this, sighed, and steeled himself to prepare Ali's remains alone. Separating the skin from the bone and muscle beneath, he reminded himself that, in so doing, he served science. Was this science? That night he was unable to sleep. Some hours after the bungalow had lapsed into silence, he found himself outside, in the dripping forest, slashing savagely at a tangle of lianas.

Not until later did he learn that somewhere during this long run of fever-soaked days, Wallace had written a paper on the possible origin of species by, as he put it, *natural succession and descent—one species becoming changed either slowly or rapidly into another. . . . Every species has come into existence coincident both in time and space with a pre-existing closely allied species.* His paper caused a stir when it was published in England that September, bringing him to the notice of such eminent men as Lyell and Darwin.

What was Alec doing while Wallace was writing? Tossing on his sweaty bed; mourning his little orangutan as he sorted and arranged his insect collections. He prepared a shipment for Mr. Barton, with a long anxious letter about the difficulty of his finances, and how much he needed to receive a good price for this batch of specimens. He wrote,

Enclosed please find:

Beetles	600 species
Moths	520 species
Butterflies	500 species
Bees and wasps	480 species
Flies	470 species
Locusts, etc.	450 species
Dragonflies, etc.	90 species
Earwigs, etc.	45 species
Total:	3155 species of insects

(note: multiple specimens enclosed of many species)

Alec never claimed that his financial difficulties kept him from such fruitful speculations as Wallace made; he knew that Wallace, like himself, spent precious hours sorting and crating specimens and was largely dependent on the income from the sale of same. Alec merely noted that Wallace had Charles, however incapable; a bungalow-palace where he might return from time to time to regain his strength; and powerful friends.

{Theories—1862}

Here is one: Two human beings, coincident in time and space, cannot simultaneously think the same thought; one always precedes the other. As Wallace always preceded Alec, except in a single case. For consolation Alec had this: that *he* was the first to bring live specimens of paradise birds to the western world. And he believed he was the first American to see these creatures in their native forests.

Although Alec thought of Wallace often and longed to see him, the Malay Archipelago is a very big place and they never crossed paths again. Not until the winter of 1860, while Alec was on Sumatra plowing stupefied through a year's accumulation of letters—his mother was ill, or had been the previous May; his brother Frank had married; Mr. Barton had sold his last shipment of insect specimens for a gratifying sum, but had advanced all the money save for a pittance to his father, at his father's request—did he again hear news of Wallace.

In a letter Mr. Barton, who kept up with the natural history journals in both England and America, recounted to Alec how at Ternate, while suffering again from the ague, Wallace had written a further essay on the origin of species and mailed it to Darwin for comments. The essay had caused a sensation, Mr. Barton said, summarizing its main points for Alec. It had been read at a meeting of the Linnaean Society, along with some notes of Darwin's expressing a similar idea.

Genius, Alec thought, sitting stunned on his wooden stool. That's what had come of Wallace's ague. Of his own, which was upon him again, there were only incoherent letters begging to know the true state of his finances. He would not repeat to anyone what he wrote to his family. To Mr. Barton he wrote,

> Thank you for your last, and for the most interesting news of Wallace's essay. You cannot imagine how tired I am after my last year's voyages. During the recent months, when I might have been resting, I have been cleaning, labeling, arranging and packing the enclosed: some 10,000 insects, shells, birds, and skeletons. Also hiring men and obtaining stores for my trip to Celebes and the Aru Islands—none of this made any easier by the fact that you have sent me hardly enough money to live on. Do not give the proceeds of this shipment to my family, but forward a full statement directly to me.

Perhaps this is when Alec first wondered why his journal had deteriorated into little more than a tally of species, interspersed with fumbling descriptions of places and people. Why all he'd observed and learned had not crystallized in his mind into some shimmering structure. Certainly he'd never lacked for facts—but he was caught like a fly in the richness around him, drowning in detail, spread too thin. If he were to narrow his gaze, perhaps? Focus on one small group of species, contemplate only them? Then he might make both his reputation and his fortune.

As a boy he'd spent hours in the Philadelphia museum staring at a skin labeled *Magnificent Bird of Paradise*: red wings, dark green breast-plumes, cobalt-blue head, a stunning yellow ruff or mantle, and behind that a second mantle of glossy pure red. Sprouting from the tail were two long spires of steely blue. He had stared not only because the skin was so beautiful, but because it had no wings or feet.

Birds with no feet—could there be such a thing? From a book in the museum's library, he'd learned that Linnaeus had labeled the skin he'd seen *Paradisea apoda*, or the footless paradise bird. A Dutch naturalist wrote that the paradise birds, wingless and footless, were buoyed up by the beams of the sun and never touched the earth till they died. How tantalizing, Alec thought now, looking up from his papers and crates. They were elusive, irresistible; and their skins were so rare as to be very valuable. Money crossed his mind, as it always had. Nearly penniless, and still without a wife or any possibility of supporting one, he seized on the prospect that the paradise birds might save him. Had Wallace married yet? He thought not. Once more he gathered the necessary supplies and prepared to disappear from sight.

After a long journey in a native *prau* from Celebes, during which his life was often in grave danger, he arrived in the Aru Islands. He shut his eyes to the fabulous trees, the astonishing moths and ants, and sought singlemindedly the Great Paradise Bird, with its dense tufts of long golden plumes raised to hide the whole body; the King Paradise Bird, so small and red, with its beautiful, emerald-green, spiral disks lifted high on slender paired shafts. The islanders with whom he was staying took him to see the *sacaleli*, or dancing-party, of the Great Paradise Birds.

In a huge tree, deep in the forest, he saw several dozen gather together. They raised their wings, they arched their necks, they lifted their long, flowing plumes and shivered them as if to music, darting now and then between the branches in great excitement. Their beauty and strangeness beggared even that of the lyre-tailed drongoshrike or the Amazonian umbrella-bird. Above the crouching, glossy bodies the plumes formed golden fans. The islanders taught Alec to use a bow, and arrows tipped with blunt knobs. He sat in the trees, dazed by the beauty surrounding him, and shot strongly, so as to stun the birds without rending the skins or staining the plumage with blood. On the ground below him, boys wrung the birds' necks as they fell.

And of course they had feet, strong and pink and sturdy. The theories about them, Alec learned, had only been misinformation. He was one of the first to see how the islanders, preparing skins for traders, cut off the wings and feet, skinned the body up to the beak and removed the skull, then wrapped the skin around a sturdy stick and a stuffing of leaves and smoked the whole over a fire. This shrank the head and body very much and made the flowing plumage more prominent. Alec prepared his own specimens differently, so that the natural characteristics were preserved. And this absorbed him so completely that only in brief moments, as he fell into sleep, would he wonder about such things as how the golden plumes were related to the emerald disks.

Rain, fungus, aggressive ants, and the ever-ravenous dogs of the region all plagued him. Still, before the fever overcame him and he had to declare his journey at an end, he salvaged four crates of excellent skins and also captured three living specimens. He might not have an hypothesis about the divergence of species, but he knew how these birds lived. At the Smithsonian Institution, where he thought to donate them, he could point to their sturdy pink feet and say, "Look. *I* was the first to bring these back."

As he hop-scotched his way across the archipelago to Singapore, he easily found fruit and insects his birds would eat. Little figs they particularly enjoyed, also grasshoppers, locusts, and caterpillars.

From Singapore to Bombay he fed the birds boiled rice and bananas, but they drooped in the absence of insect food and after Bombay even the fruit ran out. It was Alec's good fortune to discover they savored cockroaches, and for him to be aboard a battered old barkentine that swarmed with them. Each morning he scoured the hold and the store-rooms until he'd filled several biscuit-tins, and during the afternoon and evening he doled them out to the birds, a dozen at a time. As the ship headed south to round the Cape he worried that the increasing cold would bother them, but they did fine.

And if, as he learned after being back in Philadelphia for only a month, Wallace had been making his way to England simultaneously, carrying his own birds of paradise; and if Wallace's trip was shaped by the same quest for cockroaches—what did that matter? Wallace had traveled once more on a comfortable British steamer, aboard which cockroaches were rare; from his forced stops to gather them on land he made amusing anecdotes. But *I* was the one, Alec thought, who first solved the problem of keeping the birds alive.

From a London paper Alec learned that Wallace had returned to fame, as a result of his Ternate essay. His birds had taken up residence in the Zoological Gardens, where they were much admired. Meanwhile Alec had himself returned, unknown, to a country at war. To a half-country, he thought, which might soon be at war with England. His crates of skins lay uncatalogued at the Academy of Sciences. And the curators at the Smithsonian seemed less than grateful for his beautiful birds. No one had time to look at birds, their eyes were fixed on battles.

Alec wrote to Wallace once more—inappropriately, he knew; their situations had altered, their friendship had lapsed. Still he felt closer to Wallace than to anyone else in the world, and he could not keep from trying to explain himself to this man he'd meant to emulate. After giving the details of his voyage, of his birds and their fate, he wrote:

> All of this may be blamed on the war. I cannot explain how
> bewildering it has been to return, after my long absence, to

see what's become of my country. My mother died during my journey home. All three of my brothers have married, and my father has gone to live with my brother Frank, having lost through improvidence both the tavern and much of the money rightfully mine, which he obtained through trickery from Mr. Barton. Mr. Barton himself is gone, enlisted in the Army. The weather is cold and grey; the streets swarm with pallid people lost in their clothes; the air rings with boys shouting newspaper headlines, over and over again. In the Dyak longhouses, the heads of their enemies hung from the rafters, turning gently as we ate: and I felt more at home with them than here. Do you feel this? When you walk into a drawing-room, do you not feel yourself a stranger?

What I meant to do, what I wanted to do, was to visit Mr. Edwards, whose book sent me off on my life's work. He is no great thinker himself; only a man who traveled, like me, and described what he saw as I have failed to do. I thought he might help me gather some of my impressions into a book. But now I find that what I must do is abandon my collections, leave home once more, and enlist. The Potomac swarms with a great armada, ready to transport 100,000 men for an attack on Richmond.

As he mailed his letter, he thought about the legend that seemed—even before he left—to be growing up around his presence in the Aru Islands. He'd learned some of the islanders' language, and had occasionally entertained his companions by lighting fires with a hand-lens, or picking up bits of iron with a magnet, which acts they regarded as magic. And because he asked questions, even laughable questions, about the birds with no feet before he ever saw them; because he knew where beetles might be found and how to lure butterflies to a bit of dried dung; and most of all because he walked alone through the forests, for hours and days, and was comfortable there, and at peace, the islanders ascribed mystical powers to him. The birds, they claimed, came down from the trees to meet him.

One of the boys he hunted with said, "You know everything. You know our birds and animals as well as we do, and the ways of the forest. You are not afraid to walk alone at night. We believe that all the animals you kill and keep will come to life again."

Alec denied this strenuously. "These animals are *dead*," he said, pointing at a cluster of ants preserved in spirits. "Truly, truly dead."

The boy looked serenely into a golden glade dense with fallen trees. "They will rise," he said. "When the forest is empty and needs new animals."

Alec remembers staring at him; how the jar of ants dropped from his hand and rolled into the leafy litter. The suggestion seemed, in that moment, no more likely or unlikely than what Wallace had proposed for the origin of species: another theory of evolution; another theory. In that instant a line from Wallace's first letter to him returned and pierced like a bamboo shaft through his heart: *Each bird we shot and butterfly we netted was in the service of science.*

But this was only ever true for Wallace, not for him, he thinks; he has never been the scientist he'd believed himself to be, perhaps is no scientist at all. And that legend is as false as the moment, on the first leg of his first voyage home, when he hung suspended in joy. All the animals he's collected, sure that more would spring forth from the earth, are gone and will not rise. But as he packs his bags and readies himself for another murderous journey, they are what he thinks of now. The objects of his desire along the Amazon, in Borneo and Sumatra and Celebes, on the Aru Islands; his sloth, his orangutan, his birds with no feet.

Flamingos

I imagine them now
as they are sometimes seen
in great flocks flying over the Andes,
a sacred movement of birds and light.
On Sundays like this
I have glided around that point
of shaggy mangroves
off the west coast of Florida
in a canoe as the sun
slipped into the Gulf
and spread out its silks
on the water behind me,
a small boy astonished
at the world and his own mind
a few big hushed moments
in a bad year, 1956.

I like to say
I was born in 1947
just outside the city of Eureka, California
because it's true and has
a good sound. I was born
again to the strange loveliness
of this earth on that Sunday
gliding on the waters
of Pine Island Sound
around a point
through the secret opening in the mangroves
into Addison's lagoon.

My stepfather in the bow
held his finger to his lips
then pointed toward the far shore.
I held my breath and listened.
At first I didn't see them
just a rose glow on the water,
some part of the sunset broken off
and left behind.
But as we drifted quietly closer
I was filled with a single word,
Flamingos . . .
though I was wrong
and was told, in a whisper, Spoonbills.

Now I see them
preening, dipping their odd bills
into the water, swaying
in a kind of unison
on long thin legs.
Startled at the wrong word
they stiffen, bow to the water
and lift in a great shock of pink feathers
flaming into the air.
And I trail after them
all my senses stunned by the power
of a word as they fly away
toward the west
growing small and dark
on the evening sky.

BILLY COLLINS

Driving Myself to a Poetry Reading

Halfway there I pull on the headlights
and drift down the road, blazing
like the other cars in the weekday dusk.
I find something on the jazz station
and listen to the chords shifting
under the music like the many gears of the song.
The autumn air is cool and I can see
a few early stars through the windshield,
but like Caesar's Gaul, I feel divided.

There is a part of me that wants
to let go of the wheel, climb over the seat
and fall asleep curled in the back.
This is the part I would like to see
blindfolded some morning, dragged
into a courtyard, and shot.

Another part of me wants to be up on the hood,
a chrome ornament in the shape of a bird
leaning aerodynamically into the wind.
And now I can feel my voice begin to fly
ahead of the car, winging it into the night,
searching the landscape below for a podium,
a shaded lamp, a glass, and a pitcher of water.

This is the part I will still wonder about
when I am dying, staring up at the ceiling,
the part that is eager to perch on the rim
of that glass, wet its hard little beak,
and begin singing every song it ever knew.

WILLIAM HATHAWAY

The Bird Feeder

The eye of the titmouse is terribly black,
but her soft russet breast
and tufted crest is, of course, also
terribly cute. Yes, I mean it. A terrible kitsch
has been born. Reborn, of course.
Can any grand thing ever be said
in the ordinary gabble of real and forever
fallen times? (Did Dante *feel bad*
about screwing over Cavalcanti? "We can
only imagine," says the glib traducer
in his preface.) Unlike the tough-beaked finches
who cluster in to gobble, the titmouse
flutters over to the perch peg, pecks out
a black oil seed, and flutters back
to knock it open on a bare birch limb.
It's winter, and it's easy to see
all the birds twitching and flitting about
in trees stark as bones, except for white
shredded supermarket sacks flapping
like ghastly pennants ribboned
by the wind. But after a bit of that,
there's only so much to say about titmice
and such not. There's nothing to it,
really, but to just shut up for good
or get on with it and just say it—
that about half the time half my heart
is half-busting as I watch the birds flit
from branch to perch, twitching
like their whole tiny beings are being seized
moment by moment with revelations,
because half the people I've loved

that lived in the first half of my life are dead,
and there's no use for it—I just can't get
used to it. Yes, some live yet,
but gone mad, they sit as shadows
in shadow. Death in life, with their eyes
full of a terrible nothing like in the dead
Jesus brought back from the dead
just to make his point. But I won't go back
into that. I mean my heart, of course.
Your heart's another matter. Probably
you take pills for it, or something.
I don't presume. "Are you still writing?"
you're always asking me. Like,
are we still all Guelfs, or something?
The sparrows, for example, can't help
it—jerking around in little spasms
like that, that is—jumpy, like watching
old silent movies can get kids antsy,
a curious term. If airborne fungus
molts their feathers off, you can see
it's true, songbirds really are cute
tiny dinosaurs. They got them lizard nerves.
I can't help it either. Lilt, lilt, lilt
swoops the hollow-boned downy on swells of air,
and lightness tugs heavy on my heart.
Yes, but who wants to hear it?
No one does. Stick with the titmouse.
The living cannot hear the dead,
so listen: I've come halfway
from the land of the dead to tell you
what the secret Latin scripted
on the money hidden in the warm nests
of your wallet means. *I've got mine,*
it says. *Why pay more?* it asks,
and it thanks you for choosing.

PHILIP LEVINE

The Sea We Read About

Now and then a lost sea gull flutters into
our valley, comes down in a burned cotton field
and simply gives up. Once I left my pickup
by the side of the road, dug a square grave
the size of a beer case, and dropped in the bird.
Quintero, the short, husky truck farmer
from Tranquility, stopped to call out. What was I
doing in late July under the noon sun
digging in someone else's field? I told him.
Slowly he unwound himself from the truck's cab,
took up his shovel, and trudged over to see
it was done right. After we tamped down the earth
we stood speechless in the middle of nothing
while a hot wind whispered through the miles of stalks
and Johnson grass. "Can you hear what it's saying?"
Quintero asked. For the first time I noticed his eyes
were green and one didn't move. "Been hearing it
all my life, 62 years," and head down under
the straw cowboy hat he turned to go, waving
a thick forearm at the sky. I should have asked.
I'd seen him often before, stopped in his field of melons,
pensive, still, and took him for part of the place,
one more doomed farmer. An hour later, nursing
a cold beer, I stood outside the 7-11
at the four corners listening, but the voices
inside kept breaking in, two young drivers
teasing the pregnant girl who worked the register,
her laughter egging them on. Suddenly the bearded,
shirtless one began to sing a Beatles song,

"Why Don't We Do It in the Road," in such a pure voice
my whole world froze. Twenty-four years ago,
the war was ending, and though I wasn't young
I believed the land rose westward toward mountains
hidden in dust and smog and beyond the mountains
the sea spread out, limitless and changing
everything, and that I would get there some day.

T. C. Boyle

Rara Avis

It looked like a woman or a girl perched there on the roof of the furniture store, wings folded like a shawl, long legs naked and exposed beneath a skirt of jagged feathers the color of sepia. The sun was pale, poised at equinox. There was the slightest breeze. We stood there, thirty or forty of us, gaping up at the big motionless bird as if we expected it to talk, as if it weren't a bird at all but a plastic replica with a speaker concealed in its mouth. Sidor's Furniture, it would squawk, loveseats and three-piece sectionals.

I was twelve. I'd been banging a handball against the side of the store when a man in a Studebaker suddenly swerved into the parking lot, slammed on his brakes, and slid out of the driver's seat as if mesmerized. His head was tilted back, and he was shading his eyes, squinting to focus on something at the level of the roof. This was odd. Sidor's roof—a flat glaring expanse of crushed stone and tar relieved only by the neon characters that irradiated the proprietor's name—was no architectural wonder. What could be so captivating? I pocketed the handball and ambled round to the front of the store. Then I looked up.

There it was: stark and anomalous, a relic of a time before shopping centers, tract houses, gas stations, and landfill, a thing of swamps and tidal flats, of ooze, fetid water, and rich black festering muck. In the context of the minutely ordered universe of suburbia, it was startling, as unexpected as a downed meteor or the carcass of a woolly mammoth. I shouted out, whooped with surprise and sudden joy.

Already people were gathering. Mrs. Novak, all three hundred pounds of her, was lumbering across the lot from her house on the corner, a look of bewilderment creasing her heavy jowls. Robbie Matechik wheeled up on his bike, a pair of girls emerged from the rear of the store with jump ropes, an old man in baggy trousers struggled with a bag of groceries. Two more cars pulled in, and a third stopped out on the highway. Hopper, Moe, Jennings, Davidson, Sebesta: the news echoed through the neighborhood as if relayed by tribal drums, and people dropped rakes, edgers, pruning shears, and came running. Michael Donadio, sixteen years old and a heartthrob at the local high school, was pumping gas at the station up the block. He left the nozzle in the customer's tank, jumped the fence, and started across the blacktop, weaving under his pompadour. The customer followed him.

At its height, there must have been fifty people gathered there in front of Sidor's, shading their eyes and gazing up expectantly, as if the bird were the opening act of a musical comedy or an ingenious new type of vending machine. The mood was jocular, festive even. Sidor appeared at the door of his shop with two stockboys, gazed up at the bird for a minute, and then clapped his hands twice, as if he were shooing pigeons. The bird remained motionless, cast in wax. Sidor, a fleshless old man with a monk's tonsure and liver-spotted hands, shrugged his shoulders and mugged for the crowd. We all laughed. Then he ducked into the store and emerged with an end table, a lamp, a footstool, motioned to the stockboys, and had them haul out a sofa and an armchair. Finally he scrawled BIRD WATCHER'S SPECIAL on a strip of cardboard and taped it to the window. People laughed and shook their heads. "Hey, Sidor," Albert Moe's father shouted, "where'd you get that thing—the Bronx Zoo?"

I couldn't keep still. I danced around the fringe of the crowd, tugging at sleeves and shirts, shouting out that I'd seen the bird first— which wasn't strictly true, but I felt proprietary about this strange and wonderful creature, the cynosure of an otherwise pedestrian Saturday afternoon. Had I seen it in the air? people asked. Had it moved? I was tempted to lie, to tell them I'd spotted it over the school, the firehouse, the used-car lot, a hovering shadow, wings spread wider than the hood of a Cadillac, but I couldn't. "No," I said, quiet suddenly. I glanced up and saw my father in the back of the crowd, standing close to Mrs. Schlecta and whispering something in her ear. Her lips were wet. I didn't know where my mother was. At the far end of the lot a girl in a college sweater was leaning against the fender of a convertible while her boyfriend pressed himself against her as if he wanted to dance.

Six weeks earlier, at night, the community had come together as it came together now, but there had been no sense of magic or festivity about the occasion. The Novaks, Donadios, Schlectas, and the rest—they gathered to watch an abandoned house go up in flames. I didn't dance round the crowd that night. I stood beside my father, leaned against him, the acrid, unforgiving stink of the smoke almost drowned in the elemental odor of his sweat, the odor of armpit and crotch and secret hair, the sematic animal scent of him that had always repelled me—until that moment. Janine McCarty's mother was shrieking. Ragged and torn, her voice clawed at the starless night, the leaping flames. On the front lawn, just as they backed the ambulance in and the crowd parted, I caught a glimpse of Janine, lying there in the grass. Every face was shouting. The glare of the fire tore disordered lines across people's eyes and dug furrows in their cheeks.

There was a noise to that fire, a killing noise, steady and implacable. The flames were like the waves at Coney Island—ghost waves, insubstantial, yellow and red rather than green, but waves all the same. They rolled across the foundation, spat from the windows, beat at the roof. Wayne Sanders was white-faced. He was a tough guy, two years older than I but held back in school because of mental sloth and recalcitrance. Police and firemen and wild-eyed neighborhood men nosed round him, excited, like hounds. Even then, in the grip of confusion and clashing voices, safe at my father's side, I knew what they wanted to know. It was the same thing my father demanded of me whenever he caught me—in fact or by report—emerging from the deserted, vandalized, and crumbling house: What were you doing in there?

He couldn't know.

Spires, parapets, derelict staircases, closets that opened on closets, the place was magnetic, vestige of an age before the neat rows of ranches and Cape Cods that lined both sides of the block. Plaster pulled back from the ceilings to reveal slats like ribs, glass pebbled the floors, the walls were paisleyed with aerosol obscenities. There were bats in the basement, rats and mice in the hallways. The house breathed death and freedom. I went there whenever I could. I heaved my interdicted knife end-over-end at the lintels and peeling cupboards. I lit cigarettes and hung them from my lower lip, I studied scraps of pornographic magazines with a fever beating through my body. Two days before the fire I was there with Wayne Sanders and Janine. They were holding hands. He had a switchblade, stiff and cold as an icicle. He gave me Ex-Lax and told me it was chocolate. Janine giggled. He shuffled a deck of battered playing cards and showed me one at a time the murky photos imprinted on them. My throat went dry with guilt.

After the fire I went to church. In the confessional the priest asked me if I practiced self-pollution. The words were formal, unfamiliar, but I knew what he meant. So, I thought, kneeling there in the dark, crushed with shame, there's a name for it. I looked at the shadowy grill, looked toward the source of the soothing voice of absolution, the voice of forgiveness and hope, and I lied. "No," I whispered.

And then there was the bird.

It never moved, not once, through all the commotion at its feet, through all the noise and confusion, all the speculation regarding its needs, condition, origin, species: it never moved. It was a statue, eyes unblinking, only the wind-rustled feathers giving it away for flesh and blood, for living bird. "It's a crane," somebody said. "No, no, it's a herring—a blue herring." Someone else thought it was an eagle. My father later confided that he believed it was a stork.

"Is it sick, do you think?" Mrs. Novak said.

"Maybe it's broke its wing."

"It's a female," someone insisted. "She's getting ready to lay her eggs."

I looked around and was surprised to see that the crowd had thinned considerably. The girl in the college sweater was gone, Michael Donadio was back across the street pumping gas, the man in the Studebaker had driven off. I scanned the crowd for my father:

he'd gone home, I guessed. Mrs. Schlecta had disappeared too, and I could see the great bulk of Mrs. Novak receding into her house on the corner like a sea lion vanishing into a swell. After a while Sidor took his lamp and end table back into the store.

One of the older guys had a rake. He heaved it straight up like a javelin, as high as the roof of the store, and then watched it slam down on the pavement. The bird never flinched. People lit cigarettes, shuffled their feet. They began to drift off, one by one. When I looked around again there were only eight of us left, six kids and two men I didn't recognize. The women and girls, more easily bored or perhaps less interested to begin with, had gone home to gas ranges and hopscotch squares: I could see a few of the girls in the distance, on the swings in front of the school, tiny, their skirts rippling like flags.

I waited. I wanted the bird to flap its wings, blink an eye, shift a foot; I wanted it desperately, wanted it more than anything I had ever wanted. Perched there at the lip of the roof, its feet clutching the drainpipe as if welded to it, the bird was a coil of possibility, a muscle relaxed against the moment of tension. Yes, it was magnificent, even in repose. And, yes, I could stare at it, examine its every line, from its knobbed knees to the cropped feathers at the back of its head, I could absorb it, become it, look out from its unblinking yellow eyes on the street grown quiet and the sun sinking behind the gas station. Yes, but that wasn't enough. I had to see it in flight, had to see the great impossible wings beating in the air, had to see it transposed into its native element.

Suddenly the wind came up—a gust that raked our hair and scattered refuse across the parking lot—and the bird's feathers lifted like a petticoat. It was then that I understood. Secret, raw, red, and wet, the wound flashed just above the juncture of the legs before the wind died and the feathers fell back in place.

I turned and looked past the neighborhood kids—my playmates—at the two men, the strangers. They were lean and seedy, unshaven, slouching behind the brims of their hats. One of them was chewing a toothpick. I caught their eyes: they'd seen it too.

I threw the first stone.

Flight

Conor was still a Jesuit priest and during the day he said Mass, heard confessions, gave spiritual advice, and only rarely thought of bodies, his own or anyone else's. But at night he was often troubled by dreams of human flesh: of flesh falling away from the bones, of flesh rotting, of flesh transforming itself into something unspeakable; and always that flesh was his own. Lately he had begun to worry that some of the madness of his nights might—sometime, somehow— seep into the cool reassuring sanity of his days, and so once a week he saw a psychiatrist.

Conor had been a Jesuit for sixteen years, and—except for a couple recent lapses—he could say truthfully that he had lived his vows of poverty, chastity, and obedience as well as anyone could; strike that, as well as *he* could. He could say this, and he did, every week. To which, invariably, the shrink replied: "*And* you've earned a Ph.D. *And* published two books of poetry. What more do you want?" Silence. And then, "I want freedom," Conor said. "I want success. I don't know what I want."

What he wanted was to be loved, and then to be in love, but he was a priest, and so of course he had bad dreams.

On the night of his final dream, Conor had gone to bed with a terrible pain in his chest. He had been working on a poem for hours and hours—the words simply wouldn't say what they should—and it was well after midnight when he realized he was angry and frustrated and lonely and he had a pain in his chest. He poured himself a couple splashes of scotch and sat by the darkened window for a few minutes thinking his black thoughts; then he climbed into bed.

His dream that night was the usual one: he was complaining to Alix about the pain in his right leg, and as always, she said let's take a look at it, and when he slipped off his trousers they were astonished to see that his leg—halfway to his knee—was not flesh at all, but wood. And not merely wood but the rough bark of some tree. Alix was horrified and turned away, covering her face. Conor, horrified too, nonetheless bent to examine the leg. He saw that—as always—the bark was flaking off in places, that a colony of ants was carrying bits of resin from it, that there was a hole near the ankle, and coming out of that hole was a large brown beetle. It was awful, it was terrifying, because it was part of him and there was no escape. But then, all at once, Alix metamorphosed into the shrink and Conor heard him saying that things were looking much better, that the first time Conor had told him about the dream the wood had extended halfway up his thigh but in *this* dream it didn't even reach his knee. And what did he want, after all?

Conor woke now, only an hour after climbing into bed; he was shaking from the dream and from the pain in his chest. What had he been dreaming? He couldn't call it back, and in a way he didn't want to, but why was he suddenly furious with his shrink? And, good God, how was he going to get through this night? He thought of phoning Alix, but it was much too late. He thought of phoning the shrink and telling him to go to hell. He thought of dying.

He turned on the light and looked at the clock. He sat up in bed. It was at times like this that Conor wished he had a practical vice, like smoking. He poured himself a drink and closed his eyes to test how tired he was. He was very tired, he discovered, but he knew he would never get to sleep with this pain in his chest. The pain was heavy, an iron knot, a large hot something in the center of his chest and—he was working up a description for the doctor—it seemed to be sending out hot tendrils of another kind of pain into his left shoulder and arm. The classic heart attack pain. But of course this would go away and there would be no need to see a doctor. He got out of bed and sat at his desk. Automatically he reached for the sheets of paper with the unfinished poem.

This was another love poem. His earlier work had always been about death—the death of the heart, the death of the spirit—but since meeting Alix, Conor wrote only about love and its mysteries.

Possessing another: that was what intrigued him about love. Possessing and—even more astounding—being possessed. By *another*. Marvell and Donne had said everything there was to say about the mystery of possession; Conor knew that. But still there was something else, something dark, his own something, that lay just around a yet invisible turn, and he would find it, he would write it down. Again, as always, Conor's mind came back to Alix.

He was not in love with Alix, certainly; it was just that seeing her each morning at Mass, having dinner at her apartment most evenings, and, when they were apart, saving up things to tell her . . . well, it gave him some idea of what falling in love must be like. Or could be like. But he was not in love with her. She loved him, certainly, but his own feelings were something else. After all, he was still a priest, despite his recent lapses. And besides, Conor reminded himself, after they had been to bed only twice, he had successfully put the relationship back where it belonged: they were friends, not lovers. Writing love poems helped him channel all that displaced emotion.

This poem, however, was just words; it didn't work. And he didn't know what it was about, really.

> When his head split open like a rotten cantaloupe
> And seven birds flew out . . .

Well, what could you follow that with? His dreams had begun to edge over into his life, or at least into his writing.

Suddenly Conor's breath caught in his chest and he was frightened. Maybe he *was* having a heart attack. He considered the possibility with alarm and then with a kind of grim pleasure. It would resolve an awful lot of problems: his vocation, Alix, Superiors, loneliness, love. A heart attack? Good. And good riddance. Still, death was so final. Carefully, he placed the poem on his desk, and carefully, he poured himself another drink. No sudden moves. No unnecessary panic. He drew his breath in slowly and told himself he would not be having a heart attack today, thank you.

"Death, where is thy sting?" Conor said aloud, and answered himself, "Right here, and here."

He sat motionless for a long while, and then, very slowly, he moved from the chair to the bed, turned out the light, and waited to fall asleep. In only seconds he began to drowse, to give in, but just as he was going under, he had a waking vision of the flesh falling from his arm in long thin strips like bandages, but before the strips could touch the floor, some woman rolled them into neat little packets and put them in her purse. And then she flew away. Conor blinked several times in the dark and touched the firm skin of his arm. Was he going mad?

He put on the light and looked for a long while at the bottle of scotch. No. If he was going to die of a heart attack, he preferred not to have his corpse reeking of booze.

He got out of bed, sat in his easy chair, and tried to pray. That wasn't successful for long, so he picked up his Bible and flipped forward to the Apocalypse. He made his way through the seven angels, the four horsemen, and the Book of Life, and was about to launch into "new heaven, new earth," when he looked over at the window and saw the sun coming up. He had made it through the night and at least now he could die in daylight.

The pain was no worse, but it was terrible all the same. He would shower and dress and then walk to the Emergency Room of Mass. General, not telling any of the other priests in the house, making as little fuss as possible. If he was in fact dying, he wanted to do it right; and if he wasn't dying, he didn't want people thinking he went to pieces over every little pain. Make-believe virtue is better than no virtue at all.

Conor had the bathroom to himself—none of the others would be getting up until 5:30—so he felt free to moan and gasp as he eased himself into the shower stall. "Oh, oh, oh, oh, oh," he said aloud, getting satisfaction from the sounds of his pain. He stood propped against the wall, letting the hot water beat down on him; it was just too painful to use the soap and washcloth. After a while, he had had enough.

Drying himself, Conor noticed with alarm a large swelling on his left side. How had he missed it before now? He probed the swollen flesh tentatively with his right hand and cocked his head at an angle to see if it looked as bad as it felt, but he couldn't see much of anything. He wrapped the towel around his waist and went and stood in front of the mirror.

On his left side there was a swelling the size of his fist, whitish rather than discolored, and with what looked to be a thin red scar running the length of it. He turned sideways and moved closer to the sink for a better view. The pain in his chest got worse as his heart began to beat faster.

He stood there, fascinated, horrified. Even as he watched, the red scar darkened to a shade of purple. He put his finger at the top of the scar and traced its full length; when he took his finger away, it was wet. Blood? No; it was just some kind of translucent fluid; not even sticky. He looked again at the swelling with its purple scar. Where had it come from? When? And what was this stuff on his finger?

It was while he was examining his finger that Conor saw, without really looking, that the swelling had ruptured. He raised his eyes to the mirror, and yes, the purple scar had split open and out of it, very slowly, was oozing a dark black shiny fluid. Unable to turn away and yet terrified to look at what was happening to him, he took the towel from around his waist and placed it against his side just beneath the open wound. The fluid, thick and slow, oozed from his side, and when it stopped, it formed a dark and nearly solid mass on the towel. Conor examined it closely. The fluid had congealed in no particular shape; it was black and shiny, the size and color of a lump of coal. He looked in the mirror at the swelling on his side. It was nearly gone. The only proof it had been there was the scar—pale pink now, and fading—where the wound had been. And, of course, this black thing in the towel.

Conor was dressed and out of the house before anyone else was up. He felt somehow exhilarated, as if everything were over now, or nearly over. It had been a long night, with death breathing at his side; death, just as real as this towel he carried. That was all behind him now, he was sure.

The walk to Mass. General was a good twenty blocks, but the sun was bright and there was a cool breeze and, except that he was still in terrible pain, Conor felt wonderful. He set off at a brisk pace, the towel and its strange contents neatly rolled and tucked beneath his arm. Halfway to the hospital he passed Alix's apartment building, paused, and then walked on. He would like to tell her what had happened, show her this incredible thing. Would she be astonished? Horrified? No, of course not. Moreover, she would know at once how to handle this, what it all meant. He turned back.

Outside her apartment building, though he did not know why, Conor took the towel from beneath his arm and carefully unrolled it. He looked at the black thing cradled in the white towel. It was shiny still, glistening, but now it had life and form. As he watched, it shook itself, ruffled its feathers, preened first one wing and then the other with its tiny beak.

And then it flew from the towel, made a quick pass above Conor's head, and with a strange cry lit upon the windowsill of an apartment on the third floor. It was, of course—and Conor knew this—Alix's apartment.

Conor climbed the three sets of stairs slowly, the pain in his chest worse than ever. "It's over," he said aloud. "The pain and the dream and the swelling and the black bird. And now it's over. But how? How does it end?" Inexplicably, he felt filled with something very like happiness.

And so, when he walked through the open door of Alix's apartment, Conor was not really surprised by what he saw. Alix stood at the far end of the room, smiling, and beside her, suspended from the ceiling, hung a large wicker birdcage. The door of the cage was open, and inside the cage, perched on a little wooden swing, was the glistening black bird. Alix raised her hand as if to close the cage door. The bird began to sing.

KATHLEEN LYNCH

How to Build an Owl

1. Decide you must.

2. Develop deep respect
    for feather, bone, claw.

3. Place your trembling thumb
    where the heart will be:
    for one hundred hours watch
    so you will know
    where to put the first feather.

4. Stay awake forever.
    When the bird takes shape
    gently pry open its beak
    and whisper into it: *mouse*.

5. Let it go.

W. D. SNODGRASS

A Phoebe's Nest

This green is the green of live moss;
This gray is the breast-feathers' down;
This tan, tough vine-roots;
This brown, dead needles of longleaf pine;

And this, this coppery fine filament
That glints like the light-weight wire
Boys wind off a motor core,
This is my own love's hair.

       It's 7% and escrow;
       It's Mary Jane and despair;
       The ancient aunts say: headaches if
       Birds build with your hair.

Near our hedgerow, in a nest snarled
Like a fright-wig, young hawks shriek;
Great red-tails sail our winds all day
While small birds peck at their heads.

But under our kitchen floorboards
Where live wires wind through the dark
Our crewcut phoebe plaited this nest
Like a jetset high pompadour.

       Will the birds get dandruff?
        Or pubic lice?
       Will we go bald as an egg?

They'll knit a fine pucket
　　To warm up their brats;
　　You'll find out what'll ache.

This oriole's basket is woven white
Hair of our wolfhound, gone for years;
Our walls are rough plaster, laced with
The oxen's manes that worked this place.

Up under our roofpeak, birds slip
Through the roughcut cherry and beech;
Bare yards over the head of our bed
Strange bills squabble and screech.

　　It's Starlings stuck down the chimney;
　　　It's where did you go? Nowhere.
　　It's peckerholes in the siding
　　　And why did you park there?
　　It's swallows barnstorming the garage.
　　　Things get in your hair.

Sometimes you find the young birds
Gone; other times they're dead;
Ones that stay faithfulest to their nest
Just somehow never got fed. Yet

Nerve ends circuit a memory;
Phone calls lattice the night;
That phoebe shuttled our cellardoor
All day every day of her life.

　　Some say better not get involved;
　　　Send Hallmark if you care;
　　Some say they've come a long way

And haven't got much to spare;
Some say they're gonna have some fun;
Too bad you don't dare;
Some say it just isn't fair;
It stretches but it well might tear;
Get nylon or get wash-and-wear;
They want their fair share.

Polish ciocias, toothless flirts
Whose breasts dangle down to there,
Triple sea-hags say: headaches if
Birds build with your hair.

Still, my lady's brushing-in sunlight
Near our silver maples where,
Like Christmas strings or bright beadwork
We loop loose strands of her hair.

CHASE TWICHELL

Corporate Geese

When the big corporations began to build
their black glass palaces among the cow fields
of Princeton, New Jersey,

the hoof-chopped turf and muddy ponds
rippled for a moment in the heat waves
pushed by the bulldozers,

and then resolved themselves
into lakes and lawns, pure green slopes

on which executives could practice
their golf strokes during the hours
reserved for the health club and lunch.

And there was water gleaming in shapes
determined by experts to be
aesthetically pleasing, or tranquillizing,

or suggestive of the corporate logo.

These rival Edens lay on the flyway
of the Canada geese. The first year,

the ragged V's stopped on their way
south, landing on the clean new mirrors
beside the fresh squares of sod,

under which huge heating ducts criss-crossed,

melting the first snow as it fell, and making
a grid of shining grass, permanently green.

The geese stayed on, and more came.
Cars stopped to watch the vast flocks

preening and paddling, flying short aimless
missions over the town, squadrons
of gray-brown bombers landing and taking off,

the faraway north in their dog-voices.

On the corporate lawns, the slimy
cylindrical droppings began to accumulate,

clogging the mowers in spring—"organic
but non-nutritive," said the town paper—

and put an end to the mid-day golfing.

Various kinds of lights and noises
had no effect, and talk of poison and humane
relocation caused a public outcry.

So on they stayed, hundreds in each paradise:

Merck Pharmaceuticals, Cosmair, FMC,
Johnson & Johnson, Procter & Gamble,

Merrill Lynch, the Princeton Plasma Lab.

We've lost our way, said the geese
in their muted barking. Something in nature's

gone wrong, wrong. They said it
over and over, but no one heard them.

It sounded like squabbling, or mild outrage.

Teeming in their artificial south,
they gorged on breadcrumbs from the hand
of the future,

where their querulous voices
vanished in the hush of the wild grass

and the rain fell on dead cars,
the trackless contoured fields,

and, rising from a slag of black jewels,
the great steel skeletons

scrawled with the tags and logos of the dead,
picked clean by the locusts of their own creation.

KIM ADDONIZIO

The Singing

There's a bird crying outside, or maybe calling, anyway it goes on
    and on
without stopping, so I begin to think it's my bird, my insistent
I, I, I that today is so trapped by some nameless
    but still relentless longing
that I can't get any further than this, one note clicking metronomi-
    cally
in the afternoon silence, measuring out some possible melody
I can't begin to learn. I could say it's the bird of my loneliness
asking, as usual, for love, for more anyway than I have,
    I could as easily call it
grief, ambition, knot of self that won't untangle, fear of my own
    heart. All
I can do is listen to the way it keeps on, as if it's enough
    just to launch a voice
against stillness, even a voice that says so little,
    that no one is likely to answer
with anything but sorrow, and their own confusion.
    I, I, I, isn't it the sweetest
sound, the beautiful, arrogant ego refusing to disappear? I don't
    know
what I want, only that I'm desperate for it,
    that I can't stop asking. That when
the bird finally quiets I need to say it doesn't, that all afternoon
I hear it, and into the evening; that even now, in the darkness, it
    goes on.

PAUL ZARZYSKI

Bizarzyski, Mad Bard, Carpenter Savant, and Chuckwagon Wrangler of Manchester, Montana, Feeds the Finicky Birds

Unlikely that my poems will ever land
in some *Norton Anthology of Ornithology*, let alone
The Guinness Bird Book of World Bon Appétit Records,
I want all you Audubon paisanos to hear right now
who's the first mad poet to ring-shank-spike
a fat, foot-long, freezer-burned muledeer salami
to the icy top of a railroad tie corner post
where I distract rambunctious flocks
of ravenous magpies squawking happily all winter
away from the purple finch/English sparrow
birdseed feeders. Maybe I'm first
also to have learned that even a scavenger clings
to certain proprieties and will
exercise its right to decline a handout. Once,
I placed a frozen block of tofu
atop the very same post. No way. Not one minuscule
peck. Like offering menudo, paté, haggis
to a vegan. Poor tofu—it didn't get even
a second look, a quizzical magpie glance
of comical disgust or surprise. I did not know
these birds could smell, let alone whiff
tofu at 30 below. I've watched
them gobble up a bloated road-killed polecat
for brunch under a blacktop-softening sun. And so
it sat there, through 5 chinooks, through spring
and summer, until the post, I suppose, osmosised it,
almost, along with that dangerous duo

of dago hitmen, Sal Monella and his sidekick, Bocci,
who must've thunk they'd bag a bird or 2. But nothing
bit the dust, just like nothing bit the tofu. Thus,
I must confess—because I'm Catholic
and I'm unfulfilled unless I'm bearing guilt—
that I prayed very hard for scavenger forgiveness
as they laid their beady eyes upon my latest
feast and spiel: *My name is Paul. I'll be
your server this winter. For your delight,
our hammered chef tonight has spiked,
in lieu of our usual alder-planked smoked salmon
on the menu, frozen chunk of venison
sopressa over creosoted post. It's free.
I'll be right back to take your order.*

FLANNERY O'CONNOR

The Turkey

His guns glinted sun steel in the ribs of the tree and, half aloud through a crack in his mouth, he growled, "All right, Mason, this is as far as you go. The jig's up." The six-shooters in Mason's belt stuck out like waiting rattlers but he flipped them into the air and, when they fell at his feet, kicked them behind him like so many dried steer skulls. "You varmit," he muttered, drawing his rope tight around the captured man's ankles, "this is the last rustlin' you'll do." He took three steps backward and leveled one gun to his eye. "Okay," he said with cold, slow precision, "this is . . ." And then he saw it, just moving slightly through the bushes farther over, a touch of bronze and a rustle and then, through another gap in the leaves, the eye, set in red folds that covered the head and hung down along the neck, trembling slightly. He stood perfectly still and the turkey took another step, then stopped, with one foot lifted, and listened.

If he only had a gun, if he only had a gun! He could level aim and shoot it right where it was. In a second, it would slide through the bushes and be up in a tree before he could tell which direction it had gone in. Without moving his head, he strained his eyes to the ground to see if there were a stone near, but the ground looked as if it might just have been swept. The turkey moved again. The foot that had been poised half way up went down and the wing dropped over it, spreading so that Ruller could see the long single feathers, pointed at the end. He wondered if he dived into the bush on top of it . . . It moved again and the wing came up again and it went down.

It's limping, he thought quickly. He moved a little nearer, trying to make his motion imperceptible. Suddenly its head pierced out of the bush—he was about ten feet from it—and drew back and then abruptly back into the bush. He began edging nearer with his arms rigid and his fingers ready to clutch. It was lame, he could tell. It might not be able to fly. It shot its head out once more and saw him and shuttled back into the bushes and out again on the other side. Its motion was half lopsided and the left wing was dragging. He was going to get it. He was going to get it if he had to chase it out of the county. He crawled through the brush and saw it about twenty feet away, watching him warily, moving its neck up and down. It stooped and tried to spread its wings and stooped again and went a little way to the side and stooped again, trying to make itself go up; but, he could tell, it couldn't fly. He was going to have it. He was going to have it if he had to run it out of the state. He saw himself going in the front door with it slung over his shoulder, and them all screaming, "Look at Ruller with that wild turkey! Ruller! where did you get that wild turkey?"

Oh, he had caught it in the woods; he had thought they might like to have him catch them one.

"You crazy bird," he muttered, "you can't fly. I've already got you." He was walking in a wide circle, trying to get behind it. For a second, he almost thought he could go pick it up. It had dropped down and one foot was sprawled, but when he got near enough to pounce, it shot off in a heavy speed that made him start. He tore after it, straight out in the open for a half acre of dead cotton; then it went under a fence and into some woods again and he had to get on his hands and knees to get under the fence but still keep his eye on the turkey but not tear his shirt; and then dash after it again with his head a little dizzy, but faster to catch up with it. If he lost it in the woods, it would be lost for good; it was going for the bushes on the other side. It would go on out in the road. He was going to have it. He saw it dart through a thicket and he headed for the thicket and when he got there it darted out again and in a second disappeared under a hedge. He went through the hedge fast and heard his shirt rip and felt cool streaks on his arms where they were getting scratched. He stopped a second and looked down at his torn shirt sleeves but the turkey was only a little ahead of him and he could see it go over the edge of the hill and down again into an open space and he darted on. If he came in with the turkey, they wouldn't pay any attention to his shirt. Hane hadn't ever got a turkey. Hane hadn't ever caught anything. He guessed they'd be knocked out when they saw him; he guessed they'd talk about it in bed. That's what they did about him and Hane. Hane didn't know; he never woke up. Ruller woke up every night exactly at the time they started talking. He and Hane slept in one room and their mother and father in the next and the door was left open between and every night Ruller listened. His father would say finally, "How are the boys doing?" and their mother would say, Lord, they were wearing her to a frazzle, Lord, she guessed she shouldn't worry but how could she help but worrying about Hane, the way he was now? Hane had always been an unusual boy, she said. She said he would grow up to be an unusual man too; and their father said yes, if he didn't get put in the penitentiary first, and their mother said how could he talk that way? and they argued just like Ruller and Hane and sometimes Ruller couldn't get back to sleep for thinking. He always felt tired when he got through listening but he woke up every night and listened just the same, and whenever they started talking about him, he sat up in bed so he could hear better. Once his father asked why Ruller played by himself so much and his mother said how was she to know? if he wanted to play by himself, she didn't see any reason he shouldn't; and his father said that worried him and she said well, if that was all he had to worry about, he'd do well to stop; someone told her, she said, that they had seen Hane at the Ever-Ready; hadn't they told him he couldn't go there?

His father asked Ruller the next day what he had been doing lately and Ruller said, "playing by myself," and walked off sort of like he had a limp. He guess his father had looked pretty worried. He guessed he'd think it was something when he came home with the turkey slung over his shoulder. The turkey was heading out into a road and for a gutter along the side of it. It ran along the gutter and Ruller was gaining on it all the time until he fell over a root sticking up and spilled the things out of his pockets and had to snatch them up. When he got up, it was out of sight.

"Bill, you take a posse and go down South Canyon; Joe, you cut around by the gorge and head him off," he shouted to his men. "I'll follow this way." And he dashed off again along the ditch.

The turkey was in the ditch, not thirty feet from him, lying almost on its neck panting, and he was nearly a yard from it before it darted off again. He chased it straight until the ditch ended and then it went out in the road and slid under a hedge on the other side. He had to stop at the hedge and catch his breath and he could see the turkey on the other side through the leaves, lying on its neck, its whole body moving up and down with the panting. He could see the tip of its tongue going up and down in its opened bill. If he could stick his arm through, he might could get it while it was still too tired to move. He pushed up closer to the hedge and eased his hand through and then gripped it quickly around the turkey's tail. There was no movement from the other side. Maybe the turkey had dropped dead. He put his face close to the leaves to look through. He pushed the twigs aside with one hand but they would not stay. He let go the turkey and pulled his other hand through to hold them. Through the hole he had made, he saw the bird wobbling off drunkenly. He ran back to where the hedge began and got on the other side. He'd get it yet. It needn't think it was so smart, he muttered.

It zigged across the middle of the field and toward the woods again. It couldn't go into the woods! He'd never get it! He dashed behind it, keeping his eyes sharp on it until suddenly something hit his chest and knocked the breath black out of him. He fell back on the ground and forgot the turkey for the cutting in his chest. He lay there for a while with things rocking on either side of him. Finally he sat up. He was facing the tree he had run into. He rubbed his hands over his face and arms and the long scratches began to sting. He would have taken it in slung over his shoulder and they would have jumped up and yelled, "Good Lord look at Ruller! Ruller! Where did you get that wild turkey?" and his father would have said, "Man! That's a bird if I ever saw one!" He kicked a stone away from his foot. He'd never see the turkey now. He wondered why he had seen it in the first place if he wasn't going to be able to get it.

It was like somebody had played a dirty trick on him.

All that running for nothing. He sat there looking sullenly at his white ankles sticking out of his trouser legs and into his shoes.

"Nuts," he muttered. He turned over on his stomach and let his cheek rest right on the ground, dirty or not. He had torn his shirt and scratched his arms and got a knot on his forehead—he could feel it rising just a little, it was going to be a big one all right—all for nothing. The ground was cool to his face, but the grit bruised it and he had to turn over. Oh hell, he thought.

"Oh hell," he said cautiously.

Then in a minute he said just, "Hell."

Then he said it like Hane said it, pulling the e-ull out and trying to get the look in his eye that Hane got. Once Hane said, "God!" and his mother stomped after him and said, "I don't want to hear you say that again. Thou shalt not take the name of the Lord, Thy God, in vain. Do you hear me?" and he guessed that shut Hane up. Ha! He guessed she dressed him off that time.

"God," he said.

He looked studiedly at the ground, making circles in the dust with his finger. "God!" he repeated.

"God dammit," he said softly. He could feel his face getting hot and his chest thumping all of a sudden inside. "God dammit to hell," he said almost inaudibly. He looked over his shoulder but no one was there.

"God dammit to hell, good Lord from Jerusalem," he said. His uncle said "Good Lord from Jerusalem."

"Good Father, good God, sweep the chickens out the yard," he said and began to giggle. His face was very red. He sat up and looked at his white ankles sticking out of his pants legs into his shoes. They looked like they didn't belong to him. He gripped a hand around each ankle and bent his knees up and rested his chin on a knee. "Our Father Who art in heaven, shoot 'em six and roll 'em seven," he said, giggling again. Boy, she'd smack his head in if she could hear him. God dammit, she'd smack his goddam head in. He rolled over in a fit of laughter. God dammit, she'd dress him off and wring his goddam neck like a goddam chicken. The laughing cut his side and he tried to hold it in, but every time he thought of his goddam neck, he shook again. He lay back on the ground, red and weak with laughter, not able not to think of her smacking his goddam head in. He said the words over and over to himself and after a while he stopped laughing. He said them again but the laughing had gone out. He said them again but it wouldn't start back up. All that chasing for nothing, he thought again. He might as well go home. What did he want to be sitting around here for? He felt suddenly like he would if people had been laughing at him. Aw, go to hell, he told them. He got up and kicked his foot sharply into somebody's leg and said, "Take that, sucker," and turned into the woods to take the short trail home.

And as soon as he got in the door, they would holler, "How did you tear your clothes and where did you get that knot on your forehead?" He was going to say he fell in a hole. What difference would it make? Yeah, God, what difference would it make?

He almost stopped. He had never heard himself think that tone before. He wondered should he take the thought back. He guessed it was pretty bad; but heck, it was the way he felt. He couldn't help feeling that way. Heck . . . hell, it was the way he felt. He guessed he couldn't help that. He walked on a little way, thinking, thinking about it. He wondered suddenly if he were going "bad." That's what Hane had done. Hane played pool and smoked cigarettes and sneaked in at twelve-thirty and boy he thought he was something. "There's nothing you can do about," their grandmother had told their father, "he's at that age." What age? Ruller wondered. I'm eleven, he thought. That's pretty young. Hane hadn't started until he was fifteen. I guess it's worse in me, he thought. He wondered would he fight it. Their grandmother had talked to Hane and told him the only way to conquer the devil was to fight him—if he didn't, he couldn't be her boy any more—Ruller sat down on a stump—and she said she'd give him one more chance, did he want it? and he yelled at her, no! and would she leave him alone? and she told him, well, she loved him even if he didn't love her and he was her boy anyway and so was Ruller. Oh no, I ain't, Ruller thought quickly. Oh no. She's not pinning any of that stuff on me.

Boy, he could shock the pants off her. He could make her teeth fall in her soup. He started giggling. The next time she asked him if he wanted to play a game of parcheesi, he'd say, hell no, goddammit, didn't she know any good games? Get out her goddam cards and he'd show her a few. He rolled over on the ground, choking with laughter. "Let's have some booze, kid," he'd say. "Let's get stinky." Boy, he'd knock her out of her socks! He sat on the ground, red and grinning to himself, bursting every now and then into a fresh spasm of giggles. He remembered the minister had said young men were going to the devil by the dozens this day and age; forsaking gentle ways; walking in the tracks of Satan. They would rue the day, he said. There would be weeping and gnashing of teeth. "Weeping," Ruller muttered. Men didn't weep.

How do you gnash your teeth? he wondered. He grated his jaws together and made an ugly face. He did it several times.

He bet he could steal.

He thought about chasing the turkey for nothing. It was a dirty trick. He bet he could be a jewel thief. They were smart. He bet he could have all Scotland Yard on his tail. Hell.

He got up. God could go around sticking things in your face and making you chase them all afternoon for nothing.

You shouldn't think that way about God, though.

But that was the way he felt. If that was the way he felt, could he help it? He looked around quickly as if someone might be hiding in the bushes; then suddenly he started.

It was rolled over at the edge of a thicket—a pile of ruffled bronze with a red head lying limp along the ground. Ruller stared at it, unable to think; then he leaned forward suspiciously. He wasn't going to touch it. Why was it there now for him to take? He wasn't going to touch it. It could just lie there. The picture of himself walking in the room with it slung over his shoulder came back to him. Look at Ruller with that turkey! Lord, look at Ruller! He squatted down beside it and looked without touching it. He wondered what had been wrong with its wing. He lifted it up by the tip and looked under. The feathers were blood-soaked. It had been shot. It must weigh ten pounds, he figured.

Lord, Ruller! It's a huge turkey! He wondered how it would feel slung over his shoulder. Maybe, he considered, he was supposed to take it.

Ruller gets our turkeys for us. Ruller got it in the woods, chased it dead. Yes, he's a very unusual child.

Ruller wondered suddenly if he were an unusual child.

It came down on him in an instant: he was . . . an . . . unusual . . . child.

He reckoned he was more unusual than Hane.

He had to worry more than Hane because he knew more how things were.

Sometimes when he was listening at night, he heard them arguing like they were going to kill each other; and the next day his father would go out early and his mother would have the blue veins out on her forehead and look like she was expecting a snake to jump from the ceiling any minute. He guessed he was one of the most unusual children ever. Maybe that was why the turkey was there. He rubbed his hand along the neck. Maybe it was to keep him from going bad. Maybe God wanted to keep him from that.

Maybe God had knocked it out right there where he'd see it when he got up.

Maybe God was in the bush now, waiting for him to make up his mind. Ruller blushed. He wondered if God could think he was a very unusual child. He must. He found himself suddenly blushing and grinning and he rubbed his hand over his face quick to make himself stop. If You want me to take it, he said, I'll be glad to. Maybe finding the turkey was a sign. Maybe God wanted him to be a preacher. He thought of Bing Crosby and Spencer Tracy. He might found a place for boys to stay who were going bad. He lifted the turkey up—it was heavy all right—and fitted it over his shoulder. He wished he could see how he looked with it slung over like that. It occurred to him that he might as well go home the long way—through town. He had plenty of time. He started off slowly, shifting the turkey until it fit comfortably over his shoulder. He remembered the things he had thought before he found the turkey. They were pretty bad, he guessed.

He guessed God had stopped him before it was too late. He should be very thankful. Thank You, he said.

Come on, boys, he said, we will take this turkey back for our dinner. We certainly are much obliged to You, he said to God. This turkey weighs ten pounds. You were mighty generous.

That's okay, God said. And listen, we ought to have a talk about these boys. They're entirely in your hands, see? I'm leaving the job strictly up to you. I have confidence in you, McFarney.

You can trust me, Ruller said. I'll come through with the goods.

He went into town with the turkey over his shoulder. He wanted to do something for God but he didn't know what he could do. If anybody was playing the accordion on the street today, he'd give them his dime. He only had one dime, but he'd give it to them. Maybe he could think of something better, though. He had been going to keep the dime for something. He might could get another one from his grandmother. How about a goddam dime, kid? He pulled his mouth piously out of the grin. He wasn't going to think that way any more. He couldn't get a dime from her anyway. His mother was going to whip him if he asked his grandmother for money again. Maybe something would turn up that he could do. If God wanted him to do something, He'd turn something up.

He was getting into the business block and through the corner of his eye he noticed people looking at him. There were eight thousand people in Mulrose County and on Saturday every one of them was in Tilford on the business block. They turned as Ruller passed and looked at him. He glanced at himself reflected in a store window, shifted the turkey slightly, and walked quickly ahead. He heard someone call, but he walked on, pretending he was deaf. It was his mother's friend, Alice Gilhard, and if she wanted him, let her catch up with him.

"Ruller!" she cried. "My goodness, where did you get that turkey?" She came up behind him fast and put her hand on his shoulder. "That's some bird," she said. "You must be a good shot."

"I didn't shoot it," Ruller said coldly. "I captured it. I chased it dead."

"Heavens," she said. "You wouldn't capture me one sometime, would you?"

"I might if I ever have time," Ruller said. She thought she was so cute.

Two men came over and whistled at the turkey. They yelled at some other men on the corner to look. Another of his mother's friends stopped and some country boys who had been sitting on the curb got up and tried to see the turkey without showing they were interested. A man with a hunting suit and gun stopped and looked at Ruller and walked around behind him and looked at the turkey.

"How much do you think it weighs?" a lady asked.

"At least ten pounds," Ruller said.

"How long did you chase it?"

"About an hour," Ruller said.

"The goddam imp," the man in the hunting suit muttered.

"That's really amazing," a lady commented.

"About that long," Ruller said.

"You must be very tired."

"No," Ruller said. "I have to go. I'm in a hurry." He worked his face to look as if he were thinking something out and hurried down the street until he was out of their view. He felt warm all over and nice as if something very fine were going to be or had been. He looked back once and saw that the country boys were following him. He hoped they would come up and ask to look at the turkey. God must be wonderful, he felt suddenly. He wanted to do something for God. He hadn't seen anyone playing the accordion, though, or selling pencils and he was past the business block. He might see one before he really got to the streets where people lived at. If he did, he'd give away the dime—even while he knew he couldn't get another one any time soon. He began to wish he would see somebody begging.

Those country kids were still trailing along behind him. He thought he might stop and ask them did they want to see the turkey; but they might just stare at him. They were tenants' children and sometimes tenants' children just stared at you. He might found a home for tenants' children. He thought about going back through town to see if he had passed a beggar without seeing him, but he decided people might think he was showing off with the turkey.

Lord, send me a beggar, he prayed suddenly. Send me one before I get home. He had never thought before of praying on his own, but it was a good idea. God had put the turkey there. He'd send him a beggar. He knew for a fact God would send him one. He was on Hill Street now and there were nothing but houses on Hill Street. It would be strange to find a beggar here. The sidewalks were empty except for a few children and some tricycles. Ruller looked back; the country boys were still following him. He decided to slow down. It might make them catch up with him and it might give a beggar more time to get to him. If one were coming. He wondered if one were coming. If one came, it would mean God had gone out of His way to get one. It would mean God was really interested. He had a sudden fear one wouldn't come; it was a whole fear quick.

One will come, he told himself. God was interested in him because he was a very unusual child. He went on. The streets were deserted now. He guessed one wouldn't come. Maybe God didn't have confidence in—no, God did. Lord, please send me a beggar! he implored. He squinched his face rigid and strained his muscles in a knot and said, "Please! one right now"; and the minute he said it—the minute—Hetty Gilman turned around the corner before him, heading straight to where he was.

He felt almost like he had when he ran into the tree.

She was walking down the street right toward him. It was just like the turkey lying there. It was just as if she had been hiding behind a house until he came by. She was an old woman whom everybody said had more money than anybody in town because she had been begging for twenty years. She sneaked into people's houses and sat until they gave her something. If they didn't, she cursed them. Nevertheless, she was a beggar. Ruller walked faster. He took the dime out of his pocket so it would be ready. His heart was stomping up and down in his chest. He made a noise to see if he could talk. As they neared each other, he stuck out his hand. "Here!" he shouted. "Here!"

She was a tall, long-faced old woman in an antique black cloak. Her face was the color of a dead chicken's skin. When she saw him, she looked as if she suddenly smelled something bad. He darted at her and thrust the dime into her hand and dashed on without looking back.

Slowly his heart calmed and he began to feel full of a new feeling—like being happy and embarrassed at the same time. Maybe, he thought, blushing, he would give all his money to her. He felt as if the ground did not need to be under him any longer. He noticed suddenly that the country boys' feet were shuffling just behind him, and almost without thinking, he turned and asked graciously, "You all wanta see this turkey?"

They stopped where they were and stared at him. One in front spit. Ruller looked down at it quickly. There was real tobacco juice in it! "Wheered you git that turkey?" the spitter asked.

"I found it in the woods," Ruller said. "I chased it dead. See, it's been shot under the wing." He took the turkey off his shoulder and held it down where they could see. "I think it was shot twice," he went on excitedly, pulling the wing up.

"Lemme see it here," the spitter said.

Ruller handed him the turkey. "You see down there where the bullet hole is?" he asked. "Well, I think it was shot twice in the same hole, I think it was . . ." The turkey's head flew in his face as the spitter slung it up in the air and over his own shoulder and turned. The others turned with him and together they sauntered off in the direction they had come, the turkey sticking stiff out on the spitter's back and its head swinging slowly in a circle as he walked away.

They were in the next block before Ruller moved. Finally, he realized that he could not even see them any longer, they were so far away. He turned toward home, almost creeping. He walked four blocks and then suddenly, noticing that it was dark, he began to run. He ran faster and faster, and as he turned up the road to his house, his heart was running as fast as his legs and he was certain that Something Awful was tearing behind him with its arms rigid and its fingers ready to clutch.

EUDORA WELTY

A Still Moment

Lorenzo Dow rode the Old Natchez Trace at top speed upon a race horse, and the cry of the itinerant Man of God, "I must have souls! And souls I must have!" rang in his own windy ears. He rode as if never to stop, toward his night's appointment.

It was the hour of sunset. All the souls that he had saved and all those he had not took dusky shapes in the mist that hung between the high banks, and seemed by their great number and density to block his way, and showed no signs of melting or changing back into mist, so that he feared his passage was to be difficult forever. The poor souls that were not saved were darker and more pitiful than those that were, and still there was not any of the radiance he would have hoped to see in such a congregation.

"Light up, in God's name!" he called, in the pain of his disappointment.

Then a whole swarm of fireflies instantly flickered all around him, up and down, back and forth, first one golden light and then another, flashing without any of the weariness that had held back the souls. These were the signs sent from God that he had not seen the accumulated radiance of saved souls because he was not able, and that his eyes were more able to see the fireflies of the Lord than His blessed souls.

"Lord, give me the strength to see the angels when I am in Paradise," he said. "Do not let my eyes remain in this failing proportion to my loving heart always."

He gasped and held on. It was that day's complexity of horse-trading that had left him in the end with a Spanish race horse for which he was bound to send money in November from Georgia. Riding faster on the beast and still faster until he felt as if he were flying he sent thoughts of love with matching speed to his wife Peggy in

Massachusetts. He found it effortless to love at a distance. He could look at the flowering trees and love Peggy in fullness, just as he could see his visions and love God. And Peggy, to whom he had not spoken until he could speak fateful words ("Would she accept of such an object as him?"), Peggy, the bride, with whom he had spent a few hours of time, showing of herself a small round handwriting, declared all in one letter, her first, that she felt the same as he, and that the fear was never of separation, but only of death.

Lorenzo well knew that it was Death that opened underfoot, that rippled by at night, that was the silence the birds did their singing in. He was close to death, closer than any animal or bird. On the back of one horse after another, winding them all, he was always riding toward it or away from it, and the Lord sent him directions with protection in His mind.

Just then he rode into a thicket of Indians taking aim with their new guns. One stepped out and took the horse by the bridle, it stopped at a touch, and the rest made a closing circle. The guns pointed.

"Incline!" The inner voice spoke sternly and with its customary lightning-quickness.

Lorenzo inclined all the way forward and put his head to the horse's silky mane, his body to its body, until a bullet meant for him would endanger the horse and make his death of no value. Prone he rode out through the circle of Indians, his obedience to the voice leaving him almost fearless, almost careless with joy.

But as he straightened and pressed ahead, care caught up with him again. Turning half-beast and half-divine, dividing himself like a heathen Centaur, he had escaped his death once more. But was it to be always by some metamorphosis of himself that he escaped, some humiliation of his faith, some admission to strength and argumentation and not frailty? Each time when he acted so it was at the command of an instinct that he took at once as the word of an angel, until too late, when he knew it was the word of the Devil. He had roared like a tiger at Indians, he had submerged himself in water blowing the savage bubbles of the alligator, and they skirted him by. He had prostrated himself to appear dead, and deceived bears. But all the time God would have protected him in His own way, less hurried, more divine.

Even now he saw a serpent crossing the Trace, giving out knowing glances.

He cried, "I know you now!," and the serpent gave him one look out of which all the fire had been taken, and went away in two darts into the tangle.

He rode on, all expectation, and the voices in the throats of the wild beasts went, almost without his noticing when, into words. "Praise God," they said. "Deliver us from one another." Birds especially sang of divine love which was the one ceaseless protection. "Peace, in peace," were their words so many times when they spoke from the briars, in a courteous sort of inflection, and he turned his countenance toward all perched creatures with a benevolence striving to match their own.

He rode on past the little intersecting trails, letting himself be guided by voices and by lights. It was battlesounds he heard most, sending him on, but sometimes ocean sounds, that long beat of waves that would make his heart pound and retreat as heavily as they, and he despaired again in his failure in Ireland when he took a voyage and persuaded with the Catholics with his back against the door, and then ran away to their cries of "Mind the white hat!" But when he heard singing it was not the militant and sharp sound of Wesley's hymns, but a soft, tireless and tender air that had no beginning and no end, and the softness of distance, and he had pleaded with the Lord to find out if all this meant that it was wicked, but no answer had come.

Soon night would descend, and a camp-meeting ground ahead would fill with its sinners like the sky with its stars. How he hungered for them! He looked in prescience with a longing of love over the throng that waited while the flames of the torches threw change, change, change over their faces. How could he bring them enough, if it were not divine love and sufficient warning of all that could threaten them? He rode on faster. He was a filler of appointments, and he filled more and more, until his journeys up and down creation were nothing but a shuttle, driving back and forth upon the rich expanse of his vision. He was homeless by his own choice, he must be everywhere at some time, and somewhere soon. There hastening in the wilderness on his flying horse he gave the night's torch-lit crowd a premature benediction, he could not wait. He spread his arms out, one at a time for safety, and he wished, when they would all be gathered in by his tin horn blasts and the inspired words would go out over their heads, to brood above the entire and passionate life of the wide world, to become its rightful part.

He peered ahead. "Inhabitants of Time! The wilderness is your souls on earth!" he shouted ahead into the treetops. "Look about you, if you would view the conditions of your spirit, put here by the good Lord to show you and afright you. These wild places and these trails of awesome loneliness lie nowhere, nowhere, but in your heart."

A dark man, who was James Murrell the outlaw, rode his horse out of a cane brake and began going along beside Lorenzo without looking at him. He had the alternately proud and aggrieved look of a man believing himself to be an instrument in the hands of a power, and when he was young he said at once to strangers that he was being used by Evil, or sometimes he stopped a traveler by shouting, "Stop! I'm the Devil!" He rode along now talking and drawing out his talk, by some deep control of the voice gradually slowing the speed of Lorenzo's horse down until both the horses were softly trotting. He would have wondered that nothing he said was heard, not knowing that Lorenzo listened only to voices of whose heavenly origin he was more certain.

Murrell riding along with his victim-to-be, Murrell riding, was Murrell talking. He told away at his long tales, with always a distance and a long length of time flowing through them, and all centered about a silent man. In each the silent man would have done a piece of evil, a robbery or a murder, in a place of long ago, and it was all made for the revelation in the end that the silent man was Murrell himself, and the long story had happened yesterday, and the place *here*—the Natchez Trace. It would only take one dawning look for the victim to see that all of this was another story and he himself had listened his way into it, and that he too was about to recede in time (to where the dread was forgotten) for some listener and to live for a listener in the long ago. Destroy the present!—that must have been the first thing that was whispered in Murrell's heart—the living moment and the man that lives in it must die before you can go on. It was his habit to bring the journey—which might even take days—to a close with a kind of ceremony. Turning his face at last into the face of the victim, for he had never seen him before now, he would tower up with the sudden height of a man no longer the tale teller but the speechless protagonist, silent at last, one degree nearer the hero. Then he would murder the man.

But it would always start over. This man going forward was going backward with talk. He saw nothing, observed no world at all. The two ends of his journey pulled at him always and held him in a nowhere, half asleep, smiling and witty, dangling his predicament. He was a murderer whose final stroke was over-long postponed, who had to bring himself through the greatest tedium to act, as if the whole wilderness, where he was born, were his impediment. But behind him and before him he kept in sight a victim, he saw a man fixed and stayed at the point of death—no matter how the man's eyes denied it, a victim, hands spreading to reach as if for the first time for life. Contempt! That is what Murrell gave that man.

Lorenzo might have understood, if he had not been in haste, that Murrell in laying hold of a man meant to solve his mystery of being. It was as if other men, all but himself, would lighten their hold on the secret, upon assault, and let it fly free at death. In his violence he was only treating of enigma. The violence shook his own body first, like a force gathering, and now he turned in the saddle.

Lorenzo's despair had to be kindled as well as his ecstasy, and could not come without that kindling. Before the awe-filled moment when the faces were turned up under the flares, as though an angel hand tipped their chins, he had no way of telling whether he would enter the sermon by sorrow or by joy. But at this moment the face of Murrell was turned toward him, turning at last, all solitary, in its full, and Lorenzo would have seized the man at once by his black coat and shaken him like prey for a lost soul, so instantly was he certain that the false fire was in his heart instead of the true fire. But Murrell, quick when he was quick, had put his own hand out, a restraining hand, and laid it on the wavelike flesh of the Spanish race horse, which quivered and shuddered at the touch.

They had come to a great live-oak tree at the edge of a low marshland. The burning sun hung low, like a head lowered on folded arms, and over the long reaches of violet trees the evening seemed still with thought. Lorenzo knew the place from having seen it among many in dreams, and he stopped readily and willingly. He drew rein, and Murrell drew rein, he dismounted and Murrell dismounted, he took a step, and Murrell was there too; and Lorenzo was not surprised at the closeness, how Murrell in his long dark coat and over it his dark face darkening still, stood beside him like a brother seeking light.

But in that moment instead of two men coming to stop by the great forked tree, there were three.

From far away, a student, Audubon, had been approaching lightly on the wilderness floor, disturbing nothing in his lightness. The long day of beauty had led him this certain distance. A flock of purple finches that he tried for the first moment to count went over his head. He made a spelling of the soft *pet* of the ivory-billed woodpecker. He told himself always: remember.

Coming upon the Trace, he looked at the high cedars, azure and still as distant smoke overhead, with their silver roots trailing down on either side like the veins of deepness in this place, and he noted some fact to his memory—this earth that wears but will not crumble or slide or turn to dust, they say it exists in one other spot in the world, Egypt—and then forgot it. He walked quietly. All life used this Trace, and he liked to see the animals move along it in direct, oblivious journeys, for they had begun it and made it, the buffalo and deer and the small running creatures before man ever knew where he wanted to go, and birds flew a great mirrored course above. Walking beneath them Audubon remembered how in the cities he had seen these very birds in his imagination, calling them up whenever he wished, even in the hard and glittering outer parlors where if an artist were humble enough to wait, some idle hand held up promised money. He walked lightly and he went as carefully as he had started at two that morning, crayon and paper, a gun, and a small bottle of spirits disposed about his body. (*Note: "The mocking birds so gentle that they would scarcely move out of the way."*) He looked with care; great abundance had ceased to startle him, and he could see things one by one. In Natchez they had told him of many strange and marvelous birds that were to be found here. Their descriptions had been exact, complete, and wildly varying, and he took them for inventions and believed that like all the worldly things that came out of Natchez, they would be disposed of and shamed by man's excursion into the reality of Nature.

In the valley he appeared under the tree, a sure man, very sure and tender, as if the touch of all the earth rubbed upon him and the stains of the flowery swamp had made him so.

Lorenzo welcomed him and turned fond eyes upon him. To transmute a man into an angel was the hope that drove him all over the world and never let him flinch from a meeting or withhold good-byes for long. This hope insistently divided his life into only two parts, journey and rest. There could be no night and day and love and despair and longing and satisfaction to make partitions in the single ecstasy of this alternation. All things were speech.

"God created the world," said Lorenzo, "and it exists to give testimony. Life is the tongue: speak."

But instead of speech there happened a moment of deepest silence.

Audubon said nothing because he had gone without speaking a word for days. He did not regard his thoughts for the birds and animals as susceptible, in their first change, to words. His long playing on the flute was not in its origin a talking to himself. Rather than speak to order or describe, he would always draw a deer with a stroke across it to communicate his need of venison to an Indian. He had only found words when he discovered that there is much otherwise lost that can be noted down each item in its own day, and he wrote often now in a journal, not wanting anything to be lost the way it had been, all the past, and he would write about a day, "Only sorry that the Sun Sets."

Murrell, his cheated hand hiding the gun, could only continue to smile at Lorenzo, but he remembered in malice that he had disguised himself once as an Evangelist, and his final words to his victim would have been, "One of my disguises was what you are."

Then in Murrell Audubon saw what he thought of as "acquired sorrow"—that cumbrousness and darkness from which the naked Indian, coming just as he was made from God's hand, was so lightly free. He noted the eyes—the dark kind that loved to look through chinks, and saw neither closeness nor distance, light nor shade, wonder nor familiarity. They were narrowed to contract the heart, narrowed to make an averting plan. Audubon knew the finest-drawn tendons of the body and the working of their power, for he had touched them, and he supposed then that in man the enlargement of the eye to see started a motion in the hands to make or do, and that the narrowing of the eye stopped the hand and contracted the heart. Now Murrell's eyes followed an ant on a blade of grass, up the blade and down, many times in the single moment. Audubon had examined the Cave-In Rock where one robber had lived his hiding life, and the air in the cave was the cavelike air that enclosed this man, the same odor, flinty and dark. O secret life, he thought—is it true that the secret is withdrawn from the true disclosure, that man is a cave man, and that the openness I see, the ways through forests, the rivers brimming light, the wide arches where the birds fly, are dreams of freedom? If my origin is withheld from me, is my end to be unknown too? Is the radiance I see closed into an interval between two darks, or can it not illuminate them both and discover at last, though it cannot be spoken, what was thought hidden and lost?

In that quiet moment a solitary snowy heron flew down not far away and began to feed beside the marsh water.

At the single streak of flight, the ears of the race horse lifted, and the eyes of both horses filled with the soft lights of sunset, which in the next instant were reflected in the eyes of the men too as they all looked into the west toward the heron, and all eyes seemed infused with a sort of wildness.

Lorenzo gave the bird a triumphant look, such as a man may bestow upon his own vision, and thought, Nearness is near, lighted in a marshland, feeding at sunset. Praise God, His love has come visible.

Murrell, in suspicion pursuing all glances, blinking into a haze, saw only whiteness ensconced in darkness, as if it were a little luminous shell that drew in and held the eyesight. When he shaded his eyes, the brand "H.T." on this thumb thrust itself into his own vision, and he looked at the bird with the whole plan of the Mystic Rebellion darting from him as if in rays of the bright reflected light, and he stood looking proudly, leader as he was bound to become of the slaves, the brigands and outcasts of the entire Natchez country, with plans, dates, maps burning like a brand into his brain, and he saw himself proudly in a moment of prophecy going down rank after rank of successively bowing slaves to unroll and flaunt an awesome great picture of the Devil colored on a banner.

Audubon's eyes embraced the object in the distance and he could see it as carefully as if he held it in his hand. It was a snowy heron alone out of its flock. He watched it steadily, in his care noting the exact inevitable things. When it feeds it muddies the water with its foot. . . . It was as if each detail about the heron happened slowly in time, and only once. He felt again the old stab of wonder—what structure of life bridged the reptile's scale and the heron's feather? That knowledge too had been lost. He watched without moving. The bird was defenseless in the world except for the intensity of its life, and he wondered, how can heat of blood and speed of heart defend it? Then he thought, as always as if it were new and unbelievable, it has nothing in space or time to prevent its flight. And he waited, knowing that some birds will wait for a sense of their presence to travel to men before they will fly away from them.

Fixed in its pure white profile it stood in the precipitous moment, a plumicorn on its head, its breeding dress extended in rays, eating steadily the little water creatures. There was a little space between each man and the others, where they stood overwhelmed. No one could say the three had ever met, or that this moment of intersection had ever come in their lives, or its promise had been fulfilled. But before them the white heron rested in the grasses with the evening all around it, lighter and more serene than the evening, flight closed in its body, the circuit of its beauty closed, a bird seen and a bird still, its motion calm as if it were offered: Take my flight. . . .

What each of them had wanted was simply *all*. To save all souls, to destroy all men, to see and to record all life that filled this world—all, all—but now a single frail yearning seemed to go out of the three of them for a moment and to stretch toward this one snowy, shy bird in the marshes. It was as if three whirlwinds had drawn together at some center, to find there feeding in peace a snowy heron. Its own slow spiral of flight could take it away in its own time, but for a little it held them still, it laid quiet over them, and they stood for a moment unburdened. . . .

Murrell wore no mask, for his face was that, a face that was aware while he was somnolent, a face that watched for him, and listened for him, alert and nearly brutal, the guard of a planner. He was quick without that he might be slow within, he staved off time, he wandered and plotted, and yet his whole desire mounted in him toward the end (was this the end—the sight of a bird feeding at dusk?), toward the instant of confession. His incessant deeds were thick in his heart now, and flinging himself to the ground he thought wearily, when all these trees are cut down, and the Trace lost, then my Conspiracy that is yet to spread itself will be disclosed, and all the stone-loaded bodies of murdered men will be pulled up, and all everywhere will know poor Murrell. His look pressed upon Lorenzo, who stared upward, and Audubon, who was taking out his gun, and his eyes squinted up to them in pleading, as if to say, "How soon may I speak, and how soon will you pity me?" Then he looked back to the bird, and he thought if it would look at him a dread penetration would fill and gratify his heart.

Audubon in each act of life was aware of the mysterious origin he half-concealed and half-sought for. People along the way asked him in their kindness or their rudeness if it were true, that he was born a prince, and was the Lost Dauphin, and some said it was his secret, and some said that that was what he wished to find out before he died. But if it was his identity that he wished to discover, or if it was what a man had to seize beyond that, the way for him was by endless examination, by the care for every bird that flew in his path and every serpent that shone underfoot. Not one was enough; he looked deeper and deeper, on and on, as if for a particular beast or some legendary bird. Some men's eyes persisted in looking outward when they opened to look inward, and to their delight, there outflung was the astonishing world under the sky. When a man at last brought himself to face some mirror-surface he still saw the world looking back at him, and if he continued to look, to look closer and closer, what then? The gaze that looks outward must be trained without rest, to be indomitable. It must see as slowly as Murrell's ant in the grass, as exhaustively as Lorenzo's angel of God, and then, Audubon dreamed, with his mind going to his pointed brush, it must see like this, and he tightened his hand on the trigger of the gun and pulled it, and his eyes went closed. In memory the heron was all its solitude, its total beauty. All its whiteness could be seen from all sides at once, its pure feathers were as if counted and known and their array one upon the other would never be lost. But it was not from that memory that he could paint.

His opening eyes met Lorenzo's, close and flashing, and it was on seeing horror deep in them, like fires in abysses, that he recognized it for the first time. He had never seen horror in its purity and clarity until now, in bright blue eyes. He went and picked up the bird. He had thought it to be a female, just as one sees the moon as female; and so it was. He put it in his bag, and started away. But Lorenzo had already gone on, leaning a-tilt on the horse which went slowly.

Murrell was left behind, but he was proud of the dispersal, as if he had done it, as if he had always known that three men in simply being together and doing a thing can, by their obstinacy, take the pride out of one another. Each must go away alone, each send the others away alone. He himself had purposely kept to the wildest country in the world, and would have sought it out, the loneliest road. He looked about with satisfaction, and hid. Travelers were forever innocent, he believed: that was his faith. He lay in wait; his faith was in innocence and his knowledge was of ruin; and had these things been shaken? Now, what could possibly be outside his grasp? Churning all about him like a cloud about the sun was the great folding descent of his thought. Plans of deeds made his thoughts, and they rolled and mingled about his ears as if he heard a dark voice that rose up to overcome the wilderness voice, or was one with it. The night would soon come; and he had gone through the day.

Audubon, splattered and wet, turned back into the wilderness with the heron warm under his hand, his head still light in a kind of trance. It was undeniable, on some Sunday mornings, when he turned over and over his drawings they seemed beautiful to him, through what was dramatic in the conflict of life, or what was exact. What he would draw, and what he had seen, became for a moment one to him then. Yet soon enough, and it seemed to come in that same moment, like Lorenzo's horror and the gun's firing, he knew that even the sight of the heron which surely he alone had appreciated, had not been all his belonging, and that never could any vision, even any simple sight, belong to him or to any man. He knew that the best he could make would be, after it was apart from his hand, a dead thing and not a live thing, never the essence, only a sum of parts; and that it would always meet with a stranger's sight, and never be one with the beauty in any other man's head in the world. As he had seen the bird most purely at its moment of death, in some fatal way, in his care for looking outward, he saw his long labor most revealingly at the point where it met its limit. Still carefully, for he was trained to see well in the dark, he walked on into the deeper woods, noting all sights, all sounds, and was gentler than they as he went.

In the woods that echoed yet in his ears, Lorenzo riding slowly looked back. The hair rose on his head and his hands began to shake with cold, and suddenly it seemed to him that God Himself, just now, thought of the Idea of Separateness. For surely He had never thought of it before, when the little white heron was flying down to feed. He could understand God's giving Separateness first and then giving Love to follow and heal its wonder; but God had reversed this, and given Love first and then Separateness, as though it did not matter to Him which came first. Perhaps it was that God never counted the moments of Time; Lorenzo did that, among his tasks of love. Time did not occur to God. Therefore—did He even know of it? How to explain Time and Separateness back to God, Who had never thought of them, Who could let the whole world come to grief in a scattering moment?

Lorenzo brought his cold hands together in a clasp and stared through the distance at the place where the bird had been as if he saw it still; as if nothing could really take away what had happened to him, the beautiful little vision of the feeding bird. Its beauty had been greater than he could account for. The sweat of rapture poured down from his forehead, and then he shouted into the marshes.

"Tempter!"

He whirled forward in the saddle and began to hurry the horse to its high speed. His camp ground was far away still, though even now they must be lighting the torches and gathering in the multitudes, so that at the appointed time he would duly appear in their midst, to deliver his address on the subject of "In that day when all hearts shall be disclosed."

Then the sun dropped below the trees, and the new moon, slender and white, hung shyly in the west.

Worlds Apart

I can't help but believe the killdeer,
so deftly has it led me,
dragging its own wings away from a poorly
hidden nest before clenching back into flight,
and I can't help but believe in a love
that would make itself so vulnerable for its young.

It is hard to understand, but
only by leaving do we know what we love.

Before I left, you told the story
of the fledgling cuckoo who hatches on a sparrow's
nest, who spills out the native fledglings,
and is adopted by the vulnerable parents.
One night, in a city far from home,
I watched in amazement as two young men
who seemed more fierce than the cuckoo,
stooped to kiss some bag lady on the forehead
and pass her a dollar, a lady who had nested on a corner
with her dozen sacks and a cart.

Never have I felt so guilty
for what little love I could show.
That night, alone on a bus, I thought
you were the starlight nesting in the trees
holding every moment of your life.

In the pine woods along the coast north of here
starlight never touches the ground.

Somewhere in there the cuckoo will begin to sing.
I don't think there was ever a time we weren't
approaching each other through those woods.
I don't think there is a moment we have
that is not taking place somewhere else,
or a love that doesn't lead us, sometimes
deftly, further from ourselves.

JAN EPTON SEALE

Big Bird Comes to the
Rio Grande Valley in 1976

The color was white, silver, gray, brown, dark brown, black.
The height was four, five, six feet; the wingspan, twenty.
Otherwise, the bird was hairy, feathered, bald. In the pictures
drawn at school, there was the face of a bat, pig, monkey, man—
with pointed ears, eagle's beak, stork's bill, silvery red eyes.
"Pteranodon" and "pterasaurus" were librarians' nightmare.

The creature left footprints, hovered over a lagoon, hissed,
ransacked a tavern, terrified policemen, pursued children,
disappeared into a canal, perched on the Chevrolet company,
attacked two men (making one of them hot where it touched),
gave an unearthly noise, snapped its beak, ran into the brush.

There were T-shirts in four sizes and a song on a record—
the flip side an interview, old Japanese monster movies,
offered rewards and counter-rewards, vigilante groups formed,
words from the law on trigger-happiness, on endangered species,
talks about self-defense, bounty hunting, international animals.

At the end, the bird let itself be filmed in an orchard
with fifty people surrounding. Then the legend flew away.
The 6 p.m. news showed a mild blue heron gazing about.
The next day, its published demise: "Legend of Bird is Dead."
Soon the TV station had tossed the film, for more space—
(reports of drug hauls, bodies found in the Rio,
deaths of the prominent, arrests of molesters, murderers).

Then a haze clouded the eyes so the people no longer saw
the jabiru, crane, wood stork, brown pelican, condor,

and especially the great blue heron; even though these birds,
one or all, were here, in our midst: even though they came
to restore rumor, debate, declamation, the art of gossip,
the plucking of guitars, chills, *cuentos de las lechuzas*,
upstanding hair on the nape, children curved with respect
into the laps of the *viejitos* on front porches at evening.

LOUISE ERDRICH

Owls

The barred owls scream in the black pines,
searching for mates. Each night
the noise wakes me, a death
rattle, everything in sex that wounds.
There is nothing in the sound but raw need
of one feathered body for another.
Yet, even when they find one another,
there is no peace.

In Ojibwa, the owl is Kokoko, and not
even the smallest child loves the gentle sound
of the word. Because the hairball
of bones and vole teeth can be hidden
under snow, to kill the man who walks over it.
Because the owl looks behind itself to see you coming,
the vane of the feather does not disturb
air, and the barb is ominously soft.

Have you ever seen, at dusk,
an owl take flight from the throat of a dead tree?
Mist, troubled spirit.
You will notice only after
its great silver body has turned to bark.
The flight was soundless.

That is how we make love,
when there are people in the halls around us,
clashing dishes, filling their mouths
with air, with debris, pulling

switches and filters as the whole machinery
of life goes on, eliminating and eliminating
until there are just the two bodies
fiercely attached, the feathers
floating down and cleaving to their shapes.

ROBERT PENN WARREN

Heart of Autumn

Wind finds the northwest gap, fall comes.
Today, under gray cloud-scud and over gray
Wind-flicker of forest, in perfect formation, wild geese
Head for a land of warm water, the *boom*, the lead pellet.

Some crumple in air, fall. Some stagger, recover control,
Then take the last glide for a far glint of water. None
Knows what has happened. Now, today, watching
How tirelessly *V* upon *V* arrows the season's logic,

Do I know my own story? At least, they know
When the hour comes for the great wing-beat. Sky-strider,
Star-strider—they rise, and the imperial utterance,
Which cries out for distance, quivers in the wheeling sky.

That much they know, and in their nature know
The path of pathlessness, with all the joy
Of destiny fulfilling its own name.
I have known time and distance, but not why I am here.

Path of logic, path of folly, all
The same—and I stand, my face lifted now skyward,
Hearing the high beat, my arms outstretched in the tingling
Process of transformation, and soon tough legs,

With folded feet, trail in the sounding vacuum of passage,
And my heart is impacted with a fierce impulse
To unwordable utterance—
Toward sunset, at a great height.

The Cranes

"Oh!" she said, "what are those, the huge white ones?" Along the marshy shore two tall and stately birds, staring motionless toward the Gulf, towered above the bobbing egrets and scurrying plovers.

"Well, I can't believe it," he said. "I've been coming here for years and never saw one."

"But what are they? Don't make me guess or anything; it makes me feel dumb." They leaned forward in the car, and the shower curtain spread over the front seat crackled and hissed.

"They've got to be whooping cranes, nothing else so big." One of the birds turned gracefully, as if to acknowledge the old Dodge parked alone in the tall grasses. "See the black legs and black wingtips? Big! Why don't I have my binoculars?" He looked at his wife and smiled.

"Well," he continued after a while, "I've seen enough birds. But whooping cranes, they're rare. Not many left."

"They're lovely. They make the little birds look like clowns."

"I could use a few clowns," he said. "A few laughs never hurt anybody."

"Are you all right?" She put a hand on his thin arm. "I feel I'm responsible. Maybe this is the wrong thing."

"God, no!" His voice changed. "No way. I can't smoke, can't drink martinis, no coffee, no candy. I not only can't leap buildings in a single bound, I can hardly get up the goddamn stairs."

She was smiling. "Do you remember the time you drank nine martinis and asked that young priest to step outside and see whose side God was on?"

"What a jerk I was! How have you put up with me all this time?"

"Oh no! I was proud of you. You were so funny, and that priest was a snot."

"Now you tell me." The cranes were moving slowly over a small hillock, wings opening and closing like bellows. "It's all right. It's enough," he said again. "How old am I anyway, 130?"

"Really," she said, "it's me. Ever since the accident it's been one thing after another. I'm just a lot of trouble to everybody."

"Let's talk about something else," he said. "Do you want to listen to the radio? How about turning on that preacher station so we can throw up?"

"No," she said, "I just want to watch the birds. And listen to you."

"You must be pretty tired of that."

She turned her head from the window and looked into his eyes. "I never got tired of listening to you. Never."

"Well, that's good," he said. "It's just that when my mouth opens, your eyes tend to close."

"They do not!" she said, and began to laugh, but the laugh turned into a cough and he had to pat her on the back until she stopped. They leaned back in silence and looked toward the Gulf stretching out beyond the horizon. In the distance, the water looked like metal, still and hard.

"I wish they'd court," he said. "I wish we could see them court, the cranes. They put on a show. He bows like Nijinsky and jumps straight up in the air."

"What does she do?"

"She lies down and he lands on top of her."

"No," she said, "I'm serious."

"Well, I forget. I've never seen it. But I do remember that they mate for life and live a long time. They're probably older than we are. Their feathers are falling out and their kids never write."

She was quiet again. He turned in his seat, picked up an object wrapped in a plaid towel, and placed it between them in the front. "Here's looking at *you,* kid," he said.

"Do they really mate for life? I'm glad—they're so beautiful."

"Yep. Audubon said that's why they're almost extinct: a failure of imagination."

"I don't believe that," she said. "I think there'll always be whooping cranes."

"Why not?" he said.

"I wish the children were more settled. I keep thinking it's my fault."

"You think everything's your fault. Nicaragua. Ozone depletion. Nothing is your fault. They'll be fine, and anyway, they're not children anymore. Kids are different today, that's all. You were terrific." He paused. "You were terrific in ways I couldn't tell the kids about."

"I should hope not." She laughed and began coughing again, but held his hand when he reached over. When the cough subsided they sat quietly, looking down at their hands as if they were objects in a museum. "I used to have pretty hands," she said.

"I remember."

"Do you? Really?"

"I remember everything," he said.

"You always forgot everything."

"Well, now I remember."

"Did you bring something for your ears?"

"No, I can hardly hear anything, anyway." But he turned his head at a sudden squabble among the smaller birds. The cranes were stepping delicately away from the commotion.

"I'm tired," she said.

"Yes." He leaned over and kissed her, barely touching her lips. "Tell me," he said, "did I really drink nine martinis?"

But she had already closed her eyes and only smiled. Outside, the wind ruffled the bleached-out grasses, and the birds in the white glare seemed almost transparent. The hull of the car gleamed beetle-like—dull and somehow sinister in its metallic isolation.

Suddenly, the two cranes plunged upward, their great wings beating the air and their long slender necks pointed like arrows toward the sun.

A Long Sunday

Mother said *Get the paper, get the bread, you lazy bum. It's not cause it's Sunday you should stay in bed all day.* I'm outside, crossing the short garden, passing under the alamandas and the bougainvillea. The sun is low and already bright, the sky is blue gray. My eyes hurt a little. I rub them. I'm wearing a brown cotton shirt; it's too tight, so it's for when I'm not in school. I'm walking on the dusty path and I see Josef in the field across, and he waves at me with his machete and I wave back. He's bringing water to the oxen.

My foot hurts. I stop and bend down to remove a pebble that got in my plastic sandal. I walk down the path to the road, and I hear the coins Mom gave me jingling in my pocket. Old Casimir sits in front of his blue cabin; he's smoking a pipe. "Nice day, Tibitin," he says. I wave and say, "Did you see Peter and Charley?" He sucks on his pipe once or twice, his eyes almost closed, and I'm already past his cabin when he looks back at me and says, "They up to no good, you just go and do whatever your momma tells you."

I hear a car so I step to the side and let it pass. It shoots by, the engine whining and black smoke coming out, dust flying everywhere. I get back on the road and walk faster. I better hurry, or Mom will get mad. Then I think that Peter, Charley, and the others might be by the mango tree. I decide to cut through Mr. Wilson's sugarcane field. I start to run; I don't want to get in trouble for being late with the bread and paper and all.

"Tibitin! Tibitin!" I hear voices from the road. I turn my head and see Peter and Charley before I trip and crash on my face. I was running too fast, I think. My knee hurts, and I lie there without moving, just thinking and hearing "Tibitin! Tibitin!" I know Charley and Peter are approaching fast, and I want to get up before they see me like this and laugh. I put my weight on my hands and push myself up.

My right hand hurts too. I'm on my feet before they arrive, brushing the dust and pebbles off my knees and hands. "Tibitin, you okay?" says Charley, out of breath.

"Yeah, Tibitin, you fell flat on your face," adds Peter, out of breath too.

"I'm okay. Real fine." I slide my hands in my pockets. "Shit! Shit!"

"What is it?" says Charley. Both of them have their slingshots hanging out of their back pockets.

"I gotta find the money. I lost what my mother gave me when I fell." I search the area where I fell. Charley and Peter look too, but they don't really care. I get on my knees and search through the dry grass. "My mother'll give me a beating," I say.

"Sure as hell she'll give you a beating," says Charley. Peter laughs. They both laugh. I get up and glare at them. "We gotta run, we gonna get hummingbirds today."

"Yeah," says Peter, and he takes out his slingshot, bends to pick up a rock, puts it in the pouch, extends his right arm, and pulls back the band with his left hand. He aims at a frigate flying very high, and releases. The rock whizzes into the sky and disappears, but nothing happens. We're all three gazing, speechless, at the sky. Peter puts his slingshot in his pocket and turns to go.

"You gonna join us?" asks Charley.

"Later maybe. Gotta find this coin, and I don't got no sling to shoot no poor bird."

Charley laughs again, showing his white teeth. One of the front ones is missing. He's sweating.

"If you want to meet up, boy, we'll be at the mango tree after twelve." He looks at Peter who has stopped and is facing us, waiting.

"Well, gotta go, boy." And he goes, they go, leaving me alone to find the money in this field. My damn knee is aching.

I go further into the field, pushing the canes to the side, looking for the shiny coins. I know it's too far, yet I look there, just in case. I see something sparkling at the bottom of a cane, and hope it's the big coin, the five-franc one.

I bend down and pick it up. Five francs. Two more coins to find. I look and look, and it's getting late, and I think *After twelve at the mango tree. Why bother the hummingbirds? Momma'll be mad.*

Then I hear something rustling, and I see some weeds moving; I think a *serpent* and step forward cautiously, standing on tiptoe to see a little farther. I see feathers. It's a bird, a little hawk with a hook beak, and one wing dragging clumsily, like an oar, wounded. I kneel down and look at him closely; it seems his wing is broken. I take my shirt off, and holding it in front of me, I move even closer. The hawk jumps away a couple of times, but I dive on him and catch him in my shirt. The bird struggles and pecks through the shirt, but he's too weak to put up much of a fight. Holding him tightly in my shirt, against my breast, I head back to the road. Five francs will buy a newspaper, but it won't be enough for the bread. I hurry because I know Momma will already be mad, and I don't want to meet any of my friends.

At the store I step up to the counter and drop the coin on it. "I'll be needing the Sunday paper," I say loudly. I hear a rattling in the back, of cans and tins moved around, then steps. It's Wanda, big, fat Wanda. Her hair is always tied into the traditional *madras* with three bows, which means she has a man, but she still has room in her heart for another one.

"Tibitin, the paper?" she says, leaning forward over the counter, her huge pumpkin breasts stretching her madras blouse. "What you got in that shirt of yours, boy?"

"A hawk I found in Mr. Wilson's field."

"You wanna tell me about it, you and Peter and Charley and all, you always up to no good bothering them birds? You get it to your Momma and she'll sure as hell make good soup with it." Her thick lips part and her eyes sink deeper in her puffy face.

"Just give me the paper, I know my business with my bird." I step back; she is rather close and smells acrid.

"You don't wanna no bread this morning?" she asks. Her blouse is stained under her armpits.

"I fell and lost two coins, I don't got enough left." I look away because she's going to give me admonitions.

"Tibitin, Tibitin . . . ," she sighs. She takes a paper and a baguette from the shelves. "Here's your bread and paper. You bring it to your Momma and you bring me the other coin later or tomorrow." She looks at me strange. "Come tonight, boy, and it'll be okay; just come and see Aunt Wanda."

The feel of her hand, clasped around my arm, makes me shudder. She releases her grip and I grab the bread and hurry away. After a hundred meters I look back because I feel strange in my back, and I see Wanda at the counter, watching me and smiling. The bird flounders again in my shirt and almost wriggles out of my arm, so I hold him tighter. I'm almost running now—I'm late and all—and I think *Who can help me with the bird? I hope I don't meet no friends. Wanda, fat Wanda, what she want? I feel strange. My knee hurts. . . .*

"Tibitin!" calls Old Casimir. "What you got in that shirt? You up to no good?" He's sitting in the same place, except he moved his chair to stay out of the sun. That's all he does, Old Casimir, move his chair all day to stay out of the sun. Momma says that, everybody says that.

"Gotta run, Momma'll get mad." I don't look at him no more.

"You sure gonna get a beating. . . ." His voice is drowned out by the roar of a truck. I'm running now but not too fast because I don't want to drop anything I'm carrying. Then I reach the house and I hear Momma screaming something, and I know I'm in trouble.

"Tibitin! Here you are! What you got in that shirt? What you did to your knee? Got in trouble again? Get in here now and give me that bread!" She is standing at the door, stout, a blue apron on, her eyes terrible. I hand her the paper and the bread and hurry in. "Hold it!" She stops me with her arm. "What's in there?" She's pointing at my shirt, her eyes expectant and hard.

"It's a wounded hawk I found at Mr. Wilson's field," I say, looking down.

"You had no business in that field, no business with no bird! You go change your shirt and then set it free before I cook it."

She isn't that angry.

"Momma, I want to save it and keep it. Please."

"What have I done to the Lord to get a son like this!" she says. And I see she is very tired, I *understand* something. "How you gonna take care of a bird? How you gonna fix it? It's gonna die." She sighs and walks away. And I think *She doesn't look terrible now, she doesn't look big.*

I go to our bedroom and get a straw basket and put the bird and my shirt in it. I put on a fresh shirt of my brother's, a little too big. Then I get a glass of water in the kitchen and drink all of it, fill it again. In the bedroom I take the hawk in my arms and try to give it water. He drinks a little, then the water leaks out of his beak and pearls on his feathers. I look at his wing more carefully, pull on it a little, and the hawk turns and tries to peck at my hand. The wing looks broken. I put him back in the basket.

On the table is the baguette, the Sunday France-Antilles paper, and the plate with mangoes. I break off two pieces of bread, eat one and put the other in my pocket. Then I open the paper to the last page, to the ads and official services; just as we learnt in school. There is a section called *On Call & Emergencies*, and I look under the letter V. *Veterinarian on Call this Sunday, November 8th, from 8:00 am to 6:00 pm, Dr. Bourgeois, Jean; tel. 84.06.39.*

When I call the number, the phone rings three times and a lady answers. I say "Ma'am, I've found a bird, a hawk with a broken wing, where can I bring him?"

She's silent a couple of seconds, then: "*A hawk?* With a broken wing? That's what you want to bring in?"

"Yes, Ma'am. I just find him half-hour ago."

"Okay, okay. It's nine o'clock now. The doctor will be at the clinic at eleven. Sundays we try to group the calls. So you must be there, because he'll leave after he's finished with the emergencies."

I hear dogs barking on the line.

"Please hold a minute," she says. I wait, and I hear voices and barks, and she's back. "Sorry. Is everything clear?"

"Yes, Ma'am; but where you at?" I say.

"Where are you coming from?" she says.

"Gourbert."

"Okay, you just take National 5 to Pointe-à-Pitre, then Route 3 past Gosier, past St. Félix; then you'll pass the night club *Noù Ka Zouké* on the right—you know the club?"

"I find it."

"Across from it, next to the restaurant *Trattori*, you'll see a big blue cross. It's there. You follow?"

"I find it."

"It's no more than an hour. We'll see you at eleven."

"Thank you, Ma'am," I say. As I'm hanging up, Momma walks in.

"What you doing on the phone?" she says, loud. She's standing in front of me, holding a plate with a ham sandwich in her right hand.

"I called the doctor for my bird."

"You got no business calling no doctor on Sunday for no bird! Did I teach you no manners? Did I not?" She's almost yelling, and she shoves the plate at me. I take the sandwich from it.

"You just go and get rid of that bird before it dies in the house. Then you go and play! I don't want to see you no more today, or I'll give you the beating you need. Go now!" She looks at me intently, and I know she's looking at me tired, and I *understand*.

I go to my room and sit on the bed. I look at the hawk in the basket while I chew the sandwich. I tear a piece of fat off the ham and drop it into the basket. The bird doesn't move. When I finish eating, I set the basket on the bed, next to me. Tentatively I put my hand in; the hawk still doesn't budge. I put the ham near his beak. Still no movement. I sigh.

With the basket under my arm I retrace my route of earlier that morning: past Old Casimir, who is quiet and asleep, to Mr. Wilson's field, where I fell. I set the basket under a tree and search for the lost coins; I must find at least one. On my knees, I separate each blade of grass. I gaze up at the sun, bright, hot, telling me it's time to go. Just as I'm about to give up, I find both coins. I pocket them, take the basket under my arm, and walk to the road.

I'm sweating, and still I'm far from National 5. I speed up, and I hear a car. I stop and extend my arm, thumb up. A beige pickup drives by, blowing dust in my face.

A minute later I hear a moped. It's John. He stops and asks, the engine running and revving, "Tibitin! Need a ride?" I say nothing, I just get on behind him, holding the basket tightly with my left arm and his waist with my right. He revs the motor, and we go noisily forward. The wind blows in my hair and in my shirt, cooling me. As he drives John turns his head quickly and says, "Where you wanna be dropped?"

"National 5," I say. "Gotta go to Pointe-à-Pitre."

He turns his head to me again. "What you got in that basket?"

"Nothing."

"Got no girlfriend yet?"

I don't say nothing.

"You a man now, you gotta do *it*," he laughs. I think *What she want, Wanda?*

Then we're there and I get off the moped. He smiles at me, but I can't see his eyes because of his sunglasses; and he rides away, fast and loud, laughing.

On the shoulder of National 5, I wait, putting my thumb out whenever cars shoot by. I look at the sun in the deep blue sky, and my head hurts a little; I wonder what time it is. The hawk doesn't move much. I put my hand in the basket to see if he will peck, but nothing happens. I give him a name: *Soukounyan.*

I hear a car thumping music, and I extend my arm. It shoots by with a strong beat and stops fifty meters farther on. I run over to it; it is an old car, a red Citroën. The driver, a man with a mustache and glasses, yells over the music through the open window, "Where you going, man?"

I can't hear him good, so I stick my head in the window and yell, "Around St. Félix, but I be glad if you drop me at Pointe-à-Pitre."

"You come on in, man," he shouts. "I get you to Pointe-à-Pitre."

I get in, and as we drive I sit straight and hold my basket on my lap, looking ahead of me. The music is beating on my head and the whole car is vibrating with every beat. The trees shoot by quickly, *much quicker than when I walk*, I think. The wind is blowing everywhere in the car, cooling things. I worry for Soukounyan, and close my window halfway.

Glued to the dashboard of the Citroën are four pictures of naked women with big breasts. A compact disc hangs from the rearview mirror by a string, spinning in the wind and casting stars all over the car. I think *Why a compact disc there, ain't that expensive to waste?* I look at the driver's hands, with gold rings, holding on to the fur-covered steering wheel. His nails are long, especially the pinkie ones.

"My name Rand, what's yours?" he yells, turning to me, then turning back.

"Tibitin," I shout.

"So you a country boy? How old?" he yells.

"Fourteen," I say. My head hurts worse. We pass a blue sign that says *Pointe-à-Pitre 50 km.*

"What you say?" he yells. He lowers the music a little.

"Fourteen," I shout.

"You look young," he yells. I don't say nothing. We drive without speaking for a long time, and I wonder what time it is.

"What you gonna do this far?" he yells.

"Gonna see the doctor for my hawk," I yell. I look down into the basket at the bird. He doesn't budge. I feel the vibrations of the music in my whole body, and my head hurts and I'm tired now.

"What your hawk got?" he yells, glancing into the basket quickly.

"Broken wing," I yell. We drive by a sign *Pointe-à-Pitre 20 km.*

"He gonna die. No doctor can do nothing, man."

"That's for the doctor to say," I tell the man. "You don't know nothing for sure."

He laughs loud and yells, "I sure don't know nothing, man, I sure don't, I sure don't, man!"

I don't want to ask him what time it is, so I wait until he turns the wheel and the face of his heavy golden watch is visible: 10:25. My head is pounding with the music and my eyes burn. Then I see we're arriving.

The Citroën owner drops me off at the square Place de la Victoire. I get out and don't say nothing to him, and he looks at me a second, waiting for something, then drives off, taking his music with him.

The sun is burning hot and my shirt is soaked. I cross the square to a fountain, put my basket down, and drink some water, then cup my hands and fill them to splash my face. I fill my mouth with water, bend down to the basket, and spray the hawk. He jumps to the side, then doesn't move. I fill my mouth again, take hold of the bird, and let water drip on his beak. He opens his beak and drinks a little. I take a piece of bread from my pocket, soak it, and try to feed Soukounyan. He eats a little, but then spits out the rest. In the center of the square I see three boys of about seventeen. As I approach them with my basket, they watch me coming, and I feel strange.

"Where's the bus at?" I say.

"The terminal?" asks the taller one. The other two don't say nothing, they just look at my basket.

"Yeah," I say. The tall boy stares at me and I avert my eyes. When I look at him again, I focus on the pocket of his shirt.

"It's down there." He points at a brown two-story factory. "Right behind that building." He nods at the basket. "What you got in there?"

"A hawk," I say. And I *know, understand* something. The two other boys stare at the tall one, who is obviously the leader.

"It's hurt," I add.

The tall boy steps forward and peeks into the basket; the two others look at each other and say something low.

I tense up, hold my basket tighter, and turn away.

"That ain't *your* bird!" I hear in my back as I head toward the terminal. I keep on walking but I want to run.

"It's the bird I just got stolen!"

I keep on walking, my heart pounding and my throat tight.

"Hey, I'm talking to you, thief!" A hand slaps my shoulder and spins me around. I'm face to face with the tall boy. He's smirking, sneering. He grabs my basket and pulls. I hold tight.

"Little shit! Let go!" he spits out. He's real close. I thrust my head forward with all my strength and I feel his nose crack against my skull. Then I turn and run as fast as I ever have, not looking back. My eyes are burning and my ears are whistling.

I'm breathless when I reach the brown building. In the terminal behind it are only five buses, and I hide behind the first one, waiting for the boys to come, but no one comes. My heart is beating fast, and I'm soaking wet. There's a lump on my head, and I think *I must've broken his damn nose.* When I glance into the basket, Soukounyan looks okay. I wait a little more, hidden there, before emerging from behind the bus to look for an attendant. There's a man sitting in a chair holding an umbrella over his head. I approach him and ask, "Which's the bus to St. Félix?"

"Gone already, the next one's at noon."

"What time is it?" I say.

He nods toward the top of the distant church. I see a clock marking five minutes past eleven.

"Who do I pay?"

He lifts his right arm and points at a blue bus parked in the shade of a few palm trees.

The door is open, and the driver is reading the paper. "It's you I gotta pay to go to St. Félix?" I ask.

He lowers his paper and looks down at me. "Sure is," he says.

"Is this the bus?"

"Sure is."

"Leaving at noon?" I say.

"Yes."

"Can I wait in the bus?"

"Sure can," he says.

I step up and hand him my only two coins. He looks at them. "That ain't enough. You need one more franc," he says.

"That's all I got."

He looks at me a long time. "You kids," he says. "Go and sit in the back." He raises his newspaper and reads again.

I sit in the back, by an open window, with the basket at my feet. I check on Soukounyan. Then I look out the window, at the clock on the church, at the sky, deep blue with only one little bright white cloud in it. My headache is a little better, but I'm hungry. I take the remaining bread out of my pocket and eat it. I think about the day. *Wanda, the boys, all the boys. Momma is tired. Soukounyan will fly. And I feel tired.*

I lean against the window and close my eyes.

A tap on my shoulder awakens me. The bus is now half full. An old woman is staring at me through thick glasses, her eyes magnified and scary. "Young man," she says, "you all right?"

My gaze darts to the basket. Soukounyan is still there, not moving. The clock outside says five to twelve. "You was talking in your sleep," the woman informs me.

"I'm good, Ma'am," I say, looking at her mouth; she's got a mustache. My headache is back and I'm very hungry. I rub my eyes and feel my head. The bump is bigger now.

"Just making sure," says the woman, then she looks away. I look out the window. Outside, a bunch of people are roaming from bus to bus, carrying bags. Many of the people are well dressed because it's Sunday. I look at their shadows, short, trampled by their feet. A heavy woman carrying a large basket of *bouki* on her head walks along the bus saying "Five francs the *bouki*, five francs . . ." as she passes the open windows. The smell of the fried chicken dipped in manioc makes my stomach growl. She gets to my window and shouts, "Boy, wanna some good *bouki*?"

"Yes," I say, "but I don't got no money."

She's about to go on, when the old woman next to me shouts, "I want one!" She leans over me, smelling of camphor and perspiration, and thrusts a large silver coin at the vendor woman, who gives her a newspaper-wrapped *bouki* in return. The engine of the bus starts, and the driver revs it a couple of times before we lurch forward. I watch the old woman unwrap the *bouki* and take a bite. The smell fills my nostrils and teases my stomach. She chews carefully and makes a lot of noise. I watch her hairy upper lip move up and down, revealing a couple of yellow teeth. She sees me watching, so I turn to the window. Fresh air whips my face, and I breathe it in, trying not to smell the *bouki*.

I watch the people get in and out of the bus at each stop. Then I close my eyes for a while, my head out the window, and almost fall asleep.

The shifting of gears and the squeal of brakes rouses me. We're passing Gosier. I shout to the driver to let me out at the St. Félix stop. I grab the basket, clamber over the old woman, and make my way down the aisle, holding onto the handles. We pull over by a small blue sign with a white bus painted on it. The door opens and I step down to the dusty pavement. The bus growls away, trailing black, smelly smoke.

Approaching me is a man carrying a bucket of water. When he gets close I ask, "Where's *Noù Ka Zouké?*"

"You got out the wrong stop," he says, "you should've stayed till the next." He's still walking.

"How far is it?" I say.

"About three or four kilometers that way," he says, pointing toward where the bus disappeared. So I set forth walking there. When cars drive by, I extend my arm and hitch, but no one stops. They're all going too fast. I cross the road to walk in the shade, but it's very hot even there. Nobody is out. I think *They're all napping or keeping in the cool shade.* My arm is tired from holding the basket. My head feels squeezed and dizzy, and I try not to think about food, but I know I must drink.

Almost there, there'll be water and shade and Soukounyan'll be fine.

My shirt is wet and my right foot hurts. I stop and check it. A splinter has pierced the sandal, so I take it out and I feel fine now. I pick up the basket and resume walking.

In the distance is a large, bright sign that reads *Noù Ka Zouké* and another for the restaurant *Trattori*. I hurry on, to the clinic, but the front gate is closed. On the side, near a silver plate that says *Dr. Bourgeois, Jean* is a doorbell. I press it and nothing happens. I ring again and again. Nothing.

In the far distance is a Shell station. They'll have a phone, I think, and then, *What time is it?* The sun is blinding and hot, and my head feels worse.

Inside the station a young woman in a red dress sits behind the counter, reading a book with a pink cover. She looks up at me and says impatiently, "What you want, boy?"

"Can I use the phone? I gotta call the veterinarian." I think *I must go to the bathroom.*

"There's a pay phone out there." She points to a phone booth outside before starting to read again.

"I don't got nothing to put in there," I say, "and I gotta call the doctor." She looks up at me again and raises her brows.

"What's your business seeing a doctor if you don't got no money?"

"I gotta call," I say. My eyes burn, and she looks at me and purses her lips. She pulls a phone from under the counter and sets it in front of me. I dial the number and the same woman answers.

"I'm at the Shell by the clinic," I say. "Where's the doctor?"

"Are you the person that was supposed to come at eleven with a wounded bird?" she asks.

"Yeah," I say.

"Do you know what time it is?" she says patiently. "It's one-thirty. The doctor waited for you, but he's gone now."

"But I gotta see him."

She sighs into the receiver. "He's taking care of a cow somewhere in the country, he'll get back to the clinic around three o'clock."

"I wait," I say.

She sighs again. "You be there this time," she says. I hang up and look at the young woman reading the book. She's pretty. Her dress is a little transparent.

"You got bathrooms here?"

"Out in the back," she says without looking up.

When I finish, I rinse my face in the little sink and drink. I fill my mouth with water and try to make Soukounyan drink too. He swallows very little. I return to the clinic and wait under the shade of a coconut tree, leaning against the trunk, the basket between my legs. Cars zoom by, making my headache worse. I take Soukounyan in my hands and examine him. He doesn't peck; he just looks at me with his black eyes, like shiny beads. I hug him to my chest, and he doesn't struggle, though he's a little startled when my stomach growls. I hold him and look at the sky, and my eyes burn so I close them. I fear I'm going to fall asleep, so I put the hawk back in the basket. I close my eyes again.

Will the doctor have aspirin? Soukounyan. Momma's gonna kill me.

A car wakes me up. It's pulling in front of the gate. I glance down at the basket, and Soukounyan is still there.

I grab the basket and approach the car. A man and a white woman get out, slamming the doors. The woman looks at me, surprised, and says, "*You're* the person that called for the bird?"

"Yeah," I say. "I got it in here." I tilt the basket a little, but she doesn't look.

"How did you get here?" she says. She glances at the man, the doctor. He's wearing rubber boots and carrying a medicine bag. He doesn't say nothing.

"I got rides, I took the bus," I say.

The doctor unlocks the front gate and opens it.

"You waited here since one-thirty?" says the woman, disbelieving.

"Yeah," I say. The doctor leaves the gate open and enters the building by a back door.

"Go and wait in the room over there," says the woman, pointing to the front door. Then she follows the doctor.

In the waiting room are three posters of strange animals, five empty chairs, a couple of magazines on a coffee table, but no water fountain. There's a closed door that must lead to the clinic itself. Behind it, I hear muffled voices.

Soon the door opens, and the white woman smiles and beckons me in. There's a silver table, shelves full of medications against the walls, and the doctor at his desk in the back.

"Put the basket on the steel table," says the woman.

I do what she says. The doctor comes over, peers into the basket, and slides his hand in and catches Soukounyan.

"So, young man," he says, "when did you find him?" The hawk doesn't peck at him, and he moves the broken wing a little.

"This morning," I say, watching him move the wing.

"Did he drink or eat anything?" he asks. The woman hands him a piece of string.

"A little water, a little bread," I say, as I watch him tie the bird's beak.

"You must feed him meat." He turns to the woman and says, "I need some Elastoplast, and prepare me a shot of Clamoxil." She nods.

He asks me to hold Soukounyan, and then he starts to move the wing more and more. The hawk wriggles, tries to peck at him. He pulls the wing real hard and I hear something snap. Soukounyan trembles violently.

"I got it back together," says the doctor, "but it probably won't stay that way." The woman is back and she hands him a long, white bandage.

"Let go of him and watch what I do carefully, you'll have to do the same when he gets it off," the doctor tells me. I let go, and watch the doctor wrap the bandage around the wing, then tie it against the hawk's body.

"There's not much chance he'll live," the doctor says. He takes a syringe from the woman and gives Soukounyan a shot. "But it's possible, if you take good care of him, and feed him well." He looks at me, then he looks away, and I wipe my eyes.

"Keep the bandage on as long as possible, two weeks would be best."

He unties the string from Soukounyan's beak, puts him back in the basket, and hands it to me. "That's all," he says, and goes back to his desk.

The woman walks me outside and gives me instructions: "Here, take this roll of bandage, and these pills. Grind the pills and give them to him in meat—one in the morning and one at night for a week."

I take them and put them in my pocket.

"Can you get home?" she asks.

We're at the front gate. I can't see well, and my eyes burn, but I nod. "Yes."

"Are you sure?" she repeats.

I don't say nothing. I turn and walk toward the gas station. I see a blur and I clutch the basket and I run and my mouth is dry and I'm hungry and my head hurts and I'm tired and I hear her calling in my back, calling and calling.

William Archila

Bird

On the bus to Lincoln Heights,
I face a boy with a green backpack,
a geography book open on his lap,
his fingers stroking the veins of a map,
lips moving in the rhythm of a prayer
maybe a poem in Spanish,
so simple and slow I could recognize
every word from my childhood.
I also have read this book of charts
tracing every mountain and sea.

As a boy, I imagined that before Christ
and the rusty nails, before Columbus
and the gilded cross, Central America
must have been a quetzal, a young bird
with green wings and long tails,
flying over lakes, a cluster of volcanoes.

Look at the fold-out map
from *National Geographic.*
You can see its beak
northwest of Guatemala.
The legs stretch out into Panama,
its blue back of Honduras and Nicaragua.

Study the topography
and the land rises out of the water,
the names of rivers and roads sprawled
over the graphs. You can follow the train

in the rails of night, around coffee mountains,
through dark fields of corn, cane,
along rooftops burned red,
away from the soft lights of a brick house.

Search the graves and ruins,
the dark branches of palm trees
swallowing pyramids—fragments of ancient stones.
The full sun breaks on the stairs,
catches the muzzle of a shot gun,
a black ball piercing a bird
that drops in a puddle, wrecked.
A light rain falls. You can imagine
that before the insects, before the slow crumble
of bones, its legs stretch out, back curves,
the beak rises as in flight.

I go back to the boy, his black hair,
long brown nose, silver cross around his neck,
the book closed, zipped in his backpack.
He holds a sugarcane stick,
stripping the peel with his teeth.
We sit for another minute or two
while the great city cranks ahead.

At Broadway and Daily, he gets off,
runs through a crowd of women and men
coming home from work, past the mailbox,
around the corner store, arms spread apart,
chest forward. I lose him
from the yellow window of my seat.

He had the same gaze
that glides over the ocean,
the same bearing of a flight

over a crow's nest, a sailing ship
breaking waves. For miles,
you can hear a man yelling,
"Bird! Land at first sight."

DAISY FRIED

Guts

From the playground's biggest tree's biggest branch
the hawk through daylight drops to the monkeybars'
top deck, claws sunk in its plunder. The hawk

shakes its gray-brown feathers, leans, with its beak
unzips the little squirrel suit, probes into the hot mess.
Nothing bothers it. The raincoated tourist grabs

his wife's wrist knobs, gabbles a strange language,
transfixed by the bird, and the scaly foot closes down.
A mom clamps her hand over the eyes of her kid,

his face so small her hand covers it. She hustles him
bellowing away; he wrenches at her fingers,
will break them, *will*, if he can, to see. The milling

murmuring crowd snapshots, videos. "I love this,"
a man whispers, hands in his suit-pockets. "I'm a hunter
but I never get to hunt anymore, so I love this!" The hawk

from the carcass extracts a bit of bloody intestine.
Flips it long, thin, looplike, over his beak. A gewgaw.
Tilts, eats. Gets another. Loops and eats again.

JORIE GRAHAM

Detail from the Creation of Man

Even at the start, even before they hatched,
whatever there was to *know*
    was gone.
The mother was there, one yellow eye kicked up at me
    each time I lifted—barely—the hem of sage

    to see. Five eggs were there and then, one at a time,
a week apart, three birds.
    Two eggs stayed there till the end of this story,
speckled with blue like this our earth
    seen from afar—
the nest quick with twigs, grass,
    woven in to make a stream, flame,

flame with bits of dirt in it,
    each filament a reference to what follows to what came
before and disappearing now and feeding in.
    There was a fire I once saw
which was below all thought like that

and left nothing undone. It was
    of gold mosaic tile and made a nest, too, partway down
its life—
    beginning at God's feet as hair—gold hair—
and traveling down becoming rivers, wheat-fields, the hair
    of those that have to love, their love.
It flowed, burned, grew, until

darker of course, and near the end, it turned to
    blood and veins and promises, all systems
go.

Then at the very end it was, I guess, the lake
of Hell.
    But up near the top, somewhere between God's

hair and the serpentine gesture of Eve as she holds out
    the thing in her hand which is an open mouth,
or a mouth *opening*—discovering it
    opens—somewhere between or just after Eve it is
a road, dusty like the one behind our house,
    and leads to the knot which is this nest.

It burned at every stage,
    all gold enameled tile and fire. Not the trace on it of an
idea, but gold, unreasoning, something like Time
    writ down in scrawl not meant to
clear,
    communicate.
Where Adam's being made his foot is fire

becoming mud, then, slowing further, flesh.
    The rivulets firm into toes, a heel, in-
step—
    then hair on him here and there
where the waters recede.
    For three weeks I go down there every day. Some days
                                    before the news,

some not. In case you don't know this,
    they're torturing five-year-olds in the kingdom of South Africa,
they're using their sexual parts to make a point.
    A woman testifies. She raises her right hand.
Next in line is the guy about the ozone.
    The Butcher of Lyons. The Pope beatifies E. Stein.
Let x equal perhaps. Let y be the

dizziness. There's this story
     where we continue, continue, fleshy and verbal over the globe,
talk talk, wondering what have we done—and this letter is to
     confirm—.
Once I lay down on the dirt and, holding up the fringe of sage,
     placed my face at the nest, breathing in,

twigs and straw bits at my mouth. I lay there
     a long time. A bird the size of a quarter, very pink,
eyelids not opaque yet, breathed quickly at the height of my eyes
     —a breath, a breath, blue veins all over him,
him sleeping on the other eggs, her gone and watching me.
     I knew I should leave. I knew there was a scent

I left, terrible, perhaps sufficient cause for her to let
     them die—like a word that cannot be taken back,
so the ending cannot be undone—*that* scent.
     I stayed. Where in the fire is this, I thought.
What for, this tooth-sized piece of life too added
     on,

what for, looking around at all those
     woods. More under every bush. Pushing on into here.
Where the theater is empty. Where the lights are down.
     As if there were nowhere else to go. Pushed in. Has
nothing to do with love. Her sitting there some days like a

clock. *You must go in* the something says,
     pushing its thumbs in through,
making these protuberances extend—*out, out you go,*—right
     through the fabric, *in*—A madness from the other side—A

sweeping clean of some other terrain.
     In the picture I kept of Adam from the façade at Orvieto,
God has just called them and they are hiding.

He sees them of course wherever they are, but that's not
important because now He's looking for them,

He's calling and looking. He's pointing.
    They're under three bushes that make a small shade.
They're folded up into their bodies, tight.
As if they wanted to be themselves the nest, him with his hands
    over his eyes, her with her hands

over her ears. A knot of flesh, they want to be
    the nest again, but they can't, they're the thing
in the nest now, the growing pushing thing, the
    image, too late.
Their hair falls over them but it is nothing.
    Their arms fold down over their selves,

tight—
    They hide. They are what waiting is.
When I went back there today the nest was there
    but torn and rained-on, frayed. No trace of them.
A bundle of dead grass and straw. I took it up.
    I turned it for a feather, scent. Nothing. It crumbled in my

hand.
    But in the other panel, where He has just
made Adam—the moment of his making—
    Adam has not yet wakened into his madeness. His hands rest
one on the earth one on his thigh. His head is back.
    The hole in the cliff

takes its shape from him but he has no idea.
    The cliffs and bluffs arc across from the standing God
to the sleeping man as if they are
    the gesture itself which they contain—a pointing hand—You,
    you,

be now. A tree grows up out of man's mind. An angel grows
out of God's stillness—the heat He gives off as it

cools. *You*, he points,
and the finger reaches through space, and the cliffs bend, curl,
and the tree grips in, and the angel shuts his eyes, and the waters
ripple into pattern—*you, you there*—and the angel shuts his eyes
as far as is possible, further, and the man, the man . . .

Against Flight

Everyone wants to go up—but who can imagine
what it's like when the earth smooths out, begins

to curve into itself, that blue implacable ball?
Once you've adjusted to chilled footsoles,

what do you do with your hands? Can so much wind
be comfortable? No sense looking around

when you can see everywhere:
There'll be no more clouds worth

reshaping into daydreams, no more
daybreaks to make you feel larger than life,

no eagle envy or fidgeting for a better view
from the eighteenth row in the theater—

no more theater, for that matter, and
no concerts, no opera or ballet.

There'll be no distractions except birds,
who can never look you straight in the face,

and at the lower altitudes, monarch butterflies—
those brilliant genetic engines churning

toward resurrection in a foreign land.
Who needs it? Each evening finds you

whipped to fringes, obliged to lie down
in a world of strangers, beyond

perdition or pity—bare to the stars, buoyant
in the sweet sink of earth.

ROBERT DANA

Watching the Nighthawk's Dive

Not even a hawk,
but with a hawk's heart
for the dive—

how many years
of dusks have I watched you,
sucker,

fluttering,
as if short of breath,
to a height,

taking aim
on the wing, then plummeting
toward her,

toward soot
stack, schoolhouse roof, or bare
scatter of gravel,

at the last
second, popping the chute,
riding the umbrella-

strutted, down-
curved wings in a humming
skid,

a Jesus dance,
a soft bronx cheer for the void—
then

climbing again
to dive over and over and over
until the first star's gone

and I can only
hear you,
and the streetlights come on.

I could say
I've loved nothing in this whole, dumb country,
and nobody.

But it wouldn't be true,
brown soul.
—I've loved you.

GLADYS SWAN

Dreaming Crow

White Bird flapping white wings
—overtaken by darkness.
Come out, sooty one.
Charred by the darkness of the world?

I sat up with a start, head hollow, ringing with dry laughter. Sat up in alarm. Felt the bed under me, the covers in a tangle. I'd landed there in the middle of it, but from what point of departure? Felt my shoulder. Absence. "Crow," I shouted, "Crow, dammit," and in the dark heard the rustle of wings. Hadn't lost him, and if I lost him, I'd never lose him. Haunt me like a demon. But he was here. Had ridden home on my shoulder. And sat with head tucked under a wing while I took off into another crow dream. For of late, I'd been dreaming of nothing but crow.

A sudden light went on, cracking across my skull like a billy club. Hell and goddamn! The cops? The landlord? My ex-wife? Bill collector? Insurance salesman?

Just Ernie. Of course, Ernie. And what the hell was he doing in my partial awakening, the switchman turning out the black? When my eyes focused, I saw him standing at the foot of the bed, looking at me out of the silence of long waiting burdened with thought—and Crow with his claws hooked over the chair back. I was trying to reach back beyond the dream, maybe beyond the beginning of my life, that blast of birth, when the sudden, too sharp light dropped me into this year's calendar. Tried to shake the dead days out of my head. A rattling as of abandoned parts. A fog, a buzz, a falling into place: he must have brought me home from McIntyre's. Maybe, maybe not— he'd done it before.

To be on the safe side, I said, "Thanks. Thanks a lot."

"For what?"

"God damned if I know."

"Well, I sure as hell don't."

"Oh." I started to turn over, in an effort to get below the racket in my head. "I must have galloped home on the whiskey. Flown with Old Crow."

"You were roaring loud enough."

"Miracles," I said, to account for the gap between there and here. "There're still miracles in the world."

"Tell me about it," he said, slumping down into the overstuffed chair, into the distortions of springs.

I was not then of a sufficient clarity to take him on. One of his bad nights, I could tell. Had that large sad look in his eye. It would have been a waste of philosophy anyway. "Done any work on the book?" I asked him.

"Tried," he said. "Threw out the whole first section. It's about time. I've been giving myself the lie all year . . . Now I've got to start over."

"Ernie," I said. "I heard you read it." Could anything still have brought tears to my eyes, that might have had a chance.

He shook his head. "It's not there yet. Not the way it's gotta be."

Crow circled the room and landed on my shoulder. Helpful creature. A burst of distraction. Might've been good for Ernie to have a crow. Take his mind off the damned book he'd been trying to write for fifteen years. An account of his experiences: for those who weren't there in the muck and the horror. Who would never know flaming jungle and wasted life. An experience of consciousness, he called it. All this time he'd been trying to haul it back, over the distance of years and the gulf of forgetfulness—trying to get it right. Every word. A final monument for those who'd never have the chance to speak.

"How can you stand it?" he said.

"Stand what?"

"That crow flapping around."

"I'm used to him. It feels odd when he's not there. Like a growth you can't get rid of. Gets to be part of you." Performs a service. Lets you carry your darkness on your own shoulder.

"His feet are ugly."

He was in one of his moods all right. Always circled the thing that was on his mind.

"Maddy's coming tomorrow. With Roy."

His wife and kid. Separated. Still loved him. Believed in bridges, in paths around obstacles. Believed that obsessions would melt away and normal daylight return. Believed perhaps in redemption. Their visits left him in the hole for a week.

"Better get some sleep," I told him. He'd probably come up to escape his apartment, or himself. "You're welcome to the chair."

"You mean I can bounce on those springs all night."

"Suit yourself." I'd reached the limits of hospitality. I wanted to turn over. I would sleep again even though Crow would be waiting for me, something growing out of the dark, shapeless at first, then forming his image. Now in one guise, now another, a terrible suspense building, as I lay waiting. God knows what for. For him to speak? So far he hadn't spoken.

I think he must be a myna bird, if not a real crow. Your basic black bird. Someone had taken a knife and split its tongue. I have never known anyone who could do that, take a knife and slit a bird's tongue. And I have often wondered where it put you afterward. I have looked into its eye on other occasions and felt all I laid claim to split and shatter like a mirror. Once it spoke. Someone had tried to teach it to say, "All that glitters is not gold." And it had held onto the first part, flying dizzily around the room, spreading a mockery, it seemed, by saying it over and over. Only sound. Not human speech. Split the tongue and take the creature beyond the bird. To what curious sphere?

All that glitters . . . I would not have put it down as the nesting instinct, but every once in a while, I would find a little hoard of things collected: a paper clip, a silver button, a bit of cellophane, a dime.

I myself had collected enough bright objects in my time, seizing first on one, then another. All fresh and smart in the gleam of the spanking new. Love and money. Marriage and kids. House and home. All that glitters.

All fallen away. Now the kids were grown and had flown. The house, the life that went with it—collapsed. I'd dropped through the layers and folds of all that had held me up, the structures of the quotidian, and landed here, naked, a creature without a shell, in this derelict gray apartment house, where others had similarly found their level. At least momentarily. For they came and went. Except for the street, the prison, or the grave, I do not know where they could fall farther. Sometimes at night I woke and listened to the wind blowing through me, all my doors and windows banging, and a familiar, yet ghostly stranger wandering through the corridors. Martha, Jess, Lilly. Where are you?

Nothing left but Crow. And he had no words now. Not even half a platitude. For a time, I'd tried to teach him his name. Called him Charley. But he wouldn't say it, wouldn't answer to it. Only Crow. The sound of raw bird. I called him as hoarsely as he answered. Out of the mixed flickering of whiskey and dream I would wake to Crow.

"Come on, have a drink with us, Jarve," Ernie said, dragging me downstairs.

Down to family. I knew what he was after. Wanted somebody else in the room to deflect the emotional charge. I couldn't stand the voltage myself, but I went down anyway. Owed it to Maddy maybe. I liked her. She was a plain, down-to-earth type, but when she smiled a radiance lived in her briefly, though it didn't happen often. She'd set herself up for a hard life. Had the man she wanted and didn't want any other. They'd been married before Ernie had gone off to play hero, as he put it, and when he came back they had a kid, Roy, sometimes called Mickey, a thin, sallow, hazel-eyed youth, who seemed embarrassed by his father.

I had brought Crow for the sake of the kid, not that he'd likely have an interest. But this time Maddy was alone.

"Lovely to see you," I said, giving her a hug, as though I were back in the social folderol of my old life.

For a moment she clung to me as if to take some comfort from my arms around her. Then she said, "It's useless, isn't it?"

I wasn't sure what she meant specifically: her visit, Ernie's recalcitrance, or the way of things. But it looked like she'd given up on something.

"I can't make him see," she said, standing in the space between Ernie and me. Ernie's back was toward us, his gaze turned out to the back alley, where the garbage cans leaned or lay on their sides from the assault by cats and dogs. From his attitude I could read him. He wasn't looking out but in; if not to the past, to somewhere beyond the present.

"You know, Jarve," she said, as though Ernie had left the room, "I'm not coming down anymore. Finally, I know when I'm licked. And I've been a fool hanging on so long." She pressed her lips together. "It's not fair," she said, angrily for her. "If you can't let go of things and *live*"—she lowered her voice—"then what's the point?"

She grabbed her coat and rushed to the door before either of us could say a word. A shiver started through me, but I turned it off, damning Ernie for getting me involved. It wasn't any of my business. I was just going to walk out myself, but a bottle in the center of the kitchen table caught my eye. By means of the shortest distances between various points, I found a tumbler and poured myself a drink. Then another.

"She's right, of course," Ernie said, following my example.

"Then what're you doing here?"

Ernie shook his head. "Because I'm trapped—in a place I can't get out of. That you can't remember or forget. And there's no other ground. No place to call home. It's like you've lost the world, Jarve," he said, looking at me. "And there's nothing else in its place."

Couldn't say anything to that. Figured I'd lost it too. Where was some sweet spot of grass to lie on, give your body to, close your eyes and rest?

"I've got to do it, I can't go back on it. There's no peace until *they know*. It would be throwing it away. It was a sickness, Jarve." The muscles in his face tightened. "And how can you cure it if you just bury it?"

Why you? Maddy had wanted to know.

Ernie had shrugged: *Why anybody?*

I'd never gone to Maddy's neighborhood or walked past the house that waited for the return of husband and father. To which he had come back—at first. Tried for the normal. Went back to his old job. Thinking maybe he had found his spot of ground. I could imagine him picking up his old life, trying to put it together even as he had the book before his eyes. In a fever to start it. To put his malarial vision on paper. A continuation of the fever that began it, whole scenes replaying vividly before his eyes. But the more he worked, the more it eluded him. Till his whole brain was on fire. He put everything into it. Evenings, weekends, hours in the middle of the night. Ever more consumed.

He lost his job. Tried another, lost that too. Fell farther down the economic scale: short-order cook, night watchman, janitor. A sleepwalker, the book always in his head. Then he chucked it all. How could he play the part when he wasn't there?

"She deserves better," he had told me a number of times. "Why does she bother?" he said, almost angrily. "She followed me here. Couldn't let go. I thought I'd at least clear the path."

He had a disability check coming in. Grocery money. He'd work a day or two periodically, enough to collect unemployment. The rest was the book, when it was going well; the bottle, when it wasn't.

I poured myself another shot, poured one for Ernie. The good guest. Peculiar what people clung to—or abandoned. I'd left too. The newspaper office, the Kiwanis, the First Presbyterian. Just picked up one day and walked out. Let's say I'd been crushed beneath the weight of fact. Lying too long under a refuse heap. Weighty as a tombstone. The heaviness of repetition. The day's disasters, punctuated by the news of a few lottery winners. The weight of the world, yet flimsy as newsprint itself. Wrapping for the day's sink mess. For what? For Crow to pick at.

Once I hadn't gotten the facts straight—so a rival told me and sent me Crow to eat.

I see you, Crow, dragging behind you liver and lights, the message of sex, the uneven throb of the heart—all the organs exposed, globules of flesh seeking their function. Oh, it goes beyond the beat of blood, the pulsations of the nerves. These raw things . . . When love discovers you, it pulls away the skin, fingers all the tingling parts, turns outside inside.

And the eye opens, looking down through the layers. The wound and the eye meet through the hole in the flesh.

I woke up to find Ernie banging on the door. It wasn't even light yet. I moved unsteadily to the door, opened it, and leaned against the jamb.

"You mean you're just getting up?"

"What's the hurry? Can't even see by the sun."

"Hell, it's about gone down. You've slept through the whole damned day."

"Jeez, what'll I do tonight?" I said, with a sense of loss.

"Come with me down to McIntyre's. I've got a little cash. I did an article, a protest piece," he said, with great contempt. "But it's money."

When the book came to a standstill, he wrote protests—against pollution and violence and crime, against greed and corruption, against inefficiency and stupidity. It was nearly a full-time job. "Spinning your wheels," he called it. Never touched the real springs. On the contrary, you had to hit people inside, make them see. Otherwise they'd never change.

"Sure," I said. "Why not? Come on, Crow."

"Aren't you afraid he'll just take off when you're walking out in the air like that?" Ernie said, as Crow rode my shoulder.

"His choice," I said. "If he can find a good life elsewhere, I won't stand in his way." Although I wasn't sure why, I'd miss him, sign of my darkness, my faithlessness, all the things I'd given up.

McIntyre's was beginning to fill when we got there, factory workers in for a quick one on the way home, a couple of guys from the bank, their styled hairdos and shirts and ties offering a contrast to the rest of us. Slumming before they went home to the wives and kiddies. One of the fellows gave me a nod—knew him from my other life. Only now that I had Crow, I'd let go of the amenities. Marks a man. Folks stare, though all the steadies were used to me, God knows. Thought I was a little off. Harmless. Scarcely caused an eyebrow to lift unless somebody was in the mood for a little pleasantry.

Which somebody was. Just as I'd begun to put myself in the mood I'd come to get into. Had sat down and ordered a double scotch. Heading for the fog. To match the smoky atmosphere. When here comes a guy, maybe a foreman; looked like the type: well put together, arms like a wrestler's, tattoo on the left. Clipper ship. Not original. "Baby Doll" below.

"How come you got that crow?" he said, leaning over the end of our table.

"It's his sister," Ernie explained.

"Sister? What is he, some sort of environment nut?"

"Religious. Talks to the birds," Ernie went on. "And other creatures. Rabbits, even moles. All in their own language."

"Let's hear you say something."

I made a half-hearted caw.

"You're full of shit." He turned away and went to the bar.

"Only he doesn't answer," I said.

"Patience," Ernie said. "When he has something to say . . . Actually"—he raised his voice in the direction of the guy at the bar—"she really is his sister. Enchanted by a wicked magician because she wouldn't deliver. Been carrying her around for seventeen years. But when she's free," he said emphatically, "she'll tell you the secret—of crowness and black magic."

He was into it. Loved this kind of nonsense when he was in the right mood. Played with the words he had left over: jokes and puns, odd bits of anecdote. He kept it up all evening. I was just as well pleased the guy at the bar ignored us. Might've thought Ernie was making fun of him and caused trouble.

"Her name's Marigold."

All that glitters is Marigold. I ordered another scotch, to have it handy. Ernie, the same. I'd have been glad to sit quiet for a spell. I'd reached that point of silence booze brings me to before I land in the well beyond it. Half listening, I sat contemplating the scene: the colors of the bottles melting in the mirror, words and smoke intertwined. I tried to take a crow's eye view.

"Actually, she was a gift from his Aunt Caroline," Ernie said, addressing no one in particular. "Kept birds, filled up every room of her house—parakeets and lovebirds and finches. They all had free run of the place. She liked them better than folks. Less shit."

On the way home he is still making up nonsense, laughing, doubling over. Could hardly walk straight. One of his rare nights. And mine. Somehow I'd forgotten both past and future.

"O Crow!" he said, doing obeisance, "Great Bird, descending to us folks. Giver of light and life."

"Where does he get that?"

"Don't you know?" he said. "In the dark. Always in the dark."

We'd walked up the hill together, our arms around each other's shoulders, the moon tilting over the trees.

Certain things I remember vividly. The box on Ernie's kitchen table. "Maddy's stuff," he said offhandedly when I came in for a nightcap. He uncovered a little box and picked up a wedding band. "She shouldn't have hung on so long," he said. "Too many years." He sat silent for a moment, in another space. "Well," he said, back again, contemplating his glass, "here's to her. The good life . . ." He picked up the ring again. "It'll come in handy."

I figured what he'd do. Earlier that week there'd been a big set-to. Brother Crawford, who in the name of his church next door owned the apartments, had surprised two of his tenants in a compromising position. I had seen them coming and going, the girl having caught my attention with her dangling pink earrings and bright pink heels thin as toothpicks. She chewed gum and carried a transistor radio, worked as a cashier at the Dairy Bar. The lad, large, soft, ingenuous-looking type, with a shock of red hair, had been laid off from the parts plant. Brother Crawford told them he'd either marry them or kick them out—thereby offering occasion for the freedom of choice.

They had opted for a life together. Cheaper in the long run to rent only one apartment. The ceremony was the next evening, after work and before bed. The ring would be Ernie's contribution. The present inmates of the Petite crowded inside the little apartment. Patty, who worked at the Roselyn bakery, brought a day-old cake. There were balloons, somebody's notion of the festive. We listened to the ceremony, saw the ring located on the proper finger, and wished them a happy residence at the Petite.

The rest is a jumble. I remember waking up one night, raucous cries in my ears, the lashing of sounds, a terrible quarrel. Then I was looking into a silence so black I woke with an unreasoning terror and lay in the dark waiting to hear some friendly noise. The bedclothes had been fought into the usual chaos. "Crow," I called, turning on the light, trying to push aside the darkness, "say something." I didn't want to go back to sleep. Instead I got dressed and went downstairs, to roust Ernie up.

His light was on. When he was going on the book, he sometimes sat up all night. I didn't want to disturb him, just sit in the room while he was working. I turned the handle and opened the door, saw that he had fallen asleep across the typewriter, head leaning on folded arms. I knew I shouldn't awaken him. But being alone just then was too much for me.

"How's it going?" I asked him, once he'd sat up and shaken off sleep.

"Don't even ask," he said. "It's all junk."

"Maybe you need a breather," I suggested. "Get away from it and let it take you from behind."

He shook his head. "It's me," he said. "It's been in front of me so long I can't see straight anymore. I tried to get inside, to go so far in . . . Now I wonder. Maybe none of it happened like that. Or maybe it doesn't matter."

I noticed the crumpled pages lying on the floor.

I had nothing to offer. His had been the braver route, no doubt. I'd gone down a little narrow alley, found my dead end, and let it go at that.

He shook his head, played with a pen.

Maybe we were looking at two sides of the same wall. I don't know how long we sat in our separate stupors, when suddenly he rounded on me. "What're you doing down here pissing your life away? You going to rot here?"

I was caught up short. So far we'd given each other berth. With forced calm I said, "I'm supporting the Reverend."

"Come on, Jarve."

I'd done my duty by the public. Muggings, shootings, arrests, promotions. The world's a gaping maw—hungry for facts. Or maybe just sensation. A little pinch to know the blood's still in the veins. Thirty years I'd given to it. "Who the hell are you?"

The way he looked at me I knew I shouldn't have said that. He turned away. "What do you do when you can't get rid of . . . ," he said, "when you can't find . . . ?"

I was in no mood for unfinished sentences. I got up and started back to my room.

"You understand me, Jarve," I heard at my back.

But I couldn't say I did. I was too numb. "Sure," I said, and stumbled back upstairs.

That was the last I saw him. Two months ago. I think of it as a long silence. I'd climbed the stairs, untwisted the covers and fallen asleep. Then the shot rang out. I don't know whether I heard it or the commotion in the hall. Ernie had a gun, of course. These days you have to have your weapon. I flung myself out of bed and rushed down the stairs, already afraid of what I'd find. Patty was pounding on the door, a couple of others behind her. He'd locked it. I broke in the door, yelled to her not to come inside, but to call the police and an ambulance. By the time the sirens tore up the night, everybody in the house was up and people in the neighborhood had gathered on their porches and along the street, some in their bathrobes.

Brother Crawford appeared, befuddled from sleep, appalled by the noise and confusion that had descended on his property. He demanded to know what had happened. When he knew, his face paled, and he suddenly turned quiet, almost diffident, saying to the police, "Yes, sir," and "No, sir," and "Not to my knowledge, sir." Just the week before, they'd come looking for a fry cook who'd been forging checks. But when they'd gone to his room, they discovered he'd decamped, leaving his rent unpaid as well.

I recognized the reporter from the newspaper—had hired him as a kid. When he started to ask me questions, I waved him away and went back upstairs. I had managed to keep my head through the worst of the commotion, but once back in my room I couldn't control a fit of violent trembling. Following that, I sat in a stupor for hours. Somebody would have to tell Maddy, I kept thinking. Who? Images of faces rose to my mind, some of the people I had known in my youth, now long dead. And then my mind became a blank.

The time passing was no more than the rustle of crows' wings. Sometimes I slept all day and sat up all night, making a pretense of reading the books I'd checked out from the public library. Not for the sake of knowledge, not from any impulse of curiosity or imagination. Just to take up the time. Thrillers, Westerns, all the junk I could lay my hands on. I read pigheadedly, kept my eyes to the page to avoid looking out or in. My money was nearly gone, and if I didn't do something, I'd be out on the street. But I refused to move. No place to go. Nothing I wanted to do.

My life lay at the bottom of the can, no point in picking through the trash. Ernie at least had tried to capture something real. Tried to find the words. And look where it landed him. Me, I was a facts man, stuck with only a new round of facts, now as dead as Ernie himself.

"Well, Crow," I said, reaching out for him, eager for a little conversation, "you 'spose there's anything to be salvaged from all of this mess?" He cocked his head, gave me a beady stare. I wouldn't find my image mirrored from his eye. What did he see? Probably a large eye, red rimmed, staring back.

Ernie's father came to see me. He was a large man, both big-boned and solidly padded, who brought in a smell of after-shave lotion and an unwanted briskness of movement that momentarily and painfully stirred the air. He didn't belong in the Petite, where the odors congregated in the hallway, the stink of disposable diapers mingling with smells of cigarette smoke and yesterday's fried potatoes.

Maddy must've told him about me. I hadn't gone to the funeral. Easier not to go, not to see Maddy or the kid, nor to stand there in the light of not-yet-spring, looking at the bare ground. I wasn't sure why he came, what he thought I could do for him. He took off his overcoat, sat in the one armchair I could offer. Three-piece suit, silk tie— he'd done well in life. A doctor.

"A terrible waste," he lamented. "He could've gone to med school, the whole trip paid for. Wouldn't have had to struggle the way I did. I just can't understand it—all the advantages. The way he treated all of us."

He was indignant all right, the aggrieved parent. And I could understand that. Just didn't want to listen to him. Didn't even offer him a drink.

"I think something must've happened to him over there. Maybe he got off on drugs."

He sat there staring into space, until the silence became crushing. "My God, why did he do it?" he burst out, his eyes brimming.

I reached under the bed for Ernie's manuscript, what was left of it, and handed it to him. I'd rescued it, but couldn't bring myself to read it. Maybe it would only confuse him, but at least he had it. Then I brought out my bottle, and together we finished it off.

At first I thought the young couple next door woke me up. Since Brother Crawford had married them, they'd done nothing but quarrel. But I could never tell. The dramas of the day bled into the fantasies of the night till you couldn't separate one piece of nonsense from another. Quarrels and lovemaking, swearing, drunken husbands threatening screaming wives. Crazy laughter and obscenities. No matter who moved in or out, the faces you met on the stairs were always the same.

For some reason I got up and went to the window. Outside, the moon was brilliant. A clear blue-purple shadow with a gauzy sheen lay over the trees, plants in a moonlit sea. I opened the window and let the chill air flow in and around me. And I thought of Ernie, of the times we had spent together, drinking and commiserating. I remembered walking home from McIntyre's that night, our arms round one another's shoulders as we came laughing up the hill. And of other nights.

Curious how things look sometimes, the tilt of the moon in the sky, the wash of light. As though everything had arranged itself according to your feeling. As if you were in love and that gave things their hue and color. The sky and each leaf and branch shimmering in the newness of your seeing. When had I looked at the world that way? As a kid? As a youth looking into a woman's eyes and seeing something beyond even myself, something being created there? On my first job in Chicago, when the excitement of running down to the firehouse in the dead of night raised every detail of the streets to vividness? The blood must have beat in my ears then, a woman's touch awakened me, and the world laid me deep in sensation. I must have been a lover.

Now as I stood there, struck with that memory, forgetful in the shimmer of moonlight, I whistled softly. Behind me, from the curtain rod above my head, came an answering whistle.

Now that I'd had a response from Crow, I was overcome with the need to talk. Poured out my whole history, all my dissatisfactions and regrets. Guilt and frustration. Failures. Talked till my mouth was dry, my throat hoarse. And my hands empty. Got me nowhere at all. Just got thrown back on myself by that beady eye. Nothing from it. So I had to give up. I had to do something though; I had to get out. The room had become a prison.

I'd taken to standing by the window at night, looking out. But the full had passed, and we were back at the dark of the moon. Nothing out there but black branches against the darkened sky. You couldn't whistle the moon back. But I tried it in a mood of experiment, just to see what might happen. I gave a long, slow whistle. And waited.

From Crow came a long, slow whistle.

Again, in the mood of experiment, I did a long note and a short note. I stood tense with waiting. He gave that back too. Then long-short-short. He did it. I kept on, thinking now he'll quit. But he wore me out first. We'd kept going till I could hardly pucker. But no matter how complicated the pattern, he could give it back to me. I had the feeling he was enjoying himself, that I'd finally hit the spot where his real talents lay.

The next day he landed on my knee as I lay in bed working up the energy to climb out into the day. He looked at me, took me in, and gave me a whistle, two long notes followed by two shorts. I said, "Great, Crow," but he just repeated it, flew up and around, landed back on my knee, looked me straight in the eye, and repeated it again. It sounded like a challenge. I gave him back note for note. Then he did another, adding a note this time. I gave that one back too. And he went on, calling the tune, you might say. Till finally I could see what was going to happen. His whistles were getting so complicated I couldn't hold the pattern in my head long enough to repeat it. I got all mixed up trying to get it out. He cackled. He was laughing at me. He'd won.

So there I was, not knowing what to make of it. There had been communication. *All that glitters* . . . We could forget about even half a platitude. For the time being, I had run out of words.

That evening I went out with Crow for a round at McIntyre's. I hadn't been out of my room for three days or more. I'd eaten everything on the shelves, opened the last can of beans and eaten them cold, right from the container. I had spent my money down to the change in my pocket. Rent due next week. I'd be kicked out on my ear. Had to go somewhere, find something to do with myself. I couldn't put off the next move forever. But the thought of change terrified me.

"What'll you have, Jarve?" McIntyre asked me, after we'd exchanged pleasantries.

"Tell you what. How about a little contest? If this bird here can out-whistle you, you'll stand me a drink."

"What's this?"

"Really. He can do it. No shit."

McIntyre looked dubious, as though he had better things to think about.

"C'mon, McIntyre," one of the regulars said. "This joint could do with a little entertainment."

He shrugged. "What do I do?"

I showed him how Crow would imitate me. Then I said, "Whistle, Crow. Show your stuff." Crow started off easy with three notes. McIntyre had no trouble with that. Then four. Five. McIntyre had to concentrate when it came to seven and eight, Crow mixing up the long and short. He kept it up pretty well too. Got about a dozen. Then he messed up. Crow gave a cackle. I had a drink.

Others wanted to try it. One of the bank guys good with figures. But he didn't last beyond McIntyre. Then a fellow in a tweed cap and a blue denim jacket, feisty looking, pushed himself up to the corner of the bar. He'd memorized the whole of "Paul Revere's Ride" in the fifth grade and could still recite it. Damned if he couldn't out-whistle some goddamn bird. He lasted through fifteen notes before Crow got the better of him. His face had grown red, first with effort and concentration, then with defeat, and I was afraid that only a good fight would relieve his feelings. But instead he stepped back and gave Crow an admiring appraisal.

"I'm damned," he said. "He's a smart one."

I had all the drinks I wanted. Every fellow who joined the crowd had to try it. I was carrying on, roaring at the top of my lungs, "Crow, you're a gold mine."

There is always something. Deeper than wisdom, deeper than error, deeper than hope or despair. Always something that escapes your deepest notice: it was still down there, the magma of the heart—the pith, the juice, the old vinegar. Once again I had discovered complexity, only this time it saved me from something worse, from nothingness and the void.

"To Ernie," I yelled. "To the good life!" Tears were streaming down my face, and I was laughing fit to kill. Both at once.

Transmigrations

Sherman likes mayflies, admires them for their courage, their quick impulse to reproduce in the face of their brief life-span; they are sudden and fleeting things. Sherman dislikes firearms. He cannot understand how something clearly intended for wounding or killing can have its own national association and how the President of the United States can belong to such an organization.

Sherman's parents used to worry about Sherman's likes and dislikes, though they worried from a distance. They believed it unwise to get too close too fast. This is what they told Sherman. When he tried to hug them or squeeze their hands, they pushed him back by the shoulders, and Sherman's father would say, "Whoa, little man! What have I told you? You know what will happen if we spoil you rotten? People will say, 'Phew! What smells?' and they won't want to be near you." Sherman is fearful of smelling bad and driving people away, so he complies and tries not to touch. He imagines people he would like to be close to coughing from the fetid air around him, pushing him back, their arms growing and growing, stretching to such a distance they become stiff stick figures and push him into a hush of icy water.

Sherman's mother had reservations about this method of child-rearing. Sherman overheard her ask his father, "Are you sure we will be close-knit? Do you promise this will work? He's only a little boy." Sometimes at night Sherman heard his mother weeping; the sound was soft, muffled, and made Sherman think of flannel, something he could rub up against, wrap himself in.

Sherman has lived with both of his parents for the twelve years he's been alive. They recently separated and both have begun to modify their parenting techniques. Sherman's mother touches his face now whenever she sees him. His father takes him places—hockey games, observatories, putting greens, hardware stores. They are often in a car together, buckled in, looking through glass, moving forward. Despite peer pressure, Sherman loves his parents.

Five years before Sherman was born, his sister, Melanie, was born. Melanie was tiny, always the smallest person in her class, and she was very pale beneath her occasional sallow tint. In the final picture of Melanie, a tiny arm barely larger than a feeding tube rests on the raised metal guard of her hospital bed. This arm is feathered with fine, white hairs and upstages the blurred face that fades into the pillow. When Sherman looks at this picture, he focuses on the arm. It looks to him like something in an early developmental stage, something that will eventually grow and bend and sprout and flourish into a beautiful, velvet white wing. Something that could lift a person up and out of any situation and deliver her to a body of water. Something that could save her from the threat of a predator or extinction. Sherman knows it is only a tiny, sick arm in the picture, but it seems obvious to him we are all descended from a race of strong and elegant birds.

Sherman knows the story of his existence and wonders if other children know why they are here on earth, know if they've been brought for some true and special purpose or if they are only an accidental collision of elements, an extension of lineage, a repository for genes. Sherman was conceived as a means to a beginning, an instrument for prolonging life, and his parents have been quite forthcoming with the story behind his birth. There are even newspaper articles that document their intent. Melanie had leukemia and fell out of remission a year before Sherman was conceived. As the days passed and red spots bloomed on her legs and arms and her white hair thinned, family members were screened as possible candidates for the donation of bone marrow. But it is a specialized substance, and it became clear to Melanie's parents they would have to take the situation into their own hands, would have to create their own donor. Of course, there were no guarantees.

Sherman is in love with a fat girl named Cassie. There are two fat girls named Cassie at Horace Mann Elementary and one girl who claims to be big-boned named Cassandra, but it is Cassie Shockley with whom he is in love. Cassie's full name is Cassiopeia Prudence Shockley, and Sherman wishes to marry her one day and take her name as he loves the sound of Sherman Shockley. It is not quite as good as if her last name were Tank, but he has looked in the phone book to find that people with this name do not exist.

Sherman and Cassie sit at opposite ends of a see-saw. Sherman is slight and his end of the see-saw is elevated several feet off the ground. This is one of the reasons he likes Cassie. He likes to dangle his feet and imagine he is on a giant tongue depressor, a Lilliputian; or he pretends he is seated in an ancient and impossibly slow catapult. Sherman loves being up in the air. He feels indefinite and brave.

A clump of children near the merry-go-round disperses, radiating in different directions like a slow burst of fireworks. As Jason Piper passes the see-saw, he says, "Later, gators."

"Alligators can adjust their body temperatures in order to determine the sex of their offspring," says Cassie.

This is another reason Sherman loves Cassie. She knows many strange and wondrous things, though Sherman recognizes her knowledge is occasionally dubious. She once told him she knew for a fact kissing could not, in and of itself, cause pregnancy, but kissing before the age of thirteen could cause a girl's breasts to overdevelop. She could not decide whether this was an altogether undesirable effect.

"How do they know which sex to want?" asks Sherman.

"I think it all depends on their disposition. If they are prone to fatigue, naturally they want girl alligators because girl alligators are smart and quiet and contentedly sit in the cool mud. But if the mothers thirst for adventure and don't mind constant roughhousing, then they want boys. Boy alligators stick their scaly noses into everything and eat smelly things that aren't good for them." Cassie rests her elbows on puffy, pink knees.

"Well, what if one day all the alligator mothers had tired dispositions and only had girls? Then alligators would be out of business." Sherman kicks his feet as he speaks. "Anyway, it sounds prejudiced."

"I can't help my female perspective." Cassie unties her tennis shoes. "I've got blisters all over my feet from skating Saturday. Let's pop them."

Sherman swings one leg over and dismounts the see-saw. He is afraid to touch Cassie's feet. He is afraid he won't be able to control himself. He wants more than anything to wrap his arms around her waist as far as they'll go and to kiss quickly the soft putty of her cheek. He wants to bury his face in her bulging stomach. He loves that there is excess Cassie. He wants to be romantic and witty and tell her the rings of flesh around her heavenly body are lovely; she is his little Saturn. But he knows she is self-conscious and dreams of a different body, and he fears if they get too close, she will discover his soul has a terrible odor and she will be repelled.

"I've got to feed Aretha," Sherman says.

Cassie stares at her feet. "They look like they've been bubble-wrapped. Who'd have thought skating could do so much damage? I might have to go to a foot guy." Cassie pushes tentatively a blister as though it were a dead bug.

"Podiatrist."

"What I said."

"You just need to skate more often. Build up calluses."

"And have alligator feet? No way, José."

"Way," Sherman says, and smiles.

Cassie puts her socks back on. "Can I come see Aretha? My mom's at the beauty shop until 4:30."

"I don't know. This is our quiet time together. I think it'd hurt her feelings if I brought my girlfriend home at this time of day, though she probably wouldn't let it show." Sherman runs his hands through the brown tufts of his hair. Sherman's hair is coarse and prefers standing up to lying down, which it will not do without a struggle. Yesterday Cassie cut and styled it in such a way that it looks as if it grows in clusters like sage or endive. Sherman is happy it now obeys without the use of styling gel.

"Looks good," Cassie says, smiling and nodding.

"Aretha's probably screaming for her duckweed. I'll see you tomorrow, Cas." Sherman smiles and walks backwards for as long as the terrain feels safe and familiar.

Aretha is a trumpeter swan. It was a little over a year ago when Sherman decided to play outside so that his parents would not have to whisper their grievances to one another, and he walked to the lake, where he spotted a huge nest on the margin. Swans had nested there before, and he knew not to disturb them, but this mother swan was slumped over and quiet. As Sherman neared the nest, he realized the swan was too silent and supine to be alive. He petted the long, white neck and felt under her wings. Her body was still warm. He covered her with his jeans jacket and built a small fire, then he ran all the way to Lodema's, the bird lady's, house.

Lodema's trees were feathery, aflame with chickens and magpies. Sherman saw the owls and pigeons and ducks and hawks recuperating in their respective pens. Sherman loved to visit Lodema. The inside of her house was filled with beautiful domesticated birds that played on rubber rings dangling from the branches of a huge oak tree. The tree reached through the center of her living room toward the retractable skylight of her roof. Some of the birds swooped to Sherman's shoulder when he went near the tree. Others said "hello" when the phone rang or "come in" when there was a knock on the door. Colonel Klink, an African Grey, cracked nuts and fed them to Lodema. Sherman loved how the birds took care of her. He knew people thought Lodema eccentric, but he decided this was a good thing. His parents were initially wary of his association but eventually deemed it beneficial. Lodema told Sherman she had been born under the sign of Aquarius, and Aquarians were naturally eccentric. And since he was a Gemini with, she discovered, a rising sign of Aquarius, she assured him they would always get along famously.

When Lodema got to the nest, the swan was beginning to cool. Lodema kissed its black bill and bowed before it. She wrapped the clutch of four eggs in a plush towel and placed this on a hot water bottle in a cardboard box. Together she and Sherman quickly buried the mother swan in the moist earth near the lake.

"What happened to her?" Sherman asked.

"Probably ate some old lead. The hunters get them one way or another, sometimes years after they aim for them. Used to use them for pillows and powder puffs."

After several weeks Lodema gave Sherman the last egg, which showed no signs of hatching. Sherman asked to borrow an incubator just in case, and within several days Aretha was born. Sherman watched all day as she poked bits of shell out of her way and unfolded her crumpled body into the open air.

With an eyedropper he fed her a mixture of instant baby food and a powdered concoction Lodema fed her larger birds. He swirled the white fuzz on Aretha's head as he fed her.

When she opened her eyes, Sherman stared into the small black bubbles. He thought he saw himself, saw how his lips curved and jutted as if for a specialized purpose. He saw how his tiny ears were invisible beneath his unruly hair. He felt aerodynamic. He breathed deeply. He wanted to know what it felt like to glide through the air that passed through him and fueled his own movement. Aretha gurgled and yapped in scratchy tones. She inched toward him, and he kissed her black bill. She nuzzled his moist palm. She tried to pass through it, to disappear in the callused flesh. Sherman felt newly born, engendered by a baby swan, a sweet and needy cygnet.

When Sherman's parents found out he had hatched a swan and was hiding it, caring for it in his room, they were not angry. They thought it would be educational for him to have such an exotic pet; they thought it would teach Sherman responsibility, so they fixed a place for it in Sherman's father's work shed. They did not know it was an endangered species. They did not know the swan's lineage was in jeopardy, that the mother swan had been unconsciously struggling against the extinction of her race, that the baby swan's birth was purposeful.

Sherman knew, and Lodema knew. Lodema said there wasn't anything to do now that Aretha had been imprinted. Sherman knew what this meant. His image had been branded on the black beads of her eyes, and he knew her need for him had been etched in a deeper place, beneath the gray and white down, a place where sentience and instinct and emptiness collide. And he, too, felt this in the pit of himself.

Lodema told Sherman to tell people she was a basic garden variety swan and hope she wouldn't start her migrant bugling in front of anyone else who might care. "They're not as endangered as they used to be. There are several thousand of them now. They got down to a couple hundred at the time old Audubon was painting pictures of them with their own quills," Lodema said.

When Sherman gets home, Aretha is chasing squirrels in the front yard. Sherman's house sits far back from the street. His parents own the several acres of wooded land surrounding it. The house itself is sequestered by a huddle of pin oaks filled with squirrels and birds. Aretha never ventures farther than a few hundred feet away from the house without Sherman.

Sherman wonders what Aretha thinks she is. A dog or a small boy, perhaps. She has no concept of swan. She seems unimpressed by all types of birds. She frequently quarrels with the persnickety blue jays and charges robins as they tug worms from the earth.

When Aretha spots Sherman coming down the path, she lurches toward him on the black spatulas of her feet; the seven-foot wings spread dramatically, as if beckoning his embrace. Sherman cannot help but see the soap opera quality of this ritual: they are long-parted lovers with names like Lance and Ashley and tragic pasts coming together out of nowhere in a field undulating with wildflowers or wheat. It reminds him of a commercial for a feminine hygiene spray, a commercial he once saw while watching television with Cassie and which made his cheeks flush a near flamingo pink. And yet he felt comforted to know women must also worry about love and odor.

Sherman falls on the ground, and Aretha leaps on top of him, squawking and nibbling his cheeks and throat. He sits up and buries his face in her breast and kisses the squirming white pillow. "I have a surprise for you," he says. He leads her to the shed. She waddles alongside, nipping at the fingers that will feed her.

In the shed, she sits quietly on her blanket, the hooked neck poised and still. Sherman digs in his backpack. "I stopped at the lake and got you some water buttercups and elodea," he says.

As Sherman feeds her, he strokes the conveyer belt of bumps along her throat. He feels the invisible hump in her sternum housing the large windpipe that allows her to trumpet. "Cassie told me something about you today. She said that ancient Germanic peoples believed swans embodied the souls of dead people. They thought swans were sacred and holy." Sherman looks into Aretha's imprinted eyes, reflecting the world around them. "No pressure," he says. He recalls Aretha's mother, her long neck lolling over the side of the nest. "I wonder where the souls of swans go."

Sherman turns over to see the red numbers on his clock read 4:17. He expels a "hey" when he notices a figure seated at the end of his bed. He sits up and turns on the table lamp. It is his grandfather, his father's father, Elmer, a dead person. They stare at one another for several minutes. Sherman has not seen him since he was six years old.

Sherman says, "Grandpa Elmer?"

Elmer smiles.

Sherman bites into his lower lip to see if he can feel pain. He can. He reaches out and touches Elmer's hand. He can feel the knotted, leathery skin. "You're solid," he says.

"Yes."

"Are you still dead?"

"Yes."

"What are you doing here?" Sherman wonders if he is psychic, if his mind and body somehow conduct the currents of spirits. He feels light as a Kleenex.

Elmer maneuvers his false teeth and holds them between his lips. Sherman laughs at this old trick. Elmer returns the teeth to his mouth. Sherman becomes serious and silent, then asks, "Have you seen Melanie?"

Elmer nods.

"Is she okay? Are her arms bigger? Is she strong?" The fact that his grandpa still wears false teeth worries Sherman. He would have thought everything would be repaired in the afterlife.

Elmer says, "She is good. She is happy."

"Is she still sick?"

Elmer shakes his head. "She has big pink wings and webbed feet so she can land on the water."

"Do you know God?" Sherman asks.

Elmer shrugs his shoulders. "As well as anyone, I suppose."

"Have you seen Elvis?"

"Too many impersonators to be sure." Elmer smiles and squeezes Sherman's feet through the blanket.

"Is the Virgin Mary really a virgin?" Sherman smiles.

"She's given me no reason to doubt her," Elmer says. He pulls a cellophane-wrapped cigar out of his shirt pocket. He holds it out to Sherman. "They don't make these anymore," he says. He puts the cigar back in his pocket.

Sherman asks, "Why do things become extinct?"

Elmer stands. "I don't know," he says. "Just because I'm dead doesn't mean I have all the answers."

Cassie and Sherman are sitting in his front room, watching television. With remote control in hand, Sherman flips from channel to channel to channel.

"You have an abnormally short attention span," Cassie says.

"There's nothing good on anyway."

"Why can't we play with Aretha?"

"I told you, she's jealous. She'd charge you like she did yesterday."

"She needs to get used to me." Cassie reaches into the pocket of her jeans jacket.

Sherman does not want Aretha to get used to Cassie. He does not want them to bond. He knows they could give one another something he doesn't have, some secret strength. He knows they would crouch together under trees, laughing and honking, and they'd hush when they saw him approaching. Then his love for them would sour. It would begin to reek of the thing he could not give them, the thing that could lift them up and save them.

Cassie pulls crayons out of her pockets: Maize, Raw Umber, Periwinkle Blue. She says, "They've replaced these colors. I think we should start a time capsule and keep track of all the things that have been discontinued, things indicative of the sorry time we live in."

Sherman flips past more programs, a fleeting collage of moving pictures. He doesn't want to think about things that have been discontinued. He settles on a program about killer bees.

Cassie says, "The leaf-cutting ants of Central America are farmers, and they grow their own food. They gather leaves and grow a special kind of fungus that they live off. And they know how to weed the undesirable funguses out. They're quite resourceful and self-reliant. They don't need crumbs or honey or human flesh to survive." Cassie leans over and kisses Sherman on the cheek. "My mom put me on another diet," she says. "It's all rice cakes and broccoli. And carrots, carrots, carrots. It's barely enough to sustain a small breed of rabbit." Cassie stares at the layers of her stomach. "We have to be careful of my ketones this time."

Something wells up inside Sherman, and he lurches toward Cassie and knocks her back to the floor. He kisses her nose, then buries his lips in the soft center of each new breast. He jumps up and runs out the door.

He runs and runs through the woods, past the lake, across the barren highway, until he comes to the Fairgrove Shopping Center. He runs toward Safeway and collapses in the first parking space on the blue wheelchair symbol. He lies on his back and looks up at the letters that spell out SAFEWAY. There is a nest of finches cupped in the bottom curve of the S. The tiny birds flit about, squeeze through letters, and perch on the F and the E. Sunlight slants across WAY. The birds on top of the sign face the light, as though they were phototropic, as though they were drawn toward the wavy heat by something deep inside their thin, translucent bones. Sherman watches the nervous and luminous activity of the birds until an old man yells out of his car, "Hey, kid! You better get up unless you want to be squashed like a bug." Some boys walk by and laugh and say, "Road pizza."

Sherman whispers, "Dead meat."

Today is Saturday, the day and night Sherman spends with his father. Before Sherman left, his mother hugged him hard, pressing the breath right out of him, and he felt as if he'd been knocked on his back. She kissed him on the mouth, and her lips were wet and sweet. She clutched his face in her hands and said, "I love you, Sherman. I always have, and you're all that matters to me now." She let go of his cheeks, and her eyes, clear and empty as water, stared past him at his father's car in the driveway. She laughed, and her lips quivered. "You're the only reason it's not obscene for me to still be alive."

As Sherman got into his father's car, he watched his mother standing in the doorway. She held one hand over her mouth and clutched her skirt with the other. Her face was tense and furrowed, as though she were crying, though she wasn't, as though she were watching her only child go off to war and imagined him coming back with fewer limbs or relentless dreams of dying. Sherman has seen this look before, in old photographs.

Sherman and his father sit in the green-shag-carpeted living room of his father's apartment. Sherman's father drinks a beer he has heavily salted, and with the TV remote he flips from golf to tennis. "So, what should we do, Sport?" Sherman's father smiles and raises his eyebrows. He drops the remote and rubs his stomach.

Sherman blinks consciously and listens for the rumble he feels in his intestines. He thinks about how a person can feel his stomach growl before he can hear it, sort of like thunder and lightning. He doesn't like to be called Sport, though he prefers it to Little Man or Sherm.

"So? What do you say? We could go hunting. Mum's the word to your mother, of course. I just got some new boots, and we could borrow my neighbor's rifle. I don't know dick about hunting, but we could teach each other. Don't want you turning into no mama's boy, do we?" Sherman's father laughs and attempts to ruffle Sherman's stiff hair.

"No," says Sherman. "That would be tragic."

His father tightens his lips. "Well, let's hear your bright ideas, Einstein. I don't know how to entertain a twelve-year-old kid. I feel like we're on some goddamned blind date or something."

Sherman wishes he were cryogenically frozen inside a time capsule, lying next to a twisting hologram of Elvis and a stack of electric toothbrushes, waiting to be thawed by a distant culture. "I heard they were doing military maneuvers in the forest on the opening day of hunting season," Sherman says. He stares at his clasped hands.

"No shit? Anybody get hurt?"

"A lot of animals."

Sherman's father sleeps on the couch as people on television jump from bridges and dangle by bungee cords like rubber spiders. The afternoon sun angles through the sliding glass doors and spotlights his white belly. Sherman stares at the dust motes that tumble through the light and quietly sings, "We are here, we are here, we are here. Boil that dust speck, boil that dust speck, boil that dust speck." He turns the television off and walks to his father's bedroom. He runs his hand over the items on his father's dresser: a curved wallet molded by his father's hip, a pair of cufflinks, a golf tee, a Tiparillo cigar box, and cologne in green and brown bottles shaped like an old car and a horseshoe. Sherman opens the cigar box. It is full of old photographs. He looks at a picture of his father in the army. His father is thin and stiff, and his hair is cut short and neat as a newly mown lawn. The scowl on his face seems rehearsed. There is a vertical series of black and white pictures of his parents. They laugh, they kiss, they hug, they smile. Sherman thinks they look like actors demonstrating the different nuances of "happy" for a screen test. The rest of the pictures are all of Melanie. They are in chronological order from her birth picture, in which she is wrinkled and brown like an old vegetable, to a picture of her in a swimming pool. Melanie stands thin and white in the middle of the shallow end of the pool. Her face bears no expression; her eyes are closed. She holds a hand out, and it is unclear whether she is waving or asking someone to stop.

Sherman takes Aretha to the lake for a swim. He fed her beforehand so she would not be tempted to dig in the dangerous depths where the poisonous substances lurk. He knows it is risky to swim after eating, but he feels bringing a hungry swan to the site of her mother's last supper would be a bigger gamble. Besides, he is not sure it is possible for a swan to have a cramp. Sherman suspects the idea of deadly cramps resulting from swimming too soon after eating, which he himself has never experienced or witnessed, is a myth manufactured by adults who secretly hope that the lulling effects of turkey sandwiches and milk or the heaviness of meatloaf will sink their children to sleep, and make them forget about swimming entirely.

Aretha immediately paddles out into the center of the lake. She snaps at water striders and dips her head underwear. Sherman loves the shape of her head and neck: a question mark, a pitcher handle, half a heart. Sherman's own neck feels hot, inflamed. His face stings. He is thinking of a million things at once, wishes, desires, regrets bleeding together behind his eyes. There is Cassie, healthy and pink-skinned. Her mother says she is full-figured. She is ringed with flesh, and Sherman felt the feathery give of her breasts as he pressed his lips to them. There's his mother, who drinks can after can of Coke in the dark and hugs him now when she thinks he's asleep and talks to him in an altered voice, as though he were a cat or a doll. Then there's Aretha and her fragile species. He remembers the moment she first opened her eyes and he saw himself etched in the black circles; she pushed herself into the nest of his hands. Now his hands can barely cradle her head, and he fears they will only grow smaller as she ages, but he will feed her and he will love her and she will live many swan years.

Aretha flaps and honks and swims in circles. Sherman wishes he, too, had huge wings and thinks he can almost feel pinfeathers poke through the skin on his back. He wishes he were younger so he could pretend, pretend he was a swan and Aretha his mate.

Sherman begins to undress. He removes his sneakers and socks, his jacket and T-shirt and jeans and underwear. He walks into the water. The water is so cold it feels to him as if his flesh and bones were leaving him, melting, decomposing with each step, as if he were becoming part of the water.

They would live in an enormous nest atop the woven sticks of a beaver house. They would eat insects and tubers, snails and small fish. They would have beautiful children, small, fuzzy cygnets, remarkable for their blue eyes.

Aretha sees him enter the water and begins to swim toward him. His knees and elbows and ankles ache, and he wonders if Aretha can feel him course through her thin, hollow bones. Sherman extends his arms and closes his eyes. He is not sure if he is beckoning or warning.

WENDELL BERRY

The Heron

While the summer's growth kept me
anxious in planted rows, I forgot the river
where it flowed, faithful to its way,
beneath the slope where my household
has taken its laborious stand.
I could not reach it even in dreams.
But one morning at the summer's end
I remember it again, as though its being
lifts into mind in undeniable flood,
and I carry my boat down through the fog,
over the rocks, and set out.
I go easy and silent, and the warblers
appear among the leaves of the willows,
their flight like gold thread
quick in the live tapestry of the leaves.
And I go on until I see, crouched
on a dead branch sticking out of the water,
a heron—so still that I believe
he is a bit of drift hung dead above the water.
And then I see the articulation of feather
and living eye, a brilliance I receive
beyond my power to make, as he
receives in his great patience
the river's providence. And then I see
that I am seen. Still as I keep,
I might be a tree for all the fear he shows.
Suddenly I know I have passed across
to a shore where I do not live.

BRENDAN GALVIN

One for the Life List

Not a yellowthroat,
not a yellow warbler, but a
yellow-throated warbler—
it has happened again: the sky
moving out of the west
and before the clouds
migrants come scudding,
so many so fast that the pines
are mobile with blue backs
and bay breasts switching places,
undertail coverts flicking
yellow, white, twitching among
branches, impossible to locate
fast enough, but as though
at the end of summer
an East European primitivist
had painted a Christmas tree
whimsical with birds.
A yellow-throated warbler, one
for the lifelist, though
I promised myself again
I'd swear off this year.
Instead I've come back
for just one more, a failed
teetotaler of birds,
and better this stupefaction at
a lemon-bibbed ounce of
feathers than the shoddy
illusion of the aloneness

of things, wherein the sky
pours down oceanic emptiness
and the life of a grove migrates
across the road to the gas pumps:
even the common foreground
chickadee and background crow
give dimension to our days,
and not to salute such
charity of song
though it be plain as
thumbsqueaks on clear windowpanes,
not to say their names,
and the shadow of death passes
across our tongues.

RICHARD FOERSTER

The Hohntor

Bad Neustadt/Saale

For centuries the swallows have
erupted into evenings, down
from the High Tower's hollow eaves,
and soared above my father's town.

Scores twitter, flare the halflight, now
in wargame squadrons, now alone,
rapt in purposeless delight. How
will I face the dark when they are done?

I sit within the medieval
battlements and stare, no more secure
than those whom the swallows' revels
eased when the tower stood at war.

Beyond, all of my family lie
scattered in this valley's churchyards.
How should a final son reply
to a dour monument that guards

the ever changeless and the changed?
This congregation worships it
with flight ecstatically arranged
above me in the violet

nimbus of the sun's last rays.
Before night snares them, each bird ducks
beneath the tower's roof. Why praise
their roost, this constancy, this flux?

The absence surges—slackened
drive, the wayward wife, our weaseled love—
but then, around this blackened
edifice, the stars begin to move.

MACKLIN SMITH

Birding the Battle of Attu

A souvenir of this. If the moss and lichen stains
Come clean, it may seem even too abstract,
Not just how old glass ages, but in that it contains
What contained it, and was saved intact.

Knowing which side-valley we are in might tell
The story—a U.S. medicine jar
Or Japanese inkwell: there weren't any letters
From their time out here,

But some officers wrote night journals
About the wounded, rotting rice and diarrhea
In their rat tunnels,
Their wives and unseen sons, the glory of the Emperor.

Under soft mosses, somewhere here, they fill caverns
As dust and jelly. Ordnance actually floats in tundra:
Fragments, small shells, a driftwood sandal growing ferns,
And what we can't identify: this jar of rain and tundra

Vegetation squeezing out all air
Like a bunker filled with mildewed men
And the rattan chest of morphine ampules there,
A communal grave, invasions of inconsequence.

We pass it around. Tundra is merciful and just
The way it fills holes, enfolding history.
Ptarmigans lay in machine-gun nests,
Snow Buntings sing on territory;

April's neck-high snowdrifts melt
Into foxhole pools—a Kamchatka Lily
In sunshine, so we can forget the ravines burst from slit
Trenches cascading into Massacre Valley.

We drink the water, snacking on a Heath Bar.
At the half-hour, another party's CB
Might transmit Siberian Rubythroat, Far
Eastern Curlew, even a Mugimaki:

We'd doubletime for them! But we doubt
We'll have to, and it feels OK to gaze
More or less straight up. On Terrible Mountain,
Are those their holes in the scree, their snowfaces?

At radio time, no birds
On the island: Dr. Tatsuguchi, after
The injections and grenades, how he formed pious words
As his tunnel drifted with snow and white fire.

Stanley Plumly

Cedar Waxwing on Scarlet Firethorn

To start again with something beautiful,
and natural, the waxwing first on one
foot, then the other, holding the berry
against the moment like a drop of blood—
redwing-tipped, yellow at the tip of the
tail, the head sleek, crested, fin or arrow,
turning now, swallowing. Or any bird
that turns, as by instruction, its small, dark
head, disinterested, toward the future; flies
into the massive tangle of the trees, slick.
The visual glide of the detail blurs.

The good gun flowering in the mouth is done,
like swallowing the sword or eating fire,
the carnival trick we could take back if
we wanted. When I was told suicide
meant the soul stayed with the body locked in
the ground I knew it was wrong, that each bird
could be any one in the afterlife,
alive, on wing. Like this one, which lets its
thin lisp of a song go out into
the future, then follows, into the wood-
land understory, into its voice, gone.

But to look down the long shaft of the air,
the whole healing silence of the air, fire
and thorn, where we want to be, on the edge
of the advantage, the abrupt green edge
between the flowering pyracantha and

the winded, open field, before the trees—
to be alive in secret, this is what
we wanted, and here, as when we die what
lives is fluted on the air—a whistle,
then the wing—even our desire to die,
to swallow fire, disappear, be nothing.

The body fills with light, and in the mind
the white oak of the table, the ladder
stiffness of the chair, the dried-out paper
on the wall fly back into the vein and
branching of the leaf—flare like the waxwings,
whose moment seems to fill the scarlet hedge.
From the window, at a distance, just more
trees against the sky, and in the distance
after that everything is possible.
We are in a room with all the loved ones,
who, when they answer, have the power of song.

JIM HARRISON

from **Farmer**

Joseph had always spent a great deal of time trying to think analytically about his main preoccupations, which were fishing and hunting. As the years passed he found he had less and less interest in the mere act of acquiring fish and game. For instance he no longer shot ducks. Not only were they easy but they were simply too fascinating to watch on the beaver pond way back in the center of the state tract. If you spent a long time on your stalk you could get close enough to watch them for hours. It was much more difficult with Canada geese, surely the wariest of all birds. But the ducks, most commonly mallards, mergansers, teal, or blue bills, would complacently swim and speak their odd language. Joseph experimented in alarming them. Sometimes it required only an upraised hand wagging from cover but if they were feeding avidly enough you could stand and shout before they would flush. The geese always kept several scouts on the periphery of their feeding area to alert them to any danger.

On the Sunday morning after his meeting with Catherine he sat by the pond for a couple of hours watching the birds, and the peacefulness of sitting so long amid this beauty drew him to questions that seem essential to everyone. An idea that fixed him to one spot was that life was a death dance and that he had quickly passed through the spring and summer of his life and was halfway through the fall. He had to do a better job on the fall because everyone on earth knew what the winter was like. The ocean creatures he read of illustrated the point so bleakly. To devour and be devoured. But their sure instincts kept them alive as long as possible, as did those of the wild ducks before him, or the geese. Even the brook trout, the simplest of the trout family, were mindful of the waterbirds, the kingfisher and heron, that fed on them.

One afternoon he had been lucky enough to see a Cooper's hawk swoop down through the trees and kill a blue-winged teal. The other ducks escaped in a wild flock circling the pond twice while the Cooper's hawk stood shrouding its prey with its wings. Joseph watched it feed on the teal's breast then fly off to a large dead oak to preen. It was far too spectacular to be disturbing. *Once in town he had seen a car turn a corner and strike a lady pedestrian. He could still see the shocked, twisted look on her face.* A couple of hours later a few ducks circled the pond hesitantly. Soon they had all returned to their feeding.

For Joseph there were presentiments of the troubles to come even before he had begun his affair with Catherine. He had left half the apples unpicked and for the first time didn't want any school children in the orchard. What little heart he had left for teaching was gone before the end of September; he met each morning feeling a certain dread mixed with lassitude. He spent far less time in the tavern playing cards and far more time reading about distant places. All of the strictures, habits, the rules of order for both work and pleasure seemed to be rending at even the strong points.

October grouse season had always been the high point of his sporting year along with late May and early June and the heavy mayfly hatches of trout fishing. He would rush home from school leaving Rosealee to lock up, change his clothes, and hunt with old Dr. Evans until the fall light disappeared. He would hunt all day Saturday after the chores were done and on Sunday from dawn to dark. But this year the doctor had decided to give up hunting—his legs would no longer take the strenuous walking. The doctor had presented Joseph with his fine Parker shotgun in August: Joseph had coveted the expensive gun for years, the beautifully grained whorl of its walnut stock and the fine engraving of a pointing dog along the breech. But when the season began this time everything conspired against him: the weather was cold and wet, making his leg ache more than ordinary, then the weather changed into an over-warm and humid Indian summer, and grouse were near the bottom of their seven-year population cycle, though woodcock were plentiful.

It was a male woodcock that pinpointed a certain loss of nerve. After sunup one Sunday he walked along the west fence border of the farm, back toward the corner where the creek and swamp joined the state property. It was a splendid morning with white frost on the pasture; clear, cold, with the ferns finally dead and the walking easy. He approached a blackberry swale and for a moment pretended he was gesturing his old bird dog, a springer spaniel, into the blackberries to flush the birds. But the dog was long dead. Joseph stood there and stared at a weak sun climbing over the swamp. A woodcock flushed at his feet toward the sun and he lost it for a moment but then it dipped below the treetop and he dropped the bird easily. He walked over and picked up the bird but it fluttered in the tall canary grass, still alive. He caught it and began to wring its neck but the woodcock's large brown eyes followed his movements. He turned the bird around but the bird twisted its neck toward Joseph still staring at him with a glint of the morning sun shining off its retinas. Joseph closed his own eyes and snapped its spine near the neck. He shoved the bird into the game bag in his vest but he was trembling.

Joseph sat down on a pile of old fence posts and thought about the woodcock. How could he become so nervous after thirty years of hunting? He had never looked into a bird's eyes before and it had at least temporarily unnerved him. He tried to ignore how nearly human the eyes looked, but he couldn't rid his mind totally of the idea: eyes are what we hold most in common in terms of similarity to other beasts. He always cringed when he hooked a fish in the eye. When they slaughtered both cattle and pigs the eyes stayed open in death. But it was more than that; the woodcock was warm, palpable, it quivered, and its eyes did not blink under his gaze.

By mid-morning he had bagged two grouse but had missed several woodcock. He sat on a stump near the creek and slowly ate his sandwich, wondering if he had missed the woodcock on purpose. They were normally far easier to shoot than grouse. Did it mean, too, that one more pleasure was to be denied him on his already severely atrophied list of enthusiasms? He had sensed that the energies that fed his interests had somehow diminished but he believed these energies would recover and persist. Only it wasn't happening and the near frenzy that had occurred with Catherine the week before was the first "new" thing to enter his life in a long time. Sitting there on the stump with the sun warming his back and drying the dew from his pant cuffs he felt bovine, immovable; he numbered his passions: he had loved Rosealee for thirty years, he had hunted and fished for thirty-five years and worked hard on the farm nearly that long, almost assuming manhood at eight when he learned to walk again, and he had taught twenty-three years though that was more menial habit than passion. You had to count reading about subjects that were least in touch with his own life. But these simple things had truly filled his life and he knew them so intimately that an edge of panic entered him on considering that they might simply blow away like clouds. He could not comprehend it; the earth looked the same and this October day was not unlike a hundred other October days. He looked at the odd way his heels wore off his boots because of his walk. Even the stump was a familiar chair. Should he blame the woodcock's eyes or Catherine's body or his own fatuous brain for losing control? He looked at the fence which was in disrepair and again felt guilty about the apples. How many blankets had his mother quilted for his marriage to Rosealee? Why did he drink more and read less, and why did his favorite books bore him? He knew in some oblique way that he was no longer his father's son. He despaired that forty-three was too late for new conclusions, but he knew this was a lie. One of the doctor's favorite speeches when he was drunk was how grief made people lazy, torpid. Joseph wanted to believe that that was only the doctor's profession, that the doctor was vaguely buggy from seeing so much death. But it was too easy to remember the necessary deaths of so many of the farm animals he had been close to, how even the execution of an awful, cantankerous rooster had touched him.

On the way back to the house he shot another grouse. The grouse flushed toward him and flew low over some sumac. He made a difficult shot and that warmed him somewhat. Now there was enough for dinner. Rosealee was coming for dinner and he looked forward to their comforting though pointless conversations on whether he should begin farming full-time next year. They had accumulated a stack of equipment catalogs but the catalogs were far less interesting to Joseph than books on the ocean. He was startled by an urge to throw the woodcock into the weeds in order not to have to look at it again. But he hadn't fallen apart that much. To waste game was the ultimate crime: he despised hunters who shot crows for what they called "sport" or under the assumption that crows fed on duck eggs. Crows stayed on the farm the year round and after decades of studying their habits Joseph believed the crow to be the sole bird with any wit.

The unnerving incident followed him around throughout the season and the more he tried to erase the image of the woodcock the more insistent its presence became. He looked into the eyes of a dead grouse and felt nothing. The doctor thought of grouse as small gray chickens that flushed wildly and flew at fifty miles an hour. But they were without much character; if a chicken fed on wintergreen, chokecherries, wild grape, it would taste as good as a grouse. Grouse were splendid dinners wandering around in the forest waiting to be gathered and eaten. Now Joseph removed woodcock from this food category and allowed them to join the highest strata, that of the owls and hawks, the raptors, harriers, and *Falconiformes.* This made hunting much more difficult and his average bag dropped to the level he owned as a neophyte; he could no longer "point shoot" on instinct at the flush but had to wait an extra split second to make sure it was the gray flush of a grouse rather than the golden brown of the woodcock. His mother no longer asked him, how many, Yoey? when he came in from the hunting, noticing the irritation in his voice when he replied.

Little Frogs in a Ditch

Old man Fontenot watched his grandson draw hard on a slim cigarette and then flick ashes on the fresh gray enamel of the front porch.
The boy had been fired, this time from the laundry down the street.
The old man, who had held only one job in his life, and that one lasting forty-three years at the power plant, did not understand this.

"The guy who let me go didn't have half the brains I got," Lenny
Fontenot said.

The old man nodded, then took a swallow from a warm can of
Schlitz. "The owner, he didn't like you double-creasing the slacks"
was all he said, holding back. He watched a luminous cloud drifting
up from the Gulf.

"Let me tell you," Lenny said with a snarl, his head following a
dusk-drawn pigeon floating past the screen, "there's some dumb
people in this world. Dog-dumb."

The grandfather rolled his head to the side. Lenny was angry
about his next paycheck, the one he'd never get.

"They was dumber back in my time," the grandfather told him.

Lenny cocked his head. "What you talking about? People today
can't even spell *dumb*." He pointed two fingers holding the cigarette
toward the laundry. "If it wouldn't be for dumb people, modern
American business couldn't keep doing its thing selling fake fingernails and fold-up fishing rods."

"Give it a rest," the old man said, looking down the street to the
drizzle-washed iron roof of the laundry, where a lazy spume of steam
rose from the roof vent. His grandson was living with him again,
complaining of the evils of capitalism, eating his food, using all the
hot water in the mornings. The grandfather pulled a khaki cup over
his eyes and leaned back in his rocker, crossing his arms over a tight
green knit shirt. Lenny would never hold a job because he suffered

from inborn disrespect for anybody engaged in business. Everybody was stupid. All businessmen were crooks. At twenty-five his grandson had the economic sense of a sixty-year-old Russian peasant.

"No. Really. Other than food and stuff you need to live, what do you really have to buy?" He took a searing drag on the last of six cigarettes he had borrowed from his girlfriend, Annie. "A car? Okay. Buy a white four-door car, no chrome, no gold package, no nothing. But wait. Detroit wants you to feel bad if you buy a plain car. You got to have special paint. You got to have a stereo makes you feel Mr. Mozart is pluckin' his fiddle in the backseat. You got to have a big-nuts engine for the road. You got to have this, you got to have that, until that car costs as much as a cheap house. If you buy a plain car, you feel like a donkey at the racetrack."

His grandfather took a swig of Schlitz. "If you work on your attitude a little bit, you could keep a job."

Lenny stood up and put his nose to the screen, sniffling, as if the grandfather's statement had a bad odor. "I can keep a job if I wanted. I'm a salesman."

"You couldn't sell cow cakes to a rosebush." The old man was getting tired. His grandson had been out on the porch with him for two hours now, pulling cigarettes from his baggy jeans, finding fault with everybody but his skinny, shaggy-haired self.

Lenny threw down his cigarette and mashed it with the toe of a scuffed loafer. "As dumb as people are today I could sell bricks to a drowning man."

Grandfather Fontenot looked at the smudge on his porch. "No, you couldn't."

"I could sell falsies to a nun."

"No, you couldn't."

"I could sell"—Lenny's mouth hung open a moment as he looked down into the cemented side yard and toward the old wooden carport at the rear of the lot—"a pigeon."

His grandfather picked up his hat and looked at him. "Who the hell would buy a pigeon?"

"I could find him."

"Lenny, if someone wanted a pigeon, all he'd have to do is catch him one."

"A dumb man will buy a pigeon from *me*." He pushed open the screen door and clopped down the steps to the side yard. At the rear of the lot was a broad, unused carport, swaybacked over useless household junk: window fans, a broken lawn mower, and a wheelbarrow with a flat tire. He looked up into the eaves where the ragged nests of pigeons dripped dung down the side of a beam. With a quick grab, he had a slate blue pigeon in his hands, the bird blinking its onyx eyes stupidly. He turned to his grandfather, who was walking up stiffly behind him. "Look. You can pluck them like berries under here."

Old man Fontenot gave him a disgusted look. "Nobody'll eat a pigeon."

Lenny ducked his head. "Eat. I ain't said nothing about eat." He smiled down at the bird. "This is a homing pigeon."

The grandfather put a hand on Lenny's shoulder. "Look, let's go fix a pot of coffee and open up the *Picayune* to the employment ads. We can find something good for you to do. Come on. That thing's got fleas like a politician. Put it down." The old man pulled at his elbow.

Lenny's eyes came up red and glossy. "Your Ford's got a crack in the head and you can't even drive across the bayou for groceries. I'm gonna sell birds and get the damn old thing fixed."

His grandfather sniffed but said nothing. He knew Lenny wanted the car for himself. He looked at the bird in his grandson's hands, which was pedaling the air, blinking its drop of dark eye. The old man had never owned a dependable automobile, had always driven junk to save money for his kids and grandkids. He remembered a Sunday outing to Cypress Park when his superannuated Rambler gave up in the big intersection at Highway 90 and Federal Avenue, remembered the angry horn of a cab, the yells of his son and wife as they argued about a tow truck fee while Lenny sat on the floor by a misshapen watermelon he had stolen with care from a neighbor's garden for the picnic that never happened.

"This bird," Lenny said, turning it back into its nest, "is gonna get your car running."

"I told your parents I wouldn't let you get in any more trouble." He watched Lenny make a face. Maybe his parents couldn't care less. The grandfather remembered the boy's big room in their air-conditioned brick rancher, the house they sold from under him to buy a Winnebago and tour the country. They had been gone four months and had not called once.

For two days he watched Lenny sink deeper and deeper into a red overstuffed sofa, a forty-year-old thing his wife had won at a church bingo game. It was covered with a shiny, almost adhesive plastic, broadly incised with X's and running with dark, fiery swirls. The big cushions under Lenny hissed as he moved down into the sofa's sticky grasp. For Lenny, sitting in it must have been like living with his parents again. They were hardworking types who had tried to make him middle-class and respectable, who frowned on his efforts to manage the country's only Cajun punk salsa band, which was better, at least, than his first business of selling cracked birdseed to grammar school kids as something he called "predope," or "pot lite." One day Lenny had come home from a long weekend and everything he owned was stacked under the carport, a SOLD sign in front of the house. For a long while, he had lived with his friends in Los Head-Suckers, but even the stoned longhairs tired of his unproductive carping and one by one had turned him out.

Lenny folded back the classified section to the pet column and found his ad, which read "Homing pigeons, ten dollars each. Training instructions included," and gave the address. His grandfather read it over his shoulder, then went into the kitchen and heated two links of boudin for breakfast and put on a pot of quick grits. Lenny came in and looked over at the stove.

"You gonna cook some eggs? Annie likes eggs."

"She coming over again?" He tried to sound miffed, but in truth, he liked Annie. She was a big-boned lathe operator who worked in a machine shop down by the river, but he thought she might be a civilizing influence on his grandson.

Lenny rumbled down the steps, and his grandfather watched him through the kitchen window. From behind the carport he pulled a long-legged rabbit cage made of a coarse screen called hardware cloth, and two-by-two's. He shook out the ancient pellets and set it next to the steps. With his cigarette-stained fingers, he snatched from the eaves a granite-colored pigeon and clapped him in the cage. Most of the other birds lit out in a *rat-tat-tat* of wings, but he managed to snag a pink-and-gray, which flapped out of its nest into his waiting hands. The old man clucked his tongue and turned up the fire under the peppery boudin.

Annie came up the rear steps, lugging a rattling toolbox. By the time Lenny came and joined her, the old man had finished breakfast and was seated in the den beyond the kitchen. He didn't like being with both of them at the same time, because he felt sorry for the girl. He didn't understand how she could put up with Lenny's whining. Maybe he was the only man who would pay attention to her. She got a second helping and sat at the breakfast table, spooning grits and eggs into herself.

"Annie, baby." Lenny plopped down across from her.

"I saw that ad. The one you told me about." She broke open a loaf of French bread. "Why would anybody buy a pigeon? They're all over the place. Our backyard shed's full of 'em." She flipped her fluffy blond hair over her shoulders. "What are you trying to do?" she asked. "Prove something?" She looked up from her plate, her square jaw rising and falling under her creamy skin.

"I want to scare up some money to fix the old guy's car."

"And what else?" She chased a lump of grits out of a cheek with her tongue and brought her large cobalt eyes to bear on his.

He bunched his shoulders. "I don't know. It might be fun to see people throw away their money. You know. Like people do."

"You maybe want to find out why they do it? Or maybe you're just mad you don't have any to throw away. Am I reading your mind?"

He looked down at the table, shaking his head. "We been going out too long."

A voice came from the den. "I'll buy fifty shares a that."

Lenny spoke loudly. "I mean, she knows how I think." He put a hand palm up on the little table. "It's just that people throw money away on crazy stuff. It bothers the hell out of me. I could live for a year on what some people spend on a riding lawn mower or a red motorbike."

Annie took another bite and studied him. "You don't understand this?"

He looked away from her. "The more they get, the more they spend."

She put down her fork and glanced at her watch. She had to be down at Tiger Island Propeller by nine. "Lenny, in high school this teacher made the class read a play about an old guy was a king. I mean, it was hard reading, and she had to explain it or we wouldn'ta got much out of it, but this old guy gave his kingdom away to his two bitchy daughters with the reserve that he could keep about a hundred old fishing buddies around to pass the time with. After a while one daughter gets pissed at all the racket around the castle and cuts his pile of buddies to fifty. Well, he hits the road to his other daughter's place, and guess what?"

Lenny looked at the ceiling. "She gives him his fifty guys back and sucks the eyeballs out of the other bitch's head, right?"

Annie blinked. "You got snakes in your skull, man." She raised a thick hand and pretended to slap him. "Pay attention. This second daughter cuts him back to twenty-five and the old man blows a gasket and calls her a dozen buzzards and like that. Then the first daughter shows up and says, 'Look, what you want with ten, five, or even one old buddy? You don't really *need* 'em.'"

Lenny snorted. "Damned straight. What'd he say to that?"

Annie ducked her head. "He told them even a bum had something he didn't need, even if it was a fingernail clipper. That if he only had the things he needed, he'd be like a possum or a cow."

Lenny made a face. "What's that mean?"

The voice from the den called out, "When's the last time you saw a possum on a red motorbike?"

"What?"

Annie put a calloused hand on one of his. "An animal can't own nothing. Wouldn't want to. Owning things is what makes people different from the armadillos, Lenny. And the stuff we buy, even if it's one of your pigeons, sometimes is like a little tag telling folks who we are."

He turned sideways in his chair. "I don't believe that for a minute. If I buy a Cadillac, does that tell people I'm high-class?"

Again the voice from the den: "You could buy a pack of weenies."

"I said a Cadillac," Lenny shouted.

Annie Meyer stood up and pulled on a denim cap. "Time for work," she announced. "Walk me to the bus stop." She put her arm through his. "Hear from the parents any?"

He shook his head. "Nothin'. Not a check, not a postcard."

The grandfather followed them with a plastic bag of trash in his hand. When they reached the street, they saw a white-haired gentleman standing there staring at a torn swatch of newsprint. He was wearing nubby brown slacks and a green checkered cowboy shirt. He stuck out his hand palm down and Lenny wagged it.

"I'm Perry Lejeune from over by Broussard Street. About ten blocks. I saw your ad."

Mr. Fontenot gave his grandson a scowl and pulled off his cap as if he would toss it.

Lenny straightened out of his slouch and smiled, showing his small teeth. "Mr. Lejeune, you know anything about homing pigeons?"

The other man shook his head once. "Nah. My little nephew Alvin's living at my house and I want to get him something to occupy his time. His momma left him with me and I got to keep him busy, you know?" Mr. Lejeune raised his shoulders. "I'm too old to play ball with a kid."

"Don't worry, I'll fill you in," he said, motioning for everyone to follow him to the back of the lot next to the junk-filled carport. He put his hand on the rabbit cage and made eye contact with Mr. Lejeune. "I've got just two left. This slate"—he nodded toward the plain bird—"is good in the rain. And I got that pink fella if you want something flashy."

Mr. Lejeune put up a hand like a stop signal. "I can't afford nothing too racy, no."

"The slate's a good bird. Of course, at this price, you got to train him."

"Yeah, I want to ask you about that." Mr. Lejeune made a pliers of his right forefinger and thumb and clamped them on his chin. Annie came around close, as though she wanted to listen to the training instructions herself. The grandfather looked at the bottom of his back steps and shook his head, wondering if this would be as bad as the fake pot debacle, when thirteen high school freshmen caught Lenny coming out of Thibaut's Store and beat him into the dusty parking lot with their knobby little fists.

Lenny put his hands in the cage and caught the pigeon. "You got to build a cage out of hardware cloth with a one-way door."

"Yeah, for when he comes back, you mean."

Lenny gave Mr. Lejeune a look. "That's right. Now to start trainin', you got to hold him like a football, with your thumbs on top of him and your fingers underneath. You see?"

Mr. Lejeune put on his glasses and bent to look under the pigeon. "Uh-huh."

"You go to your property line. Stand exactly where your property line is. Then you catch his little legs between your forefingers and your middle fingers. One leg in each set of fingers, you see?" Lenny got down on his knees, wincing at the rough pavement. "You put his little legs on the ground, like this. You see?"

"Yeah, I got you."

"Then you walk the bird along your property line, moving his legs and coming along behind him like this. You got to go around all four sides of your lot with him so he can memorize what your place looks like."

"Yeah, yeah, I got you. Give him the grand tour, kinda."

Annie frowned and hid her mouth under a bright hand. His grandfather sat on the steps and looked away.

Lenny waggled the bird along the ground as the animal pumped its head, blinked, and tried to peck him. "Now, it takes commitment to train a bird. It takes a special person. Not everybody's got the character it takes to handle a homing pigeon."

Mr. Lejeune nodded. "Hey, you talking to someone's been married forty-three years. How long you got to train 'em?"

Lenny stood and replaced the bird in the cage. "Every day for two weeks, you got to do this."

"Rain or shine?" Mr. Lejeune's snowy eyebrows went up.

"That's right. And then after two weeks, you take him in a box out to Bayou Park and set his little butt loose. You can watch him fly around and then go home to wait. He might even beat you there, you know?"

The man bobbed his head. "Little Alvin's gonna love this." He reached for his wallet. "Any tax?"

"A dollar."

Mr. Lejeune handed him a ten and dug for a one. "Ain't the tax rate eight percent in the city?"

"Two percent wildlife tax," Lenny told him, reaching under the cage for a shoe box blasted with ice-pick holes.

When the man and bird had left the driveway, Lenny's grandfather cleared his throat. "I wouldn'a believed it if I didn't see it with my own eyes."

"That's capitalism—"

"Aw, stow it. You took that guy's money and he got nothin'." He started up the steps, pulling hard at the railing, but stopped at the landing to look down at them.

Lenny turned to the girl and said under his breath, "He'll feel better when I get that old Crown Vic running again." Turning to the carport, he fished out a young pigeon from the eaves, one the color of corroded lead.

"You think what you told him will work?" she asked, bending down for her glossy pink toolbox.

"Hell, I don't know what a bird thinks. Say, you got any cigarettes on you?"

"They don't let us smoke on shift." She looked at his back, which had begun to sag again. "I got to get to work," she said. "Try not to sell one to a cop, will you?"

That day Lenny sold pigeons to Mankatos Djan, a recent African immigrant who repaired hydraulics down at Cajun Hose, Lenny's simple cousin, Elmo Broussard, who lived across the river in Beewick, and two children who showed up on rusty BMX bikes. The next morning an educated-looking man showed up, made a face at Lenny's sales pitch, and got back into his sedan without a bird. Several customers had behaved like this, but by the third day he had sold a total of twenty-three pigeons and had enough to fix the leaf-covered sedan parked against the side fence. He had given everybody the same directions on how to train the birds. He told his grandfather that after two weeks, when the birds wouldn't come back at the first trial, they would chalk things up to bad luck, or maybe a skipped day of training. Not many things could take up your attention for two weeks and cost only eleven dollars, he argued.

Thirteen days after the ad first appeared, Lenny counted his money and walked up to the front porch, where his grandfather was finishing up a mug of coffee in the heat. He looked at the cash in Lenny's outstretched hand. "What's that?"

"It's enough money to fix the car."

His grandfather looked away toward the laundry. "I saw you take over twenty dollars from some children for a lousy pair of flea baits."

"Hey." Lenny drew back his hand as though it had been bitten. "It's for your car, damn it."

"That poor colored guy who couldn't hardly speak a word of English. Black as a briquette, and he believed every damned thing you told him. My grandson sticks him for eleven bucks that'd feed one of his relatives living in a grass shack back in Bogoslavia or wherever the hell he was from for a year." He looked up at Lenny, his veiny brown eyes wavering from the heat. "What's wrong with you?"

"What's wrong with me?" he yelled, stepping back. "Everybody's getting money but me. I ain't even got a job, and I come up with a way, just like everybody else does, to turn a few bucks, not even for myself, mind you, and the old fart that I want to give it to tells me to shove it."

"You don't know shit about business. You're a crook."

"All right." He banged the money against his thigh. "So I'm a crook. What's the difference between me and the guy that sells a Mercedes?"

The grandfather grabbed the arms of his rocker. "The difference is a Mercedes won't fly off toward the clouds, crap in your eye, and not come back after you paid good money for it."

Lenny jerked his head toward the street. "It's all how you look at it," he growled.

"There's only one way to look at it, damn it. The right way." His grandfather stood up. "You get out of my house. Your parents got rid of you and now I know why. Maybe a few nights down at the mission will straighten you out."

Lenny backed up another step, the money still in his outstretched hand. "Gramps, they didn't get rid of me. They moved out west."

"And it was time they did. They shoved you out the house and got you lookin' for a job, you greasy weasel." He grabbed the money so hard he came close to falling back into his chair. "I'll take that for the poor folks that'll start comin' round soon for their money back."

"They'll get eleven dollars' worth of fun out the birds."

"Get out." The old man brought his thin brows down low and beads of sweat glimmered on his bald head. "Don't come back until you get a job."

"You can't put me on the street," Lenny said, his voice softening, his face trying an ironic smile.

"Crooks wind up on the street and later they burn in hell," the old man said.

Lenny walked to the screen door and stopped, looking down North Bertaud Street where its narrow asphalt back ran toward Highway 90, which connected with the interstate, which connected with the rest of the scary world.

He kicked the bottom of the screen and his grandfather yelled. A half hour later he was standing on the sidewalk in front, holding a caramel-colored Sears suitcase, listening to the feathery pop of wings as the old man pulled pigeons out of the rabbit cage and tossed them toward the rooftops.

He walked to Breaux's Café, down by the icehouse, drank a cup of coffee, and read the paper. Then he wandered his own neighborhood, embarrassed by the huge suitcase banging his calf, enduring the stares of the women sweeping porches. He swung by Annie's house even though she was still at work. Her father sat on the stoop in his dark gray plumber's coveralls, drinking a long-neck in the afternoon heat. He watched Lenny come to him the way a fisherman eyes a rain-laden cloud. "Whatcha got in the suitcase, boy?"

Lenny set it down on the curb and motioned down the street with a wag of his head. "The old man and me, we had a discussion."

Mr. Meyer laughed. "You mean he throwed your ass in the street."

Lenny tilted his head to the side. "He's mad at me right now, but he'll cool down. I just got to find a place to stay for a night or two." He glanced up at Mr. Meyer, who looked like a poor woman's Kirk Douglas gone to seed. "You couldn't put me up, you know, just for the night?"

Mr. Meyer didn't change his expression. "Naw, Lenny. What with Annie in the house and all, it just wouldn't look right." He took a long draw, perhaps trying to finish the bottle.

"That's okay. When it gets dark, I'll just go back and sleep in his car. The backseat on that thing's plenty big enough."

"You sell all your birds?"

"He put me out of the bird business. I was just doin' it for him. I thought it was a good idea. I didn't see no harm in it."

"That's what got him hot."

"What?"

"You didn't see no harm in screwing those people. I talked to Mr. Danzig over by the laundry. He said you didn't see no harm in putting one, two extra creases in a pair of slacks. He told me on Monday some pants had more pleats than a convent schoolgirl's skirt. The trouble with you is, you ain't seeing the harm. You see what you want to see, but you ain't seeing the harm."

"I worked cheap for that old bastard. He could expect worse."

Mr. Meyer stood, took a last swig, then put the bottle in his hip pocket. "You hurt his business, boy."

"Business," Lenny said with a snarl. "It's bullshit. A business for people too lazy to iron their own clothes." He kicked his suitcase and it rolled over onto the grass, flattening an old dog dropping. Mr. Meyer threw back his head and laughed.

That night, the grandfather couldn't sleep, and he rolled up the shade at the tall window next to his bed, looking into the moonlit side yard at his old car parked against the fence. He thought about how Lenny was sweating and rolling like a log on the squeaky vinyl of the backseat, trying to sleep in the heat and mosquitoes. The old man knelt on the floor and folded his arms on the windowsill, thinking how Lenny should be back at the cleaners, smiling through the steam of his pressing machine. He remembered his own work down at the light plant, where he tended the thundering Fairbanks-Morse generators for forty years. Down in the yard, the Ford bobbled, and he imagined that Lenny was turning over, putting his nose in the crack at the bottom of the seat back, smelling the dust balls and old pennies and cigarette filters. The grandfather wondered if some dim sense of the real world would ever settle on Lenny, if he would ever appreciate Annie Meyer, her Pet-milk skin, her big curves. He had seen her once at her lathe, standing up to her white ankles in spirals of tempered steel as she machined pump rods and hydraulic pistons. Lenny talked with longing of her paychecks, nearly $2,400 a month, clear, all of which she saved. The grandfather climbed into bed but couldn't sleep because he began to see images of people Lenny had sold birds to—the dumb children, the African—and wondered why the boy had done them wrong. It was only eleven dollars he'd gotten. How could you sell your soul for eleven dollars?

At dawn he went down into the yard and opened the driver's door to the car. Lenny had used his key to turn on the power to the radio, the only thing in the car that still worked. He was listening to a twenty-four-hour heavy-metal station that was broadcasting a sound like the exhaust of a revving small-plane engine overlaid with an electrocuted voice screaming over and over something like "burgers and fries."

"That sounds like amplified puking," the old man said.

Lenny lay back against the seat and put his arm over his blood-shot eyes. "Aw, man."

His grandfather pushed on his shoulder. "You get a job yet?"

Lenny cocked up a red eye. "How'm I gonna get a job so soon? How'm I gonna get a job smelling bad, with no shave and mosquito bites all over me?"

The old man considered this a moment, looking into his grand-son's sticky eyes. He remembered the inert feel of him as a baby. "Okay. I'll give you a temporary reprieve on one condition."

"What's that?" Lenny hung his head way back over the seat.

"St. Lucy has confessions before seven o'clock daily Mass. I want you to think about going to confession and telling the priest what you done."

Lenny straightened up and eyed the house. The old man knew he was considering its deep bathtub and its oversized water heater. "Where in the catechism does it say selling pigeons is a mortal sin?"

"You going, or you staying outside in your stink?"

"What am I supposed to tell the priest?" He put his hands in his lap.

His grandfather squatted down next to him. "Remember what Sister Florita told you one time in catechism class? If you close your eyes before you go to confession, your sins will make a noise."

Lenny closed his eyes. "A noise."

"They'll cry out like little frogs in a ditch at sundown."

"Sure," Lenny said with a laugh, his eyeballs shifting under the closed lids. "Well, I don't hear nothing." He opened his eyes and looked at the old man. "What's the point of me confessing if I don't hear nothing?"

His grandfather stood up with a groan. "Keep listening," he said.

After Lenny cleaned up, they ate breakfast at a café on Tulane Avenue, and later, walking back home, they spotted Annie coming up the street, carrying her toolbox, her blond hair splashed like gold on the shoulders of her denim shirt.

The old man tipped his cap. "Hi there, Miss Annie."

She smiled at the gesture. "Mr. F. Good morning."

Lenny gave her a bump with his hip. "Annie, you're out early, babe."

She lifted her chin. "I came to see you. Daddy told me you were wandering the street like a bum." She emphasized the last word.

"The old man didn't like my last business . . ."

"It wasn't business," she snapped. Annie looked down at a work boot as though trying to control her emotions. "Lenny, yesterday morning I went walking over by Broussard Street. You know what I saw? Shut up. Let me tell you." She put down the tool box and held out her hands as though she was showing him the length of a fish. "That old Mr. Lejeune, on his knees with that damned bird you sold him, wobbling down his property line."

Lenny laughed. "That musta been a sight."

Annie looked at the grandfather, then at Lenny's eyes, searching for something. "You just don't get it, do you?"

"Get what?" When he saw her expression, he lost his smile.

She signed and looked at her watch. "Ya'll come on." She picked up her toolbox and started down the root-buckled sidewalk toward Broussard Street. After nine blocks they crossed a wide boulevard, went one more block, and stopped behind a holly bush growing next to the curb. Across the street was a peeling weatherboard house jammed between two similar houses separated by slim lanes of grass.

"This is about the time of day I saw him yesterday," Annie said.

"Who?" Lenny asked, ducking down as though afraid of being recognized.

"The old guy you sold the pigeon to."

"Jeez, you want him to see me?"

She looked at him with her big, careful blue eyes. The grandfather thought she was going to yell, but her voice was controlled. "Why are you afraid for him to see you?" She was backed into the holly bush, fresh-scrubbed for the morning shift and looking like a big Eve in the Garden.

Across the street, there was movement at the side of the house, and Mr. Lejeune came around his porch slowly, shuffling on his knees like a locomotive. The grandfather stood on his toes and saw that the old man was red in the face and that the pigeon looked tired and drunk. "Lord," he whispered, "he's got rags tied around his kneecaps."

"Yesterday I saw he wore the tips off his shoes," Annie told him. "Look at that." Behind Mr. Lejeune walked a thin boy, awkward and pale. "Didn't he say he had a nephew?" The boy was smiling and talking down to his uncle. "The kid looks excited about something."

"Two weeks," Lenny said.

"Huh?" The Grandfather cupped a hand behind an ear.

"Today's two weeks. They'll probably go to Bayou Park this afternoon and turn it loose."

Mr. Lejeune looked up and across toward where they were standing. He bent to the side a bit and then lurched to his feet, waving like a windshield wiper. "Hey, what ya'll doing on this side of the boulevard?"

The three of them crossed the street and stood on the short stretch of capsizing walk that led to a wooden porch. "We was just out for a morning walk," Lenny told him. "How's the bird doin'?" The pigeon seemed to look up at him angrily, blinking, struggling. Someone had painted its claws with red fingernail polish.

"This here's Amelia," Mr. Lejeune said. "That's what Alvin named her." He looked at his nephew. The grandfather saw that the boy was trembling in spite of his smile. His feet were pointed inward, and his left hand was shriveled and pink.

"How you doing, bud?" the grandfather asked, patting his head.

"All right," the boy said. "We goin' to the park at four o'clock and turn Amelia loose.

Lenny forced a smile. "You and your uncle been having a good time training old Amelia, huh?"

The boy looked over to where his uncle had gone to sit on the front steps. He was rubbing his knees. "Yeah. It's been great. The first day, we got caught out in a thunderstorm and I got a chest cold, but the medicine made me feel better."

"You had to go to the doctor?" Annie asked, touching his neck.

"Him, too," the boy volunteered in a reedy voice. "Shots in the legs." He looked up at Lenny. "It'll be worth it when Amelia comes back from across town."

"Why's it so important?" Lenny asked.

The boy shrugged. "It's just great that this bird way up in the sky knows which house I live in."

"Hey," Mr. Lejeune called. "You want me to put on some water?"

"No thanks," the grandfather said. "We had coffee already."

The old man struggled to his feet, untying the pads from his knees. "At least come in the backyard and look at the cage." He shook out his pants and tugged the boy toward the rear of the house to a close-clipped yard with an orange tree in the middle. Against the rear of the house was a long-legged cage shiny with new galvanized hardware cloth.

"That took a lot of work to build, I bet," the grandfather said to Lenny, who shrugged and said that he'd told him how to do it. The corners of the cage were finished like furniture, mortised and tenoned. In the center was a ramp leading up to a swinging door. The pigeon squirted out of the old man's hand and flew into the cage, crazy for the steel-mesh freedom.

"We'll let her rest up for the big flight," Mr. Lejeune said.

Lenny glanced over at Annie's face. She looked long at the pigeon, then over to where the boy slumped against the orange tree. "You know, if you decide you ain't happy with the bird, you can have your money back."

Mr. Lejeune looked at him quickly. "No way. She's trained now. I bet she could find this house from the North Pole."

Lenny smiled. "I knew it. Another satisfied customer."

The grandfather told Mr. Lejeune how much he liked the cage.

"Aw, this ain't nothin'," he said. "Before my back give out, I was working for Delta Desk and Chair, thirty-six years in the bookcase division. Man, you could pass your hand over my seams and it felt like glass if you closed your eyes." He waved a flattened palm over the cage is if he was working a spell.

The grandfather touched Annie's shoulder and they said their good-byes. On the walk home, she was silent. When they got to his grand-father's, she stopped, rattled her little toolbox, and did not look at either of them. Finally, she looked back down the street and asked, "Lenny, what's gonna happen if that bird doesn't come back to the kid?"

He shook his head. "If she flies for the river and spots them grain elevators, she'll never see Broussard Street again, that's for sure."

"Two weeks ago you knew he was buying Amelia as a pet for a kid."

Lenny turned his palms out. "Am I responsible for everything those birds do until they die?"

The grandfather rolled his eyes at the girl. She wasn't stupid, but when she looked at Lenny, there was too much hope in her eyes.

Annie clenched and unclenched her big pale hands. "If I was a bad sort, I'd hit you with a crescent wrench."

Lenny blinked twice, perhaps trying to figure what she wanted to hear. The grandfather knew that she paid for their dates when the boy was out of work. She bought his cigarettes and concert tickets and let him hang around her house when something good was on cable. Often she looked at him the way she studied whatever gadget was whirling in her lathe, maybe wondering if he would come out all right.

Lenny lit up a cigarette and let the smoke come out as he talked. "I'm sorry. I'll try to think of something to tell the kid if the bird don't come back."

She considered this for a moment, then leaned over and kissed him quickly on the side of his mouth. As he watched her stride down the sidewalk, the grandfather listened to the Williams sockets rattling in her toolbox, and he watched Lenny wipe off the hot wetness of her lips.

That night, a half hour after dark, Annie, Lenny, and his grandfather were watching a John Wayne movie in the den when there was a knock at the rear screen door. It was Mr. Lejeune, and he was worried about Amelia.

"I turnt her loose about four-thirty and she ain't come back yet." The old man combed his hair with his fingers and peered around Lenny to where Annie sat in a lounger. "You got any hints?"

Lenny looked at a shoe. "Look, why don't you let me give your money back."

"Naw." He shook his head. "That ain't the point. The boy's gonna get a lift from seeing the bird come back." Alvin's pale face tilted out from behind his uncle's waist.

Annie, who was wearing shorts, peeled herself off the plastic couch, and the grandfather put a spotted hand over his eyes. Lenny turned a serious face toward Mr. Lejeune.

"Sometimes those birds get in fights with other birds. Sometimes they get hurt and don't make it back. What can I tell you? You want your money?" He put a hand in his pocket but left it there.

The old man sidestepped out onto the porch. "Me and Alvin will just go and wait. If that bird'd just come back once, it'd be worth all the crawling around, you see?" He held the boy's twisted hand and went down ahead of him one step at a time. Annie moved into the kitchen and broke a glass in the sink. The grandfather tried not to listen to what happened next.

Lenny went into the kitchen to see what had caused the noise, and met a rattle of accusations from Annie.

Then Lenny began to shout. "Why are you bitching at me like this?"

"Because you gypped that old man and the crippled kid. I've never seen you do nothing like that."

"Well, you better get used to it."

"Get used to what?" She used a big contrary voice better than most women, the grandfather thought.

"Get used to doing things the way I like."

"What, like stealing from old people and kids? Acting like a freakin' slug? Now I know why your parents left your ass in the street."

Lenny's voice came through the kitchen door, thready and high-pitched. "Hey, nobody left me. They're on vacation, you cow."

"People on vacation don't sell their houses, leave the time zone, and never write or call. They left because they found out what it took me a long time to just now realize."

"What's that?"

And here a sob came into her voice and the grandfather put his head down.

"That there's a big piece of you missing that'll never turn up."

"You can't talk to me like that," Lenny snarled, "and I'll show you why." The popping noise of a slap came from the kitchen and the grandfather thought, *Oh no*, and struggled to rise from the sofa, but before he could stand and steady himself, a sound like a piano tipping over shook the entire house, and Lenny cried out in deep pain.

After the grandfather prepared an ice pack, he went to bed that night but couldn't sleep. He thought of the handprint on Annie's face and the formal numbness of the walk back to her house as he escorted her home. Now he imagined Mr. Lejeune checking Amelia's cage into the night, his nephew asking him questions in a resigned voice. He even formed a picture of the pigeon hunkered down on a roof vent above the St. Mary Feed Company elevator, trying with its little bird brain to remember where Broussard Street was. About one o'clock he smacked himself on the forehead with an open palm, put on his clothes, and went down to the old carport with a flashlight. In the eaves he saw a number of round heads pop into his light's beam, and when he checked the section from which Lenny had plucked Amelia, he thought he saw her. Turning off the light for a moment, he reached into the straw and pulled out a bird that barely struggled. Its claws were painted red, and the grandfather eased down into a wheelbarrow to think, holding the bird in both hands, where it pecked him resignedly. He debated whether he should just let the animal go and forget the Lejeunes, but then he imagined how the boy would have to face the empty cage. It would be like an abandoned house, and every day the boy would look at it and wonder why Amelia had forgotten where he lived. He held the bird and thought of Lenny's parents probably parked in a Winnebago in some canyon in Utah, flown off that far to escape him, his mooching and his music. Why had they really left him? The old man shook his head.

At two-fifteen the grandfather walked down the side of Mr. Lejeune's house, staying close to the wall and out of the glow of the streetlight. When he turned the corner into the backyard, he was in total darkness and had to feel for the cage, and then for its little swinging gate. His heart jumped as he felt a feathery escape from his palms, and the bird squirted into the enclosure. At that instant, a backyard floodlight came on and the rear door rattled open, showing Mr. Lejeune standing in a pair of mustard-colored pajama bottoms and a sleeveless undershirt.

"Hey, whatcha doing?" He came down into the yard, moving stiffly.

The grandfather couldn't think of a lie to save his soul, just stood there looking between the cage and the back door. "I wanted to see about the bird," he said at last.

The other man walked up and looked into the cage. "What? How'd you get ahold of the dumb cluck? I thought she'd be in Texas by now." He reached back and scratched a hip.

The grandfather's mouth slowly fell open. "You knew."

"Yeah," Mr. Lejeune growled. "I may be dumb, but I ain't stupid. And no offense, Mr. Fontenot, but that grandson of yours got used-car salesman writ all over him."

"Why'd you come by the house asking about the bird if you knew it'd never come back?"

"That was for Alvin, you know? I wanted him to think I was worried." Mr. Lejeune grabbed the grandfather by the elbow and led him into his kitchen, where the two men sat down at a little porcelain-topped table. The old man opened the refrigerator and retrieved two frosty cans of Schlitz. "It's like this," Mr. Lejeune said, wincing against the spray from the pull tabs, "Little Alvin's never had a daddy and his momma's a crackhead that run off with some biker to Alaska." He pushed a can to the grandfather, who picked it up and drew hard, for he was sweating. Mr. Lejeune spoke low and leaned close. "Little Alvin's still in fairy-tale land, you know. Thinks his momma is coming back when school takes up in the fall. But he's got to toughen up and face facts. That's why I bought that roof rat from your grandson." He sat back and began rubbing his knees. "He'll be disappointed about the little thing, that bird, and maybe it'll teach him to deal with the big thing. That boy's got to live a long time, you know what I mean, Mr. Fontenot?"

The grandfather put his cap on the table. "Ain't that kind of mean, though?"

"Hey. We'll watch the sky for a couple days and I'll let him see how I take it. We'll be disappointed together." Mr. Lejeune looked down at his purple feet. "He's crippled, but he's strong and he's smart."

The grandfather lifted his beer and drank until his eyes stung. He remembered Lenny, asleep in the front bedroom with a big knot on the back of his head and a black eye. He listened to Mr. Lejeune until he was drowsy. "I got to get back home," he said, standing up and moving toward the door. "Thanks for the beer."

"Hey. Don't worry about nothing. Just do me a favor and put that bird back in its nest." They went out and Mr. Lejeune reached into the cage and retrieved Amelia, dropping her into a heavy grocery bag.

"You sure you doing the right thing, now?" the grandfather asked. "You got time to change your mind." He helped fold the top of the bag shut. "You could be kind." He imagined what the boy's face would look like if he could see that the bird had returned to the cage.

Mr. Lejeune slowly handed him the bag. For a moment they held it together and listened. Inside, the bird walked the crackling bottom back and forth on its painted toes, looking for home.

SARAH GETTY

That Woman

Look! A flash of orange along the river's edge—
"oriole!" comes to your lips like instinct, then
it's vanished—lost in the foliage,

in all your head holds, getting on with the day.
But not gone for good. There is that woman
walks unseen beside you with her apron

pockets full. Days later, or years, when you least
seem to need it—reading Frost on the subway,
singing over a candled cake—she'll reach

into a pocket and hand you this intact
moment—the river, the orange streak parting
the willow, and the "oriole!" that leapt

to your lips. Unnoticed, steadfast, she gathers
all this jumble, sorts it, hands it back like
prizes from Cracker Jack. She is your mother,

who first said, "Look! a robin!" and pointed
and there was a robin, because her own
mother had said to her, "Look!" and pointed,

and so on, back to the beginning: the mother,
the child, and the world. The damp bottom
on one arm and pointing with the other:

the peach tree, the small rocks in the shallows,
the moon and the man in the moon. So you keep on,
seeing, forgetting, faithfully followed;

and you yourself, unwitting, gaining weight,
have thinned to invisibility, become
that follower. Even now, your daughter

doesn't see you at her elbow as she walks
the beach. There! a gull dips to the Pacific,
and she points and says to the baby, "Look."

B. J. BUCKLEY

In June, In Summer

Two afternoons ago. The gravel road to Carlton Creek, narrow
ditches on both sides running high with irrigation overflow.
A bird—folded into the grass, not bloody, as if it had just
fallen toward the common mercy of gravity's worn teeth,
though I was sure some pickup's shiny grill had caught it
and flung it down. Magpie. Green embers burned
in the midnight sapphire of its head and bent long wing
and tail, and the breast was white, so white, like the company
tablecloth at Thanksgiving, or snow, or stars. There were ants
making quick inroads beneath the feathers, and tiny black
round beetles, and two of its own kind patient on the fence
till my departure should give them leave to open the unmarked
belly with their razoring beaks. To feast. To peck out the eyes.
And soon would come for what had ripened in the long day's
shimmering heat, small others—stealthy, fleetfoot, furred.

I'd stopped for the feathers, a looter, a thief like any other,
then looked too long—at the downy fuzz, almost imperceptible,
where its bill met the sleek head, the small feet curled
around a branch of air, the scaly eyelids and the insect hurry,
at the grass bent to shelter it, a better nest than that mess
of sticks in life it was content with—and I couldn't take them.
Let its ghost go flying. I wanted then to offer
some apology, some murmur like a prayer, a soft last word.
But in the face of raucous beauty quieted, subsiding
already sweetly toward decay, it came to this—
I knelt to lay my breath against its breathless body
and spoke nothing.

Tonight in a field of fragrant timothy its mate will tear
a bit of carrion from a broken rabbit, and then from a perch
in jackpine or leaning cottonwood she'll search the purple
air for wings as the last light goes. A thing like grief
must overtake her. Silent somewhere waits a widowed bird.

Maxine Kumin

Bringing Down the Birds

For Christopher Cokinos

Does it make you wince to hear
how the last of the world's great auks
were scalded to death on the Newfoundland coast
in vats of boiling water so that
birdshot would not mutilate the feathers
that stuffed the mattress your great-grandparents
lay upon, begetting your forebears?

Are you uncomfortable reading how
the flocks of passenger pigeons
that closed over the sky like an eyelid
the millions that roared like thunder
like trains, like tornados were wiped out, expunged
in a free-for-all a hundred years gone?
Can you bear the metaphor in how it was done?

Pet pigeons, their eyelids sewn, were tied
to stools a few feet off the ground until
hordes of their kind swooped overhead.
Released, their downward flutter lured
the multitude who were smothered in nets
while trappers leaped among them
snapping their necks with pincers.
The feathers from fifty pigeons
added up to a pound of bedding.

Does it help to name the one-or-two-of-a-kind
Martha or Rollie and exhibit them in a zoo
a kindly zoo with moats in place of wire

or clone from fished-up bits of DNA
a creature rather like the creature
it had been, left to the whim of nature?

Would bringing the ivory bill back from deep woods
to a greenhouse earth placate the gods?
The harlequin-patterned Labrador duck
the dowdy heath hen, the gregarious Carolina parakeet
that once bloomed like daffodils in flight,
if science could reconstruct them, how long
would it take us logging and drilling and storing up
treasures to do them all in again?

ANDREW HUDGINS

Raven Days

These are what my father calls
our raven days. The phrase is new
to me. I'm not sure what it means.
If it means we're hungry, it's right.
If it means we live on carrion,
it's right. It's also true
that every time we raise a voice
to sing, we make a caw and screech,
a raucous keening for the dead,
of whom we have more than our share.
But the raven's an ambiguous bird.
He forebodes death, and yet he fed
Elijah in the wilderness
and doing so fed all of us.
He knows his way around a desert
and a corpse, and these are useful skills.

Richard Wilbur

The Writer

In her room at the prow of the house
Where light breaks, and the windows are tossed with linden,
My daughter is writing a story.

I pause in the stairwell, hearing
From her shut door a commotion of typewriter-keys
Like a chain hauled over a gunwale.

Young as she is, the stuff
Of her life is a great cargo, and some of it heavy:
I wish her a lucky passage.

But now it is she who pauses,
As if to reject my thought and its easy figure.
A stillness greatens, in which

The whole house seems to be thinking,
And then she is at it again with a bunched clamor
Of strokes, and again is silent.

I remember the dazed starling
Which was trapped in that very room, two years ago;
How we stole in, lifted a sash

And retreated, not to affright it;
And how for a helpless hour, through the crack of the door,
We watched the sleek, wild, dark

And iridescent creature
Batter against the brilliance, drop like a glove
To the hard floor, or the desk-top,

And wait then, humped and bloody,
For the wits to try it again; and how our spirits
Rose when, suddenly sure,

It lifted off from a chair-back,
Beating a smooth course for the right window
And clearing the sill of the world.

It is always a matter, my darling,
Of life or death, as I had forgotten. I wish
What I wished you before, but harder.

Emory Bear Hands' Birds

My name is Julio Sangremano. I was at the federal prison at Estamos, California, when the incident of the birds occurred, serving three to five for computer service theft, first offense. This story has been told many times, mostly by people who were not there that day, or by people who have issues about corruption in the prison system or class politics being behind the war on drugs, and so on. The well-known Mr. William Hanover of the Aryan Brotherhood, he was there, and also the person we called Judy Hendrix; but they sold their stories, so there you're talking about what people want to buy.

I didn't leave that day, though I was one of Emory's men. Why I stayed behind is another story, but partly it is because I could not leave the refuge of my hatred, the anger I feel toward people who flick men like me away, a crumb off the table. Sometimes I am angry at people everywhere for their stupidity, for their buying into the American way, going after so many products, selfish goals, and made-up desires. Whatever it was, I stayed behind in my cell and watched the others go. The only obligation I really felt was to the Indian, Emory Bear Hands. Wishako Taahne Tliskocho, that was his name, but everyone called him Emory and he didn't mind. When I asked him once, he said that when he was born, his fists came out looking like bears. He was in for theft, stealing salmon. Guys who knew the history of what had happened to the Indians thought that was good; they said it with a knowing touch of irony. Emory, he didn't see himself that way.

I was put in his cell block in 1997 when I went in, a bit of luck, but I want to say I was one of the ones who convinced him to hold the classes, to begin teaching about the animals. Emory told us people running the country didn't like wild animals. They believed they were always in the way and wanted them killed or put away in zoos, like they put the Indians away on reservations. If animals went on living in the countryside, Emory said, and had a right not to be disturbed, then that meant the land wouldn't be available to the mining companies and the timber companies. What they wanted, he said, was to get the logs and the ore out and then get the land going again as different kinds of parks, with lots of deer and Canada geese, and lots of recreation, sport hunting, and boating.

I'd never heard anything like this, and in the beginning I didn't listen. Wild animals had nothing to do with my life. Animals were dying all over the place, sure, and for no good reason, but people were also dying the same. I was going with the people. Two things, though, started working on my mind. One time, Emory was speaking to a little group of five or six of us, explaining how animals forgive people. He said this was an amazing thing to him, that no matter how much killing and cruelty animals endured—all the songbirds kids shot, all their homes plowed up for spring planting, being run over by cars—they forgave us. In the early history of people, he said, everyone made mistakes with the animals. They took their fur for clothing, ate their flesh, used their skins to make shelters, used their bones for tools, but back then they didn't know to say any prayers of gratitude. Now people do—some of them. He said the animals even taught people how to talk, that they gave people language. I didn't follow that part of the story, but I was familiar with people making mistakes—animals getting killed in oil spills, say. And if you looked at it the way Emory did, also their land being taken away by development companies. It caught my interest that Emory believed animals still forgave people. That takes some kind of generosity. I'd wonder, when would such a thing ever end? Would the last animal, eating garbage and living on the last scrap of land, his mate dead, would he still forgive you?

The other thing that drew me in to Emory was what he said about totem animals. Every person, he told us, has an animal companion, a sort of guardian. Even if you never notice it, the animal knows. Even when you're in prison, he said, there's an animal on the outside, living in the woods somewhere, who knows about you, and who will answer your prayers and come to you in a dream. But you have to make yourself worthy, he said. You have to make a door in yourself where the animal can get through, and you have to make sure that when the animal comes inside that way, in a dream, he sees something that will make him want to come back. "He has to feel comfortable in there," Emory said.

Emory didn't say all this at once, like you'd read in a book, everything there on the page. If someone asked him a question, he'd try to answer. That's how it began, I think, before I got there, a few respectful questions. Emory conducted himself in such a way, even the guards showed him some respect. He wouldn't visit with the same people every day; and when guys tried to hang with him all the time, he discouraged it. Instead, he'd tell people to pass on to others some of the animal stories he was telling. When someone was getting out, he'd remind them to be sure to take the stories along.

The population at Estamos was changing in those days. It wasn't quite like the mix you see on the cop shows. Most everybody, of course, was from the street—L.A., Fresno, Oakland—and, yeah, alot of Chicanos, blacks, and Asians in for the first time on drug charges. And we had hard-core, violent people who were never going to change, some difficult to deal with, some of them insane, people who should have been in a hospital. The new element was people in for different kinds of electronic fraud, stock manipulations, hacking. Paper crime. I divide this group into two types. One was people like me who believed the system was so corrupt they just wanted to jam it up, make it tear itself apart. I didn't care, for example, about selling what I got once I broke into Northrup's files. I just wanted to scare them. I wanted to hit them right in the face. The second group, I put them right in there with the child molesters, the Jeffrey Dahmers. Inside traders, savings and loan thieves who took money from people who had nothing, people who got together these dime-a-dozen dreams—Chivas Regal for lunch, you know, five cars, a condo in Florida. Every one of them I met was a coward, and the cons made their lives miserable. Of course, we didn't see many of these real money guys at Estamos.

We had the gangs there, the Aryan Brotherhood, Crips, Dragons,

Bloods, all the rest. These could be very influential people, but the paper and electronic criminals, the educated guys, almost all white, they passed on it. If one of these guys, though, was a certain type of individual to start with, he might help a gang member out. Even mean people. Even not your own race. Prepare their appeals, lead them through the different kinds of hell the legal system deals you.

Emory, who was about fifty, was a little bit like those guys. He spoke the same way to everyone, stayed to himself. Even some of the Aryan brothers would come around when he talked. The only unusual thing I noticed was a few of the more educated whites made a point of ignoring Emory. They'd deliberately not connect with him. But there were very few jokes. Emory was the closest thing to a real spiritual person most of us had ever seen, and everybody knew, deep down, this was what was wrong with the whole country. Its spiritual life was gone.

When I first asked Emory about teaching, he acted surprised, as though he thought the idea was strange, but he was just trying to be polite. My feeling was that by telling stories the way he could, he was giving people a way to deal with the numbness. And by identifying with these animal totems, people could imagine a way over the wall, a healing, a solid connection on the outside.

Emory declined. He said people had been telling these stories for thousands of years, and he was just passing them on, keeping them going. Some of the others, though, talked to him about it, kept bringing it up, and we got him to start telling us, one animal at a time, everything he had heard about that animal, say grizzly bears or moose or even yellow jackets. Some guys wanted to learn about animals Emory didn't know about, like hyenas or kangaroos. He said he could only talk about the ones he knew, so we learned about animals in northern Montana where he grew up.

Emory spoke for about an hour every day. The guards weren't supposed to let this go on, an organized event like this, but they did. Emory would talk about different kinds of animals and how they were all related and what they did and where they came from—as Emory understood it. Emory got pretty sophisticated about this, and we had some laughs too, even the guards. Sometimes Emory would imitate the way an animal behaved, and he'd have us pounding on the tables and crying with laughter, watching while he waddled along like a porcupine or pounced on a mouse like a coyote. One time he told us there was so much he didn't know, but that he knew many of these things had been written down in books by white people, by people who had spoken to his ancestors or by people who had studied those animals. None of those books were in the prison library, but one of the guards had an outside library card, and he started bringing the books in so Emory could study them.

For a couple of months, a long time, really, it went along like this. People wanted to tell their own stories in the beginning, about hunting deer or seeing a mountain lion once when they were camping. Emory would let them talk, but no one had the kind of knowledge he had, and that kind of story faded away. The warden knew what Emory was doing and he could have shut it right down, but sometimes they don't go by the book in prison because nobody knows what reforms people. Sometimes an experiment like this works out, and the warden may get credit. So he left us alone, and once we knew he was going to leave Emory alone our wariness disappeared. We could pay attention without being afraid.

That tension came back only once, when Emory asked if he could have a medicine pipe sent in, if he could share the pipe around and make that part of the ceremony. No way, they said.

So Emory just talked.

Two interesting things were going on now. First, Emory had drawn our attention to animals most of us felt were not very important. He talked about salamanders and prairie dogs the same way he talked about wolverine and buffalo. So some guys started to identify with these animals, like garter snakes or wood rats, and not with wolves. That didn't make any difference to us now.

The second thing was that another layer of personality began to take hold on the cell block. Of the one hundred and twenty of us, about sixty or sixty-five listened to Emory every day. We each had started to gravitate toward a different animal, all of them living in this place where Emory grew up in Montana. Even when we were locked up we had this sense of being a community, dependent on each other. Sometimes in our cells at night we would cry out in our dreams in those animal voices.

I identified with the striped skunk, an animal Emory said was slow to learn and given to fits of anger and very independent in its ways. It is a nocturnal creature, like me. When I began dreaming about the striped skunk, these dreams were unlike any I had had before. They were long and vivid. The voices were sometimes very clear. In most of these dreams, I would just follow the skunk, watching him do things. I'd always thought animals like this were all the time looking for food, but that's not what the skunk did. I remember one winter night (in the dream) I followed the skunk across hard-crusted snow and along a frozen creek to a place near a small treeless hill where he just sat and watched the stars for a long time. In another dream, I followed the skunk into a burrow where a female had a den with two other females. It was spring, and there were more than a dozen small skunks there in the burrow. The male skunk had brought two mice with him. I asked Emory about this, describing the traveling and everything. Yes, he said, that's what they did, and that's what the country he grew up in looked like.

After people started dreaming like this, about the animals that had chosen each of us (as we understood it now), our routine changed. All the maneuvering to hold positions of authority or safety on the cell block, the constant testing to see who was in control, who was the most dangerous, who had done the worst things, for many of us this was no longer important. We'd moved into another place.

Emory himself didn't make people nervous, but what was happening to the rest of us now did. The guards, just a little confused, tried to look tougher, figure it out. Any time you break down the tension in prison, people can find themselves. The gangs on our block, except for the Aryan Brotherhood, had unraveled a little by this time. People were getting together in these other groups called "Horned

Lark" and "Fox" and "Jackrabbit." Our daily schedule, of course, never changed—meals, lights out, showers—but all through it now was this thing that had gotten into us.

What was happening was, people weren't focused on the prison routine anymore, like the guards playing us off against one another, or driving each other's hatred up every day with stories about how we'd been set up, who was really to blame, how hard we were going to hit back one day. We had taken on other identities, and the guards couldn't get inside there. They began smacking people around for little things, stupid things. People like Judy Hendrix, who thrived on the sexual undercurrents and the brutality on our cell block, started getting violent with some of their clients. The Aryan brothers complained Emory had stirred up primitive feelings, "African feelings," they called them. Their righteousness and the frustration of the guards and the threat of serious disruption from people like Judy Hendrix all made Emory's situation precarious.

One day the story sessions just ended. They moved Emory to another cell block and then, we heard, to Marion in Illinois. With him gone, most of us fell back into the daily routine again, drifting through, trying to keep the boredom at bay. But you could hear those dream calls in the night still, and people told stories, and about a month after Emory left one of the guards smuggled the letter in from him that everybody has heard about, but which only Emory's people actually read. And then we destroyed it. He told us to hold on to our identities, to seek the counsel of our totem animals, to keep the stories going. We had started something and we had to finish it, he said. By the night of the full moon, June 20, he wrote, each one of us had to choose some kind of bird—a sparrow, a thrush, a crow, a warbler—and on that night, wherever he was, Emory was going to pray each of us into those birds. We were going to become those birds. And they were going to fly away.

There were some who accepted right away that this was going to happen and others who were afraid. I would like to say that I was skeptical, but I was one of those who was afraid, a person for whom fear was the emotion on which everything else turned. I could not believe.

We got the letter on the fourteenth of June. The beatings from the guards, with people like Hanover and Judy Hendrix having a hand in it, none of that affected the hard-core believers, the guys they put in solitary. Especially not them. In solitary they'd turn themselves into the smallest birds, they said, and walk under the doors.

In that week after the letter came, a clear line began to divide us, the ones who were leaving, the ones who were going to stay.

The night of the twentieth, about eight o'clock, sitting around in the TV room, I was trying to stay with a game show when a blackbird landed on the table. It cocked his head and looked around the way they do. Then I saw a small flock of birds like finches out in the corridor, swooping up and landing on the hand railings on the second tier. A few seconds later the whole cell block was full of shouting and birdsong. The alarms started screaming and the guards stormed in. They beat us back into our cells, but by then birds were all over the place, flying up and down, calling out to the rest of us. My cellmate, Eddie Reethers, told me he was going to be a wild pigeon, a rock dove, and it was a pigeon that hopped through the bars and flew past me to the window of the cell. He kept shifting on his feet and gazing down at me, and then he stepped through the bars out onto the ledge and flew away. I ran to see. In the clear air, with all that moonlight, I could see twenty or so birds flying around. I jumped back to the cell door. As many were flying through the corridor, in and out of the cells. The guards were swinging away at them, missing every time.

Five minutes and it was all over. They shut the alarms off. The guards stood around looking stupid. Seventy-eight of us were at the doors of our cells or squeezed up against the bars of the windows, watching the last few birds flying off in the moonlight, into the darkness.

In the letter, Emory told us the birds would fly to Montana, to the part of northern Montana along the Marias River where he grew up, and that each person would then become the animal that he had dreamed about. They would live there.

MAYA SONENBERG

Beyond Mecca

Down past Mecca there is a tremendous inland sea. I know because
I've seen it, the Salton Sea, stretching way across the desert valley in
the morning, flat and blue. I drove there all unawares, a series of accidents—*farblondjet*, Mama would have said, *like a chicken with her
head cut off*—but now I'm going back. "Meshugge," my older sister
Rose said when I told her. I was on my way to visit her when I saw it
first. "What do you need it for?" she said. Yes . . . but I'm on my way
now, driving from the two-bedroom in Santa Monica that she wanted
me to share. Something happened there, in Santa Monica, where the
ocean glittered, and the palm trees were coddled and ornamental, and
the crowds of young people biked and skated and bared their bellies.
Or maybe something happened in the desert—before I even got to
the ocean. But today, after a week of Rose insisting I live with her—
"the best place in the world," she said; a week of mornings sitting on
a bench, waiting for her friends to find us and chat; a week of afternoons with Rose first asking for a magazine, then a book, then the
television on, then off, then the radio turned just to one particular
station and a nice hot cup of tea—I fled. I got back in the rental car
and drove east, through one suburb after another, past the exit for
Disneyland.

When I was in New York, my niece Phyllis called—the hysteri-
cal one—and then my nephew Danny—the doctor like his father:
"Come. Your sister Rose needs you. She's been so difficult since Dad
died."

"Of course I'll come," I agreed. I am alone, after all, the healthy
sister, the one without any obligations, and I felt sorry for them—so
many years of their mother looking after them, and now they had to
look after her. I knew what that was like. And both of them busy
with their own lives: the children, the work, the husband away on

business for six months overseas. And I had just retired after thirty-five years of service, had been given a gold-plated pen by Mr. Jenson and a chocolate bar in the shape of a typewriter. I left my bookcases in New York, the set of Dostoyevsky I've been saving to reread, and flew to Phoenix. There, for a week I stayed with our cousin who's turned the desert into a beautiful garden just like the one she tended in New Rochelle. Beautiful roses—"They grow even better out here," she said, "as long as you water them enough." In the mornings, I always found her outside with her hose. She wanted me to stay, too. "So many people retiring here now, nice people," she said. But I remembered how I had never gardened anything, not even a window box, and I left with the promise I'd come for another visit—when, I couldn't say. In the Phoenix airport, the plane was late, not even taking off from Chicago yet, so I went to the Avis counter instead of the ticket counter. Do you see what I mean by an accident? But at that moment I just thought, a nice drive, a vacation that I deserved after all these years, and besides, by the time that plane gets here, I might already be with Rose. "Tsuris, nothing but tsuris," Rose said, "asking for trouble," when I explained, but it turned out the drive was easy, all the way to the California border. Eight o'clock, a balmy spring night. Back in New York, it's still winter, freezing rain, snow maybe, certainly cold. And on the map California looked so skinny, so easy to drive across and come to Rose's while still she was watching the *Tonight Show.* When I noticed the gas getting low, I pulled out the map again to look at. The road was short to Mecca and I could have a little break. I could stretch my legs, get a cup of coffee, and visit the ladies' room.

But Mecca was further than I thought, and the road was very dark and narrow when the highway lights disappeared. I was scared but mostly of running out of gas and then the next day, where would I be? Stranded alone in the desert. "What mishegoss!" Rose said when I told her I ended up sleeping in the car's backseat, my skirt wrapped around my knees, but what else could I do, other than wait for morning? "Like a bag lady," she said, but I hadn't thought of that. I was too busy trying not to be frightened. Before I fell asleep, I heard scurrying things outside but I knew they couldn't be people, so I locked all the car doors and hoped for the best. In the morning, I fixed hair and lipstick in the rearview mirror and headed on instead of back, which is what any sane person would have done—gone back to the main road. But I went on, looking for that gas station, because, God knows, it couldn't be far.

And you see, this is how I kissed an egret and how I ended up with Donna, but I'll get to that. The road ran between hills of sandy rock that had been made into craggy shapes—from too much scouring, I thought, like with a steel wool pad. There were a few dry squeaking trees, brown signs with no words, wheel tracks heading off into the canyons, and above a blue sky like its own river up there between the banks of the hills. I tried to tell Rose about the cool dry morning and how ahead of me were purple shadows made by strange shapes in the rocks and behind me was nothing but hot sun, but she said, "Oy, I don't understand this whole business of driving. You were supposed to fly. You know, the stewardesses tell jokes—funny ones even—while they show you how the seatbelt works." Then she said, "But you're here now," and we looked at each other, we who hadn't seen each other since after Mama died, maybe a dozen years, a long long time. "You're here now," she repeated. "We're too old for such adventures. You're seventy years old, Rachel. My *children* are too old for such things now—sleeping in a car. Even the *grandchildren* have more sense; they at least bring a tent, a sleeping bag." Between talking, she wheezed. "It's not becoming," she said, and stared at me just like she did when we were children and I did something wrong. Such a long time ago and the same look. She wanted me to stay, every day she told me. Her children wanted me to stay. I could take the other bedroom. The weather's so much better here, they said, and I would have things to do: I could let in the night nurse, do the shopping and cooking, and call the doctors for appointments. I could pick the grandchildren up from school while Rose napped and wait for them at their piano lessons. "You're so good at taking care of things," Phyllis said. When Rose dozed off, I got up and looked out her window at the ocean and the palm trees and all the people in the park above the beach exchanging pictures of their grandchildren and playing canasta. I hadn't played since I don't know how long, but I remembered it used to be fun. If I stayed, I'd have to learn again. We'd been down there earlier—me with a magazine and Rose with her oxygen canisters. Very pleasant—not too hot, the sun not too bright.

But I kept thinking about Mecca, a little nothing of a town laid out in the desert, where on Thursday morning every child in the county was coming for school—little ones in shorts and T-shirts, dragging their backpacks on the dusty ground, teenage girls in short skirts, and boys driving up fast in pickup trucks. I drove around and around, avoiding those meshuggener teenage drivers and looking for some place to have breakfast, a cup of coffee at least, but there were no restaurants. Can you imagine—a town with no restaurants! Not even around the park, a little dried-up square of brown grass where some dark men lounged in their big hats and their dogs sat in the shade with their tongues hanging three-quarters out of their mouths.

Finally on the edge of town, I found a store, clean at least, attached to the gas station. Inside, like a deli—back home we'd call it a deli—but here there were cookies, frosted pink and with a look like packed sand, and a glass case full of some type of sandwich wrapped in bright yellow paper where there should have been bagels and cream cheese. I bought a cup of coffee and a big cookie with sprinkles and pointed to one of the sandwiches in the case. "Burrito?" the girl behind the counter asked, and I got through the rest of the transaction with sign language, lots of nodding, and a *gracias*, though I was worried—was I pronouncing it properly? I tried to remember my high school Spanish, but nothing. I tried to remember what Spanish I'd learned on the streets of New York, but every phrase made me blush. When I handed over my money, she said "Thank you" in perfect English. What had I been thinking? California, I needed to keep reminding myself, not Mexico! Now I laugh at my foolishness. I walked around the town, what there was of it. Like a tourist! When I had seen the stucco houses, the gas station, and the little drugstore— a *farmacia*—then I stood by the school fence, eating my burrito and watching all the little ones getting off the buses, because where else could I go in that poor ugly town? What would those men have said—very nice men, I'm sure—about an older Jewish lady sitting down under their tree with them to eat? No, I couldn't do that. "Oy, Rachel, such chozzerai," Rose said when I told her about my breakfast. "A burrito is full of lard. Terrible for the heart, my Danny says." But, I said, the coffee tasted of cinnamon. Maybe they would have talked to me, would have let me rub the dogs' bellies with a stick.

Later in the day, again Rose started in, between complaining about the wait at her doctor's and about the friends who would be coming for cards. "You'll be staying," she said again, like an order more than a question. "I don't need much. Just someone here to make sure I don't stop breathing. I'll just stay in my room, and the whole apartment will be yours."

I said, "I'm here, Rosie. Don't worry."

"And why, Rachel, why did you keep driving? Why didn't you stop earlier? Why not stay in a motel a second night, you can afford this, no? Still I don't understand."

"What's to understand?" I said. "I thought I would be here faster," but she waved her hand at me as if something smelled bad, because already she understood, before I did even, that I would be leaving.

In Mecca I stared at the dingy Chamber of Commerce sign: "Eastern Gateway to the Salton Sea," it read. "Largest Body of Water in California." And I picked up a brochure. The lake was formed, it said, in 1905 when an irrigation canal failed. The flooding lasted sixteen months, until boxcars filled with rocks were used to dam the flow. Sixteen months of water flowing into a valley that used to be under water. It was flowing back toward its home. Largest body of water? It was—forty-five miles long and twenty-five miles wide—but I'd never heard of it.

At the gas station, I asked the quickest way to Route 10 and Los Angeles, and the man pointed me north, not back the way I came. "Are you sure?" I asked.

"*Sí,* up through Indio. Takes you right there."

And there, another little mistake, following his advice—shorter maybe, but the road took me so that I could glimpse this Salton Sea. Maybe my sister was right—what normal person would drive around in the heat, in the desert, already the asphalt shimmering, prickly things and gray bushes piled up against fences? I drove alongside a railway track on which freight cars rumbled. Then the road turned right, and there it was, a pale blue lake so long I couldn't see its southern end, a mechiaeh—like a turquoise in a ring. Really, it was pretty, and I skipped my turn-off. Again crazy instead of sane. The road drove through green fields of something growing but I didn't know what, then desert again, then groves of oranges and palm trees. When I told Rose I'd seen orange groves, she said, "Oranges I can get you here, as big as your head nearly, nothing like those hard green balls we got in Brooklyn as kids. And remember how Mama always made us eat them with a glass of milk. The acid wasn't good for our stomachs, she said. Well I've learned since then, it's just not so. For once, Mama was wrong."

When I told her I'd walked through groves of date palms, she sighed again. "Palms, schmalms," she said. "There are palms here," and she lifted her hand above her head. We were outside as usual in the early morning, in the park, and there were palm trees all around, sprinkling us with their shade. "And dates . . . here I can buy you dates all the way from Arabia, you want dates." She tapped my knee.

"You'd like it, Rosie, so much to look at. Maybe we could go back there for a visit. You know, just like Israel, they turn the desert into a garden. Then there's a fence, the water stops, and boom—desert again. So strange . . ."

"Yes, irrigation. I know about irrigation, Rachel."

"And it's so bright . . . ," I said, but then I remembered—her conversion. My sister had raised her children by the backyard pool, but since her best friend got skin cancer fifteen years ago, she has not left the house between ten in the morning and four in the afternoon. Similar to her conversion from Reform to Conservative that happened when David, her husband, died.

She said, "So what do you need with that? You know how terrible sun is for the skin. And you especially, someone who spent her whole life indoors. Besides," she said, "there's plenty light here, just open the curtains. And here, it's so close to the hospital, just in case—God forbid—anything should happen. And what would you do there? Here, there's the library for books, and a synagogue. Here you can hear the symphony at the Hollywood Bowl. I can't go—the walk from the bus, it's all uphill, and besides, the seats there are so hard, three cushions you need to schlepp. But you, Rachel, you're younger." I didn't understand how with each sentence I felt older, not younger, until, finally, I felt my age. The fog came in off the ocean and I felt the arthritis in my fingers. The sun went down and I couldn't see. I woke in the middle of the night and couldn't sleep, so hobbled around the apartment, afraid I would trip and fall and break a hip. I kept thinking, the life here *is* better than Mama's in the home in New York where she couldn't go outside all winter, not even up on the roof because of the ice. But when Phyllis came the next morning, my favorite niece, I didn't want to talk to her. At breakfast, I complained the orange juice was pulpy, the lox cut too thick, and the coffee too strong. Already, I too was a kvetch.

And then at the sign for Salton City, I turned off the main road. I kept driving because once I saw the water, I wanted to get closer. "Water," I thought, "lunch. I might as well." Streets ran off, with a neat sign at each corner: Tilapia Avenue, Paradise Lane, Oleander Drive. And there really were pink flowering bushes—oleanders?— growing, and down one street, a tank truck even, watering them, but hardly any houses anywhere. The streets were waiting for them to be built. Closer to the water, there were signs with the price of a lot, the price of a house, and then some houses—just one here, one there, along all those streets—all the blinds drawn, some cactus in the yard, a scrawny tree, and a boat pulled up to the top of the driveway.

And the man I met at the dock, in his greasy garage coveralls, kinky hair gone gray, skin a nice mahogany color but dusty—Rose would think that was crazy, too, just talking to him. And why did I, anyway? Rose would have tossed her head the way she did in high school when a boy she didn't like came to speak with her: she'd toss and walk away. And from riding the subway all these years I have made my own way to fend off strangers: I clutch my handbag to my stomach and look right through them. But this time I didn't. I saw him fishing, then I went and stood behind him. In a white plastic bucket, I could hear something thumping. Finally he said, "Pretty lucky today," without turning around, and I crouched down and watched him fish. It was hot, dry like an oven, so I fanned myself with a map from my purse to make a little breeze and watched the little blue waves lapping all along the treeless shore and the sun move around and hit the mountains, brown like corrugated boxes, on the eastern side of the lake, pretty even, so long as you didn't breathe through the nose—it didn't smell very nice. To tell the truth, the whole place smelled fetid, like sulfur and salt and dead things. I could see there were dead fish floating near the shore. And it was hotter and hotter. When I could feel the perspiration run down my chest and my stockings stick to my legs, I remembered suddenly that Rosie wouldn't approve. I had to get going, and I stood to walk away.

"Don't go yet. Dontcha want to see me catch something?" He chuckled, and goodness knows why, I stayed to see, though my head kept telling me, "Rosie will be worrying about you. Already it will be dark by the time you reach her." But maybe I got sunstroke or some other sickness out there. Or maybe the ugly smell from the lake was some sort of a drug, because I stayed and stayed. Finally he reeled one in, a gray and scaly fish, the size of his two dark hands. He unhooked it and held it out to me, still flopping and flapping. "Whoa," he said, and grabbed it tighter. "That's tilapia. That's some good eating. Pretty much the only fish that'll stay alive in here." He waved it at me, smiling, and I stood up so fast, I got dizzy. "Take it. Take it," he said, "come on now. But don't kill it till you get home." When he saw me shrinking back, he laughed, put it in a plastic bag with some water. "Now come on, take it," he said, and laughed some more and patted me on the arm with a slimy, fishy hand, until I had to take it, just to make him stop. What do you do with a live fish when you don't have a knife to kill it with or a kitchen or even a bucket to keep it alive in? I thought of slipping it back into the lake. But I didn't want to hurt his feelings, either. I was embarrassed to think of him watching me put his catch back in the water, so I just thanked him and started to walk away.

"If you're not from around here, you can take that to Johnson's Landing and Donna'll cook it up for you," he called after me. "It's about the only restaurant around, just around that bend."

Well, okay, I thought, it was past lunchtime anyway. "Now you're eating poisoned fish!" my sister said when I told her. "And when there's a new deli here that, I swear, makes kreplach like you haven't tasted since Mama died."

My mouth began to water. Mama would spend a whole day in the kitchen and come out dusted with flour. To the table, she would bring the bowls of chicken soup and kreplach, chewy dough filled with ground meat, onions, chicken fat. On special occasions—on Purim or to break the fast on Yom Kippur—she drew hopeful messages, Hebrew letters, into the dough so that Rose and I and our brother Itzhak would swallow God's blessings. "She's in a better place," I said, remembering her last years in the nursing home that you had to check every day were they bathing her and changing her clothes when she soiled them. She lived to ninety-five, but she could recognize me, thank goodness, at least enough to know I was the one to complain to. Rose visited once every year, the same time she came to visit Papa's grave. I always got to the home early that day, made sure Mama was clean and dressed in her best, wearing the latest piece of jewelry Rose had sent that otherwise I kept at home, or her roommate, an even older lady but cunning, would steal it.

I stumbled along the shore, wishing I'd changed into some other shoes, until I saw it—a white shack on salt-crusted pilings out over the water with a big red sign and flowering cactuses all along the front. It was right in the sun, but inside the air-conditioning was on and it was cool and dark. There were some canned goods on shelves, a soda machine, a bar, two covered pool tables with, in the middle of each, a vase of flowers. A young woman bent over the counter, her long dark hair falling and covering her face. She was reading a magazine, and when she looked up, I saw she was Japanese. Maybe I was in the wrong place. In the background, I heard a television going. Then I realized I was holding the fish in its bag in front of me like something dirty. "Oy, how silly," I said, waving the bag. "Are you Donna?" I asked, unsure.

"Who else?" She smiled at me. "Did Vick give that to you from the lake? Ugly, isn't it? I don't eat those—I hear the water's full of chemicals from all the farming round here. Do you want it for your lunch?"

"Oh, no, thank you. I don't think so," I said.

"Well, here, give it to me." She held out her hand for the bag. "I'll have the kids take it back to the lake when their show's over. I can't drag them away from it. They're home sick from school today. I'll put it in the sink for now." Then she came back with her order pad, and I noticed she was looking me up and down, leaning over the counter, even, to see my bottom half—my skirt all wrinkled from sleeping, my heels all coated with mud. "You're not from around here, are you?" and before I could answer, she asked, "You're not lost?"

"Oh no, I have a map," I said. "I'm going to visit my sister in Santa Monica, but I got off the highway to . . . well, it's too long a story. Now I see I might was well drive to San Diego and then north. I need to start again soon."

"Well, San Diego's pretty nice. Least that's what the kids tell me. Their dad lives there."

"Oh," I said, and looked down at her order pad. Her hand was still poised to write. Her fingernails were painted pale pink, the color of carnations. "I'll have a turkey sandwich." I watched her paint mayonnaise onto the bread slices. I'd never seen someone make a sandwich so slowly. It would take forever and when would I get back on the road? "My, I'm hungry," I said, but she didn't fix the sandwich any more quickly. "Well, it's nice and cool in here, anyway, isn't it?"

"Deadly out there. I keep the lights low, too. That helps."

When she brought the sandwich over, she had a sad look, and she kept looking at me as I started to eat. "I'm sorry," I said.

"Sorry?"

303

"About your husband," I said.

"My ex? He's okay. He sends money when he can. And he's good to the girls, takes them for a couple weeks every summer, takes them to Disneyland at Christmas, too. He's a trucker, so even if we were still together, they'd hardly see him. It just didn't work out with us is all. He never even yelled that I can remember."

She took it all so smoothly. "Oh" was all I could think to say.

"Maybe that was it," she said, thoughtfully. "Someone *not* yelling can be terrible, can't it?"

We laughed together, and I ate the sandwich. Soon her children came into the dining room and climbed up on two stools at the end of the counter—two girls about eight and twelve. Both with her mouth and eyes, but with freckles, too, and brown hair done up in braids that looked as though they'd been slept on. They didn't look a bit sick.

"What have you been watching?" I asked.

"*The Mole People*," the one closer to me said, the littler one. "It's really neat. There're these people who live underground. They're all white and these other guys find them, sort of by mistake, I think. They're evil—the mole people, I mean—but the other guys get them with this big flashlight."

When she paused for breath, her mother said, "I think that's enough, Sue. We barely know what you're talking about."

"But Mom, she asked."

"Why don't you do something for me? Get out of the house for a few minutes and take this fish back to the lake, will you?"

"Aw, it's so hot out there," the older girl complained, but she slid off her stool and pulled her sister after her. They took the fish in its plastic bag, but they lingered, kicking the screen door open and letting it slam shut. Their mother went over, put her hands on their shoulders. "Hey, you're letting all the hot air in." She gave them a little shove out the door. "You can have ice cream when you come back," she called after them.

"What nice girls," I said.

She wiped her hands on a towel. "Sometimes I just let them stay home," she said. "They keep me from talking to the radio. It's not too busy round here, you can see. Sometimes I get a crowd on the weekend when the fishing's good and sometimes a couple people want to stick around late playing pool but otherwise . . ." She'd been there for over ten years, she said, first with her husband and now alone. Still, she wasn't really thinking of leaving. "Some fools—me included—thought this could be a second Palm Springs! You know, lots of rich white people on vacation, spending money!"

"But it's so quiet here," I said. "Wouldn't people come just for that?"

"You've got to be kidding," she said, and laughed. "It's hot. It's smelly. And it's miles from anywhere. My parents won't even come visit from L.A. They say the desert reminds them of the camps."

"The camps?" The word is a curse, involuntary cringing.

"You know. They were in Oklahoma during the war," she said, "before I was born."

When the girls came back in, they got up on the stools again, waved their hands wildly in front of their faces. "It's hot out there, Mom. Where's that ice cream?" the older one said.

The younger one came over and stood in front of me silently, rubbing her damp hair out of her face. "Do you know how to make braids?" she asked. "These are a mess."

"Leave the lady alone now," Donna said. "She needs to leave soon," but the girl didn't move. She just stood in front of me, tugging on the ends of her braids.

"Of course I know how to make braids," I said. I held my arms out to her, and she turned around and stood between my knees. While I struggled with the tangles, Donna turned the radio on to a country station. It was foreign-sounding music to me but it certainly had a beat. When the song changed, she grabbed her daughters. "This is it," she said, "the song I've been telling you about. Come on, Sue, Misha, I'll teach you that dance." They stomped and kicked and twirled across the floor, the girls giggling every time they got the steps wrong, their mother yelling, "That's it, that's it," every time they got it right.

I sat, uncomfortable on my stool at the counter, watching them dance, waiting to pay my check. "I never had children," I thought suddenly, and it was as if someone pulled a plug and tears came to my eyes. "Of course, you didn't," I thought. "How could you with no husband? And working all the time. And besides, there were Itzhak's kids, those three beautiful babies who ended up with no father. And then later Rose's kids came east for school and stayed with you summer vacations while they worked in the city. Remember how you liked to take Phyllis shopping for her winter college clothes at Gimbel's and how you liked it when Danny took you out to dinner, just the two of you like a mother and son on a date. And now, all the grandnieces and grandnephews," I thought, and started to list their names in my head. The tears disappeared again, and by the time the song was over, I was fine, just fine. "Let me finish those braids," I said. And when a waltz came on the radio, I said, "Would you like me to teach you?" and Sue nodded her head vigorously, and I was happy to show her and her sister the fundamentals of the waltz. Rose and I had often practiced the waltz and the fox-trot together, and the tango, too, when Mama wasn't looking. We dreamed of reincarnation as the dancing Levine sisters.

When the news came on, Donna turned the radio off. "Well, you girls need to call up and find out what your homework is. I'm not letting you stay home another day," she said. "And I've got to get to those books. It's almost tax time, and it always takes me forever 'cause I never really know what I'm doing, even after all these years."

"And I need to go to my sister," I said.

Donna walked me to the door. Outside, the sun had gone down. Can you believe it? I'd spent that much time without even noticing. The sky in the west was turning pink. To the east, the lake and the Chocolate Mountains behind it were all one creamy brown-pink smear, like a Necco wafer. When I pulled the car keys from my purse, Donna said, "It'll be getting dark soon, you know. You don't really want to be driving all that way in the dark, do you?"

And that was that. That's how I came to stay with her. One night, I thought, but then I started to help with her taxes and stayed three days. After helping Mr. Jenson with his books twenty years, the skills came in helpful, helpful to someone who really needed some help, not just useful to someone, Mr. Jenson, who could afford to pay someone to do this work. When we put the finished forms in the mail, Donna gave me a big hug. I shrank back, but she said, "You don't know what a help you've been. Now, tell me what I can do for you."

"Where have you been?" my sister insisted when I finally arrived at her apartment Monday noon, in time for the first seder. "We've been waiting and waiting."

"Ah, our missing person," Danny joked when he came from the kitchen holding a glass of something dark over ice.

"We even called the police we were so worried," my niece said, "but they wouldn't start looking for another day."

I reminded them I'd called—I did call and say I would be delayed. I explained it was an accident, a series of little accidents all piling up, and everything else—really, I myself didn't know how it had taken me so long to reach her, but Rosie sighed with exasperation. "Like a crazy child," she said. "Just like you always were, Rachel," she said. "You remember Aunt Mildred? How she used to go to the store in her slippers and come back with only a box of cookies, not even kosher? Listen, Rachel, you stay here and Danny will help."

I remembered we laughed at Mildred, but now I think maybe that was all she wanted, a box of Mallomars.

Rose's voice was the same as I remembered, coarser but still reedy like an oboe is reedy, musical, that is. And my head, as I stood in her living room, it was still full of the sound of the typewriter bell when it hit the end of the carriage and the buzzing of the computer when it saved a file. It was full of sirens and subway trains and the garbled voices that come over the loudspeakers in the subway stations, especially Union Square. *Beware of the moving platform* . . . I could still hear the voices of all my nieces and nephews, too, at all different ages— the babies when they clamored for something sweet, the older ones with their stories of parties and classes. And Mr. Jenson wishing me good morning and then his friendly bellow: "Oh Rachel, oh Rachel, you're needed here." So many noises inside my skull. Why wouldn't they go away?

I have only one thing left to tell you, really, and that is how I kissed the egret. Sunday, Donna took us for a drive. "Come on," she said, "Margolita's here to watch the place. Let me show you around." We got in her car and drove south along the lake's western shore, past green growing fields and orange and grapefruit groves with the fruit shining between the leaves like Christmas decorations, the girls in the backseat.

Desert passed by with little dry bushes growing in sand. Then when water glistened in ditches, there were brilliant green fields. "That's alfalfa, I think," Donna said. Then another field.

"That's onions!" I said.

"More onions!" Sue and Misha cried.

I saw row after row of green onion stalks, and in the dirt I could see the white onions, almost like eggs or bones. The car filled with the smell of onions, as if you had just cut one in half to grate for latkes. "This soil must be very good," I said, looking at all the growing things.

"Only because they irrigate," Donna said. "Only because of all that stuff they pour into it, fertilizers and I don't know what else."

"And all the water's stolen from the Colorado River," Misha added. "It used to run into the gulf and it's not supposed to be here at all. They built about six dams, though, so now all the water comes here to grow things and to L.A. so all the movie stars have water to drink. Now it's just a swamp where the river used to go into the gulf."

When the road curved, we drove through a town that was nothing but shacks, tin warehouses, garages, fertilizer stores, and one dusty motel—even uglier than Mecca, even less than Salton City. Then we turned again and headed to the lake, now from the south. In the distance, there were some buildings with concrete domes, clouds of white steam coming from them. "What are those?" I asked.

"Geothermal plants," Donna said. "The Magma Energy Company—isn't that a goofy name? The kids got to go to one for a field trip but I had to stay with the store. Misha, you explained it to me. How does it work again?"

"There's hot water, really hot, deep down in the ground, and they . . . do you really want to hear about this?"

"Yes." I turned around to see her. "Tell me how it works."

"They pump the hot water up, and when it hits the air, it turns into steam, and the steam turns the turbines. All the heat gets turned into electricity—somehow. I don't remember that part so well. People used to think it was a really clean way to get energy but it makes air pollution, too. And noise. And when they put the cold water back into the ground, it can make earthquakes happen."

We kept driving, and I realized I was in a very strange place, where things did not go together in the way I was used to, ugly and pretty at the same time so I couldn't figure out should I smile or not, where Japanese mothers danced some country music jig, where you needed a shmatte bobby-pinned on to keep the hot wind from blowing your hair, where you brought the smell of living vegetables and dead, salty fish into the house with you every time. "Where are you taking me?" I asked.

"Just around. You'll see," was all Donna said.

"I know where," Sue said. "It's a surprise."

We were driving on smaller and smaller roads until we pulled up at a bird sanctuary. "This is one of my favorite places," Donna said. We walked along a marsh—Donna lent me gym shoes this time—scaring rabbits, lizards, and roadrunners out of the underbrush, then the grasses split and there was the lake. White pelicans swooped overhead and avocets dipped with the black and white stripes along their backs and grebes swam and sandpipers poked along in the mud. I looked them all up busily in a pamphlet I'd picked up. The girls ran around in circles. At the foot of a hill, we saw a burrowing owl sitting calmly on a post. It eyed us but didn't move until I pulled my camera out. Already I wanted a photo to prove to Rose there was more here than dust. Then we all sat on a bench near the water, and a cool breeze blew. It seemed thousands of ducks were floating on the lake—a convention, a conference, all headed in the same direction. Even the girls were quiet. Then out of the sky, a great white bird came sweeping, wings spread wide wide wide. It landed near us on long skinny legs and ruffled the long plumes on its back, and we sat so still it didn't fly away. Sue held my arm tight. Donna leaned close. "An egret," she whispered in my ear. Slowly, I held out my hand—I don't know why. My hand was empty, no fish to entice it, but the bird came closer, until it looked right up at my face with that quick pecking birdie look that even sparrows in Central Park have. It looked at me like my nieces and nephews used to look at me when I baby-sat, when they wanted something and neither of us could figure out what it was. I moved my hand but the egret stayed. I remember Mama wanting a hat with egret plumes, a blue hat so it looked like a bird on water, but she could never afford it. And I learned later almost all these birds died to make such hats. I touched the bird's neck, its crest, but it didn't startle. It actually stepped closer and tipped its beak up. If it had opened its mouth and spoken, I wouldn't have been surprised, but it didn't. It just stood there, so I bent down and kissed it, kissed the spot right above the beak. The feathers were soft—of course they were—and I smelled fish and salt and a completely new smell that must be the smell of live birds. I heard Donna gasp and the girls gasp, so I gasped, too—what *was* I doing? "Feh!" Rose would say, "dirty." And then the egret hopped back and flew off, disappearing into a great flock of other egrets wheeling above, as if it had never been there in front of us.

Monday noon I arrived in Santa Monica, and six days later, I called the family together in Rose's living room. "I've decided," I said. "I'll come visit, but I won't stay. This time, I am the one to leave." My voice was shaking, and I needed to sit down in the middle of my speech.

"All these years," Rose said. "So you were upset that I left. Who would know? But Rachel, you were the baby, you were always the favorite, that's why I left."

Her children were silent. They looked at their hands.

"Me, the favorite?"

"Yes, it was true. Mama always made a dish special for you. Papa gave you books. Me, he gave something little he didn't care about, a hair clip, a sewing kit. Ah, enough of that. This place you've found, I don't understand, but if you like it . . . And you know you're always welcome here."

On the dock, I sit, just sit, happy to be back. Happy? What is that? I don't know. The lake is blue and the waves make little lapping sounds—otherwise silence. As usual the water smells bad. The dead fish float but maybe not so many as last week. I sit on the dock anyway, where Vick baits hooks and spills gasoline for his boat, where birds have relieved themselves. Just a few days ago, I came here in my nylons and could barely think to crouch. Now I have on an old black cotton skirt, the one I used to wear only for housecleaning, and no shoes, and I'm sitting right on this smelly dock. Up above, the sky is pale yellowish blue like always just after sunset, and the Chocolate Mountains fade pink into the lake. Overhead there are the silver glints of jets flying from the Naval Air Station in San Diego ("Don't go driving off onto the bomb range, now," Donna told me when I was heading for Indio to get us some groceries). I wish I could say it was all very nice, but this place isn't like that, not right off. It will take a long time for all the noises in my head to go quiet, all the people talking to me and all the machines I've heard clanging and banging and whining and whistling, all the radio programs and television programs; it will take many days of reading, walking, and continuing the dancing lessons with Sue and Misha. The sky turns orange, then pink, then violet, and the colors reflect in the lake's water like flowers, like double flowers. I am like them—an accident, a switch being turned in the brain by mistake, water pushing through a levee, like a medication that pushes the cells apart, like blooming. On the way back from seeing the egret we stopped at a date grove, and seventy feet up, I saw a man working, with his hands buried in a cluster of bright yellow flowers. "He's pollinating," Donna said. He tied the male flowers into the female and placed a net bag over all, no good relying on wind to do the job. I thought, the man's hands must get filthy, coated with golden pollen.

Suddenly Daniel, I have never told anyone about Daniel, our decade-long Thursday afternoons affair, Daniel with the limp that kept him from the war, but he made me open, like the brightness here—everything tight loosening up. My legs spread wider and wider, my hands grasped the headboard. Why would I remember that now? I'm afraid even Donna might find it sordid, the hotel room with a window opening on the airshaft, my dream that never happened of one time spending a whole night with him in one of the big rooms overlooking Gramercy Park. Sometimes it would be his child's birthday and he would come with a present, a big box wrapped up in paper. He'd try to hide it from me, to spare my feelings, and that made me almost cry, almost as nice as if the present were for me (though what would I have needed with a doll or a toy railroad, I don't know). Still, once we were undressed, once we were in bed . . . And now forty years without it, my goodness, forty years! The other day, when Donna touched my wrist—that's the feeling I had. Oh, not as strong of course, not really the same of course, but still it was skin on skin. Ah, all that was years, no, decades ago, and now gone with the others—Itzhak; our parents; Itzhak's daughter to leukemia; my best friend from high school, Leah, who died trying to get rid of a baby; Rose's husband David; and Rose soon, too. She sounds sharp to me, but Phyllis says how difficult it is for her to breathe (how could she have stopped sunning but not smoking!). "No use crying," Papa always said, and snapped his *New York Times* out full width to read. But some things are worth crying over, I think, and I remember his bald head, all freckled. I see a silver glint high up, another jet. Here, they practice bombing things, they suck energy up from the ground and let chemicals seep down into it and into the water so things can grow, they pay people nothing nearly to pick those fruits, which is terrible, but still, there is a space to breathe. It's almost dark now, just an orange glow up there, up above. A few tears, and then suddenly, absurd, I realize I'm filled with some feeling I don't know. Each cell pulses. They move fast. I can't imagine how they stay together in this one body. The world tastes sweet and there's so little time. Breathless, I think, stunned, "This is joy!"

AMY CLAMPITT

A Hermit Thrush

Nothing's certain. Crossing, on this longest day,
the low-tide-uncovered isthmus, scrambling up
the scree-slope of what at high tide
will be again an island,

to where, a decade since well-being staked
the slender, unpremeditated claim that brings us
back, year after year, lugging the
makings of another picnic—

the cucumber sandwiches, the sea-air-sanctified
fig newtons—there's no knowing what the slamming
seas, the gales of yet another winter
may have done. Still there,

the gust-beleaguered single spruce tree,
the ant-thronged, root-snelled moss, grass
and clover tuffet underneath it,
edges frazzled raw

but, like our own prolonged attachment, holding.
Whatever moral lesson might commend itself,
there's no use drawing one,
there's nothing here

to seize on as exemplifying any so-called virtue
(holding on despite adversity, perhaps) or
any no-more-than-human tendency—
stubborn adherence, say,

to a wholly wrongheaded tenet. Though to
hold on in any case means taking less and less
for granted, some few things seem nearly
certain, as that the longest day

will come again, will seem to hold its breath,
the months-long exhalation of diminishment
again begin. Last night you woke me
for a look at Jupiter,

that vast cinder wheeled unblinking
in a bath of galaxies. Watching, we traveled
toward an apprehension all but impossible
to be held onto—

that no point is fixed, that there's no foothold
but roams untethered save by such snells,
such sailor's knots, such stays
and guy wires as are

mainly of our own devising. From such an
empyrean, aloof seraphic mentors urge us
to look down on all attachment,
on any bonding, as

in the end untenable. Base as it is, from
year to year the earth's sore surface
mends and rebinds itself, however
and as best it can, with

thread of cinquefoil, tendril of the magenta
beach pea, trammel of bramble; with easings,
mulchings, fragrances, the gray-green
bayberry's cool poultice—

and what can't finally be mended, the salt air
proceeds to buff and rarefy: the lopped carnage
of the seaward spruce clump weathers
lustrous, to wood-silver.

Little is certain, other than the tide that
circumscribes us, that still sets its term
to every picnic—today we stayed too long
again, and got our feet wet—

and all attachment may prove at best, perhaps,
a broken, a much-mended thing. Watching
the longest day take cover under
a monk's-cowl overcast,

with thunder, rain and wind, then waiting,
we drop everything to listen as a
hermit thrush distills its fragmentary,
hesitant, in the end

unbroken music. From what source (beyond us, or
the wells within?) such links perceived arrive—
diminished sequences so uninsistingly
not even human—there's

hardly a vocabulary left to wonder, uncertain
as we are of so much in this existence, this
botched, cumbersome, much-mended,
not unsatisfactory thing.

The Quail

Lost in the brush, bound by the other path
To find the house,
You let me know how many voices,
How many shifting bodies you possessed,
How you could flit away to follow birds,
And yet be near.

A quail implored the hollow for a home,
A covey of dark to lie in under stars;
And, when it sang, you left my hand
To voyage how softly down the even grass
And see the meadow where the quails lie down,
Flushed in the dark by hunters' broken guns.

You left my side before I knew the way
To find the house,
And soon you called across the hollow
To say you were alive and still on earth;
And, when you sang, the quail began to cry,
So I lost both.

The blue dusk bore feathers beyond our eyes,
Dissolved all wings as you, your hair dissolved,
Your frame of bone blown hollow as a house
Beside the path, were borne away from me
Farther than birds for whom I did not care,
Commingled with the dark complaining air.

I could have called the simple dark to fade,
To find the house,

And left you standing silent;
But stained away by maple leaves, and led
From tree to tree by wands of luring ghosts,
You knew my love,

You knew my feet would never turn away
From any forest where your body was,
Though vanished up the disembodied dark.
And when I found you laughing under trees,
The quail began to trill and flute away,
As far away as hands that reach for hands;
But, when it sang, you kissed me out of sound.

SEAMUS HEANEY

Drifting Off

The guttersnipe and the albatross
gliding for days without a single wingbeat
were equally beyond me.

I yearned for the gannet's strike,
the unbegrudging concentration
of the heron.

In the camaraderie of rookeries,
in the spiteful vigilance of colonies
I was at home.

I learned to distrust
the allure of the cuckoo
and the gossip of starlings,

kept faith with doughty bullfinches,
levelled my wit too often
to the small-minded wren

and too often caved in
to the pathos of waterhens
and panicky corncrakes.

I gave much credence to stragglers,
overrated the composure of blackbirds
and the folklore of magpies.

But when goldfinch or kingfisher rent
the veil of the usual,
pinions whispered and braced

as I stooped, unwieldy
and brimming,
my spurs at the ready.

WILLIAM WENTHE

Birds of Hoboken

Here there is space, and what innocence
I can hold on to, alone—
neither Adam nor Ecclesiastes.
The tremendous fact that is Manhattan
shimmers across the river's crumpled foil;
but the dweller upon vanity could find enough
behind him on this world that ends
at the concrete bumper of a railroad wharf—
a flatcar load of rusted wheels,
or the derrick of a half-sunk
wooden ship, unable to raise itself
from its berth of silt.

There is a recoverable grace
in the fine joinings of wood, soft grains
bleached by sun and the river's chemicals.
That it has remained this long
seems a bit of a miracle, but the very water
of this place has been abandoned,
a trapped rectangle, rainbowed only
with petroleum seepings, obsolete
to anyone, it seems, save myself—

and the birds, now half my reason
for coming here. It is too far
to call back the first time
the appearance of a bird above the river
opened a new world. It may have been
the croak of a heron, flying to roost
at seven o'clock, that struck me so out of time
as if the sky itself had spoken.

Now in winter, I stand in the disused
shadows of Pullmans painted the old
green, my fingers stiffened on binoculars,
to watch small rafts of scaup
and others brought here in the amplitude
of migration. There are black ducks, goldeneye,
mergansers, occasional pairs of tiny
bufflehead sheltering among still-rooted
pilings, abiding here on their commute
that measures a continent in a year.

As darkness obtains, I look more
for the significant flashes of white—
the pure body of the canvasback,
or the half-hid speculum
in the gadwall's folded wing, or, once,
the white crown worn like a lily petal
by a widgeon that had flown from extreme
spaces of tundra, of muskeg lakes.

The birds speak that way (oblivious
to my desire, to the whole city
brighter now in dark) of remotenesses
we haven't killed yet. They know nothing
of abandonment, and yet I think
they want this place simply
because we have wasted it
even of ourselves.

                    They allow me
to watch them, though by now I can see only
the way bodies keep their even keel
in waves that may be killing them.
They don't exclaim: again, as if
willing to forgive, they arrive.

REGINALD GIBBONS

No Matter What Has Happened This May

I love the little row of life along the low rusted gardenwire fence that divides my small city backyard from my neighbor's. The wild unruly rose, I hacked like a weed last spring; then it shot quick running lengths of vine in every direction and shuddered into a thickness of blown blossoms—the kind you can't cut and take in because they fall apart—so I think I should cut it back as if to kill it again. The violets, just beautiful weeds. Then there are yellow-green horseradish leaves, they rose as fast as dandelions in today's rain and sun; and the oregano and mint are coming back, too, you can't discourage them. Last year's dry raspberry canes are leaning, caught in the soft thorns of the new, at the corner. And beyond them, the mostly gone magnolia in the widow's yard, behind ours, the white petals on the ground in a circle like a crocheted bedspread thrown down around the black trunk.

I went out to see what the end of the day was like, away from everything, for a minute, and it was drizzling slowly. I touched the ground, just to feel it wet against my palm; and the side of the house, too. It was quiet, and I saw two robins bringing weeds and twigs to a nesting place in the new leaves at the stumpy top of a trimmed buck-eye limb. How little they need—weeds and some time—to build with.

In a month I may find a new one not yet fully fledged, lost from the nest, and put it on the highest limb I can reach, but not high enough to escape harm's way, I imagine, when the harm is a shock within it, a giving up already; and it will be dead before morning. That's happened before. But these robins were just building, and one came with a full beak and paused a moment on a lower branch and cocked its head and looked upward and shifted as if it were a muscled cat, of all things, about to leap, and then it did leap and disappeared into the clump of leaves, and shook them, as the single drops of rain were gently shaking them one by one, here and there.

I was getting wet but I felt held outside because I could hear, from inside the house, a woman and a child—my wife and my daughter—laughing in the bathtub together, their laughter not meant for me but brought out to me like a gift by the damp still air so I could see that like the rain and the robins and the row of weeds they too were working and building. I'm not going to mention, now, any harm or hurt they have suffered; no winter nor summer government; no green troops nor trimmed limbs of trees; no small figures beaten or fallen. I wiped the dirt off my palms and I picked up again the glass of wine I had carried out with me. I rejoiced. There was no way not to, wet with the sound of that laughter and whispering in the last light of a day we had lived.

MARK HELPRIN

A Dove of the East

They rode up to the Golan every week on Friday or Saturday, in an old army truck with two rows of hard wooden seats. In summer the heights were cooler than the Bet Shan Valley, which like a white strip of ivory is set into mountains as if they had been wounded, and cartilage exposed. Nothing is hotter than an afternoon by the Jordan, neither chilly nor deep but green and rapid like an African river.

When Israel took the Golan she found it to be dry and wasted, brush fire slopes gold only to God and pilots, so she put cattle there, since anyway she had few elsewhere. The price of meat was high; the grass had gone uneaten. Men had to watch the cattle and tend them otherwise. They stumble and cannot get up. They fall in gullies. They become trapped in labyrinthine ravines. Ticks make mockery of them, since they have no hands. They step on mines and must be shot. They lose themselves in reverie and cannot find grass to eat. They easily get lost, and at night they are frightened, like primitive men.

The farmers of Kfar Yanina, a settlement in the Bet Shan Valley, sent a proportion of their number to take care of their steers. There had been economic trouble, crops not coming in with all good speed, a shortage of labor as the young left the settlement for the pains of city life, dry years, and fires set by artillery. In a memorandum entitled *What Is to Be Done?* the secretary suggested allocation of loan capital to build a herd of cattle to roam about the hills in the north, where the mountains had snow.

A herd was created. In the first year it numbered four hundred, in the second, six hundred, and in the fourth, one thousand, at which it stabilized for lack of further resource. The farmers already knew how to make fences and enclosures, and how to deal with the animals and encourage their health and reproduction—since at the settlement cows had been in residence from 1936 onwards, the same family, remarkably content to give all that milk and end up as roasts in the ovens; and that is by no means funny, for if you look into the eyes of a cow you see a gentle being, perplexed and confused, and although they are hardly full of grace and beauty they order pity in a human heart for their very thickness and incapacity.

Being practical, the men of Kfar Yanina did not worry about the fates of their charges but rather tried to nurture them into robust meatiness. In the breeding and feeding they were already expert, but they had to learn how to ride and rope, and this they took up rapidly if only for its romance and publicity in films. There were a few accidents. Once, red-haired Avner crashed his horse head-on with a fat steer, causing minor injuries in order of increasing seriousness to the steer, the horse, and Avner, who rode chuckling in an ambulance to the nearest X-ray machine. But all in all they were good herdsmen, and they developed into a permanent elite group within the settlement. Perhaps in doing so they struck a natural balance, for they became extraordinarily desirable to women, who were irresolute and nervous in their presence. This may have been because they saw the women so rarely. For whatever reason, hot fires were lit when the Golan crew returned suddenly out of the dusk for alternation, hot showers, conversation, movies, and dalliance.

But they left their women after a day or two and rode back in the old truck to a little camp of tents and trailers. It was usually on Friday or Saturday. They rested for the evening, then got up the next morning and began to work.

Each day a scout was sent to trace ahead the paths by which the herd, or parts of it, would move the next morning. In that way the scout and the herd moved out simultaneously, the herd stopping at a place determined the day before, the scout continuing into fresh country. As many steers as they had could not have been moved spontaneously and freely—it was hardly a place for Isadora Duncan—for various reasons. The first was the availability of watering places. Sometimes they were wet, sometimes not, and the scout was obliged to find a wet one within a certain distance. The second was the condition of march. One is always surprised by the agility of cattle and their willingness to confront the steep and narrow, but they are after all not goats and it is not possible to drive them over too difficult a path. The third is pasturage, which must be suitable and green; green, that is, in a Middle Eastern sense, which can be yellow. The fourth is that a herd should be able to find new pastures without too much backtracking, an act which is a waste and which tends to upset them. The fifth is that the herd and the riders must be fairly well protected from saboteurs. Occasionally a steer will fall, victim of a long and casual rifle shot. In that case the riders must turn their own guns against it, and call immediately for a truck to take it for butchering. Steers have been known to set off antivehicular mines, resulting in an awful sight, but there is little danger to the men, whose weight even if combined with that of a horse will not trigger the fuse.

A scout must balance these conditions, weighing and judging, until he reaches an acceptable result. He then rides back to camp, sometimes late at night, for he has his work cut out for him. It is a good job though, because he can be alone and he usually rides all day on the mountains and in the canyons, stopping only for a small lunch, to rest his horse, or for the hell of it to sing and eat chocolate and to know he stands alone for as far as he can see and sense.

And for every Jew who did this a terrible joy descended. He was a cowboy, standing with a rifle, a rope, a horse. He was strong, tanned, able to move with lightning speed over long stretches of ground, tough, alert, and dirty. And yet he was incredibly sad and thought perhaps he was wrong to ride rather than reflect. Being in the saddle was a fearsome thing. And no matter how natural it seemed or how rough and arrogant he was, he feared deep down that he had succeeded, and fearing his own success he rode harder and was more daring and it seemed that he was extraordinarily capable upon a horse.

A favorite and excellent scout, a hard and trustworthy man, was Leon Orlovsky, a French Jew who had been at Kfar Yanina since the Second World War, who spoke little, and who often did the work of two men. He was one of those people with neither past nor future. About him the young, the middle-aged, and the old never thought very much or hard for he was self-contained, a little irrational, and he absented himself from normal society by means of superior work. Had he only been able to deal with people he might have been elected secretary many times, for he was well educated, and although in his fifties, as handsome and masculine as a man could be, like the rare film star who had aged well, or the fit professional soldier who hasn't a mean look. Yet he did not even speak to women, and appeared shy and confused by them. Many women had fallen in love with him from a distance, but momentarily, for he was clearly not to be sought.

For most people he was just a brusque and silent ex-European, an ill-fitting refugee who had strange habits. In his case it was that he wore a tremendous coat into the dining room (when he was on rotation from the mountains) and filled its pockets with all manner of things—eggs, bread, scallions, salt shakers, tomatoes, and whatever else he could fit in—and then left to eat alone in one of the watch towers or among the date trees.

Whatever his peculiarities, and they were many, the young men, army officers in the reserve with new families, knew that they could trust him. As a scout he was unmatched, for he had not only vigor but wisdom. He had in twenty-five years become senior on the land, a master farmer and horseman, as knowing of the winds, soil, and animals as a man can be—and yet he was from Paris.

This Parisian, who walked no longer among the shimmering autumn trees of the Jardins du Luxembourg but instead in the pale green and sulfurous orange date orchards ripe with heat and sweet decay, packed his canvas saddlebags and laid on his equipment with the thoroughness of a legionnaire. "If a man is to be independent," he was fond of saying, "he must be the master of his kit, and pack lightly but with great care."

His horse, the offspring of a Texas quarterhorse and a pure-bred Arabian, had the strong chest and mathematical curves of a desert animal, along with the somewhat thicker neck and sturdy legs of the American mount. A chestnut mare who would have been at home in Virginia, she carried her rider with great speed and over difficult terrain despite the heat and hills. A locally made saddle, cool for the horse, with a palm-wood pommel and an English halter and bit, could not have weighed more than five pounds altogether on her.

His saddlebags were of white duck and in them he carried a liter vacuum bottle of cool water purely for the pleasure of it since he carried two plastic bottles also a liter apiece in the bags and a similar one on his belt. In a little tin box he always put some wheat biscuits, half-dried beef, dried apricots, peaches, and bananas, chocolate, and a Cuban cigar cut in two. He carried an aluminum cup in which were four teabags, a small sack of sugar, and matches. In the other half of the bags he had three long magazines of ammunition for his automatic rifle which was in a leather case on the saddle, a small and powerful Carl Zeiss pocket telescope, his book for the week, some toilet articles, and whatever else might end up there (for instance a newspaper or an interesting-looking rock he had found). A warm leather jacket was rolled inside two cotton wool blankets resting over the top of the bags; on his belt in addition to a canteen he had a parkerized knife in a leather sheath which held also a pliers-wirecutter, a stainless steel awl, and a pocket whetstone. A white although vaguely cream-colored leather lariat which smelled just like his horse hung near his rifle, where he also often put his shirt. He brought the lariat mainly out of habit but also because he sometimes came upon strays, which in a long and frustrating process he eventually led home.

With all this, or rather with only this, he stayed away from his companions for a full day, often two, and sometimes three, depending on what he was supposed to find and how easy things were or how difficult. For him this was a great delight. In solitude he could remember, and hope, and in rapturous moments in the early mornings or late afternoons when the sun did not impose its glaring reality he sometimes even dared to plan.

"I'm going up ahead," he said to Yossi, the head of the crew, "about five or ten kilometers. I don't think that at this time of year it will be hard to find water. At least it wasn't last year at this time; the damn thing was overflowing. I'll be back late this afternoon."

Yossi nodded his head and said "Okay, see you then," and Leon, whose Hebrew was not quite perfect and who spoke in a deep and rather sad voice, mounted his horse and rode away. He had arisen before the others, shaved while they slept, eaten while they were shaving, and left while they were eating, with only a few words to Yossi. He passed by the herd quietly and then rode hard and fast for some distance until, surrounded by silence, beige rocks, and fast-rising heat, he came to a ridge, which he climbed and followed, seeking out a decent route suitable for cattle.

After an hour or two he thought he had found a good path and rode on it toward the place where the steers were being driven. He could see far off in the distance a light cloud marking their transit. Had he been new, he might have departed from the path to that night's resting place at the point where the two were closest. But he could see that although he and his horse could pass through the ravine in between, the herd couldn't. So he left the path a good mile or two before most people would have and followed a gently rolling hill along its topmost ridge. In order to get to his destination along an easy way he sometimes had to travel in the opposite direction, waiting for the hill to curve around again and send him to where he was going. This reminded him of something he had heard a long time before, in Switzerland. He had taken it as a figurative lesson for his life, and then in the Golan he found himself all the time acting out its literal sense.

"In Switzerland," said a tall, bland-looking man whom the children called "Monsieur Yaourt," "one must often go down in order to go up." The lights switched off and a projector beamed a blinding ray at a glass-beaded screen. Leon covered his eyes until he heard the film winding through the sprockets and could smell the warm celluloid; he saw on the screen a black and white meadow, and mountains. He recognized on the wall what he saw each day in colors untranslatable in depth and perfection. He then saw a boy much like himself, about twelve, blond, in leather shorts, walking across a log bridge to the beginning of a trail. Klaus, as "Monsieur Yaourt" called him in his narration, was a Swiss boy about to climb a small nondangerous mountain. Otherwise, he judiciously added, he never would have gone alone. Klaus knew when to set out, when to return, how to climb, and what to take. Klaus had asked his parents or some other higher authority if he could climb the small nondangerous mountain alone. They had said yes only because he was a Swiss boy used to living in the country. And children from Paris would have to wait until they were older to climb mountains by themselves, small, dangerous, or otherwise. Klaus held up several completely unidentifiable packages and "Monsieur Yaourt" said, "He has taken with him for the ascension cheese, bread, meat, and fresh fruit." Klaus was pictured going down in order to go up and later, after he had raised a large Swiss flag on a heavy pole waiting for him at the summit, going up in order to get down.

Leon noticed the strange mottled gray of the Swiss flag, a flag he knew to be scarlet red, a color not naturally common in the Alps, a color which in black and white has a peculiar heat and grain. And he stared at it with feigned intensity, but not more than that of the girl next to him who had an equally serious look. Each was sure the other was looking and wanted to appear grim and reflective. He was perfectly content to sit in the pinewood hall listening to the rapid clacka clacka clacka of the projector for as long as any film would run even if it were not a Charlie Chaplin because sitting next to him was a girl also from Paris, from the 16th as was he, a girl he had noticed in the station even in the midst of his fear at being packed away to the cool green Alps, a girl with dark red auburn hair and thin long legs and arms. She was tan and beautiful, and was prone to giggling, and tried to show that she did not care that he existed by doing cruel little things like walking away from him abruptly as he spoke, or making fun of him. But she cried every night and clasped her arms around his imagined presence because she loved him so much, so much that it frightened her, for it was a very deep and serious love for a child. Her name was Ann.

In Austerlitz Station, a Paris June, and lines of children waiting for special trains to take them to Brittany, Germany, and the Alps.

Leon had come with his father to await the train. The little boy carried a small bag in which was a carefully packed tin of sandwiches, chocolate, a penknife, and a French translation of Mark Twain's *A Connecticut Yankee in King Arthur's Court.* He wore schoolboy's shorts, a Bristol blue shirt, and an enameled pin glowing red and white with the Swiss flag and the name "Suisse." He was young enough to half think, half imagine that the pin and small military bag would set him apart as a youthful Swiss official returning gravely to the country he knew so well, on a mission vaguely connected with banking, military affairs, and the prevention of German rearmament. And so he acted haughty and serious, silent, and in a way he thought to be adult. His father, a gentle but tough-looking man who had seen the Great War almost from its very beginning to its absolute end as a press officer assigned to all battles on all fronts, accompanied him and stood there in a gray suit with a Legion of Honor pin he had earned by filing thousands of dispatches to inform the public of the carnage. He had started with fine description, casting a good eye on the rapid clash of those two armies and the suffering countryside underneath, and had ended half-alive, with reports as clipped and sad as Morse code. But during the war he had fathered a son, an only son, who brought him back alive and restored his humor.

While standing by his boy he passed greetings to other fathers he knew or with whom he was acquainted, and this included a doctor of considerable wealth and age who lived in the same district and frequented the same restaurants and bookstores. The doctor's daughter was tall and looked older than her age: she had the most beautiful mouth and eyes Leon's father had ever seen, and when he saw her as he greeted her father, he felt as if he were looking simultaneously into the past and the future. He was understanding what his son could only feel, that the life of their generations was here reborn, and blessed, and compassed; Leon in his confusion had only a sense as strong as memory of all his life, while shattering whistles reverberated between shafts of dusty light as trains ended or began what trains exist for.

They did not reach Kreuzlingen on the Baden-See until the middle of the next day, when the children were exhausted and gray despite the freshness of the air and the hunting-horn atmosphere. They could see Germany on the far side of the lake, and since borders were for him always the most exciting places in the world, clear demarcations promising something different and new throughout their entire lengths, he spent much time that summer watching the high clouds crossing to Germany with the grace of gliding dirigibles. And the light from them was so much more superb, separating into currents, corridors, and rays of gray and silver. The frontier was then a place of prosperous romance, the fields of Bavaria enameled green and settled nightly with cold clear mist as joyous and beautiful as a twelve-year-old boy could have wished. He was a Jew from Paris and beginning to open up on the world, with these his first views royal—something he considered later, achingly, a mean trick of a God whose savage beauty made sharp mountains of ice and rock rise suddenly out of soft green fields.

When he came finally upon the place he had found several days before and to which he had guided one of the men (who was then in the process of guiding the herd), he dismounted to rest and water his horse. He removed the bridle and bit, unfastened the rifle scabbard and saddlebags, hobbled the horse, and let her drink.

In the same way that he had years before rationed out his lunch on the way to Kreuzlingen so that different sandwiches were assigned to various cities and the chocolate was divided between Lausanne and Zurich, he had determined that upon reaching the watering place he would have four squares of chocolate, one biscuit, a dried apricot and banana, five sips of water from his belt canteen, and one cup of cold water (because it was the middle of the day and as hot as new steel). He ate slowly and with great pleasure—one thing after another, orderly, disciplined, and lasting. He was the same with his meals, which he planned, and with his room, which was as neat as his kit. This was because there was something of a German in him: he loved ordered beauty and success in objective things. When a young man he had learned German to study science. And he looked English, so that he was often mistaken for a Briton or a German, this giving him great satisfaction for it has always been popular in one way or another to be a master of the world or even just to resemble the type. But more important than that, he simply was an orderly, organized man and always had been. Many people disliked that or saw it as a sickness, but he could not see why, and anything under his control became almost immediately as shipshape as the bridge of an English cruiser. This was good for running things, judging disputes, understanding the way things worked. He was a good scout because he ordered the shape of the land in his mind and made calculations as to where and when to go. People who simply threw themselves at the land and did not weigh and judge its characteristics usually fell in the ravines or ended up red-faced on the army road. "In that case," said Leon, "it would have been just as wise to have sent a cow."

After about half an hour he packed up and rode out, backtracking along the winding ridge to the path he had found earlier, arriving after several hours on a wide plateau with soft earth and a few palms scattered here and there. He was riding in a little grove of trees, trying to find open water or a well, when he noticed that it was getting late. Perhaps, he thought, I will sleep here for a few hours and then go back when the moon has risen. It's clean here, and the leaves make a nice sound in the wind. In fact he was very happy about camping in the grove because it seemed somehow European. It was several acres of small trees, some palms, and many pines, and quite a few deciduous saplings whose leaves were like bronze medallions. Then he began galloping his horse through the brush, to beat it down, to find water, to find the best place to sleep, and just for the sake of galloping itself.

He was an excellent horseman, having studied for eight years at a Viennese riding academy in Paris, and although the trails past Versailles were not as rocky and hilly as those on the Golan he had absolute confidence. When he had arrived at Kfar Yanina—a half-bearded, ragged Frenchman spit from the hold of an illegal immigrant ship— the man who tended the few horses told him, fearing an accident, to keep off. He had done it with such contempt and superiority that

Leon grabbed one of the saddled horses from him, mounted it suddenly, and began to go as far as he was able through his graduation exercises. Needless to say, the saber charges, jumps, mountings and dismountings while on the run, and highly controlled form were the beginnings of his reputation at Kfar Yanina.

And there in the grove he drew his lariat as if it were a saber, this perhaps the most exciting instant in the life of horse or horseman, waited the tense moment, and then charged with great speed—cavalry, another fine and useless art he had inherited from the past, part of his world which had vanished. He was like cavalry, speeding by trees and charging down another row with the quick turn only a quarterhorse can make; both horse and rider became heated and their blood ran fast. It was good to be sometimes like a Mongol, a Scythian, any hard fighter who used everything to find strength where there was no strength, courage where there was no courage, swirling cold air to beat against the fire of his activity. He shot down the rows breaking the grasses, the horse's hoofbeats echoing callously through the trees. He took his rope and with it beat at the trunks of the palms, strapping them fiercely as if they were an enemy. And then he paused at one end of the grove, red and wet, his blood surging through him, his lower jaw trembling, and he began to scream at the trees. He said no words but his voice, like that of an attacking animal, could be heard at a great distance—even though no man was there to hear. The horse was frightened and her eyes went round and back. The wind stopped, and almost as if he had been trying to drown its rustling through the branches above him Leon stopped too and tears began to fall from his eyes all over the saddle and his horse's wet back. He cried for a long time, and then dismounted and slept.

When he awoke, it was dark. He could see by the light of the stars his horse standing a few feet away, looking at him as if to say, If you do this again, I'll go. He stood up and tended the horse, reassuring her, and then, feeling as tired and drained as he could, he began to make his own little camp. He broke some branches to build a fire for tea, which he drank while he ate some biscuits and beef. Usually when he made camp it was as tight as a drum, but this time everything was scattered. He was just too tired to impose a design on the few things he had lying about him. He spread his blankets, jammed a magazine of ammunition into his rifle, and lay down to listen for an hour or so to enter the frame of mind which would assure him alertness to any strange sound, even while he slept. Rifle by his side, he started the silence.

In between shudderings of the trees he heard a whistling, a weak deathlike wheeze at regular intervals off on his left. He waited, not knowing what it was. It sounded like a child's idea of a witch's sigh, a frightening noise from and within the darkness. It was, and this he sensed for sure, a steady death rattle. He waited more, and his lethargy fled from him as fast as alcohol disappears on the ground. Now he was planning and alert; like a bat he turned his head to and fro, searching the coordinates of the sigh to see if it were moving, while all the time checking the opposite silent sides where he expected surprise. No grasses rustled except in the wind, but perhaps it moved only then? It didn't, because it stayed in the same quarter.

If it were an enemy, what would be the sense in alerting him— perhaps to frighten him and steal his wits away, perhaps to confuse? But the man who could make such a noise was beyond Leon's imagination or experience. So terrible and pathetic was it that he thought perhaps he was mad. Remembering how he had screamed at the trees and beat them, he feared that they were whining in the darkness, and bleeding, and wailing like broken bodies. His fear grew white in front of him.

Then in a half beat of his heart he became less afraid and instead angry; he could see the darkness again, and the stars. He pulled his boots all the way on, and determined but fearful started toward the sound ever so quietly, rifle in hand with its safety off and his finger on the trigger, ready to fight without fear when the moment came, as he had done several times before in war. Yet he knew that he had to judge finely, for it could be an innocent making that hideous noise. He, of all men, was alert to that. And perhaps because of that he did not fire when he ranged in on it and fixed its exact location, but kept walking toward it, transfixed by its steadiness and by its weakness, as if the faint whistle were air rushing past the fine points of the stars. It was closer than he thought and without intending to he came directly upon it. He saw what it was.

"Oh God in heaven," he said. It was a dove. He had trampled it with his horse and it was dying.

Having only the light of the stars, he could see no colors. But he had lived in the same shade as doves for a quarter of a century, and was able to deduce from patterns and shadings in the black and white the colors he knew so well—a process which signified for him the depth of his life. It was an Eastern dove, not a shock of white and pure line as in the West, but many-colored, as deep contradictions ran through, and it was beautiful.

The wings of a dove are white-tipped, slate gray, brown as the Nile, then bronze along the back to a gold rim at the neck. A turn of the head changes the colors. The neck feathers have a shimmering purplish tinge. Similarly, the slate gray tends to green or blue. Watching it fly is like watching a storm on a tropical sea; the rich hot colors well up and spread across its surface like rain on blue green. Its head, as smooth as a hawk's silken hood, or an airman's leather helmet, with large brown eyes, is patterned with circlets and triangles and rims of white—like a Persian woman made up. It is always tending itself, and flies gracefully amid the olive trees and to date palms, winging and gliding in the clear air of the white hot valley.

But this dove was sick and silent, except for its sigh which had stopped when Leon came upon it, as if it had expected to die. Its wing lay extended, clearly it had been broken, and at the point where wing and body fused Leon could see a deep unnatural depression. Its head was tilted to one side somewhat strangely, and its eyes half closed in pain and waiting. It lay on a fallen palm branch, legs wedged between the thin green leaves.

He simply could not leave it there in its labored breathing to die in the cold and dark, with no one, no other dove, to form a chain from eye to eye, to show love at the last moment, to be there until one was

not needed. To die alone is to die a perpetual death, forever unfinished like a straight course into the black of the sky. To die alone is
not to have lived. So he took his knife and clipped the palm branch
to form a tray, pruning off the extremities and the weak pointed tips
of the leaves, and he carried the dove back through the underbrush to
his camp. There he rekindled the fire and put the dove and its tray on
a folded blanket. He could see in the firelight all the colors he had assumed, and the white ringlets. The dove stopped sighing, and with
renewed energy managed to open its eyes a little and turn its head to
watch the fire, and Leon, and the white nettles and grasses which
were shining in the light of the flames.

For a long time he just stared at it. He tried to give it cool water
but it would not drink. He tried to give it fruit he diced with his
knife, but it would not eat. Then he laid aside the fruit and water
and, after putting more twigs and some heavy branches on the fire,
lay down propped on his elbow near the dove, and stared at it trying
to decide what to do.

He could not heal it; that was impossible. He could, however,
wait with it until it died or until it got better. The chances that it
would live were greater that way, since he thought it would eventually take food from him and thus not starve. But it might take days,
he thought to himself, and meanwhile Yossi and the herd are waiting
for me. If I don't come it will be bad for all the animals, each one of
them a thousand times this light dove, and dozens of men will be
sent to look for me. And they probably would not find me. When I
returned, what would I tell them? And if they did find me, what
would I tell them then? They would think me crazy and never trust
me again, but how can I leave this dove?

Leaving the dove was out of the question. When he looked at it he
knew he would have to wait with it, despite ugly things that would be
said, and stories that would go around. Life was not rich there, and
people depended on the welfare of the animals. Were they to know
why he stayed away from the herd for days and days, jeopardizing its
course and making everyone worry, they would never forgive him.
And where would he go? And what profession would he follow?

They would say, Why so much trouble just for a dove? Do you not eat meat, and chicken? And since he did, he would not be able to answer them. They would say, You were irresponsible in your job, and you paid no attention to the welfare of several hundred men, women, and children. For what? For a dove that was going to die in any case? And he would not know what to say to them. But he could not leave the dove, and as the night passed he lay by it as if it were a sick child, tired himself, half dreaming. He lay there as if in a fever, breathing as slowly as the dove, determined to see it through.

Passing a gun shop in the Champs de Mars one fall he felt a great longing to be quail shooting. But he had not had, and had never had, nor would he ever have the slightest desire actually to shoot the quail. He wanted to be dressed in strong leather boots, in khaki pants with pockets on the thighs, to wear a rust-colored tweed jacket with shooting patches, a bandolier of copper bullets, and to carry a deep black shotgun of fine craftsmanship and light weight. He wanted to make his way across country (there was a specific image of gold and yellow grass and a view of low hills and apple orchards) and to come out of the darkness finally with cheeks reddened from the cold and an alert demeanor, to a fire and hot tea. But he had no desire whatever to shoot them. Hunting was merely a slaughterhouse with country accoutrements. Why not simply abstract and abandon the slaughterhouse? And yet he ate meat, and would continue, for cruel inconsistency was part of what made life. He became sick when he tried vegetarianism. A proselytizing friend of his who suggested it was thin and the color of ashes in the fireplace flue. Those who saw him immediately thought of the morgue; there was just something smooth and dull about his gray face—a lack of stolen energy and the evil sparkle of the predator. But for sport? Never, it was just the equipment, the sounds of walking through dry clean brush, the ice cold small rivers by which to halt.

And he loved so much to love that he wondered if he were drawn to it by all but love itself. Walking in the Champs de Mars, a place of orange and blue awnings and quiet curving streets, he felt at twenty so hypnotized by love, by its idea, by the beauty of the women he saw. He stared at them—not with the pompous, self-worshipping, suspiciously homosexual gaze of the Mediterranean strutter, but rather with an openness and humility, a simplicity which for a numbing moment worked its way even to his fingers and back and caused the whirling of an electrified moment to become a feeling of history. History, the means by which he loved, the recollection of all men and all women gazing at one another in times past; the graveyards of Paris, strangely untended and quiet as before a war, full of charted lives which had seen such hot permanent moments as he felt on the Champs de Mars, the hollowness and waste of societies of men and their deeds in the face of these breathless confrontations when the world went silk and eyes moved as if they could feel.

And how refreshing it was afterwards to go back and reflect once again on things and quantities, the books in his shelves, the small everyday machines, speculation, conversation, a new suit of clothes, buttered bread and tea in a café on mornings before school, the grandeur of what he studied, and the excitement of a winter night at work under his light inscribing equations in fine pen across the pages of a blank book.

But these were only the general, and Ann the specific. He had fallen in love with her in the station years before, and then again at the camp when she had spurned him, if only because she loved him too much. With Ann it was not a question of silken moments, but just Ann, not a single association, just Ann. Her singing at Kreuzlingen had so much entrapped him in a lifelong love that he remembered each day several times the way she was sitting at night by the fire, in a blue jacket, her dark auburn hair falling beyond her shoulders. Her voice was clear and especially beautiful, and she was embarrassed to sing, but she sang and her French songs rang out among the hills. For him they still sounded there, having survived all the years of ice and snow, the new roads and buildings, the children getting older and dying. Her songs were still heard.

Later in Paris he knew her at school, loving everything she did.

But for several years it was just dreaming, for they hardly even spoke and their manner was such that anyone else never would have had the vaguest notion that they were aware of one another, much less passionately in love. And then one day she broke her ankle on the playing field and he carried her up the steps to his car and drove her to the hospital. He had never touched her except accidentally or to take something from her hand. When he held her, her arms around his neck, he sensed for the first time that far from hating him she loved him; that she thought of him just as he had thought of her, in enveloping dreams; that she was thrilled by his presence as much as he had always been by hers; that she wanted to kiss him; that he was loved back. Then there was a golden fall when he scouted for perfect places in the woods and took her there on weekends. Her hair, lightened in the summer, fell from her blue student's cap. The weather was dry and cool and wavelike winds moved the trees and grass like breathing as they lay together for the first time in the diminishing October sun, its rays weakening into a cool sigh.

His aspirations were as great as his experience was little, but he could do no more than enjoy the impressions he felt so keenly. Life was a powerful confusion with rewards to those who did not control it. Those times were marked by the strangest remembrances: the heavy wooden door of her house, the black metal of his car, the letters they wrote, how Spain had passed them by and they had been hated for being so finely able to achieve what all the world's revolutions and all the red armies, what neither fascists nor pilots nor propagandists, nor the righteous or the daring or the obsessed, could do—and that was to create a heaven on earth. They had been hated for not noticing the definitive and terrible approach of the whitest winter ever to be seen. But had they feared and been oppressed by just the pressure of its advance, then they would have had nothing at all.

In no time they had finished university and found themselves hurtling through the Juen fields of Normandy on a fast black train, one car of which was filled with their families and friends on the way to the wedding at Honfleur. He was uncomfortable at the wedding itself: they thought it too beautiful and too much a part of the nineteenth century to be their own, but they wanted the old men and women—for whom the white dresses and morning suits, the flowers and childrens' carts, the canopy, glass, and ring, were real—to be happy and to remember, as memory was all they had. But the great thing for Leon and Ann was the train ride itself, something which had not been planned as enjoyment.

They all met at the North Station early in the morning when the streets were still wet and being swept. A cool wind came into the train shed from the north, and everyone was dressed informally but Leon, who wore a three-piece black suit with two fountain pens in the vest pocket. He had just published a paper in an important journal of biochemistry and won recognition as the *Majeur* of his department. This was published with his picture in all the newspapers of Paris and people had been recognizing him on the street—not many people, but some. The car they had reserved was supplied in each compartment with champagne, fruit, and cheese. Leon and Ann went from one group to another, being toasted in each compartment and drinking back until they became riotously intoxicated and staggered down the corridor as the train lurched back and forth, sending them crashing into walls and doors. In one place they played cards for half an hour with an old uncle of hers, in another they received gifts—for her a black gem of some sort set in a gold foil, for him more fountain pens, the kind with an edelweiss on both ends which looks just like a Star of David. All the time unbeknownst to them they passed the rusted cannon and common graves of the Great War. The old men and not so old men looked out the windows at places they had heard of or fought in, never dreaming that they would have the opportunity to glide by so peacefully in a car laden with champagne. They thought quietly and looked at the new summer fields; some of them managed to smile.

After the wedding they stayed at Honfleur boating and swimming. When they returned to Paris, it was the middle of summer and they settled down to work. She often wore a white silk dress and a white hat. They went to museums and walked in the parks at night—it was almost as if Paris were again the city of the century before. But winter came, and then the next summer, and the twentieth century clicked suddenly back into place like the sharp closing of a rifle bolt.

Again they were on a train, he and Ann, with just the beginnings of real fear about what Paris would become. Early one morning his father had driven to their apartment and burst in during breakfast looking like someone they hardly knew. "You must get out of Paris now, immediately," he screamed. His son's reaction was one almost of dumbfoundedness; he began to compose himself for analysis of the risks and probabilities, but the father took him by his dressing gown and lifted him from the chair. "Listen to me. I tell you to leave and go south. It is not at all like the last time, for Paris is going to burn, and we will burn first of all. You must leave."

"But how can we, Papa? You are here, and Mother, and Ann's parents and the family. The banks are closed, what nonsense, I am not even dressed," he said somewhat sheepishly before he was slapped across the face and knocked down. He then began to understand his father's understanding.

"All right," he said with a red eye, "we will leave." They dressed, he took his bank books and magazine article, and the three of them drove to the house of Ann's father, who agreed to leave that day because he too felt it was the opportunity, and "if they don't take Jews as I suspect they will, then we can return. We will always be able to say, if anyone should think to ask, that we are on holiday." He thought because he was so old that he should take charge.

"Monsieur Orlovsky, take the children to the station. We will follow later today after I arrange some business. If all goes well, shall we meet in Aix at the house of Pellegrin?"

"Good idea," said Leon's father, a bit of the fight returning to him, "we will all go separately and meet at the Pellegrins. The children this morning, we in the afternoon as there is some business that I too must finish before leaving, and you at night."

He took them to the station and gave them money enough for

several weeks' travel. "I want to see Mother," said Leon, and his father replied that he would see her at Aix and shortly. And then as it became clear that the train was going to leave, the father kissed Ann as he would have kissed a little girl, and turned to his son.

"Until Aix," he said, but just stood there with his hands at his sides. "At the house of Pellegrin." A column of soldiers marched into the back of the station, filling it with the rough cloth color of their uniforms. The father, who had seen and lost so much, embraced his son and they gripped one another as if for the last time. Leon remembered his father's tweed jacket, and the smell of cigars even on the shoulder. He remembered how suddenly his father looked so old, and how the old man had grasped his hand with a pathetic strength as if to say, Although we could never communicate and cannot communicate now, I love you very much. And then he backed away and said, lifting his head a little, "Your wife." Leon nodded, climbed on the train with Ann, and turned to see his father for the last time standing in a Paris station looking hopeful and childlike, in a black and white tweed jacket which was easy to see against the soldiers' cloaks of the darkest gray. The train pulled away, and Leon feared for him. When they had embraced he noticed how the power of his father's grasp had so lessened with the years. And he thought of the tweed jacket pushing its way through the masses of soldiers.

This train fell southwards instead of climbing north. The fields and trees were crazily indifferent to streams of refugees along the roads. It seemed to Leon that this was yet another battle in the Great War, for much of the equipment looked the same and the feeling was that the dead had risen to take revenge upon the living, that the trenches had suddenly burst open from the pressure of all that had grown within, and that a hideous rotted whiteness was about to envelop the land.

Unlike their wedding train, this one was not rapid. It often pulled over onto sidings for several hours, sometimes for the night, and it had a curious habit of going backwards for scores of kilometers and then coming to a dead halt in the middle of countryside as quiet and lush and black with night as in a dream. Then the conductors would walk up and down with red lanterns, the current would cease, and a tiny old man's voice would weave its way through the corridors, saying, "Stop for the night. Sleep outside or in. Leave at daybreak."

The trainmen replied to all questions with upraised shoulders and eyebrows. "It is war," they would say, "not a café."

"All the trains have been requisitioned," said Ann authoritatively, "and therefore our parents must have gone in a car. This must be. They are already in Provence." Leon kept busy buying food, bribing conductors to return to him his seat, and looking over and over again at his article as if it might have given him answers. On one of the seats a soldier had left a pea-green great coat with many pockets. With the practice of an established refugee Leon appropriated it, and used the pockets on food-gathering expeditions. He even brought back a bottle of good perfume for Ann, who was as overjoyed as if she had been impoverished all her life. He remained clean-shaven because a barber was also fleeing Paris and had brought his artillery. When the train halted the barber cut down oak branches and heated fresh river water in a large vat he had paid a soldier to steal, and then shaved most of the men on the train in return for food or money, and sometimes for free, just because he missed his home and his shop and the streets he knew so well.

Several days passed, and although Leon and Ann had been used to leaving Paris in the morning and arriving at Aix that evening, they were still somewhere in the middle of France—surrounded by cursing farmers, refugees, and confused army detachments hurrying in retreat as if to a battle already won. The life itself was not so bad, somehow there was always fresh food, the weather was good, but his impatience was tremendous regarding the house of Pellegrin, good friends in Provence sure to help. He was sure that his parents, even if they had started by train, would have then taken a car and gotten to Aix after a pleasant journey through the countryside in new summer. Undoubtedly they were in Pellegrin's garden, reading and talking. "My country is being invaded, and yet she contrives to be beautiful." It was early then for Provence, perhaps a little quiet, but a summer bursting out amid the mountains and white-faced cliffs. "I am sure they are there, and they must wonder about us. It is war after all and the sirens are real enough."

Ann, on the other hand, did not seem to worry, but was instead very quiet and happy. This angered him but he said nothing, thinking her very selfish for her lack of concern: she behaved like a school-girl on an outing, a little crazy, and he thought that callous indeed, but it only made him love her more.

There was a halt again after yet a few more days, in a small town which they guessed to be in the Midi (it was difficult to tell after being shuffled around for days on nameless sidings and rusted one-track lines). The engine hissed down, the electricity ceased, and the voice of the little old man passed through the train, "Leave tomorrow morning, express South, all tracks now clear, no hotels here." In an instant the passengers had their cooking tools and orange crates alongside the train turning the freight yard full of military trains and matériel into a temporary camp. But this was not unusual as all of France had become a camp of one sort or another.

Leon threw on the coat and checked his wallet. "I will get some food," he said, "before it's all gone."

"Please, try to get some meat or fish."

"Maybe there will be a restaurant. Then I will return with just an invitation—steak, watercress, and wine."

"Of course. I'll dress for the occasion in my dress. Go before it's too late."

He jumped from the train and ran enthusiastically over the many tracks and through the munitions until he came to the town, where restaurants were closed, except for one just for soldiers. There were some farmers with old trucks, selling vegetables and poultry. He bargained with them and afterwards stuffed a chicken, leeks, and potatoes in his big pockets. The coat was unbearably hot but the pockets served well. Again it would be chicken soup, not bad, but he wished he had some beef, especially since Ann had asked for it. Because it was hot he walked slowly back to the yards singing to himself a Jewish song he had learned in camp: "The Day Will Come." Off to his right he heard a humming noise like swarming bees but with a sharpness which offended the ear. Over the glowing terra-cotta tiles of an old house he saw six dots coming almost directly for him from a sky of very pleasing blue. They came so fast that he hardly knew what was happening until they began in terrifying immediacy to strafe and bomb.

At first he had no idea of the target, but then his sense of general danger became a much greater fear. Obviously, they were after the train yard. He began to run, his heart giving him much energy by its beating and fear. It was only after he saw the fighters diving at the yards that he decided to throw off his heavy coat with all the food, and even then he paused for half a second to take his wallet, without which he knew he could not survive.

Bombs were exploding all over the yard, tracer bullets, barely visible in the sun, making puffs and ricochets on the earth and steel. It was the part of a bombing attack comparable to starting a cold engine. Inside, things had not begun to catch, and bombs often fell isolated and without effect. But there were six planes and it was not long until the engine began to go—secondary explosions, walls of flame, freight cars blown apart so that their sides and doors flew like chaff.

He was running as fast as he could, with the incredible grace and energy of instinct. He never in his life had run so fast, nor had he been as sure of foot or as quick to dodge as then in the freight yard.

The train on which he had spent the previous few days was pulling away. The engine had gotten up steam, a track had opened, and it was gathering speed. Ann was in the window of their compartment, throwing things out the window and herself about to jump. "Leave them," he shouted, "stay," even though he was far away and the train was really beginning to move. He cut over toward it with incredible speed. He could hear feet that seemed not to be his own pounding the earth and stones. All was well; he had gone between the fires and bombs and shells, and he was running magnificently. "Stay," he screamed to Ann even as she pulled away with the train, because he knew he would make it. He tried to open one of the doors, but it was shut tight. He began to panic, for he knew there wasn't time for her to help him and the train was passing over cross switches on which he lost a lot of speed.

But then she said, "Other side, other side," and he felt great relief remembering that there the doors were open. He stopped for breath, nodded his head to her confidently, and pointed to the other side of the train. He would wait, get some wind, and then when the back of the train had passed him, make a break for the open doors. She understood this and they were confident that he would succeed. He stood there while the accelerating train passed him car by car and the bombs fell all around. But not one had struck the train, and he had not been wounded at all.

When the last car passed he set out with everything he had, leaping across the rails in one jump, and running furiously to an open door which was banging to and fro. He had room and time to spare. Even though the train was already going fairly fast he could have run beside it and entered by any door, but he wanted to be safe and he began to close on the first. He knew he could do it. It had become a great adventure—what a story to tell. He was sorry about the coat and the food, but he still had his wallet. He and Ann would be safe; he smiled.

And then he heard a terrific roar. A fighter plane's engines came so close he thought it was going to hit him. The deafening noise was followed by a string of explosions rapidly overtaking him. They were incendiary bombs, phosphorus. One exploded some meters in front of him and the world went white. He could see nothing, and he tripped and flew forward, crashing onto the railbed of stones and slate. He heard whistles, bombs, and engines, and then lost consciousness thinking he was dead.

When he opened his eyes, it was pitch dark except for some orange fires far away. He could hardly see, but that was nothing. Ann was gone.

The old conductor had said the South of France. He raised himself and tried to sense what was around him, thinking only of how to get to the house of Pellegrin in Aix where she and his parents would be waiting.

With much difficulty he stumbled across the rails until he heard a train passing slowly in front of him. He judged it a freight and somehow managed to catch hold of a ladder on its side and climb to a hatch through which he let himself fall without much caution. He landed on bales of some sort of cloth, perhaps felt or even velvet, and lay on them quite comfortably except for his wounds and some burns on his feet and ankles. He could see the sky through the opening, but not the stars, as he was partially blinded. The train had been a shadow, but since they had lived in the summer near the railroad he was always able to distinguish different trains even without sight of them.

Passenger trains were light shells, whisked effortlessly after the engine in delightful relief. The slower freight trains continued to grind the track as had done the engine, with little contrast. Once in a great while he had seen flatbed trains loaded with tanks and half-tracks. Always on these one could see soldiers perched on the vehicles. Regardless of the time or place they seemed to have the same expression, a combination of the joy of riding carefree and a grim feeling of predetermined death. They would be either eating, casting off nut shells or fruit pits into the wake of their convoy, or scanning the countryside while at the ready on double-barreled machine guns in flimsy sand-bagged positions. It was like riding the back of a dragon. Before the war he had echoed Ann's feelings, that there were too many tanks and soldiers and that these were likely in themselves to bring about conflict, like the spontaneous generation of snakes from a horse's hair in rainwater. But lying on bales of cloth which had been packed before the war and would be unpacked during the war, he wished there had been more tanks and guns, since a lack of them hadn't stopped anything. And he wondered why Ann, who was so weak and willing to be weak, had been attacked as if she were armed to the teeth. With this thought, and a terrible hollowness and fear that at last he had been broken, and in one blow, he fell asleep on his bales under stars he could not see on a train which by pure luck was quickly making its way south.

He was startled suddenly upon waking up in a motionless silence. A blue sky shone through the hatch, and for the first time in days he was able to see perfectly. He had been lying on bales of black felt. Several bees had flown into the car and were having difficulty finding their ways out. The air was different so that he knew he was far away from the yard and sidings of the bombing attack. He looked at himself and felt his face. The cuffs of his pants were burned away and his ankles blistered. His clothes were ripped and full of dried blood, and he felt a wound on his skull and across his forehead. Really awakening, he breathed in tensely and thought of Ann. He felt his wallet in his pocket, cursed himself, and prayed that her train had gone directly south. He climbed out of the dark into a freight yard in Provence, in a town he knew well. For some reason, even though he had money, he set out by foot for Aix, fifty kilometers distant. But he was more exhausted than he thought and when he stopped to rest by a bridge he fell asleep and did not awaken until evening. Then he drank water from a cool stream and his rest, the fresh water, and the descent of evening made him feel again like a man. Nevertheless he did not look like one, and when he stopped a truck loaded with mirrors for a ride to Aix, the driver would take him only if he rode in the back. "You are ugly, that's why," the man said, and Leon watched himself for an hour or more in the very dimly lighted mirrors. He looked like a Napoleonic infantryman in the Russian winter. This, the fact that he had survived, and the joy at closing the distance between himself and his wife whom he imagined in the garden at the house of Pellegrin made him laugh out loud over and over. He was rugged. What a tale to tell the Pellegrins. He was alive and soon he would see Ann. But his wounds began to pain him and he realized how hungry he was.

The driver rapped on the panel of his compartment. "Aix, Aix," he said, and Leon climbed out just before the truck drove off into the dark. He was in the main square by the fountain and could not believe what he saw.

Literally scores of young men and women, in tuxedos and white ball gowns, were clustered around the fountain, talking and laughing, with champagne glasses in their hands. Telling the virtues of the town, the fountain splashed clear water on clear light. The night was one of those early summer nights which is thick and beautiful and yet cool enough to accommodate the pale light of the moon. They had just graduated. To him it was unbelievable.

He went to the fountain and washed himself. Several of the young people came up to him and one boy handed him a glass of champagne, saying, "Don't drink from the fountain, drink this." Leon drank it with the speed of a trout catching a fly, and he was poured another, and then several others until his pain was gone and he began to feel some energy and a great deal of dizziness. They had gathered around and were looking at him as if he were a nice little dog. He felt no anger, and just looked at them and at the lights and water. "I was one of you," he said, "indeed I was, and in just a few days I have become someone else, never to return. Consider that. Consider that here in your summer of trees and fountain." He was swaying back and forth, not unpleasantly, and his eyes could not focus.

"There is an ice age up there, you know, in the North. It's falling down here and will slide over here any time. You know that. You know what's happening." The boy closest to him nodded. He had finally spoiled their party, a spoiled party anyway. Here was a wretched creature who said he was from the North, and they became frightened down to the soles of their patent leather shoes. "There's a war, a war, and I was in it," he said. He began to weep, swaying back and forth, staring into the fountain and its intoxicating random envelopments, stunning the adolescents all around him. "Take me to the house of Pellegrin," he commanded forcefully. Two boys helped him to their car.

The effects of champagne retreated as the little car weaved its way, headlamps beaming, through the walled and gardened countryside quiet but for a din of crickets and the rushing of dark overhead branches. They left him at the gate and he walked up a familiar stone drive to a familiar house which was shut, and dark, and terrifying; and he wailed a cry of despair and horror which silenced the night animals, for even they could sense the upwelling of Hell.

In September of 1947, after he had been with the Free French, and then for several years searched as best he could the D.P. camps and the German records, he went to Palestine. Both sets of parents had never left Paris except on a train to Poland. Beyond names and numbers there was nothing more to be heard of them. They had vanished into the soil. They had not even a grave. He returned to the family houses to find other people living in them, quite happily; all the furniture had been taken; the books, diplomas, letters, photographs were gone. He found that under law he still owned his house. An eager lawyer told him of how it could easily be regained. Leon thought for a moment and then simply said, "What would I do with it?" and walked out.

He went to photographers in the neighborhood to try to find a photograph of his wife or his parents. They made him pay exorbitantly to search through their files. Thousands of men, women, and children stared out at him, but he found nothing. He had been arrested and his papers had been confiscated. Because of that he hadn't even a picture, or signature, or anything at all of his wife or parents. He remembered his father in the station, in his jacket. Where was his jacket?

He went to friends to inform them that he was alive and to seek information. They had none. He did not wish to hear of his mother and father, for they were dead and there was no point in reconstructing those days when he had been absent. But Ann was still alive. Of this he was convinced, since there was no record of her anywhere. No one had seen her, her name was to be found on no lists, there were no rumors.

It was said that beautiful women survived better than anyone else and he hoped for this. She might have been in England, Russia, France, America, Palestine, anywhere. People in the camps were going to Palestine. He knew that she might not even have been able to return to France, and hoped that she had been in Palestine all during the war. On the train they had discussed it, for although their first choice was America they knew they had no chance of entry. He spent weeks and months imagining her healthy and dark, farming the land and changed. And anyway, although he loved Europe he could not bear to put one foot down after another there. He left for Palestine from Trieste, illegally, but by then he had a talent for such things.

The Mediterranean—bright and dark, covered with mists of glowing air, surrounded by coasts of white rock and fish-eating cities, divided by islands of pine and citrus, rapid carrier of heat and conflict—enlivened him for a time. Three weeks on the deck of an old ship, with men and women as broken, defeated, and numb as the rusting iron and toothless rails, made him aware of his strength once again. He was moving once more, as rapidly as when he had fallen into France by silken parachute, or followed an armored column across the Rhine. These wretched refugees even sang, and despite its age the ship went forward, and the waves went eastward, waves which would become a new state, sweeping through it as it grew. They sang "My Thoughts Are Free," and they sang "The Day Will Come," and many other songs, so that at night on the small ship by yellow lantern light the new state took shape, in waves of feeling and energy, like a song. The children were given life, born here. And Leon, who had begun to crumble, had a part of him braced. He was again in the deep flux of history, nurtured only by events and hopes. The sun rose and beat upon the green sea. It set, and left its mark of bronze and red on the faces of those who had cast their eyes always to the East. I love, he thought, I must love. If I cannot love Maman, and Papa, and Ann, then I must at least love this land a little.

And the days passed as they hid behind islands and kept off the sea lanes until one late afternoon as the sun lit the East they found themselves, gasping as if at a stage play, face-to-face with land on which waves broke hard. A hot sweet wind came off the beaches and mountains. They could see trees ashore. They were face-to-face with the cliffs of Rosh HaNikra, and the British awaited them with trucks and lights while doglike patrol boats made wakes in lariats and loops and figure eights across their bows and off their stern. They were to be detained. But some decided to take to the water.

Leon was the first. As part of his training in England before he was sent into France he had to swim a mile every day. After many months of delays he became an excellent swimmer—much more so than he had been, and he had been good. He decided to swim around the British cordon. Although loudspeakers said he would drown, and some unfortunates did, he knew it was just a question of a few hours in the water. He tied his shoes around his neck and jumped into the sea. A second later he felt a splash beside him and from a froth of white emerged a girl's head. She said in Italian, since that was the language of the ship, "To swim beyond, no?" and he just began. They started straight north, parallel to the shore. She kept on wanting to go in, but he insisted that they clear the cordon and land where the cliffs came down to the sea. "That's dangerous," said the girl swimmer, who was about twenty. "Exactly," he replied, "there will be no police dogs there."

The waves were crashing against the rock as if in a great storm, and some of them flowed into caves where their breaking was trumpeted to the sea. It was getting dim when they made for a large cave, thinking to hide in it for the night and then swim out the next day. The entrance was narrow and surrounded with sharp rocks. They centered themselves as best they could and were swept inwards, almost crashing on a wall of rock. They swam for a while until they reached the back of the grotto and a ledge to which the water reached out and then receded gently. They climbed out and found themselves in a roaring mist. The air was wetter than the sea, the rock salty and moist. In the remaining light he looked at his companion and discovered a beautifully proportioned, darkly tanned half-naked girl. They were exhausted; the waves, noise, and depth of the cave were counters to inhibition. They had after all accomplished a great feat and they were landed. They stared at one another, both of them trembling from the hours of swimming, and she slowly wrung out her shirt. It was in fact a dream situation, but he rapidly found himself feeling nothing. His greater loyalties surfaced as if from the sea. He just stared at her, his heart contained by an open question. All was cold, and dead, and over. He would not marry ever again, or make love, or fall in love. Such would ruin his chances. He simply could not take certain breaths, for fear of toppling Ann into hopelessness. What had she apart from his faith? So he stared dully at this girl who truly was able to impart deliriousness, and the night passed miserably. If he had felt temptation, and if he had felt longing for Ann, they had mixed to become as clean, smooth, and monotonous as the moist green stone which had been ground down by the waves.

Before dawn broke he had passed through many an ecstasy and sustained many a second wind. But with the coming of the light he felt drained and quiet, breathing hard and slowly like the dove. He feared that it had been chilled when the fire burned down, and overheated when he built it up again. It looked so much, in its expression, like a human invalid, that he found himself sometimes imagining that he was by the bed of a sick child. But he glanced at its Oriental luminescence, the warmest of colors, reminding him that it was indeed a dove and that he had chosen to remain by its side waiting despite the consequences.

He had sometimes exercised his wants despite consequences and tugged at the patience of friends, if they could be called that. Unbelievably, he shirked guard duty for a decade or more, being allowed to do so because of his reputation as an intense eccentric. It was not that he wished to avoid work, for work was the only thing left to him, but rather that he genuinely feared to stand watch. He thought the crucial seconds between his sentry's challenge and a response would be wasted and that he might be killed. This was because he knew he would not shoot a shadow moving toward him on a moon or star lit night, thinking it might be Ann, come to find him.

She had long ago assumed these proportions, of a shadow or a shade, a walker on the floor of the valley without touching it, a descender from the deep sky, pale and sad, a ghost, a weeping gossamer, as white as powder and as quiet. This was unavoidable, a debt to pay, for in his stronger imaginings she was red as all life, moving, bursting into laughter, singing, fighting him, loving him—and imagination's pendulum had to sway.

When he had first come to the Bet Shan Valley he had found, as if in coordination with everything else, that the climate was unbearable and the land an infested swamp. But he worked hard to clear it where it was not already cleared. For him it was as if the more beautiful the valley became the more likely that she would suddenly arrive. There was always the faintest hope, like one star on a black night, which sometimes in his dreams became a wall of white light blinding him with happiness as if the next day he would see her, for one never knew. These, while they lasted, were his best times, although extraordinarily bitter afterwards.

And yet his dreams did not run in place. He knew that everything moves forward, and he had grown and developed despite himself over the years. A film which in 1950 or 1960 had seemed to him to be richer and fuller than life itself, and certainly as real, was upon reshowing no more authoritative as to the depth of things than a fast-moving montage of African and Asian postage stamps—colorful and interesting, but with the flow and humanity of a cogwheel. Things moved forward, and although most of his life had been the history of solitude, a long unbroken color, and although his wisdom had served only to heighten the quality of his sadness, he continued to think that perhaps there would be a day when his unraveled life would again be whole.

The practice of years on the land made him look up. On a distant hill he saw horses and riders in the heat of middle morning, raising threads of dust. They would soon be upon him. He looked at the dove, its eyes three-quarters closed, and surmised that despite its gentleness it was willed to die.

And what would the horsemen say, seeing him beside a dove dying rapidly on a palm branch he had cut? These young men would not understand. They did not know what he thought and felt. He was beyond their concern and that was in his view quite right. For they had to grow up and pass their scores of years and enter into history. They too would be old, touched by events younger ones could not understand. They too would go to their graves alone, obsessed with remembrances of a life which in its incredible variation had pushed them out beyond the society of men into quiet places where they could only reflect. Starting on the surface of a sphere, crowded and touching, each man moved outwards so that the longer his life the greater the loneliness around him. Nothing can be done, and there is no comfort in it. There is no comfort in dying, no comfort in growing old. In the end there is no solace even in history. But a young man and an old man are moved before they die to finish the task of their life. And this, Leon, far from Paris and far from his love, could do.

A pair of horsemen came down a near hill, raising dust in the white morning sun. They were approaching the grove of trees. Leon looked at the motionless dove, and then at the horses and men galloping toward him.

The gentleness of a dove is something we cannot understand. Sometimes a fighter, it is not all of one color. But most of all it is moved by quiet love and a wish for simple life among the trees. And when it dies it breaks us apart, for it never thinks of itself. But God protect it if it should die alone, and God protect its poor family.

The Season of Phantasmal Peace

Then all the nations of birds lifted together
the huge net of the shadows of this earth
in multitudinous dialects, twittering tongues,
stitching and crossing it. They lifted up
the shadows of long pines down trackless slopes,
the shadows of glass-faced towers down evening streets,
the shadow of a frail plant on a city sill—
the net rising soundless as night, the birds' cries soundless, until
there was no longer dusk, or season, decline, or weather,
only this passage of phantasmal light
that not the narrowest shadow dared to sever.

And men could not see, looking up, what the wild geese drew,
what the ospreys trailed behind them in silvery ropes
that flashed in the icy sunlight; they could not hear
battalions of starlings waging peaceful cries,
bearing the net higher, covering this world
like the vines of an orchard, or a mother drawing
the trembling gauze over the trembling eyes
of a child fluttering to sleep;
                                        it was the light
that you will see at evening on the side of a hill
in yellow October, and no one hearing knew
what change had brought into the raven's cawing,
the killdeer's screech, the ember-circling chough
such an immense, soundless, and high concern
for the fields and cities where the birds belong,
except it was their seasonal passing, Love,
made seasonless, or, from the high privilege of their birth,

something brighter than pity for the wingless ones
below them who shared dark holes in windows and in houses,
and higher they lifted the net with soundless voices
above all change, betrayals of falling suns,
and this season lasted one moment, like the pause
between dusk and darkness, between fury and peace,
but, for such as our earth is now, it lasted long.

Contributors' Notes

KIM ADDONIZIO is the author of three books of poetry, the most recent of which, *Tell Me*, was a finalist for the 2000 National Book Award. She has published a book of stories, *In the Box Called Pleasure*, and is co-author, with Dorianne Laux, of *The Poets' Companion: A Guide to the Pleasures of Writing Poetry*. She currently teaches private workshops in the San Francisco Bay Area.

SHERMAN ALEXIE is a Spokane/Coeur d'Alene Indian from Wellpinit, Washington, on the Spokane Indian reservation. He is the author of sixteen books, most recently the story collection *Ten Little Indians*. He is also a screenwriter, director, stand-up comic, and four-time winner of the World Heavyweight Poetry Bout. He lives in Seattle with his wife and two sons.

WILLIAM ARCHILA lives in Los Angeles and earned his M.F.A. in poetry from the University of Oregon. His poems have appeared in *The Georgia Review*, *Rattle*, *Drumvoices Revue*, *Bilingual Review*, and the anthology *Another City: Writing from Los Angeles*.

ANDREA BARRETT lives in Rochester, New York. She is the author of *Servants of the Map*; *Ship Fever*, which won the National Book Award; and *The Voyage of the Narwhal*. Barrett has been a fellow at the Center for Writers and Scholars at the New York Public Library. In 2001 she was awarded a MacArthur Fellowship.

CHARLES BAXTER is the author of four novels, most recently *Saul and Patsy*, and four books of stories. He lives in Minneapolis and teaches at the University of Minnesota.

WENDELL BERRY is a Kentuckian who wrote and taught in California and New York before returning to the Kentucky River region, where he has lived for two decades. In his essays he has emerged as an eloquent spokesman for conservation, common sense, and sustainable agriculture, and he has written of the Kentucky River country in his novels, including *Nathan Coulter* and *A Place on Earth*, and in the short story collection *The Wild Birds*.

ELIZABETH BISHOP remains one of America's most celebrated and admired postwar poets. She won both the Pulitzer Prize and the National Book Award for her verse and served as Poetry Consultant at the Library of Congress in 1949–50. She died in 1979.

DAVID BOTTOMS's first book, *Shooting Rats at the Bibb County Dump*, won the Walt Whitman Award. His poems have appeared widely in such magazines as *The Atlantic Monthly*, *The New Yorker*, and *Poetry*. He teaches at Georgia State University and co-edits *Five Points* magazine. He lives in Marietta, Georgia.

T. C. BOYLE is the author of ten novels and six collections of stories. His most recent titles are *Drop City*, *After the Plague*, and *A Friend of the Earth*. He received his M.F.A. and Ph.D. degrees from the University of Iowa and is currently a member of the English Department at the University of Southern California. His just completed novel, *The Inner Circle*, will appear in 2004.

JOEL BROUWER is the author of *Exactly What Happened* and *Centuries*. He lives in Tuscaloosa and teaches at the University of Alabama.

B. J. BUCKLEY is a poet and writer who lives in a small cabin in the Bitterroot Valley of Montana. Her publications have appeared in many small magazines and anthologies. She is the 2003 winner of the Rita Dove Poetry Prize from the Center for Women Writers at Salem College.

ROBERT OLEN BUTLER has published ten novels and two volumes of short stories, one of which, *A Good Scent from a Strange Mountain*, won the 1993 Pulitzer Prize for Fiction. Among his other awards is a National Magazine Award for Fiction. He teaches creative writing at Florida State University.

ETHAN CANIN is the author of *Carry Me Across the Water*, *For Kings and Planets*, *The Palace Thief*, *Blue River*, and *Emperor of the Air*. He is on the faculty of the Iowa Writers' Workshop and is also a physician. He lives in Iowa.

HAYDEN CARRUTH has published twenty-nine books, chiefly poetry but also a novel, four books of criticism, and two anthologies. *Collected Shorter Poems 1946–1991* won the National Book Critics Circle Award; *Scrambled Eggs and Whiskey* won the National Book Award for Poetry. He lives in upstate New York.

AMY CLAMPITT was born and brought up in Iowa, graduated from Grinnell College, and from that time on lived mainly in New York City. Her first full-length collection, *The Kingfisher*, was followed by *What the Light Was Like*, *Archaic Figure*, *Westward*, and *A Silence Opens*. In 1992 she received a MacArthur Fellowship. She died in September 1994.

BILLY COLLINS was born in New York City in 1941 and now lives in Somers, New York. He is the author of several books of poetry, most recently *Nine Horses*.

His poems have appeared in a variety of periodicals, including *Harper's* and *The New Yorker*, and have been selected three times for *Best American Poetry*. He served as the eleventh Poet Laureate of the United States.

ROBERT DANA was born in Boston in 1929. His poetry has won several awards, including two National Endowment for the Arts Fellowships, the Delmore Schwartz Memorial Poetry Award, and a Pushcart Prize in 1996. His books include *What I Think I Know: New and Selected Poems*; *Yes, Everything*; *Hello, Stranger*; and *The Morning of the Red Admirals*.

RITA DOVE served as Poet Laureate of the United States and Consultant in Poetry to the Library of Congress from 1993 to 1995 and was reappointed Special Consultant in Poetry for 1999–2000. Her literary and academic honors include the 1987 Pulitzer Prize in Poetry, the 1996 Heinz Award in the Arts and Humanities, the 1996 National Humanities Medal, and the 2001 Duke Ellington Lifetime Achievement Award in the Literary Arts. She is Commonwealth Professor of English at the University of Virginia.

LOUISE ERDRICH grew up in North Dakota and is a mixed blood enrolled in the Turtle Mountain Band of Ojibwa. She is the author of eight novels, including the National Book Critics Circle Award–winning *Love Medicine* and the National Book Award finalist *The Last Report on the Miracles at Little No Horse*, as well as poetry, children's books, and a memoir of early motherhood. She lives in Minnesota with her children, who help her run a small independent bookstore, the Birchbark.

RICHARD FOERSTER lives in York Beach, Maine. He is the author of four books of poetry, the most recent of which is *Double Going*. He has received many awards for his work, including the "Discovery"/*The Nation* Award and *Poetry Magazine*'s Bess Hokin Prize.

DAISY FRIED's first book of poems, *She Didn't Mean to Do It*, won the Agnes Lynch Starrett Prize. She has received fellowships from the Bread Loaf Writers' Conference and the Pew and Leeway Foundations. Her poems have been published in *Threepenny Review* and *Triquarterly*, among others. She teaches at Haverford College and the University of Pennsylvania and lives in Philadelphia.

BRENDAN GALVIN is the author of thirteen collections of poems. His recent books are *Place Keepers*, *The Strength of a Named Thing*, and *Sky and Island Light*. He lives in Truro, Massachusetts, and is at work on a collection of his bird poems, *Whirl Is King*.

TIM GAUTREAUX's work has appeared in *Harper's*, *The Atlantic Monthly*, and the *O. Henry* and *Best American Short Stories* annuals. His new novel is *The Clearing*. He lives in Louisiana.

SARAH GETTY's first book of poems, *The Land of Milk and Honey*, published as part of the James Dickey Contemporary Poetry Series, won a Cambridge Poetry Award. Her poetry has appeared in *Paris Review*, *Western Humanities Review*, *The New Republic*, and several anthologies. She lives in Bedford, Massachusetts.

REGINALD GIBBONS is the author of seven books of poetry, most recently *It's Time*, and a novel, *Sweetbitter*. With Charles Segal he has translated Euripides' *Bakkhai* and Sophocles' *Antigone*. He is a professor of English at Northwestern University in Chicago.

ALBERT GOLDBARTH lives in Wichita, Kansas. He has been publishing notable books of poetry for over thirty years; two have received the National Book Critics Circle Award. He is also the author of a novel, *Pieces of Payne*. "27,000 Miles" will be included in his forthcoming volume of poetry, *Budget Travel Through Space and Time*.

JORIE GRAHAM was born in New York City and spent her youth in Italy. She is the author of numerous collections of poetry, most recently *Never*. *The Dream of the Unified Field: Selected Poems 1974–1994* won the 1996 Pulitzer Prize for Poetry. Her many honors include a MacArthur Fellowship. She teaches at Harvard University.

JOY HARJO is a poet, musician, writer, and performer. She has published several books, most recently *How We Became Human, New and Selected Poems*. A saxophone player, she performs nationally and internationally solo and with her band. She is a member of the Muscogee Nation and the Tallahassee Wakokaye Grounds and is a full professor at the University of California at Los Angeles. She lives in Honolulu.

JIM HARRISON's *Off to the Side* memoir recently appeared in paperback.

ROBERT HASS is the author of several books of poetry, including *Sun Under Wood: New Poems*. He is also the author or editor of several other collections of poetry, essays, and translations. He served as Poet Laureate of the United States from 1995 to 1997. He lives in California and teaches at the University of California at Berkeley.

WILLIAM HATHAWAY has published seven books of poems, all of them teeming with squawking and strutting birds. He lives in Surry, Maine.

SEAMUS HEANEY's recent works include *Electric Light*; his acclaimed translation of *Beowulf*, which was an international best-seller; *Diary of One Who Vanished*, his version of the text for a song cycle by Leoš Janáček; and a comprehensive selection of his poetry, *Opened Ground: Poems 1966–1996*. Heaney was awarded the Nobel Prize for Literature in 1995. A resident of Dublin, he teaches regularly at Harvard University.

MARK HELPRIN is author of numerous books of fiction, including *Memoir from Antproof Case* and *The Veil of Snows*. A contributing editor of *The Wall Street Journal*, he is also a senior fellow of the Claremont Institute, a fellow of the American Academy in Rome, and a former Guggenheim Fellow.

ANDREW HUDGINS has published a collection of literary essays and five books of poetry, most recently *Ecstatic in the Poison*. *Saints and Strangers* was a finalist for the 1985 Pulitzer Prize for Poetry; *After the Lost War* received the Poets' Prize in 1989; and *The Never-Ending* was a finalist for the 1991 National Book Award. He lives in Columbus, Ohio, and teaches at Ohio State University.

RICHARD JACKSON's seventh book of poems is *Unauthorized Autobiography: New and Selected Poems*. He teaches at the University of Tennessee at Chattanooga and has won Guggenheim, Fulbright, and Witter Bynner Fellowships, among others. In May 2000 he was awarded the Order of Freedom Award from the president of Slovenia for his editing and humanitarian contributions in Slovenia and the Balkans.

SHERI JOSEPH is the author of a cycle of stories, *Bear Me Safely Over*. Her short fiction has appeared in numerous literary journals and in *After O'Connor: Contemporary Georgia Stories*. "The Elixir" was a finalist for the 1999 National Magazine Award. She lives in Atlanta and teaches at Georgia State University.

BARBARA KINGSOLVER's eleven published books include novels, short stories, poetry, essays, and oral history. Her work has been translated into more than two dozen languages and has earned numerous literary awards. She, her husband, and two daughters live outside of Tucson, Arizona, and on a farm in southern Appalachia.

MAXINE KUMIN lives on a farm in central New Hampshire. She has published thirteen volumes of poetry, most recently *The Long Marriage*, as well as a memoir, novels, short stories, and essays on country living. She was awarded the Pulitzer Prize for Poetry in 1973 and has been a poetry consultant for the Library of Congress and Poet Laureate of New Hampshire.

LI-YOUNG LEE was born in 1957 in Jakarta, Indonesia, of Chinese parents. In 1959 his father, after a year as a political prisoner, fled Indonesia with his family. They arrived in America in 1964. Li-Young Lee's book *Rose* won the 1986 Delmore Schwartz Memorial Poetry Award; *The City in Which I Love You* was the 1990 Lamont Poetry Selection of the Academy of American Poets. He lives in Chicago with his wife, Donna, and their two children.

PHILIP LEVINE grew up in Detroit. He is the author of sixteen books of poetry, most recently *The Mercy*. Among his honors are the Pulitzer Prize, the National Book Award, twice the National Book Critics Circle Award, the Lenore Marshall Poetry Prize, and two Guggenheim Fellowships. He lives in New York City and Fresno, California, and teaches at New York University.

JOHN L'HEUREUX is the author of seventeen books of poetry and fiction. His most recent novel, *The Miracle,* won the 2003 Commonwealth Award of California. "Flight" will appear in his next book of short stories. He teaches at Stanford University.

ROBERT HILL LONG was raised and educated in North Carolina. His books include *The Power to Die*, *The Work of the Bow*, and *The Effigies*. He has been awarded fellowships by the National Endowment for the Arts and several state arts councils. His work has been anthologized in *Best American Poetry*, *Flash Fiction*, and *Web del Sol* and has appeared in journals across America. He lives in Eugene, Oregon.

BARRY LOPEZ is the author of six works of nonfiction and eight works of fiction. His writing appears regularly in *Harper's*, *The Paris Review*, *Double Take*, and *The Georgia Review*. He is the recipient of a National Book Award, an Award in Literature from the American Academy of Arts and Letters, a Guggenheim Fellowship, and other honors. He lives in western Oregon.

KATHLEEN LYNCH is the author of *How to Build an Owl*, *Alterations of Rising*, *No Spring Chicken*, and *Greatest Hits*. A poet, fiction writer, and artist, she lives in Carmichael, California.

PETER MEINKE has published twelve books of poetry, six in the prestigious Pitt Poetry Series, the latest of which is *Zincfingers*. His book of stories, *The Piano Tuner*, received the 1986 Flannery O'Connor Award for Short Fiction; his recent story, "Unheard Music," is in *New Stories from the South: The Best of 2003*. He lives in St. Petersburg, Florida.

WILLIAM MEREDITH was born in New York City in 1919. He is the author of nine books of poetry, including *Effort at Speech*, which won the National Book Award, and *Partial Accounts: New and Selected Poems*, which won the Pulitzer Prize. He lives in Connecticut and Florida.

HOWARD NORMAN is the author of three novels—*The Northern Lights*, *The Bird Artist*, and *The Museum Guard*—and a story collection, *The Chauffeur*. He has twice been named as finalist for the National Book Award and has received a Lannan Literary Award for Fiction. He lives with his family in Vermont and Washington, D.C.

LESLIE NORRIS was born in Wales and was educated there and at the University of Southampton. He is University Poet in Residence at Brigham Young University and lives in Orem, Utah, with his wife. His poems and stories are widely published.

FLANNERY O'CONNOR was born in Savannah, Georgia, in 1925. When she died at the age of thirty-nine, America lost one of its most gifted writers at the height of her powers.

GREG PAPE is the author of *Border Crossings*, *Black Branches*, *Storm Pattern*, and *Sunflower Facing the Sun*. He teaches at the University of Montana and in the brief-residency M.F.A. program at Spalding University, and he lives with his family in Montana's Bitterroot Valley.

STANLEY PLUMLY's book of essays is titled *Argument and Song: Sources and Silences in Poetry*. He is a Distinguished University Professor at the University of Maryland.

PATTIANN ROGERS's tenth book, *Song of the World Becoming: New and Collected Poems 1981–2001*, was a finalist for the *Los Angeles Times* Book Prize. Among many other honors, she has received a Guggenheim Fellowship, a Lannan Fellowship, and five Pushcart Prizes. Her next book, *Generations*, will be published in 2004.

MAXIMILIAN SCHLAKS grew up on the island of Guadeloupe. He is a graduate of the Iowa Writers' Workshop, and his fiction has appeared in *The Missouri Review*,

Manoa, *The Sun*, and *The Massachusetts Review* and is forthcoming in *The Atlantic Monthly*. He received the 2003 Pennsylvania Council on the Arts Fellowship for Literature.

JAN EPTON SEALE lives in the Rio Grande Valley, where she writes and teaches writing. She is active in environmental work and is the editor of *Creatures on the Edge*. Other books include *Homeland* (essays) and *Airlift* (short stories), as well as three volumes of poems.

MARTHA SILANO is the author of *What the Truth Tastes Like*. Her work has appeared in *Paris Review*, *Green Mountains Review*, *Beloit Poetry Journal*, and the anthologies *American Poetry: The Next Generation* and *Red, White, and Blues: Poetic Vistas on the Promise of America*. She lives in Seattle, where she teaches at Edmonds Community College.

MACKLIN SMITH, a devoted bird-watcher and obsessive birder, also teaches medieval literature, poetry and poetics, and creative writing at the University of Michigan. His poems have appeared in various journals and in *Transplant*.

R. T. SMITH's *Messenger* received the Library of Virginia Poetry Prize in 2002. His new books include *The Hollow Log Lounge* and *Brightwood*. He lives in Virginia and edits *Shenandoah* for Washington and Lee University.

W. D. SNODGRASS's first book, *Heart's Needle*, won the Pulitzer Prize in 1960. Since then, he has had numerous publications and occasional awards, most recently for *Selected Translations*. His two most recent books are critical studies, *De/Compositions* and *To Sound Like Yourself*. Retired from teaching, he lives with his wife in Erieville, New York, and winters in Mexico.

MAYA SONENBERG's story collection, *Cartographies*, received the Drue Heinz Literature Prize. Her more recent fiction has appeared in *Alaska Quarterly Review*, *Passages North*, *Other Voices*, and *American Short Fiction*. She lives in Seattle with her family and is director of the Creative Writing Program at the University of Washington.

GLADYS SWAN is both a painter and a writer. She has published five collections of short fiction and two novels, *Carnival for the Gods* and *Ghost Dance: A Play of Voices*. Her most recent book is *News from the Volcano*, which was nominated for the PEN/Faulkner Award. She lives in Columbia, Missouri.

CHASE TWICHELL is the author of five books of poetry, the most recent of which is *The Snow Watcher*. *The Lover of God*, by Rabindranath Tagore, co-translated with Tony K. Stewart, is forthcoming. In 1999 she quit teaching at Princeton to start Ausable Press, which publishes contemporary poetry.

DAVID WAGONER is the author of seventeen books of poems, most recently *The House of Song*, and ten novels, one of which, *The Escape Artist*, was made into a movie by Francis Ford Coppola. He teaches at the University of Washington.

DEREK WALCOTT was born in St. Lucia in 1930. His *Collected Poems: 1948–1984* appeared in 1986; his subsequent works include the book-length poem *Omeros* and *The Bounty*. He received the Nobel Prize for Literature in 1992.

ROBERT PENN WARREN was born in Kentucky in 1905. He won the Pulitzer Prize three times, twice in poetry and once in fiction for *All the King's Men*. In 1985 he was appointed the first Poet Laureate of the United States. He died in 1989.

KELLIE WELLS's *Compression Scars* won a 2001 Flannery O'Connor Award for Short Fiction and was selected for the Great Lakes Colleges Association's New Writers Award for Fiction in 2003. She is also the recipient of a Rona Jaffe Foundation Writer's Award. She teaches in the writing program at Washington University in St. Louis.

EUDORA WELTY was born in Mississippi, where she lived most of her life. She is the author of, among many other books, *One Writer's Beginnings*, *The Robber Bridegroom*, *Delta Wedding*, *The Ponder Heart*, *Losing Battles*, and *The Optimist's Daughter*, which won the 1973 Pulitzer Prize for Fiction. Eudora Welty died on July 22, 2001, at the age of ninety-two.

WILLIAM WENTHE has two books of poems, *Birds of Hoboken* and *Not Till We Are Lost*. He has won fellowships from the National Endowment for the Arts and the Texas Commission on the Arts, and two Pushcart Prizes. He lives in Lubbock, where he teaches at Texas Tech University.

RICHARD WILBUR was born in New York City in 1921. After graduating from Amherst, he served with the 36th Infantry Division during World War II. Having taught at Harvard, Wellesley, Wesleyan, and Smith, he has now retired to rural Massachusetts and Key West. In 1987 he served as Poet Laureate of the United States. His poetry has twice received the Pulitzer Prize, and his latest book of poems is *Mayflies*.

JAMES WRIGHT was a native of Martins Ferry, Ohio. He was a Fulbright Fellow, a two-time Guggenheim Fellow, and a member of the Academy of American Poets. Among his many books, *Collected Poems* won the 1972 Pulitzer Prize. He died in 1980 in New York City.

PAUL ZARZYSKI, who received his M.F.A. in creative writing at the University of Montana under the mentorship of Richard Hugo and Madeline DeFrees, has authored eight collections of poetry and a spoken-word CD, *Words Growing Wild.* His latest book is *Wolf Tracks on the Welcome Mat.* He lives west of Great Falls, Montana, where he feeds a trio of horses and large herds of birds.